OTHER BOOKS BY HENRY DENKER I'll Be Right Home, Ma
My Son the Lawyer
Salome: Princess of Galilee
That First Easter
The Director
The Kingmaker
A Place for the Mighty
The Experiment
The Physician
The Starmaker
The Scofield Diagnosis
The Actress

PLAYS BY HENRY DENKER Horowitz and Mrs. Washington
The Headhunters
Time Limit!
A Far Country
A Case of Libel
Venus at Large
What Did We Do Wrong?
Second Time Around

ERROR OF

JUDGMENT

Henry Denker

SIMON AND SCHUSTER   NEW YORK

Library of Congress Cataloging in Publication Data

Denker, Henry.
Error of judgment.

I. Title.
PZ3.D4175Er [PS3507.E5475]   813'.5'4   78-21220
ISBN 0-671-24130-3

To Edith, my wife

ACKNOWLEDGMENT

For the scientific and medical research that served as a basis for this novel, the author wishes to express his deep appreciation to Herbert J. Buchsbaum, M.D., F.A.C.S., F.A.C.O.G., Professor of Obstetrics and Gynecology, Director, Division of Gynecologic Oncology, University of Texas, Southwestern Medical School.

Chapter One

Tall, black-haired, a scowl turning his handsome face craggy, Dr. Craig Pierson glanced impatiently at the large wall clock as he raced down the hospital corridor. Already ten minutes past seven. He had not completed his morning rounds of postsurgical patients, and he was due to assist in the O.R. at eight. One damned interruption after another, this latest most irritating of all. Now he caught sight of the distressed young intern waiting outside the patient's room.

As he reached him, Pierson demanded angrily, "What is it this time, Blinn? Can't you take a simple presurgical history?"

Willis Blinn was black, but he could not conceal his embarrassed blush. That blush became a rebuke to Craig Pierson. It reminded him that only two years ago, he too had been an insecure intern. He must learn to control his impatience with younger, less experienced men. But then, he also had days when he was impatient with older colleagues as well. The staff surgeons and the attendings. There were days, many days, when Craig Pierson was also impatient with his own limitations, as well as with the present state of what some euphemistically termed the healing art.

The realities of this science called Medicine and the way it was practiced would never match his boyhood dreams. Constantly, he had to remind himself that science or art, Medicine was a craft practiced by mere human beings. With the best of intentions, they were bound to make mistakes. As a second-year resident in Ob-Gyn, he had already made his share.

He was impatient now with Blinn, a willing young man who worked harder than any other intern on staff. Still, he was not yet up to the demands and challenges of the job. Undoubtedly, Pierson thought, Blinn had been admitted to medical school with somewhat less than the usual stringently demanded qualifications. Nor would Blinn's academic record normally have earned him an internship at such an excellent institution as State University Hospital. But Pierson acknowledged that exceptions had to be made to give the disadvantaged their chance. He was simply impatient with the problems it added to his days and nights, already overburdened with more patients than he could handle, in addition to the surgery he had to assist at or perform.

Still, it was his duty as a second-year resident to cope with such inadequacies. Next year, when he became a senior resident and, he hoped, Chief Resident, he could devote more of his time to surgery. He would even have the privilege of selecting only the most interesting and complicated cases. The residents under him could worry about interns who had not yet mastered the simple task of taking a medical history.

Painfully aware of Pierson's impatience, Blinn attempted to explain. "Sorry to bother you. But she's highly emotional. I couldn't get her to answer any questions."

"Of course," Pierson said, not agreeing but dispensing with Blinn's excuse.

Blinn acknowledged the rebuke. "Maybe it's because . . ." He did not complete the thought.

Nor did he have to. Pierson turned on him sharply. "Look, Blinn, if you're going to be sensitive, being a black gynecologist dealing with white women, choose another specialty! G-y-n is fraught with the patient's emotional problems. We don't have to add the doctor's as well."

Blinn glared back, but did not respond. Instead, dismissed, he turned and started down the corridor. At once, Pierson felt a rush of guilt. He decided to take the patient's history himself rather than add to Blinn's embarrassment by having another intern do what he had failed at.

Pierson looked up at the room number. 442. Through the half-open door he could see that the bed was still neat, its corners tightly squared. It had obviously not been occupied. There seemed to be no patient. He pushed the door open a bit wider. He discovered her.

A young woman; hardly more than a teen-ager, to judge from the general size and contour of her body. She stood turned away, staring out the window. She

13

did not appear to hear him. Or, having become aware, she was determined to ignore him.

He picked up the chart.

PATIENT: *Horton, Cynthia.* BIRTH DATE: *May 12, 1956.* AGE: *22.* ADMITTING PHYSICIAN: *Dr. H. Prince.*

Another of Old Goldfingers' early admissions, Craig Pierson observed. She would spend three or four days in hospital before Prince would get around to doing surgery on her.

Old Goldfingers! That title had been bestowed on Dr. Harvey Prince both by young residents who stood in awe of his brilliant surgical technique and by older staff surgeons who envied his huge annual six-figure income.

The next and only other entry on the otherwise blank history form arrested Craig.

ENTRANCE COMPLAINT: *Ovarian mass.*

PROCEDURE: *Exploratory laparotomy.*

Seemingly innocuous words, he thought: *mass . . . exploratory . . .* Some days he wondered, Why don't they simply say in cold bold type: *This young woman probably has ovarian cancer.*

Gently, as reassuringly as he could, he began, "Miss Horton?" She refused to face him. "It is *Miss,* isn't it?" he pursued, hoping to evoke some response.

Without turning to him, in a voice strained with great tension, she accused, "I shouldn't even be here!"

"Dr. Prince seems to think it's necessary." Craig coaxed: "Miss Horton?"

Slowly she turned to him. He was struck by her beauty. Finely cut features in a pale face were accented by deep violet eyes and lustrous black hair. She appeared even younger than twenty-two.

"I shouldn't be here!" she repeated, as if blaming

14

Craig for her confinement. "I should be getting the final fitting on my wedding gown this afternoon. Instead, I'm going to die. I know it. It's a curse, a curse!"

The word unleashed a flood of tears. She buried her face in her hands.

When all other resources fail them, doctors resort to statistics.

"Miss Horton, no need to be so upset. It's really a simple procedure. Most patients are out of bed in two days. And home in four. As to the possible findings, statistically three out of four of these are benign. And even if Dr. Prince finds something, it's undoubtedly very early and probably can be completely removed. He's an excellent man. The best G-y-n surgeon around."

Cynthia Horton looked up at him. Though the plastic badge on his white lab coat identified him, he introduced himself: "I'm Dr. Pierson."

She did not acknowledge the introduction but responded, "It's an accident that I'm here at all. Mother said it was a good idea, before Pete and I got married, for me to have a physical. So I went to Dr. . . . ."

She could not control her tears again, turned away, hid her face. Craig tried to ease things for her.

"So you went to your family doctor. He did a routine examination, including a pelvic, and discovered something. Did he do a smear?"

She nodded.

"And it came back negative?"

Again she nodded.

"That's a good sign," he encouraged. She did not respond. "Miss Horton?" She adamantly refused to face him again. "I have to ask you some questions. Will you answer them? Please?"

15

"I'll try," she said, but began crying again.

Following the hospital's form for Gynecological History, Craig began:

"Onset of menstrual periods?"

"I was twelve."

"At what intervals?"

"Twenty-eight to twenty-nine days."

"Duration?"

"About four days."

"Flow?"

"Usual, I guess. Moderate."

"Pain?"

"Only on the first day. Not bad, though."

"And you did have a Pap smear. When?"

"A week ago."

"Pregnancies?"

"None!" the girl retorted, sounding a bit belligerent, then admitting, "Yes. One."

"Do you use any contraceptive technique?"

"The pill."

Craig noted on the form, *O.C.*

"Any previous operations?"

"Tonsils, that's all."

He moved on now to questions concerning her present condition.

"Noticed any weight loss in the last month?"

"No."

"Any changes in bowel or voiding habits?"

"No." She seemed to become impatient; he realized it was due to her tense state.

"Pressure on the bladder?"

She hesitated. "Yes," she admitted, "but I thought that was due to the pill. Is that important?"

"Probably not," Craig said, hoping to calm her fears. "Miss Horton, did you notice any other effect of this mass on your bodily functions? Any bleeding?"

"I didn't even know there was a mass!" she protested hostilely, as if the physician who first discovered it had inflicted it on her. "Mother kept saying, before a girl gets married she should have a complete physical. To make sure there are no impairments. That's the word she used, 'impairments.' 'Impairments to what?' I asked. And she said, 'Impairments to your sex life, to having children.' "

Cynthia Horton now turned to face Craig. On her face a small smile that seemed to contradict her tears. "She's a dear woman, my mother. But of another generation. 'Impair my sex life.' Isn't that quaint? For almost two years, Pete and I . . . but I couldn't tell her that. No, my sex life is not 'impaired.' Nor my childbearing ability. But I never told her. I wouldn't want to hurt her. She's a great lady, my mother. So how could I tell her there was an abortion? Perfectly legal, of course. Still, I couldn't tell her."

Suddenly she stared hard at Craig. "Doctor, I want an honest answer. Could my abortion have caused this?"

"Absolutely not," he reassured her. He also changed the subject to put her at ease. "What kind of work do you do? Or are you still a student?"

"I work in an ad agency. Assistant to a media executive." Then she admitted, "Secretary, really."

"Parents still living and well?"

"Yes."

Craig noted on the form, *Parents, L & W.*

"Any family history of cancer? Especially breast or vaginal cancer in your mother or any aunts?"

Instead of answering, Cynthia Horton turned away.

"Miss Horton? Any family history of cancer? It would be important to know."

When she finally tried to answer, she faltered. "I . . ." Then she admitted, "I don't know."

17

"You mean, if there had been, your mother and father would have kept it from you?" he asked, surprised.

"I mean what I said, *I don't know.*"

"Miss Horton, the time when people were ashamed of admitting there was cancer in the family is gone. If there had been, I'm sure . . ."

She interrupted him with a fierceness born of inner torment. "I told you, I don't know! I don't know! I don't know!" She was weeping again. "Now, leave me alone."

He permitted her to weep freely. It would do no good to pressure her. Eventually she recovered sufficiently to say, "*I* don't know because *they* don't know."

"Your mother and father don't know?" he asked, surprised.

"Do I have to spell it out for you? I'm adopted! I don't know my family history. Neither do they."

"I understand," Craig Pierson said sympathetically.

"*Do* you?" She turned on him. "Do you really?" she demanded vehemently. "I wonder! I wonder if you know how it feels to go through your life with half of it missing! All those times when you're being asked questions, simple questions, like the ones you just asked me, and I have to say, I don't know. The worst is not *admitting* I don't know. It's *not knowing.*

"Don't you think I've read the pamphlets? Don't you think I know that if your mother or your sister had breast cancer that puts you at greater risk? That it can run in families? It was the first thing I thought of when Dr. Corbin discovered that mass. I wanted to find her and ask her, 'What kind of drugs did you take when you were pregnant with me? Did you ever have cancer? Before I was born or after?'

18

"But where do you go? Who do you ask? Who?" she demanded.

She was now so tense that Craig decided he must get a sedative into her as soon as possible. Eventually the rigidity drained out of her young body. She resumed shallow but quite even breathing. Her voice became gentler, no longer accusatory.

"I thought . . . I know it doesn't make sense, but I thought marrying Pete would end all that. Our children would know who they were, where they came from. Their family history. Getting married was going to wipe out my past.

"Then this happened. . . . I thought, I've never seen her. But she won't let go. She's put a curse on me. From the day I was born. I am never to be like other girls. Even now, twenty-two years later, somehow she reached out to destroy my marriage. I won't even live to get married."

"Miss Horton, your fear is quite unrealistic," Craig reassured her. "You'll have surgery. You'll recover. You'll be married. Probably even without postponing the date."

She stared at him, disbelieving.

"We do this operation every day. It's a simple procedure. Quite safe. You'll be home by the end of the week."

"And if you *find* something?" she asked.

"The odds are greatly against its being anything serious," he said truthfully.

"If there's a way to destroy me, she'll find it," the girl said grimly. "Sometimes I decide I'll search for her. Find her. Find out why she gave me up. Why she won't let go of me, even now. But Mother and Dad might misunderstand, might feel hurt. I couldn't do that. They've been so good to me. Maybe sometime after I'm married, it might hurt less. I'll try to find her.

It's not impossible, you know. Adoptees do it all the time."

"I know," Craig said.

"Do you?" she challenged, as if her plight were exclusively her own.

"Yes," Craig said. "I know because I did it."

"Did what?" Cynthia asked, obviously dubious.

"Searched. Found her."

"You mean you're adopted too?"

"Members of the same club," he said, smiling to put her at ease. He held out his hand to her. She stared at him before she took it.

She did not relinquish his hand as she asked, "What was it like? When you found her?"

"I was apprehensive," he admitted. "And I was eager. I felt guilty about my own parents. I felt anger toward her. Plus a certain amount of pity. After all, maybe she didn't want to be found. Maybe she had a family of her own, children of her own. I could be an unwelcome intrusion, a shocking reminder. I thought of all those things.

"Then I saw her. She turned out to be a rather plain woman. Small. Frail. I don't resemble her at all. We had nothing in common. We couldn't even make conversation. She seemed relieved that I had grown up well. She was impressed that I was a physician. But that was all. She had no impulse to embrace me or kiss me. And I had no feeling toward her. We were strangers. At that moment I knew who my mother and father really were.

"So I went back home to my real parents. I told them. They weren't surprised. They had expected I'd do it one day. They never wanted to interfere for fear of inhibiting me, so they never asked. But they were relieved that it was over."

20

"That's all there was?" Cynthia Horton asked.

"That's all," Craig admitted. "Except afterward, I felt a bit foolish."

"Why?"

He smiled. "I forgot to ask her about *my* family medical history," he admitted.

Cynthia Horton now relaxed sufficiently to smile with him.

"You didn't make all this up, did you? Just to put me at ease?"

"No," he said, quite soberly. "I *am* adopted, I *did* go find her. And it felt just like I said."

The pretty, dark-haired girl was pensive for a moment. "Will I be able to get married?" she asked suddenly.

"As far as I know, yes."

"And have children?"

"As far as I know," he reassured her, honestly.

"I want children. I want children who will grow up free of all the uncertainties, fears, and doubts I've always had," she said intently.

"I see no reason why you can't have them."

In the normal course of a history and physical on a new admission, Craig Pierson would have done a thorough bimanual pelvic examination.

However, since this girl was in such a highly emotional state, he chose not to add to her tension. He terminated the interview: "Miss Horton, I want you to know there's no more capable surgeon for this procedure than Dr. Prince. If you were my own sister, Prince is the man I'd have do it."

He started down the corridor glancing into every room until he found Blinn taking a blood sample from a young pregnant woman who was two weeks overdue and who, they expected, would have a difficult deliv-

21

ery. Once Blinn had sealed the test tube and handed it to the technician, Craig beckoned to him.

Blinn came to the door, on his black face an anticipatorily defensive look.

"I thought about what you said," Blinn began. "I guess I should consider transferring to another specialty."

"I wouldn't," Craig contradicted. Blinn was surprised. "I wanted to tell you, it wasn't your fault. She's extremely apprehensive. Highly emotional. And for good reason. So forget it. Sorry I blew my top."

When that distress call from Blinn had first summoned him, Craig was starting to examine the woman in 407. He returned to resume with the patient whose chart identified her as *Keegan, Mrs. Theresa J.*

Blond, slight, with a pinched face, she had eyes that gave her the appearance of being constantly on guard. Many women presented themselves that way on the Ob-Gyn Service. As if they all had only one question which they dared not ask: "Doctor, is it malignant?"

"Mrs. Keegan, sorry for the interruption. You were describing your pain . . ."

The woman edged up in bed, pressed against the metal head frame. She spoke of her pain as if it were remote. When he asked exactly where the pain occurred, she pointed to vague areas in her lower abdomen. He distracted her by asking a few more questions.

"How many children do you have, Mrs. Keegan?"

"Six."

"Any other pregnancies?"

"Oh, I would never have an abortion," she protested as if she had been accused.

"I meant pregnancies that terminated in miscarriage."

22

"Once, yes. Between the second and the third, there was one. Doctor said it would have been a girl."

"Now, about that pain. Just show me once more, and describe it, please?"

She pressed the same general areas and described it in the same vague way.

"Ever take anything for it?"

"I don't believe in pills. Most pills," the thin blond woman said, "they make you drowsy. And when you have six little ones, you can't afford to be drowsing off. Except at night. And even then, a whole night's sleep is rare."

"I can understand that," Craig said as he proceeded with his examination. The woman presented no signs, swellings, or palpable masses of any kind, not even any tender areas.

He examined her chart again. Her doctor had sent along his X-ray findings. All were negative. Craig would not order an exploratory on the basis of such a history.

There was one other course open. He would have to check out his suspicion first.

"How long has this pain persisted, Mrs. Keegan?"

"Months."

"Has it gotten any worse?"

The woman considered her answer before she said, "No. About the same. It's always about the same."

"Comes and goes?"

"Yes, it . . . it comes and goes . . ." she said, searching Craig's face for some hint.

He pretended to study her chart, but actually glanced beyond it to fix on her thin face.

"Mrs. Keegan, what kind of work does your husband do?"

"My husband?" she repeated, taken unaware by Craig's question.

23

"Is his job covered by a health insurance plan?"

"Yes. Why?" she asked, fear distorting her face now. "You think it's serious. I need an operation. You think it's ... it's ..." She could not bring herself to speak the word.

"No, I don't think it's that at all. But I do think that your pains may be associated with pregnancy and childbearing. So it might be desirable to do a procedure that would prevent you from having any more children," he said, watching for her reaction.

"I'd have to talk to my husband about that. Or maybe you should. Would you, Doctor? I wouldn't know what to say. And of course, there's Father Ogilvy. I'd have to talk to him," she said thoughtfully.

"I think he'll approve after I explain," Craig reassured her.

"Would you really explain it, Doctor?" she asked.

"Tell me what church and where I can reach him."

"Thank you, Doctor, thank you."

Relieved, she slid down from the rigid position she had assumed throughout the interview.

Craig Pierson had confirmed his diagnosis. She was a conflict-ridden woman whose strict religious upbringing made her feel guilty for wanting to be relieved of the burden of bearing and caring for more children. But she could not bring herself to disobey the dictates of her church. So, unconsciously, she sought another way out. Pain, of undetermined origin, would justify the sterilization she desired, while avoiding any guilty consequences.

Craig had no doubt that to her, the pain was real. Vague, but real. He would talk to her husband, then to her priest. The procedure itself was simple, safe and painless. Her life would be a good deal happier thereafter.

24

Chapter Two

Pierson had completed his morning rounds. He had then scrubbed and assisted at four surgical procedures. One, a simple hysterectomy, he had performed himself with the woman's surgeon standing by to observe. The surgeon complimented Craig on his technique and his proficiency. Yes, the surgeon had been quite pleased, and he would now send the woman a bill for a thousand dollars and consider it quite modest when compared with her husband's annual income.

His long day done, Pierson changed from his O.R. greens. Instead of reassuming his white lab coat, he slipped into his gray tweed jacket. He was ready to depart for the night. There was no rush. Since Kate was away at a seminar, he could go back to his small, clean—if not neat—bachelor apartment and catch up on the high stack of medical journals and papers that seemed more than any doctor could hope to cope with. Every month each specialty produced a prodigious number of new findings. Ob-Gyn was among the most prolific. What specialty in Medicine, Craig used to joke, had a better right to be so productive?

He was crossing the crowded lobby of the hospital when he felt a sudden need to see that Horton girl again. Though he had reassured her, to himself Craig had to admit the serious possibilities inherent in her case.

Statistically, women in their early twenties did not

often present gynecological malignancies. Yet in her case, at least one ovary was suspect. And ovarian malignancies, though third in frequency among gynecologic cancers, were fatal in more cases than all others combined.

He reached her room, heard voices—low, soft, and trying desperately to be bright and reassuring. The door was slightly ajar. Craig knocked nevertheless.

"Yes?" a man's voice called, suddenly guarded, apprehensive.

"May I come in?"

"Dr. Prince?" a tall young man asked as he opened the door.

"I'm the resident. I saw the patient this morning. I wanted to check on her before I left."

"Of course," the young man said, stepping back. He was tall, taller even than Craig's six feet one. He was rangy, with a bony face and the tanned, weathered complexion of a man who did most of his work out of doors.

Cynthia Horton was sitting up high in her bed. She turned to the young man and started to say, "This is Dr. . . . ," then laughed and said, "I forgot your name."

"Pierson, Craig Pierson."

"Dr. Pierson, this is Pete. Peter Tompkins. My fiancé."

"How do you do?" Craig said, shaking hands with the young man, who was no more than twenty-six but had a maturity and physical presence that made him seem older. Quite unconsciously, Craig thought, It's good he's so mature. She might need a man like him now.

"We were expecting Dr. Prince," Pete explained. "He said he might drop by this evening if he had time."

"Good," Craig replied, pretending he expected Prince to fulfill his promise. Though it was not like Prince to visit the hospital in the evening unless some serious emergency developed in a post-op patient.

However, Craig was relieved to observe the improvement in Cynthia Horton's attitude. The sedation had evidently done its work. She smiled easily, and when she did, he appreciated even more how unusually beautiful she was. He could not help thinking that with her beauty and Pete's physique they were going to have magnificent children.

His thought was interrupted when Pete said, "Cynthia told me about the coincidence."

"Coincidence?" Craig was surprised.

"You both being adopted."

"Oh. Not so remarkable. After all, there are several million of us. We may be a minority. But I call us the only *over*privileged minority."

The three of them laughed. Conversation was light, casual and general after that. When Craig excused himself, Pete volunteered to walk him to the elevator. Smiling, he kissed Cynthia, saying, "Be right back, honey."

Once outside the door, Peter Tompkins turned grim and direct. "Doctor, you can tell me the truth. Is it bad? How bad? I swear I won't tell her."

"We won't know a thing until Prince does the exploratory."

"I called a friend of mine," Pete said, "guy I roomed with at college. He's a doctor now. When I said 'exploratory laparotomy,' he was stunned."

"Tompkins, exploratory laparotomy simply means performing an exploratory by opening up the abdominal cavity. The term itself is nothing to be frightened of."

"But if you find—" Pete started to say.

27

Craig interrupted him sharply. "We don't speculate. That's why we go in. As for what we might find, there's been no bleeding. No pain. No obstruction. If anything's there, it must be very early. And cases like that we can cure."

"But it *is* possible there's something there."

"Two doctors have found a palpable ovarian mass. But that's no reason to panic. Possibly the luckiest thing that ever happened to her is that she went for a checkup so that it was discovered in time."

Craig realized that he was becoming impatient. He could not blame the young man, who less than a week ago had been eagerly looking forward to marrying this rather unusual girl. Now he suddenly confronted the possibility, at least, of consequences that might be dreadful indeed.

Fortunately, the elevator arrived. Unfortunately, as the door opened a middle-aged couple emerged. The woman threw her arms around Tompkins, saying, "Oh, Pete, Pete . . .," and she began to weep.

Tompkins embraced the woman, introducing the couple to Craig at the same time.

"Mr. and Mrs. Horton, Cynthia's folks. This is Dr. Pierson, Dr. Prince's assistant."

"Just a resident," Craig explained. He shook hands with Mr. Horton, a harried man, with dark hair running to gray now that he was in his fifties. Tompkins and Mrs. Horton started down the corridor toward Cynthia's room. Horton lingered, his hand on Craig's arm to detain him.

"Doctor . . .," he blurted out, then stopped as suddenly.

"Yes?" Craig encouraged.

"Doctor, I'm Cynthie's father. You can tell me the truth."

"Mr. Horton, why does everyone assume that doctors go around lying? I didn't lie to Cynthia. Nor to Pete. There's something there. We have to find out what. When it comes to finding out, Prince is the best man there is. That's the truth, the whole truth, and nothing but the truth."

"Thank you, thank you," Horton said, his eyes filmed over with tears of relief. "She's our only one. If anything happened to her . . . well, her mother would never be able to take it. Never."

Craig recognized instantly that the man was projecting his own emotions onto his wife.

"People talk about your own flesh and blood. I don't know a family with kids of their own that love them more than we love Cynthie. She's like . . . I don't know how to say it . . . a gift. You look at Barbara and me. We're plain-looking people. If we had ever had a daughter of our own, she wouldn't be half as beautiful as Cynthie. Or as lovely. To us, she's always been a gift, a treasure to take care of. If anything were to happen to her now . . ."

Horton could not allow himself to contemplate the consequences.

"Just tell me she's going to be okay, Doctor. And I'll believe you."

Rather than indulge in an easy lie, Craig Pierson said, "The odds are in her favor, Mr. Horton."

"Thanks, thanks very much," the relieved man said, and started down the hall.

Craig Pierson could appreciate Horton's feelings. His own folks felt the same way about him. Which reminded him, he had not called home in almost three weeks. He determined to call as soon as he arrived at his apartment.

But he became engrossed in the medical paper he

29

read while eating the sandwich that was his dinner. When he looked up again, it was past eleven. Dad would probably be asleep. His modest landscaping business called for him to be up at six to get his men routed for the day and to make sure all equipment was in working order.

Not that his folks would mind a late call. They did not call him as often as they would like, for fear of imposing on him an obligation for having raised him, loved him, educated him, and given him advantages beyond their means. They never wanted to appear to ask him for anything in return, not even love.

For himself, and because he felt secure, Craig did not often ponder his relationship with his parents. In his youth he had come to recognize and love his father for the man he was. Stolid, hard-working, only a generation removed from a rugged stony farm in northern New York, Bill Pierson had accidentally drifted into landscaping, a profession he came to love.

Once he had achieved a comfortable financial status, his wife, Anna, began gently urging that since they had no children, they consider adopting.

At the outset, it was not for his own sake but for Anna that Bill Pierson did it. But once they were handed an unnamed male infant for their own, Bill Pierson discovered emotions within himself that he had not suspected. The first time he watched Anna diaper the infant Craig, Bill Pierson looked at his own huge gardener's hands and wondered if he dared touch so fragile a being; it seemed he would endanger it. Before the week was out he was changing the infant, holding him, feeding him, and tiptoeing about the house for fear of waking him.

At the end of the first month, he was already making plans for the boy's future. By the end of the first year,

30

he had set up a modest savings account for his education. He was determined, should there ever be such a tragic time as a Depression again, that unlike himself, his son would not be denied an education. He would become far more in this world than a gardener with two small trucks and four men working for him.

One thing Bill Pierson felt, but could not articulate even to his wife: the child had done more to give them something in common than even their love for each other.

From an early age, Craig Pierson had been made aware that he was an adopted child. It was Anna's idea. In all matters unrelated to his landscaping business, Bill always deferred to Anna, who read a great deal. When it came to home and family, always, "Anna knows about such things."

Craig's conflicts did not arise until much later. In his growing-up years he had nights when he lay awake pondering where he had come from, why he had been given up. But in the end he felt glad that he had been given to such loving people as Anna and Bill Pierson.

Through high school, though coaches urged Craig to go out for baseball and football, sports for which he had natural aptitude, he declined in favor of helping in his father's business. The physical exercise involved in gardening was as great as it was in athletics. The satisfaction of contributing to the well-being of the family was far greater.

His dad tried to suggest there was no need to feel any obligation. But he was not an easy man with words and could never make it sound right. Nor could he disguise his pride when customers praised Craig's excellent work.

Always, Bill Pierson was happy to reply, "Well, he

won't be at it long. That boy is going to medical school. He's going to be a doctor. Not a gardener like his dad."

When the time came to consider colleges, Bill Piersen went to call on two of his customers, both physicians, who had large homes and well-cared-for grounds in the finest area of town. Dressed in his best dark suit, his shoes polished, wearing an unaccustomed tie and shirt, Bill Pierson requested an audience with each physician.

A man who was only a gardener did not know much about colleges and medical schools. Which was the best college to go to in order to qualify for the best medical school? There was never any doubt in Bill Pierson's mind that his son Craig would be accepted by the best.

Impressed by his straightforward, if naive, approach to the problem, the doctors agreed to help. They had both observed young Craig working on their property. They knew him to be industrious, rugged, quite handsome, and most conscientious. They were delighted to send on his qualifications to their respective alma maters. He was accepted by both. He chose the university that had the best medical school.

When Bill and Anna drove their only son to college for the first time, they felt sad and satisfied. They had achieved the goal of a lifetime. Yet both had the feeling that what had begun that day when the woman at the social agency placed a small, dark-haired infant in Anna's arms was beginning to end on this day.

From now on, he would not be coming home from school every afternoon and calling, "Mom?" He would not be helping out on the trucks every Saturday and during vacations. He would not be getting dressed up to go to parties and coming down from his room to kiss them both good night before he went off.

32

Nor would they hear that reassuring sound of the door opening and closing in the dead of night which told them he was safely home again.

There would no longer be the sense, the silent sense, of someone in the home even though he was out of sight, up in his room studying or reading.

They would go back to being just the two of them. Anna and Bill. As it used to be in the early days of their marriage.

They walked around the university grounds staring at the old ivy-covered buildings, with dates on their cornerstones going back more than a century. Here was tradition that Bill Pierson respected, as he did the church in which he worshiped. To disguise both his pride and his inferiority, he kept remarking on the expert care of the university grounds and the excellent condition of the ivy.

It came time for them to leave. Their son walked them back to the car. He kissed them both. His mother began to weep. His father, who could be as easily moved to tears, covered his feelings by shaking hands and saying, "Remember, son, anything you need, don't hesitate to ask. There's money enough."

At the last moment, Bill Pierson embraced his son and did have to blink back tears.

Craig was never told what his parents spoke of on the long drive back home. But knowing them both, he could imagine the conversation.

"Bill, I feel . . . I feel like we've just given him back."

When Bill did not answer, she must have said, "I hope he doesn't grow away from us. After all, we did the best we could. And if we're not so educated, we made sure he had the best. I hope he knows that. Did you see some of the cars those other boys came in? Two even had chauffeurs. I wonder, did we push him

33

too much? Maybe some other college, not the best, would have been better for him. More comfortable for him."

His father, stolid as ever, most likely said, "Did you see that ivy, Anna? And those grounds? Beautiful. I wonder who does their work." Then, after a few moments of silence, he probably said, "Must be their own staff. Too big a job to give to any outside contractor."

When they arrived home, just before turning out the light for the night, Bill Pierson probably said, "Anna, I hope the boy won't feel out of place."

During summer vacations from college, Craig returned home and insisted on working in the business. His father demurred. How would it look for a college man to be dragging hose, tilling soil, running a noisy lawn mower, his naked back sweating in the hot sun? A man who studied hard all year should rest during his time off, save himself for the difficult times ahead. But Craig insisted on dragging hose, tilling soil, pushing a noisy lawn mower. Not the least reason for his insistence was that he noticed that increased wages had forced his father to employ only three men instead of four and that he was again doing a great deal of the work himself.

At the end of a hot day's work they would sit out on the back patio and have a cold drink before dinner. His folks would ask questions about college: how it was going, how he enjoyed it; had he made inquiries about getting into medical school? Always there was the unspoken yet keenly felt guilt that they had never done enough for him, that their station in life was a detriment to his future.

Several times Craig had tried to discuss it with his father. But Bill Pierson was not a man given to intimate conversation. With him, it was all feeling. You sensed what he felt. He had no need to say it.

Bill Pierson's greatest joy during those summers was when one of the doctors who had given him advice would come out of his house, cross the wide lawn, and strike up a conversation with Craig. Sometimes they talked for minutes. Once one of the doctors took Craig back to the house and they talked for more than an hour over coffee. Bill Pierson stood off, watching while he worked and thinking, He's being accepted; one day our Craig will be as good as any of them.

After Craig entered medical school, Bill Pierson absolutely forbade him to work at landscaping. It was not fit work for a doctor. So Craig took up work in a summer playground for disadvantaged children. It was a welcome break from the confinement of classrooms, lecture halls, labs, and nights of study.

Working with children aided Craig's study of pediatrics. For a time he contemplated it as his specialty. But the year his mother had a cancer scare he began to delve into gynecological oncology, and he decided in favor of that field of research and practice. Fortunately, his mother's case was well handled by his professor of Ob-Gyn, and she recovered completely. When it was over, his dad had said to him, "Anything we ever did for you, son, you repaid a million times over. I don't know what I would have done without your mother."

That simple confession made Craig determined to preserve the close family they had been until his profession intervened to separate them.

Tonight, having been sharply reminded by his meeting with Cynthia Horton, Craig decided to call despite the late hour. The phone rang four times. That meant they were watching the eleven-o'clock news, so Dad had to cross the length of the living room and take the call on the kitchen phone. Dad answered all late-night calls, since it was usually one of his men reporting in sick and unable to work tomorrow.

"Hello," Bill Pierson said, expecting trouble.

"Dad?"

At once, Bill Pierson called out, "Mother, it's Craig!" Craig heard her cry out, "Don't say a word until I get on the extension!"

Her first question was "What's wrong, son?"

Craig laughed to calm her fears. "Ma, Ma, does there have to be something wrong for me to call home?"

"No," she said, reassured. "Only to call so late, I thought..." But she didn't say what she thought, since it concerned all the worst fears mothers have about children no longer under their protection.

"I've had no chance to call before."

"They keep you that busy?" his father asked, obviously proud that his son's services were so much in demand.

"Busy? Every day is like trying to save a stand of saplings in a hurricane. Never lets up."

"Can't do no harm," his father said. "The more you do now, the better equipped you'll be when you go out on your own."

Craig made a mental note that one day soon he must tell his father that he was considering not going into private practice but staying on at the hospital on staff and to do research. So for him there would be no huge house, no large, well-cared-for acreage that his father had always assumed was the just due of any successful doctor.

They talked of many things, catching Craig up on

what had happened to them in the three weeks since he had called last. They asked how his work was going. Suddenly he found himself telling them about Cynthia Horton, her condition, and her fears about being adopted.

He ended by saying, "I guess that's really why I called. If people love each other maybe they don't have to say it. But I want you to know how I feel."

"It never hurts to say it, son," his mother replied. He could envision the tears in her eyes.

His father said, "Take good care of that girl. See that she's okay."

"Sure, Dad."

"Talking of girls, son," his mother said. Craig knew what was coming. He made no attempt to discourage her. "Is there a girl yet?"

"A girl?" Craig asked. "Or *the* girl?"

"You know what I mean, son," she answered. "After all, even for a doctor, life shouldn't be all work. There's a time for marriage. And a family. Otherwise suddenly you find yourself too old for your own children. And that's not good."

Craig knew she was referring to the time his folks had had serious discussions about adopting a little girl. Until his mother confessed, "Bill, it wouldn't be fair to her. We couldn't give her what she needs—the time, the patience. We're just too old."

Now Anna Pierson feared that her son might let his career so dominate his life that he would suddenly find himself too old for the children he should have.

If Craig had resolved that question, he would have been delighted to share the answer with them. There was a girl. *The* girl.

But how could he explain to his simple, honest parents how the world of men and women had changed in thirty years? How much more free and open it had become. And hence, how much more complicated.

Without understanding that, they would never understand about Kate.

Chapter Three

Just past midnight, when Craig Pierson finished talking to his family, Cynthia Horton was still awake in her bed in Room 442. The night nurse had given her the medication prescribed on her chart. But Cynthia's anxiety had defeated the mild dose.

She stared up at the pale green ceiling, watching the reflection of the dim corridor lights that leaked through the small opening left by the door. Occasionally she heard the swift whisking of rubber-soled shoes along the tiled floor as a nurse raced to answer some late-night emergency.

Cynthia breathed guardedly, fearing that to draw a single deep breath might disturb and spread the *thing* that was growing in her. She had moments when she could convince herself it was nothing. But always those moments were overwhelmed by sheer panic of such frightening depth that she considered leaping out of bed and fleeing. As if she could leave behind her whatever the *thing* was.

At moments, she blamed her mother. Who ever heard of having to go to a doctor for approval to get married? It was ironic. Comic, in fact.

When her mother first suggested she see Dr. Corbin for a checkup, she and Pete had joked about it. Wouldn't it be funny if Corbin discovered that she really couldn't have sex with Pete? That what had been happening for two wonderful years was really impossible? Old Corbin had been their family physician ever since Cynthia could remember. Yet when the time came to go on the pill, she had gone to a younger doctor recommended to her by one of her friends. Still, it was natural that when her mother thought of a checkup, she had suggested Corbin. And just as natural that Cynthia would respect her wishes.

Old Corbin had done what seemed a perfunctory examination. But one of the first questions he had asked was "Of course, you're on the pill?"

"Yes."

"Uh-huh" was all Corbin had said, going gravely about the rest of the examination. Meantime, he asked questions about her mother and dad. Were they going to Europe again this spring? Did they expect to go back to the lake house this summer? Was her dad overworking, as usual? Though to Arthur Horton, an attorney with a large law firm, trial work must be enjoyable, since he seemed to thrive on it, Corbin had to admit.

Suddenly, during the course of her pelvic examination, his attitude changed. For the first time his questions changed from casual to strictly medical. His experienced fingers had obviously detected something that startled him. He went back, pressed again, probed again.

Ovarian mass, his fingers told him. His alert mind raced through all the possibilities. She was on the pill; hence it could not be a harmless follicle cyst. Nor a corpus luteum cyst. If he recalled correctly (and he must look it up the moment she left the office), in a patient this young such a mass would most likely be a benign cystic teratoma, a harmless dermoid cyst.

He took a Pap smear, determined to rush it to the

lab. He completed his examination, making sure once more that what he felt was truly a mass. Once she was gone, he locked himself in his consultation room, surrounded by large volumes on specialized areas of medicine, and carefully studied two texts on gynecological diseases.

They confirmed his recollection. They also raised another alarming possibility. Both books warned that ovarian malignancies while not always presenting pain or bleeding could still be quite virulent and aggressive.

He rushed the Pap smear through. He was somewhat relieved when it came back negative. He called Barbara Horton and, as casually as he could, suggested, "I think it would be advisable for Cynthia to see a gynecologist."

"Why? What's wrong? Is she going to have trouble conceiving?" her mother asked.

"It may be nothing at all," old Corbin had said. "But I'd like to get another opinion. Quickly!"

"Dr. Bacon?" Barbara Horton asked, suggesting her own gynecologist.

"This time I'd rather it were Harvey Prince," Corbin said firmly. If surgery proved necessary, he knew no more skillful man.

Corbin called Cynthia at her office, told her that though her Pap smear was negative, he thought she should get another opinion. Cynthia was inclined to laugh it off. But when Corbin became quite stern and fatherly, she no longer resisted. She agreed to keep the appointment Corbin had arranged for her at one o'clock the next day.

Throughout the rest of the day, Cynthia Horton chose to believe it could be nothing serious. Most likely old Corbin was too self-conscious to make a proper examination and would rather a stranger do it on a more impersonal basis. She finally called her mother, caught her at the country club making arrangements for the wedding reception.

"Mom, did Dr. Corbin say anything to you? I mean, *really* say anything?"

"Why, no, darling. What's wrong?"

"He wants me to see this Dr. Prince tomorrow. Even made an appointment for me. I just wondered..."

"You know old Corbin—conservative to the end. No pills, no antibiotics, no injections of any kind unless absolutely necessary. It's his way. Nothing to worry about, I'm sure. So see Prince tomorrow and call me the minute you leave his office. I'll be home waiting.

"Of course, Mother."

Somehow her mother's glib reassurance left Cynthia disquieted. She would have been even more disturbed if she had known that as soon as she hung up, her mother immediately called Dr. Corbin and asked him forthrightly, "About Cynthia, be honest with me."

The old doctor sighed. "There's something there. I want another opinion from a man who can go in and take a look."

"Then it could be something," Barbara Horton said, not wanting to use the hated word.

"It could also be nothing," Corbin tried to reassure her.

Two hours later, after considerable self-torment, Barbara Horton called Cynthia.

"Darling, tomorrow..."

"Yes, Mother?"

"I'd like to go with you when you see that Dr. Prince."

Cynthia hesitated for a moment. Then, because she needed it, badly, she was relieved to agree. "Please, Ma."

They had to wait till long past two before Prince could see them. Twice Cynthia phoned her office to say she would be a little late getting back from lunch. She discovered Pete had called three times, left no message, except that he would pick her up for dinner. She felt guilty about not telling him of her visit to Corbin, her presence at Prince's office.

Finally she was shown into one of the eight examining rooms that opened onto the corridor of Prince's long suite of offices. One of the nurses told her to disrobe and gave her a white gown. She asked her to climb onto the gynecological examining table. The fresh muslin sheet felt cold and coarse to her skin.

Minutes later, minutes that seemed much much longer, she heard a voice—a man's voice, efficient, crisp, and quite businesslike—ask, "This one?"

"Dr. Corbin's patient."

"Oh, yes, he called me about her. Check her history. Did he do a Pap smear?"

"Yes. Negative," the nurse replied.

"Good."

The door opened wider and Dr. Harvey Prince entered, in a white lab coat. He was a tall, dignified man with an impressive white moustache. He exuded an air of authority that transmitted itself to Cynthia at once. She would believe him if he said there was nothing wrong. And if there were something wrong, she had every confidence he would fix it.

He smiled warmly, asked the same routine questions Corbin had asked: pain, pressure, bleeding. With each answer, he smiled and nodded. She felt

42

determined to please him, and thus earn a favorable verdict, so that her wedding could proceed on schedule and the life for which she had been prepared could go on endlessly.

Prince asked questions in an easy manner, but his examining hand seemed more grave and purposeful. He pressed areas of her abdomen. Then, efficiently but gently, his gloved hand entered her vaginal canal as he asked her about the pill.

When he was done, he turned to dictate a brief, cryptic note into his machine: "Ovarian mass. Seven to eight centimeters. Mobile. Tensely cystic. Suggesting ovarian neoplasm."

The words, most of which were foreign to Cynthia, alarmed her. Yet she hardly dared ask.

"What did you find, Doctor?"

"Get dressed and go into my consulting room. That's your mother out in the waiting room, isn't it?"

"Yes. Why—"

Before Cynthia could verbalize her question, Prince said, "Well, we'll have her in too."

They waited almost an hour for Prince to join them. Meantime they sat in the lavishly furnished consulting room not daring to speculate on the possibilities. Her mother camouflaged her fear by describing the plans for the wedding. She talked so incessantly that Cynthia realized how grave she suspected the situation actually was.

Meanwhile, Cynthia stared at the volumes in the bookshelves. *Tumors of Female Sex Organs. New Concepts in Gynecological Oncology. The Classification of Malignant Tumors. Carcinoma of the Uterine Cervix, Endometrium and Ovary.*

Though the word *Oncology* was new to her, she knew well what tumors and carcinoma meant. Sud-

43

denly she found herself interrupting her mother's ceaseless chatter about wedding plans with a tense and tearful "Mother, please!"

Her mother was not surprised or hurt. She embraced her, saying, "It's going to be all right, all right."

But it was a prayer, not a firm statement of assurance.

Prince entered moments later.

"Well, now," he began, once he had settled himself in his luxurious leather desk chair. He seemed to require a moment to recall to which patient and what set of facts he was addressing himself. "Oh, yes. Miss Horton. Dr. Corbin's patient. Well, I like to be quite open about these things. I'll be as frank with you as I am going to be with Dr. Corbin."

He lifted his phone, pressed one of many buttons, and said, "Carla, get me Dr. Corbin. About the Horton girl."

While they waited for the call to go through, Prince asked a number of inconsequential questions and seemed only the slightest bit concerned when he discovered that she was planning to be married in four weeks. His phone buzzed.

"Corbin? Harvey Prince.... Fine. And you?... Good. Now, about the Horton girl. She's sitting right here. I want her to hear everything I say to you.

"By the way, I wish all the patients you send me were so pretty. Lovely girl. She's blushing now. Frankly, so am I. I wish I were twenty years younger."

He smiled at Cynthia. "About my findings. You were right. On bimanual, she presents an ovarian mass. I'd say seven to eight centimeters. I think we should go in and take a look. I'd like to send her into the hospital tomorrow. Fortunately, I have an empty bed right now and we might as well get it over with so she can proceed with her wedding plans. I'd like to meet the lucky man. I envy him.

"So if it's okay with you, I'll send her in tomorrow."

Prince hung up. He smiled reassuringly. "There, that's all there is to it. Miss Reigle at the front desk will arrange the hospital. All you have to do is show up first thing in the morning. We'll want to run some tests. I'll probably operate the next day or the day after, depending on whether I have any emergencies. But don't worry about a thing."

They were about to rise when Prince said, "Oh, by the way, I always like the patient to know what it is I am going to do.

"Very simply, the procedure will be done under a general anesthetic. The incision will be in the abdomen. Horizontal. Trust me to leave a very small and not disfiguring scar. I am noted for my small, neat scars."

He laughed. "So there'll be nothing to spoil the honeymoon. Once in there, we'll find that pesky little thing and remove it. We have a regular procedure we have to follow at that point. It goes to the pathologist, who does a frozen section. Once it comes back negative, we close you up and that's it. A few days later, you're up and out of bed. Then you're home good as new."

"Of course"—Prince was no longer smiling—"if the path report comes back positive, we look around carefully and stage the disease—that is, map out the extent of it. Then we do the operation to remove it. And that is usually that."

"Exactly what *do* you do?" her mother asked.

"What the surgeon does depends on what he finds. You have to trust me at that point," Prince said soberly.

"Of course," Cynthia replied numbly. Then she

asked, "Shall I . . . Dr. Prince, do you think I should tell my fiancé?"

"I would," Prince advised in warm, fatherly fashion. "I always advise my patients to be quite open about these things. In the long run it's best."

"Have it done and get it over with, darling!" had been Pete's advice. "Make sure. Then we can go on with our plans."

He had embraced Cynthia, and for the moment she felt safe in his powerful arms. Later that night, alone in her own bed, when the Horton house was still, the frightening feelings of her childhood returned to overwhelm her. She had not been deserving enough, not good enough for her natural mother to keep her. Now that she was diseased, she would not be good enough to marry.

She began to sob uncontrollably. She could be heard beyond the intimacy of her own room. In a while her father came in. Even in the dark, the look in his eyes told her he had not slept all night. He sat on the side of her bed, gathered her up in his arms.

"Cynthie, Cynthie baby, it's going to be all right. We've been through a thing or two as a family. We'll get through this. And it'll be fine. Fine! I was talking to one of my partners only this afternoon. He has a niece who went through the same thing. They operated and found it was nothing. Nothing at all. She's been married six years now and has two terrific kids. Believe me, it'll be all right. You know your dad would never let anything bad happen to you."

A man used to arguing the cases of clients was suddenly bereft of anything of positive value to speak on his own behalf, except promises meant to be reassuring which sounded weak and unconvincing during this terrifying night.

46

"Listen, darling, Prince is a member of the same country club as one of my partners. I'll have him arrange for me to meet Prince away from his office where we can talk uninterruptedly, man to man. I'll get the whole truth."

"I've always been a trouble to you and Mother."

"Never say that! Never even think it! Without you, this house, this . . . this life . . . would have been without meaning. What you think were troubles were really privileges for us. The times you were sick as a child were times of great pain to us. But times of great love as well. Great love."

Horton hesitated before confiding, "Cynthie, darling, there come times in a marriage when people feel empty. When a man and his wife wonder how or why they ever married to begin with. In those times, you held us together. Don't ever tell your mother I said that. But it's true.

"And there are times a man's career doesn't seem enough. Times I wonder, What the hell kind of profession am I in? My main function is to protect clients who I know have broken the law. I have to assist them—subtly, of course—to invent the kind of lies that judges, juries, or government administrators like to hear. So that one way or another my client can beat the law. It's a profession in which my success is determined by whether my guilty client can outwit the law. The worse *his* actions, the greater *my* success.

"I ask, is that a way for a man to spend his life? But then I come home and Barb is here, you are here. And it's not so bad anymore. You two are the part of my life that makes the rest bearable.

"Trouble? It's been a privilege to be your father. I want you to know that. All your life, I want you to remember that. It's been a privilege, Cynthie, darling."

She pressed against his shoulder, her tears wetting through his pajama top. The pain of her weeping scalded him as if her tears were acid.

Tenderly he set her down on her pillow. He kissed her on the brow, as he always did at night. At the door he paused long enough to say, "First thing in the morning I'll arrange to talk to Prince."

It had been almost dawn when she had finally fallen asleep, her hand on her belly trying to contain whatever it was that she felt was threatening her life.

Tonight, in Room 442 in State University Hospital, twenty-two-year-old Cynthia Horton again lay with her hand on her belly. Wondering what they would discover in there. Finding it impossible to believe that all this had happened to her so suddenly.

From the excitement and intoxication of making wedding plans to this. In only three days.

It was unreal. Yet she felt she had known all along that something dire would happen. That special destructive fate which had marked her since infancy had overtaken her again.

Chapter Four

It had been a usual harried morning for Dr. Craig Pierson. He had made his rounds of patients on the Ob-Gyn floor, checked on an experiment he was working on, been interrupted with a call to Emergency Admitting to save the life of a young woman who had tried to abort herself in a particularly dangerous way. She was now resting comfortably in Intensive Care with a chance for complete physical recovery.

Craig was not so confident of her emotional recovery from the near-fatal event, and it concerned him deeply.

Every patient on his service had to be viewed psychiatrically as well as physically. In any Gyn situation, a woman's sense of self was at stake at all times. Wife, mother, lover—her fulfillment as a woman depended on that part of her.

Craig had seen some of the most ardent fighters for equal rights who, when faced with a surgical decision of gynecological importance, were always concerned with one thing: How will it affect me as a *woman*? Then not equality with men, but equality with all other women was the only important criterion.

Emotional problems on the Ob-Gyn service presented themselves in many ways. The woman in 403, thirty-six years of age, was scheduled for a total hysterectomy to remove leiomyomata uteri, commonly called fibroids. Not dangerous, but uncomfortable and painful. And better removed than allowed to become a risk. Despite the fact that her ovaries would remain intact and functioning, all she thought of was, What will it do to me as a woman at such an early age in my life?

The girl of fifteen, in Room 427, had been born with an uncommon but by no means rare condition: the absence of a uterus and vagina. She would have to have a vaginoplasty, during which a skin graft would be performed to create a vagina so that she could, in the future, have a normal sex life though she could never conceive.

Always it came to the same thing in Craig's specialty: Doctor, save my life, but keep me a woman.

Don't remove or damage that part of me uniquely mine and the purpose for which I was born.

That problem, emotional and physical, was always compounded when the possibility of a malignancy presented itself. Craig was reminded of Cynthia Horton. Though she was not in need of medical attention this morning, she had seemed so disturbed last evening that he decided to drop by and reassure her. Her door was opening and Chief Resident Dr. Burt Carlyle was just emerging.

Carlyle was a light-skinned black man, lean and of slightly taller-than-average height. The same mixture of genes, black and white, that had endowed him with his color had also given him regular and handsome features. He carried himself with a dignity and confidence that were almost aggressive. No one could accuse Burt Carlyle of having arrived at the privileged rank of Chief Resident by virtue of any affirmative action, except his own. He had been an excellent student in medical school and had since absorbed all the surgical technique that Harvey Prince and other fine surgeons loved to demonstrate for the younger men.

Carlyle was a good surgeon. Better than good. He was excellent. The times when he experienced difficulty with white patients who objected to having a black man perform delicate examinations on them were very few. Carlyle's ability and confidence dispelled most prejudices or reservations.

Craig disapproved of only one trait in Burt Carlyle: he was always tougher on black interns than on other members of staff, feeling that their shortcomings or errors were, somehow, a reflection on him.

The rare times when Craig Pierson was unduly sharp with a young black intern, like Blinn, he suffered pangs of liberal conscience. But Carlyle never seemed to.

As soon as Carlyle saw Craig, he explained at once, "Prince asked me to have a look. Seems her father called him this morning. Kept him on the phone for fifteen minutes. You know how old Goldfingers is with families. Nice. But only up to a point. Time is money, he always says."

"Who should know better?" Craig joked. "How is she?"

"Tense. It was difficult to do a bimanual on her."

"And?"

"No question. Ovarian mass. Goldfingers says seven or eight centimeters. I say nine or ten."

"Making any bets on the biopsy?"

"A girl that young, I'd hate to." Carlyle added optimistically. "But then, it could be nothing. Like with LuAnne."

Carlyle referred to his own wife, a beautiful black girl who, until she married him, had been an outstanding fashion model. Then, only eighteen months ago, she had suddenly begun to present the same signs as Cynthia Horton. Except that in LuAnne's case there had been pain and some bleeding.

Carlyle had become terrified at the possibilities. As a professional courtesy, Dr. Prince had operated. Carlyle had asked Craig to assist. It turned out to be a benign tumor and no danger at all. Now she was seven months pregnant and gave no indication of any difficulty.

"Yes, like LuAnne, she could be lucky," Carlyle repeated. "But she is tense. Maybe you should increase her Valium."

"I'll have a look first."

"Sure," Carlyle agreed. "As an expert on beautiful

women, I can tell you that is one pretty girl. I would hate to see anything happen to her."

"Me too," Craig said, starting into the room.

Cynthia Horton was lying on her side, facing away from him. He thought she did not hear the soft hiss of the door. But without turning, she said, "I don't want any more doctors! I don't want to be poked at or pried into! I want to be left alone!"

"Good morning, Cynthia."

She turned. "Oh, it's you. You can come in. Only don't examine me again. Please?"

"I won't."

He stood over the bed, subtly trying to appraise her condition, yet not wanting to be too obvious since she was already so sensitive.

"There was a black doctor in here," she said. "He said Dr. Prince sent him. Was that true?"

"Of course."

"He wanted to examine me. At first I was going to say no. But then I realized I would hurt his feelings. So I . . . I let him," she said apologetically.

"He's Chief Resident and a damn good doctor. Wouldn't be surprised if Goldfingers tapped him for his office at the end of the year."

"Goldfingers?" she asked.

Craig laughed. "Dr. Prince. He's such a fantastic surgeon that we younger men call him that. It's an experience to watch him work."

She seemed encouraged by that.

"Well, how are you today?" he asked warmly. "Have a good night?"

"Not bad," she evaded.

"You did something for me yesterday," Craig said.

"What?" she asked, puzzled.

"Made me call home."

"I did?"

"The talk we had gave me a renewed appreciation of what terrific people mine are. You feel the same way about your folks?"

"Yes." But she sounded tentative and uncertain.

"You an only child?"

"Yes."

"Me too. It creates a responsibility. As if their whole lives were centered around you. You ever feel that way?"

"Yes."

His efforts at bringing her out had not succeeded. With each monosyllable she seemed to withdraw more. He considered for a moment having one of the psychiatric residents come see her. But there was so little time before the operation, it could accomplish nothing.

Of course, Kate might help. She was marvelously effective in emergency situations. Being a woman, she did especially well with patients on the Gyn service. Though there were times when Craig wished she would organize her own life first.

He took Cynthia's pulse and found it racing. Not unusual under such strain. Carlyle was right: he should increase her Valium. He must check first with her anesthetist to make sure it would not conflict with what he intended to use.

Craig was on his way to the residents' station to make his call when he passed young Blinn, who greeted him pleasantly. But there was a hint of guilt in the black intern's eyes. To discover if he had reinstated himself in Craig's favor, Blinn stopped to ask, "How is she today? Any calmer?"

"A little," Craig conceded. "Sorry about yesterday."

"That's okay. My daddy used to say the best learning come with a little pain. I guess that's what he meant." Blinn laughed.

It eased the tension and made Craig feel better.

"Think Prince would mind if I scrubbed?" Blinn asked.

"Of course not. The bigger the audience, the better he likes it," Craig said. "Sometimes I think he might insist on doing all his procedures in the amphitheater. And take bows at the end."

"Would you ask him for me?"

"Why not ask him yourself?" Craig suggested. He lowered his voice not to be overheard. "Blinn, you want some good advice? Don't be shy. Look at Carlyle. Chief Resident. That's the best you can be at his stage of a doctor's career. He didn't get there by being shy or humble."

"He didn't get there by being brash and aggressive," Blinn pointed out. "I don't know how to explain it to a white man. But there's a fine line for black men. You live your whole life walking that line. Between too little and too much. Either one is a crime. Carlyle has the formula down pat. But then, Carlyle's an exceptional doctor. Isn't he?"

"You're saying he made it on his own."

"There must be a certain confidence that comes from that," Blinn said.

"Blinn, look at it this way. They gave you the chance—an extra chance if you want to call it that. But *you* went to college, *you* went to medical school, *you* graduated. *You* took your National Boards, *you* passed them. Other men who entered on the same basis you did have failed. That has to mean something, doesn't it?"

Blinn nodded. Craig Pierson could see doubt still in the young intern's eyes.

54

"You ask Prince," Craig advised. "The worst he can say is no. But at least he'll know there's an intern around here named Blinn who's interested and anxious to learn."

"Okay, I will." Blinn was about to turn away, but hesitated. "You know what's so strange about it?"

"About what?" Craig asked, puzzled.

"I could never have had this conversation with Carlyle. Why?"

"I don't know. *Why?*"

Blinn shook his head, still puzzled. He readjusted his silver-framed glasses and headed down the corridor, presenting the classic silhouette of a young intern, white jacket with stethoscope dangling from his pocket.

As Craig watched him, he thought, Of course Prince will give him permission.

Craig would never forget the first time he scrubbed with Prince. It had been fascinating. The neat, horizontal incision which when healed would fold naturally into the abdomen leaving a minimal scar. The deft way he worked through layers of fat, muscle, and other tissue to get to the source of the trouble. The precise excision of a sample biopsy.

Then, once it was in the specimen tray and on its way to the pathologist's lab, Prince was as relaxed as if he were waiting to tee up because there was another foursome ahead of him. He had been genial and expansive during the entire ten minutes they waited for the results of the frozen section, speaking to Craig as if he were a concerned and caring father.

"Let me tell you, Pearsall . . ."

"Pierson," Craig had to correct him, to make sure Prince would remember his name.

"Pierson. Of course. Let me give you the best medical advice you are ever going to get. Start investing when you're young. You residents these days get fortunes compared with what I got when I started out. All I got was room, board, and fifty dollars a month. Not twelve and fifteen thousand a year like you fellows.

"So I say, with that kind of money, whatever you save after taxes, put it into the market. Don't take flyers. Buy only good stuff. Blue chips. And energy stocks. For the rest of your life buy energy. Put 'em away. Don't trade. Don't get nervous when the market goes down. In fact, that's the time to buy more, not pull out.

"Keep piling up equity. Then when you're fifty you can decide if you want to continue to practice or retire. Myself, I don't ever want to retire. But I do want to know that I have that freedom. That's the thing that counts. Yes, Piersall, freedom."

"Pierson," Craig had had to remind him once more.

"Yes, of course, Pierson." Prince accepted the correction graciously.

At that moment the phone had buzzed. The pathologist was on the line. The frozen section had come up positive. Endometrial carcinoma.

Prince returned to the table and, as though he had never interrupted the operation, he proceeded to perform a total hysterectomy, staging it first to make sure the carcinoma was localized, confined to the immediate area.

While he worked swiftly and with great skill, he continued to talk, not of surgery but of practical plans for young doctors.

"Another thing, Piersall," Prince said through the mask that covered his mouth and his elegant white moustache. "When it comes time to go into practice ... you *are* going into private practice, aren't you?"

"I haven't decided yet."

"That's where the money is. If you do go into practice, don't put all your available cash into office equipment and furniture. Get a bank loan. Interest is deductible from your income taxes. So you benefit two ways. The interest comes off, and meantime your own money is working for you in the market. Or in tax-exempts. Though for the first couple of years you won't want to bother with tax-exempts. You won't be in a high enough bracket. Anyhow, don't forget, borrow the money for your office.

"I know a couple of doctors who bought their own CAT scan machine. Six hundred and fifty thousand dollars. Financed by a bank. The interest comes off their taxes. Their fees for scans are three hundred dollars a crack. At the end of ten years they'll own the machine outright and be a million and a half net ahead of the game.

"Yes, Piersall, these days practicing medicine is only half what a doctor does. The other half is trying to outwit the government. Patients complain about high fees, but between malpractice insurance and taxes, a good man is lucky to net a hundred thousand at the end of the year. Do you know what it costs me just to open my office in the morning? Five nurses and an office manager. Two assistants. Eight examining rooms. My nut for the year, counting malpractice insurance for three doctors, rent, salaries, and other expenses, including paying off equipment, is three hundred twenty thousand. And that's before I net a dollar for myself.

"They're destroying us, Piersall, destroying us. Some days I think the worst enemy I have is the United States Government!"

Through the entire financial lecture, which Craig Pierson hardly listened to, he had watched with awe as Prince completed the surgery cleanly, efficiently, and with great finesse.

The procedure completed, Prince was stripping off his surgical gloves as he said, "Piersall, if you decide to go out on your own, let me know. I might have room in my office for a bright young man like you."

"Thank you," Craig Pierson had said. It was a flattering suggestion from a man as important as Prince.

As Prince tossed his gloves into the unsterile-waste container, Craig felt obliged to remind him, "By the way, sir, the name is Pierson. Not Piersall."

"Oh, yes," Prince had replied affably, "of course. Pierson. I'll remember next time."

After that first day, Craig Pierson knew precisely why, from the beginning of Prince's affiliation with State University Hospital eleven years ago, all the older doctors had called him "Goldfingers."

Burt Carlyle, who had scrubbed along with Craig Pierson that day, must have read his thoughts. Once Prince left, Burt advised Craig, "Don't let it throw you. Just watch his fingers while he's talking finance and you'll learn a hell of a lot about surgery. Listen to him talk finance while he's doing surgery and you'll learn a hell of a lot more about how to become a successful doctor."

"Is he always like that?"

"When you've got his technique, you can talk about anything and still be better than most surgeons. He's precise, accurate. He makes quick judgments and he performs. Man, that's the thing to remember. He performs," Carlyle said admiringly. "One day I'm going to be that good! There's a reason he has more beds in Ob-Gyn than any other surgeon."

Days later, when Craig had scrubbed with Prince a second time, he heard him utter a bit of advice that he would always remember. Prince had just received an equivocal report from the pathology lab. He paused for only an instant before he said, "When in doubt, take it out!" Prince had then proceeded to do surgery which Craig considered far too radical for the situation. Later, when he raised the question with Carlyle, Burt had said, "Study Prince's record. His cancer patients have a remarkable five-year survival rate."

Dr. Harvey Prince came striding down the corridor of the Ob-Gyn floor greeting nurses, residents, and interns. He was attired in what had become his trademark when he made his visits to the floor. He always wore one of his half-dozen neatly pressed, custom-made, light gray flannel suits, with a budding red rose in his lapel. He always pretended a warmth and affability which he believed won him the admiration and cooperation of the entire staff. If his older colleagues and competitors envied or resented him, he strove to make the younger men admire and respect him. He was especially warm in greeting Craig Pierson.

This time he lingered long enough to ask, "Pierson, do you play golf?"

"Afraid not. But I've taken care of many a fairway and green. My dad's in the landscaping business."

"Oh? Really?" Prince pretended to be pleasantly surprised. "I thought if you were free Wednesday afternoon, you might like to come out to my club. An afternoon of golf, then dinner out on the veranda. They serve a marvelous buffet Wednesday evenings."

"I'd love to," Craig said. "But I'm a tennis buff myself."

"Tennis!" Prince reacted, delighted. "Wonderful! Carol's a tennis player. A hell of a good one. She was ranked in college. She'll give you quite a game. See if you can arrange Wednesday."

"I'll try." Craig avoided a firm commitment. He had been warned about Prince's daughter Carol. She was a nice, homely girl, and as resentful of her father's matchmaking propensities as were the young residents and interns upon whom he imposed from time to time.

Prince asked suddenly, "Have we got a signed consent from the Horton girl?"

"I'll check and see."

"Do that. Her father's a lawyer. A nervous lawyer. Had me on the phone again for half an hour early this morning. I do not like to operate on the family members of lawyers. They sue for malpractice at the drop of a hat. So make sure we get that consent signed right away. Though I may have to delay her for another day or two. Three emergencies in a row. All referred last evening. Never got out of the office until past eight o'clock. Get that consent signed." Prince started away, turning back only to call out, "And let me know about Wednesday, so I can tell Carol to sharpen up her game."

Craig Pierson knocked softly on the door of Room 442. There was no answer. He opened the door slightly. "Cynthia?"

He heard her answer. But when he entered she was not in her bed.

"Cynthia?"

"Yes," he heard her answer from the bathroom.

The door was open. He found her staring into the mirror over the washbasin, examining her face very carefully. She drew down the skin that covered her cheekbones, the better to stare into her eyes. She

60

pressed her cheeks, as if attempting to make a diagnosis. Finally she turned to face him.

"I look the same. Surely if there were something wrong, really wrong, it would show. I'd be able to detect it. All I can see is red. I've done a lot of crying," she confessed.

"That's why it's best to have the surgery. Get the suspense over with," he encouraged.

She came out into the small sunlit room. Though she wore a loose blue silk robe, he realized she was a nicely proportioned, very feminine girl, even more attractive than she appeared lying in bed. Despite her eyes, which did betray considerable weeping, her face was more than pretty. She was quite beautiful— and so young.

Craig himself was only thirty. But twenty-two seemed a long time ago, and anyone that age was very young.

"Do I have to stay in bed?"

"Of course not."

"Bed is depressing. Makes you feel like an invalid."

She dropped into the armchair, more casual and self-contained than when last he had seen her. The euphoria induced by the Valium had set in. Good.

"Cynthia, there's a standard procedure in all hospitals. Before a patient can be operated on, she has to sign a form. An informed consent."

"Yes, I know. Daddy told me."

"I assume Dr. Prince explained everything to you. The procedure. Its purpose. The questions that might come up in the course of the operation. The importance of the pathologist's report."

"Yes, yes, he did," she said, impatient to get over the preliminaries.

He handed her the blue sheet.

G-117 CONSENT FOR OPERATION OR PROCEDURE appeared at the top in bold black type. After the date, her name, her hospital number, and her birth date, she could read:

1. I AUTHORIZE DR. HARVEY PRINCE OR SUCH AS-SOCIATES AS MAY BE SELECTED BY THE DOCTOR, TO PERFORM UPON MYSELF THE FOLLOWING OPERATION/PROCEDURES: EXPLORATORY LAPAROTOMY, SURGERY PERFORMED THROUGH THE ABDOMEN FOR THE PUR-POSE OF DOING A BIOPSY ON THE RIGHT OVARY.
2. IN THE EVENT DEVELOPMENTS INDICATE FUR-THER OPERATIONS/PROCEDURES MAY BE NECESSARY. I AUTHORIZE THE PHYSICIANS TO USE THEIR OWN JUDGMENT AND DO WHATEVER THEY DEEM ADVISABLE DURING THE OPERATION/PROCEDURE FOR THE PA-TIENT'S BEST INTERESTS, EXCEPT THE FOLLOWING:

After the printed words ended, the word NONE had been typed in.

Cynthia looked up at Craig. "That word 'none': does that mean if they do find . . ." she faltered over the word, "something, cancer, they might do some drastic things to me?"

"Extensive surgery might be deemed advisable," he said as gently as he could.

"Like what?" she challenged.

"It might be necessary to do what we call a bilateral salpingo-oophorectomy," he said gingerly.

Nervous, she tried to laugh, as she said, "You can talk clearer than that, Doctor." The joke died on her lips.

"It would mean excising both tubes and ovaries. We might possibly remove the uterus as well."

"That would mean . . ." Cynthia Horton dared: "I'd never be able to have children—wouldn't it?"

"We're dealing in *ifs*. *If* there is a malignancy, *if* Dr. Prince finds other involvements, *if* he decides that's the proper course to take . . . Remember, it could be benign, nothing at all."

Her blue eyes sharpened angrily. "We're making quite a fuss over 'nothing at all,' aren't we?"

"Only in the interest of making sure."

Cynthia Horton was thoughtful for a time. She made another attempt to study the form. She tried to do so bravely, but the wavering form betrayed her trembling hands. She could not continue.

"I can't. I won't." She turned away to hide her tears.

"We can't help you without it," Craig urged.

"I won't!" Cynthia Horton said firmly.

Craig decided to have Kate talk to her.

He was on his way to the phone when Dr. Prince came down the corridor. One could tell when he was having one of his crowded operating-room days. He approached Craig, asked crisply, "The Hooten girl?"

"Horton," Craig corrected.

"Yes, of course, Horton. I just looked at her chart. There's still no consent form."

"She hasn't signed it yet."

"Why not?"

"She's tense. Emotional. It's a big decision. The most important she's ever taken," Craig tried to explain.

"Hell! Patients do it every day! I may want to squeeze her in tomorrow if my first few procedures go off without a hitch."

"She's only twenty-two, and this is a shock. She has to get adjusted to the idea."

"I explained everything. I reassured her. Now, get that consent!" Prince ordered.

"I'm calling Dr. Lindstrom now."

"Who the hell is Dr. Lindstrom?" Prince exploded in an indignant whisper.

"She's on the Psychiatric Service. Resident."

"Okay. Call her. But get that damned thing signed before the day's out. I've got a busy day tomorrow and I can't wait for last-minute forms to be signed."

Craig watched as Prince strode down the hall to disappear into the room in which the wife of a State Senator was recuperating after the surgery Prince had performed four days ago. It was noted and remarked upon among residents that though Prince left the aftercare of most of his patients to the staff, he always made it a point to bestow unusual post-op attention on the wives of influential men. Among them he was known as a most considerate and concerned surgeon. Which led to a great number of profitable referrals.

Chapter Five

Katherine Lindstrom was a disarmingly small blond young woman of twenty-nine, who appeared to be years younger. Standing somewhat more than an even five feet, with a slender but quite feminine body, she was destined to be taken for a college junior for the next five years of her life. Actually, she had been graduated from a Midwestern university *cum laude*, had been accepted by its medical school and had broken off her relationship with a law student to concentrate on her own career.

Her mother, who had lived all her life on a farm in eastern Nebraska, understood that. Her father, who considered himself a practical man, would never understand. He had met the young law student once during a summer vacation and had judged him a suitable husband with good prospects for the future. Why his only daughter would ask any more out of life he did not know. When his wife tried to explain that in these times women had different plans for their lives, he asked, "Laurie, do you have any regrets? Aren't you satisfied with your life?"

It would have been difficult for her to explain without hurting his feelings, so she always insisted she had no regrets. Secretly she admired her daughter and envied her. The time Kate had been arrested for chaining herself to the founder's statue on campus to protest unfair entrance conditions for women into professional schools, her mother agreed with her. But her father was shocked and outraged. However, he did get into his half-ton truck and drive three hundred and fifty miles to the university to bail his daughter out. He had almost been arrested himself for telling off the judge who had dared to chastise Kate and her fellow protesters on the day of their bailing.

Before he drove back home, he let Kate know what he would not admit to the judge: that he was most critical of her conduct. It was the kind of thing her mother never would have done, he declared.

"Don't you understand, Dad?—it's because Mother never did it that we have to."

Dad did not understand. He pressed twenty dollars into her hand and said, "Get yourself some new jeans. Those are pretty torn and dirty. Better still, get yourself a skirt or a dress."

He kissed her warmly, got into his truck and drove the three hundred and fifty miles back, shaking his head most of the way and wondering if it had been

65

wise to send her off to the university in the first place. Women, he kept muttering. And especially these days. It must be television. Any problem that would not allow itself to be satisfactorily explained was blamed on television.

When Kate came home at the end of her junior year and announced that she had decided to go to medical school, her father listened, shook his head, glanced at her mother, whose look warned, Don't say a word, Carl. And he did not. When Kate announced that that would mean breaking off with her young man, her father glared at her mother. But her mother remained impassive.

Late that night, in the quiet privacy of their own bedroom, Kate's mother lay awake and restless while her father tried to get some sleep so that he could be up by dawn to resume his chores. After a while, it proved useless. They were both too restless. They had to discuss it. In whispers, lest Kate overhear.

"Carl, I want you to give her permission," her mother said softly.

"I didn't say no, did I?"

"I mean more than not saying no. I mean saying *yes*. I mean a real firm yes."

"When you were her age, we'd been married four years and had a son," her husband reminded her.

"When I was her age, I'd been through high school and no further. Those were different times. The war was just over; you came home from the army. Every girl who had a man was getting married. Nowadays they go to college."

"And what good does it do? It only makes them want to go on," he said. "A doctor," he considered disapprovingly. "Nobody wants to go to a lady doctor. A nurse maybe. But not a doctor."

66

"It's what she wants, Carl."

"Maybe that's the trouble: being the only girl, she's always had her own way," her father grumbled softly.

"That's not why. She's had her own way because she's strong-minded. And smart. She did better in high school than Ted and Junior. She'll be good at anything she wants, if she wants it enough."

"Oh, she wants it," her father admitted grudgingly. "I wish she wanted it less. A doctor, Laurie. Do you know what that means? Having to examine men so . . . so intimately?"

"A girl brought up on a farm knows all she needs to. She won't be shy."

"No, she won't," her father agreed, though it was not meant as praise. "Talking about such things, Laurie, that young man who came to visit last summer—do you think Kate and him . . . you know . . . these days that's all you hear about kids in college."

"You mean, were they living together?"

"I didn't exactly mean living together," he protested. "I meant . . . okay, yes, living together."

"She hasn't said anything. She's a very private girl. But she has good sense. And you keep saying 'these days.' You're forgetting, Carl, how it was with us after you came home."

"But I'd been away for three years. The war and all. That was different."

"Do you think *my* father thought it was different?"

"We were always planning on getting married. There was never any doubt about that, was there?"

"No," Laurie Lindstrom conceded.

"Well, then," Carl Lindstrom said, as if he had won his argument.

"What if Kate and her young man were planning on getting married? Would that make it all right?"

"Not exactly all right, but somewhat better."

"Get some sleep, Carl. You have to be up early."

He turned over on his side, reached back to pat her on the behind, the last thing he did each night before dozing off. It was a small gesture, but it reassured them both.

Just before he fell asleep, he asked, "How much does it cost to send a girl to medical school?"

"The same as it costs to send a boy," her mother said softly, putting an end to any further discussion.

It was Laurie Lindstrom's boldest stroke for the equality of women in her time. And she never regretted it.

Kate Lindstrom had entered medical school, had done well in all four years, and had been graduated with high grades. She had selected psychiatry as her specialty and, a year ago, had become only the second female resident in the history of the Psychiatry Department.

She met Craig Pierson during a Grand Rounds session which had been devoted to postpartum depression, an area in which the departments of Ob-Gyn and Psychiatry had a commonality of interest. He was struck by her from the moment she walked into the auditorium. She was an uncommonly attractive girl. She also turned out to be quite forthright and firm in her opinions and her contribution to the session. He came away greatly impressed.

She would confess to him later that she had not even noticed him during that session. Tall men, good-looking men were not as exceptional in such a meeting as was a pretty, and bright, young woman.

He called her after that meeting. But she was always too busy to see him. It was no strategy, no game. She was simply busy. She did not spare herself, either in the clinic or on the wards. She made it a point to keep up with the literature in her own and allied fields. As she would explain to him one night, "Every illness creates its own psychiatric consequences. So I have to know all I can about all illnesses."

He had started dating her with only romance in mind. Within a few weeks he ended up admiring her as well as being in love with her. She was a determined little girl. He would always call her that, even though it annoyed her.

The first time they made love together, it was she, not he, who made it quite clear that there would be no permanent commitment until she had settled her professional future. When he persisted in wanting to formalize their relationship, she was quite gentle and considerate in pointing out that being an adopted child, he needed that kind of assurance. But that was no basis, she declared, on which to make important lifelong commitments.

But without spoken demands or agreements, they remained faithful to each other. They remained aloof from each other's professional duties and decisions. Except at those times when Craig felt the need of psychiatric assistance in coping with an especially distraught patient.

Cynthia Horton was such a case. Kate examined Cynthia's chart in detail, studied the findings of all three physicians—those of Corbin, Craig, and especially Harvey Prince.

She had her own private reservations about Harvey Prince. He had once made a pass at her after she had observed at one of his more intricate surgical procedures. This despite the fact that Rita Hallen, his chief scrub nurse, was within earshot. Everyone in the hos-

69

pital knew that Rita was Prince's mistress and had been for nine years. When staff members gossiped about it, there was never any criticism of Rita. But there was always an undercurrent of disapproval of Prince, who carried on flagrantly with Rita despite the fact that he was married. It was also well known that he had had brief affairs with other, younger, nurses and, at times, with patients as well.

Aware of all this, Kate respected Harvey Prince only for his work at the operating table. She had to grant, as did everyone, that there he was superb.

Once she was thoroughly familiar with Cynthia Horton's chart, Dr. Kate Lindstrom knocked gently at the door of 442. She entered and found Cynthia lying on her side, facing away from the door, her arm trailing over the edge of the bed. Motionless, she seemed asleep.

"Miss Horton?" Kate asked softly.

"I didn't ring for a nurse," Cynthia said.

"I'm not a nurse."

Cynthia turned to stare. Kate realized at once that what Craig had said was true: Cynthia was a remarkably beautiful girl. Her inner torment added pathos to her beauty.

"I'm Dr. Lindstrom."

"I don't want to be examined by any more doctors! I am not a specimen! Or a ward patient! I don't want to be used as a practice dummy!"

"I'm not here to examine you."

Cynthia Horton glared at her, openly distrustful.

"I understand you refuse to sign the consent form for your operation."

"It's not *my* operation. It's *their* operation. *His* operation. I'll bet he does a lot of operations that are unnecessary! I've read about doctors like him," the patient said venomously.

70

"I've examined your chart. There's no doubt surgery is indicated. But I'm more interested in your reaction than I am in the surgery itself. Being a woman, I think I know what you're going through."

"Oh, do you?" Cynthia demanded, trying to sound combative—but not succeeding, for she was on the verge of tears.

"The fact that I'm a doctor doesn't mean I'm any less a woman. I examine myself every month to make sure I have no alarming lumps in my breasts. I go to my gynecologist every six months for a checkup and a Pap. I've had two occasions when I thought I felt something in one breast and had that pang that Maybe this is it. Then that flood of fear—burning fear that maybe they were going to take my womanhood away from me. So I do know the feeling."

Cynthia Horton turned to face Kate Lindstrom.

"Yes," Kate reassured her, "I know how you feel. Because we both have our lives ahead of us. Which means marriage, and childbearing. We may have jobs, professions, or careers, but we're essentially women. To fulfill ourselves, we want to be wives and mothers."

"I was supposed to be married in four weeks," Cynthia explained softly.

"Why do you put it in the past tense?" Kate asked, slipping into the chair so that they could talk more intimately.

"Because I have a feeling it won't happen."

"The surgery can be done and you can be home in less than a week. There may be no need to change your plans."

"There will be, if they find it."

"Find what?" Kate pinned her down.

"That thing."

"What thing? Say it."

The girl hesitated. Finally, she said, "Cancer"—but said it softly.

"The odds are—"

The girl interrupted sharply, "I know about the odds! I want to know about *me*. Do *I* have it?"

"Instead of tormenting yourself with doubts, let the doctors find out. It may be benign."

"And it may not!"

"True. But the best chance for a cure lies in early detection. This may be the most fortunate thing that could have happened."

"They all say that. But somehow I know . . . I just know . . . it won't turn out right. Won't!" she insisted.

Kate betrayed no hint of the concern she felt. She knew, as every psychiatrist knew, that the psychological state of the patient could be highly important if it did turn out to be cancer. Patients with an affirmative attitude could develop a factor which, for want of a better name, had been dubbed *host resistance*. If that affirmative attitude was lacking in the patient, she might develop *host acquiescence*, making herself a more submissive victim to the deadly disease.

This girl, Kate thought, has already resigned herself to the worst of all prognoses.

"I understand you couldn't give Dr. Pierson a complete medical history."

"Oh, you know I'm adopted?"

"Yes. And I understand your fear. But you're an intelligent girl. Surely you must realize that what you're reacting to now is not the possibility of the disease. It's the fact that you feel deprived. Cast out. Never good enough. Else why did your natural mother give you away? So you fear that somehow, up in that operating room, the same thing will happen. They won't care. Because you're not good enough. They'll let some terrible thing happen to you again."

Cynthia did not dispute her.

"Who'll let it happen? Your mother and father, who love you? Your fiancé, who wants to marry you? Dr. Prince? Dr. Carlyle? Dr. Pierson? Men who devote their lives to saving people? Are they going to single you out and say, No, this one we'll cast out, we'll reject, desert? Does that make sense?"

Cynthia shook her head.

"Unless you sign that consent, none of them can help you. And they want to; they all want to."

Kate drew the blue consent form from the pocket of her lab coat.

"That line," Cynthia said. "The one that says, 'Restrictions: none.'"

"It means you give the surgeon permission to exercise his professional judgment on what's to be done once he gets the pathologist's report."

"He could do anything . . . remove anything . . ."

"He would take whatever steps are necessary to protect your health and your life. That's all we're interested in. You have to trust us, Cynthia."

Cynthia Horton stared down at the form. Without a word, without looking into Kate's eyes, she held out her hand for the pen.

As she finished signing, the door opened tentatively.

"Cynthia?" a woman asked.

"Mama?" Cynthia Horton responded like a frightened child.

Barbara Horton entered. Cynthia looked up at her, tears forming in her eyes. "I signed it, Mama. I signed it."

"Good. It's the best thing," her mother agreed, trying to smile.

Kate Lindstrom went out to the nurses' station. After she herself had signed *Dr. K. Lindstrom* in the space provided under SIGNATURE OF PHYSICIAN SECURING THIS CONSENT, she placed the signed consent form in Cynthia Horton's chart.

She called Craig. He was greatly relieved. They both assumed that Kate had completed her work on the case.

They were wrong.

Chapter Six

Rita Hallen had sharp, neat features which were accented by the severe headdress she was required to wear in the operating room, where she presided as chief scrub nurse. When she was not in her required hospital garb, her face was more apt to be described as pleasing. Never soft, but quite attractive. She was dark-haired and tall. Her femininity, concealed by green O.R. gowns, became quite apparent in the dresses she chose for social occasions. Though she had turned forty, she impressed strangers as being in her mid-thirties. But tense young interns and nurses, whom she dominated during surgical procedures, considered her to be closer to sixty.

Blinn had once said, "It would take that long to make a woman that tough."

A tyrant in the O.R. Rita Hallen had proved most inept in her private life. She had first met Dr. Harvey Prince when he had joined the hospital eleven years before. She had been twenty-nine at the time. And he forty-four. Not as distinguished as he now appeared, Prince had always been handsome, tall, and brilliant with a scalpel. His addition as an attending surgeon at State University Hospital had been considered a triumph. He had had an excellent reputation in the Northeast, having been affiliated with a most prestigious hospital there. His reason for leaving was hardly unique. He had grown weary of the hassle of life in a large old city. He preferred a newer community where he and his family could live graciously in pleasant suburbs only ten minutes from the hospital. And where he was only minutes from the country club for his usual Wednesday and weekend golf.

When Harvey Prince first met Rita Hallen, she had just recovered from a long and tragic relationship with a young resident who had died of a self-administered overdose in a hospital utility room at a time when he was supposed to be on duty. For a time it had been rumored Rita would be terminated as a result of the scandal. When it was proved that she had had no part in the doctor's addiction, she had been granted a six-month leave of absence and restored to the staff thereafter.

To prove herself when she returned, Rita Hallen had become a despot in the operating room. She was the essence of professionalism. She had no personal attachments in the hospital or outside. She avoided cultivating friendships. She lived alone. Some termed her a recluse.

She would have lived out her life that way if Harvey Prince had not joined the hospital.

Their first meeting outside the hospital had taken the form of a much-needed after-hours drink. Prince had just completed a long, difficult procedure. A Stage Four ovarian cancer. The procedure, which included an omentectomy, a total hysterectomy, and the bilateral excision of both tubes and ovaries, had consumed more than three and a half hours.

He had left the O.R. perspiring furiously. In the locker room, he had stripped off his sweaty, bloody O.R. outfit and sunk down on the bench exhausted. He recovered eventually, took his shower, and dressed in his gray flannel suit, red rose in place.

He was just emerging from the locker room when Rita Hallen came off duty and passed by. She stopped long enough to do something she had never done before. She complimented the surgeon.

"If she has any chance at all, you gave it to her," Rita had said.

"Tough case," Prince admitted. "But I never could have done it without you. You're the best scrub nurse I've ever had. No one in the East can touch you."

"Thank you, Doctor," Rita had said, unused to receiving compliments, only respect.

Prince sighed wearily. "I'm too keyed up. I'd like a drink. Would you join me?"

Rita hesitated.

"Please?" he insisted. "For my sake? I need someone to talk to."

She nodded finally, breaking a vow she had made never again to become social with any doctor. And never, never to become involved.

In a dark booth in a small cocktail lounge not far from the hospital, they drank and talked. Mainly Prince talked. About his training, his past, the way his wife had worked to help him through medical school. The main reason he had left the East. Professional jealousy, hospital politics. All he wanted was to practice his specialty as best he could without having to fight a constant rearguard action against other, lesser surgeons who made up for their lack of skill by advancing themselves politically.

"I'm not a politician. If God has given me any talent at all, it's in my hands."

He had stared down at them as if they were disembodied instruments, scientific *objets d'art* to be admired.

"You were fantastic this afternoon," Rita said. "I've never seen a surgeon who could have done it half as well or so swiftly."

He took her hand. His touch excited her.

"I work with such confidence only because you're there. Rita, I've felt something for a long time. But never had the courage to say it. I think there was an element of fate involved in my coming here. In meeting you. The first time I saw you I felt it. By the time I'd worked with you for a month I knew it. We understand each other. We need each other."

Rita had remained tense and breathless throughout his declaration. She was powerfully tempted, yet terrified. For she knew how strongly attracted to him she had been from the start. His skill had earned her admiration. His attractiveness had evoked her desire. But she knew that once she let down her reserve, she would have no defenses at all against this overwhelming man.

She should have chosen to withdraw her hand. Instead, she had closed her hand over his.

Encouraged, Prince continued, "I've heard the sad story of your past experience. I know what you must have gone through. But Rita, my dear, you can't go on this way. You're a young woman. A beautiful young woman. A capable young woman. The best in your profession. But a woman is no woman at all without a man. You're punishing yourself for his crime. You can't go on doing that. I won't let you. It's not fair. To you. *Or* to me."

At those last words, Rita looked into his eyes.

"Rita, darling, I'm saying it as plainly as I can. I love you. I need you. Not just in the O.R. You have no idea how many times a day I say, Oh, if only Rita were here to share this with me. You know how it is when you love someone. You need that one person to give everything else meaning.

"I've been a man without meaning for months now. Surgery, yes—that has meaning. Because you're there. I can see the look of approval in your eyes. And the sadness, too, when we both know that no matter what I do the patient hasn't a chance. Like the day that young girl died because of that stupid anesthetist's mistake. All that night I relived that terrible moment when I had to explain to her family. But I consoled myself, No matter if they blame me, Rita knows. And that was enough. That's how much you mean to me."

He took her back to her apartment. He made love to her. For the first time in several years she felt like a woman again.

At first, nothing was said about his wife. For Rita it was enough that she had him to herself for a little part of every week. By the end of the second year of their affair, she realized that for a woman in her thirties, theirs was a relationship that held out little promise for the future. Yet she needed him. So she continued. Waiting for the odd moments when he could get away to see her. Willing to meet him in small, out-of-the-way places where they would not be observed. Forgiving the times when he promised to meet her, then at the last minute phoned to say he could not because some emergency had arisen.

A frustrating existence, it was still fuller than it had been before she had taken him into her life.

She had seen Margaret Prince only twice. Once when the hospital dedicated a new building. Once at the Christmas party given on the hundredth anniversary of the founding of the hospital. Both times the entire staff had been invited, with wives or husbands, so the crowd was large enough to make their meeting safe and innocuous.

On the second occasion, Margaret Prince, small, dark-haired, expensively dressed, if not pretty, had said, "Oh, Miss Hallen, I've wanted to meet you. Harvey talks about you often. He says you're the finest nurse he's ever worked with!"

"Thank you," Rita said, modestly accepting the compliment. But silently she said, You idiot, don't you know? Don't you even suspect? What's wrong with you that you can't give him the love he needs?

From that time Rita Hallen had begun a persistent campaign demanding that Harvey divorce his wife and marry her. Many times she threatened to break off their relationship unless he did. Always he had ready excuses. The scandal would endanger his career. God knew, there was enough gossip about gynecologists; to give substance to it in his case might cause him irreparable damage. But one day soon. Soon . . .

So, because she needed him, Rita had permitted their affair to continue, enduring the deprivations, frustrations, lonely holidays, and hospital gossip, as well as his lies and evasions.

When Harvey Prince felt a strong enough urge for her, and could gracefully manage the time, he would see her. The night before he planned to do the Horton girl was one of those times.

He had called Margaret from his office late in the

afternoon. His pretext was that he had an unusually complicated case early the next morning and he wanted to devote the evening to examining all the X-ray films and scans, discussing the proper anesthesia, and a hundred other details, since the woman had an unfortunate combination of problems, including an earlier heart involvement. So he would be home late. Possibly very late. Margaret was not to hold dinner for him. Or wait up.

For Harvey Prince and Rita Hallen, the evening began with a few drinks, then dinner in a small French restaurant never frequented by members of the hospital staff. He did most of the talking, as usual. She drank little, ate little, as usual. He detected that this might develop into one of her morose evenings, when she took most of the joy out of sex. So he talked of an invitation he had received to address a convention of Ob-Gyn men in Las Vegas three months from then. If he could arrange it, he would like Rita to come with him. That would mean finding some reason for Margaret not to go along. But Margaret had never liked Vegas anyhow. So it could be managed. If Rita could arrange to take her vacation at the same time, it would be perfect. Yes, they must plan on going to Vegas together.

The prospect did not diminish Rita's resentment. She persisted in moody silence throughout the meal and for most of the night, except in her most passionate moments, when she gave way to him completely. Afterward, he talked, as he always did afterward, about the day when he could finally be free of Margaret, free to marry Rita. He always talked that way, but over the years his reasons had subtly changed. Whereas, earlier, possible damage to his professional reputation had stood in the way, in more recent times his problem had become how to divorce Margaret without giving her legal grounds to take most of his substantial holdings.

Once more he promised to talk to his lawyer. But he had not yet done it. And, Rita suspected, he might never do it. She knew what she ought to do. She also knew that she never would.

Harvey Prince was dressing to go home. He stared at himself in the mirror to make sure that no telltale sign of lovemaking remained. He doused himself with the bottle of Dunhill's strong after-shave, which he kept at Rita's for the express purpose of obliterating any of her fragrance that might linger after his shower.

"Have you seen the schedule for tomorrow, darling?" he said.

"I know you have that exenteration first thing," she called to him as she slipped out of bed and into the expensive red chiffon peignoir he had bought her two Christmases ago.

He came out of the bathroom, buttoning his shirt as he said, "Then there's a total hysterectomy." He smiled, a bit proud as he added, "The mayor's wife. He called me himself only yesterday. Wanted to know what effect the operation would have on her. So I said, 'At thirty-eight, she's had all the kids she wants. So she's not going to miss whatever I take out. In fact, you can now enjoy sex even more.'"

He was chuckling until he noticed Rita was neither smiling nor amused. She was thinking, I'm past forty. Whatever they take out of me, I won't miss it either.

To smooth over the awkward moment, he continued blithely and quickly, "Oh, yes, if there's time and I don't feel too tired, there's that other case. Young girl with an ovarian mass. Shouldn't take long. Routine exploratory. I doubt if it's malignant. So it should be over quick."

He had finished dressing. Rita's silence made him

81

aware that the unfortunate comparison with the mayor's wife still lingered. He knew what was called for now. He lifted her from her bed and embraced her as he whispered to her.

"Darling, believe me, I would if I could. But it's not possible right now. Unless we left here. I think about that. But after all, I'm not forty-four now, I'm fifty-five. I can't think about starting up someplace new. Not at my age. I'm so well established here. It would be a crime to give it all up."

"*She* could leave here," Rita said flatly. Rita never referred to Margaret Prince by name.

"I wish I had some way of making her. But there are the girls."

That was always his last refuge. His daughters. One in her last year in high school. The other just graduated from Smith. That he was truly fond of them Rita had no doubt. But that he used them as an excuse for inaction she did not doubt either. Yet she had never before dared to openly question his loyalty to his daughters.

He was gone. Rita Hallen put the cups and saucers into the dishwasher, turned out the kitchen light, and went into the living room to see if there was a good movie on the late late show.

There was. She watched it until she fell asleep. She woke a little past three, to find a completely different movie on the tube. The tinny sound track told her it must be a film from long ago. It was also in black and white and featured stars all of whom had been dead for years now.

She went back into her bedroom. She sat before her dressing-table mirror. Forty years old. And hopelessly involved with a man who had no plans to marry her. There were times—this night was one of them—when she thought the best thing she could do was quit and go back home to the small coal-mining town in West Virginia where she had been born.

Instead, she fell asleep thinking of tomorrow's O.R. schedule.

First a long, complicated exenteration, then a total hysterectomy, and if there was time, that young girl with the ovarian mass.

Chapter Seven

Kate Lindstrom never stayed over at Craig Pierson's apartment. But he had stayed at her place many times. In her mind, for some reason she had never been able to explain to him, she insisted on that arrangement because it gave her a greater sense of control over her life. There was something more reassuring and right about receiving a man into her own bed than there was in getting into his.

The night before surgery on Cynthia Horton, Craig and Kate had been to dinner. A modest dinner, with an inexpensive French wine. They had talked about the hospital, the latest administrative gossip, cases of interest.

Lastly, they talked of themselves. Craig did. Kate made it a point to avoid any conversation that might commit her to a course upon which she had not yet decided. Like most residents at the hospital, she had to choose soon between private practice and full-time academic medicine. Stay on or move to another hospital in another city. It would depend on a combination of her ambitions and what offers might be forthcoming.

Craig Pierson had just about made that decision for himself. If they would have him, he would stay on. He saw a good future here at the hospital and the medical school. On the basis of the qualifications and the ages of the men who outranked him in the Ob-Gyn Department, he could even see himself one day assuming the Chiefship of the department.

That would never mean great wealth. He would not become the next generation's Harvey Prince with the chauffeur-driven car, the expensive parties at the country club, and the red rose in his lapel. But Craig had never had such ambitions.

What he had started out to be, what he still strove to become, was an excellent physician and surgeon, ministering to women in that area of their bodies which combined the miracle of birth with the battle to survive.

Their joys and their burdens were centered there. Nature had so arranged it that each month they received new assurance of their unique ability to reproduce the race. Nature had also chosen that area in which to visit upon them many deadly diseases. Every woman lived in fear of it. Every doctor who ministered to women was constantly aware of it. His eyes as well as his trained fingers kept probing, hoping to find nothing, fearing to find something. More often than he liked, sensing and tracking down a foreign intruder, which, until it was identified with scientific particularity, was designated simply as a mass.

By the time the physician had detected it, there was already the fearful presumption that it might be too late. Health-minded organizations could urge early detection, but how early was early detection when many times the disease gave no sign until it was too late?

Craig Pierson had chosen that specialty precisely because it was so baffling. Although in recent times he suspected his choice had been related to a favorite aunt who had died when he was very young. Died of a mysterious disease that his mother would identify only as something that happened to women.

Now, lying awake in the middle of the night, with Kate's head resting against his shoulder, Craig thought, That Horton girl: she's almost the same age Aunt Helen was when she got sick and died.

Cynthia Horton troubled him greatly. He had that feeling—that instinct—that sense in his fingertips— that her mass was malignant. But he had been wrong before. Many times. As all Ob-Gyn men were. Times they breezed through a procedure sure the growth was benign, only to receive the unhappy news in the O.R. that the pathologist's findings spelled doom. He had seen experienced surgeons refuse to accept that and go charging down the corridor from the O.R. to the Path Lab to peer into the microscope and see for themselves before accepting the verdict.

He had also been there when the surgeon had lifted a mass from a patient, held it up to the intensely inquisitive view of residents and interns, as one would lay evidence before a jury. Then the surgeon consigned it to the specimen tray, which an orderly would rush to the lab. The surgeon would use the ensuing fifteen minutes to gravely explain the procedure he would now follow, since the mass seemed malignant. He planned to stage the extent of the disease, making every effort to determine how deeply embedded it was; how far it had spread; had it affected the adnexal area involving the tubes and ovaries? had it spread to the lymph nodes, or throughout the abdominal cavity? Then the phone had rung and an unsterile nurse held it to the surgeon's ear. His face changed. Craig could see it in the eyes that peered over the surgical mask. The eyes reflected doubt, then finally relief. *Benign.*

But most times there were no happy surprises. The doctor knew, or had a sense, as to what he would find. Unfortunately, he was more apt to be right when it was grave than when it was hopeful.

Tonight Craig wished he did not have that nagging fear about Cynthia Horton.

Kate was snoring. Lightly. She did on occasion. It was a delicate snore, not annoying but amusing. Craig liked to tease her about it. She always denied it. Now he nudged her gently. She whispered faintly, "I know, darling," turned her head slightly, and was asleep again at once. Tomorrow when he kidded her about it she would deny she had awakened, had spoken, or even that she snored.

It was Kate who had started them on running. Not mere jogging. He had resisted at first. But she had made it a rule. Oftentimes he tried to seduce her into making love in place of running. She made love. Then insisted on running afterward. And he had to oblige.

Much as he had resisted, Craig had to admit now that on mornings when he had to be in surgery very early, he actually missed running. He missed having Kate alongside, her face damp, her blond hair hanging down, her appley cheeks, her breasts bobbing up and down in a rhythm that was both serious and delightful.

Tonight, tired as he was from a long day at the hospital, and facing a longer, tougher day assisting Prince in the O.R. tomorrow, he devoutly hoped Kate would not insist on running tomorrow.

He fell asleep trying to reassure himself that a mass

like Cynthia Horton's, not accompanied by pain or bleeding, could damn well be benign. Could. Could, he kept insisting; his last conscious thought before he drifted off.

In a comfortable Tudor-style house in a northern suburb of the city, Barbara Horton slipped out of bed very cautiously, thinking, Arthur is asleep. And a good thing. He will need his strength for tomorrow. But she was scarcely at the bedroom door when he called out softly, "Barb?"

"Sorry, darling. I didn't mean to wake you."

He rose, went to her, kissed her. She clung to him, trying in her own way to reassure him.

"The odds are all in her favor. Corbin told me so again today."

"You talked to him today?"

"Yes," she said defensively. "I had to!"

"So did I," he admitted. "He told me the same thing."

"Then we have to have faith."

"Faith in what, Barb?"

"I don't know. Just . . . just faith, I guess."

"We've never been religious before. Not really. We're belongers, not believers. We belong to the right church. Just as we belong to the right country club. That's all become clear to me the last few days."

She started to weep.

"Barb, no—please?" He placed his comforting hands on her shoulders. "Remember what we said? Tomorrow when we visit her she is not going to see red eyes, or pity, or fear. We're going to send her up there with every hope, every chance, every bit of courage we can muster."

They were both silent for a time.

87

"I wonder," Barbara began. "Would it have made any difference if we'd known more about her mother?"

"No."

"How do you know?"

"The attorney for the adoption agency, he's a friend of one of my partners. I asked. He searched the records for her medical history. No mention of any kind of malignant disease. Of course, she was only twenty, the last record they have of her."

"What if we tried to find her?"

After an uncomfortable silence, Arthur Horton admitted, "I've already tried."

"And?"

"She died a few years after."

"Oh, God," Barbara Horton whispered. "Did they say from what?"

"Suspicious circumstances. Suicide possibly."

"I hope not."

"Why did you say that?" he asked.

"I don't know. I just hope it wasn't, that's all."

Burton Carlyle, Chief Resident on Ob-Gyn, had just finished reading the last medical paper on some new findings on cancer of the endometrium. He turned out the light in the small living room of their modest apartment and went into the bedroom to join LuAnne, who was already asleep. In the dim glow from the night-light, he admired her delicate profile, her nicely carved lips, and her flaring nostrils, which added a look of pride as well as beauty to the face that had made her one of the most highly paid black models in the fashion world.

She was proud, as he was proud of her. He would have had no other kind of woman for his wife. That was his grandmother's doing.

When he was a boy of four and onward, while his mother was out working in other women's homes, his grandmother would drum it into him. "Be proud. And be smart. Even if you go without food, get learning. Because learning is what is going to make a man out of you. Not merely a growed-up colored person. If you got learning, you can have pride. And if you got both, there's no limit to what you can do.

"So even where other kids don't learn nothing, you will learn. And what you don't know in school you will come home and ask. And if I don't know, and your mama don't know, we will ask other people until we find out.

"But we will make you smart. Because once you smart you going to be what we want you to be. And that is a doctor."

Through the rest of his life he would live with the ambition his grandmother had instilled in him. He carried himself proudly. He made no apologies for his race or his background.

That was why it infuriated him when he was confronted by young affirmative-action interns like Willis Blinn.

Burton Carlyle could see ahead of himself a lifetime in which, by one means or another, he would have to explain, I am one black doctor who made it on ability. I stood fifth in my class at college, third in my class at medical school. My grandmother wouldn't have it any other way. So judge me, not my skin, not any government program. I am as good a physician as any man on that staff, and I want people to know it!

Especially he wanted Dr. Harvey Prince to know it. For it was common word around the hospital that Prince's chief associate was leaving at the end of the year so Prince would be looking for a promising new associate. And Prince was not getting any younger.

When he retired, his associates would inherit the most lucrative practice in the city. Burton Carlyle wanted a share of that practice.

It would make him intimate physician to the wives and daughters of some of the city's wealthiest and most important men. It would set him up for life—financially, but most of all in status, in acceptability. His children, the one now being nurtured in LuAnne's womb, would go to the best private schools, the finest prep schools, Ivy League colleges, and from there anywhere they wanted! Carlyle's last thought before falling asleep was to hope Prince would let him do one of those cases tomorrow. He might even let him do the exenteration. But Carlyle now decided, a procedure as complicated as that gave Prince too much of a chance to display his virtuosity. He would not let anyone else do that one. Probably only that scheduled hysterectomy. Carlyle had done so many of those they no longer constituted a challenge. Or maybe he would be stuck with the simple exploratory on that young Horton girl.

On the night before her surgery, Cynthia Horton lay dozing in Room 442 of the Ob-Gyn wing. Sedated by 100 milligrams of Nembutal, she was still far from deep sleep.

She had already been prepped—the silky hair shaved away so that she seemed a girl of ten again. She pressed her side, seeking to isolate the enemy lurking there. Four men, three of whom she did not even know, had probed the most intimate part of her, found something, and none of them could tell what it was. They would have to open her up.

When they finally got to the *thing*, what would it look like? How would it feel?

Perhaps she should have read up on it before she came to the hospital. Or asked more questions. Now, in the dead of night, she thought of a hundred questions she would ask if only the doctors were here. But they weren't. She would have to endure the night alone.

Terror overtook her. She began to tremble. The next twelve hours could spell the end of everything. Marriage, Pete. Mother. Dad. Life.

She gripped the sides of the bed to control her trembling. She had only one thought: it if was bad, she hoped she would never wake up. Never wake up.

Finally she turned on her side, wet her pillow with tears.

Why me ... why me ...

Just past five, before the first light of dawn, Cynthia Horton fell asleep, not from sedation but from exhaustion, repeating to herself, over and over, a single prayerful word: "benign ... benign ... benign ..."

Chapter Eight

It was only seven o'clock when Dr. Harvey Prince began to scrub carefully to ensure complete sterility for his first procedure of the morning. Alongside him Burt Carlyle scrubbed. Two washbasins away was Craig Pierson. This was one of those early mornings when Prince envied them. They were young, energetic. He was reaching the age at which, despite his success, every procedure had become a chore. He should seriously contemplate retirement.

He might, he considered, leave here and move south, give up surgery altogether. Or become a consulting surgeon, letting other, younger, more eager, ambitious men do the work. To move would mean to give up Rita. There were nights when he was tempted to do that. Rita had become more demanding of late. Not for gifts or money; not even for a measure of financial security. But she was approaching menopause. Most women faced that with a degree of emotional instability. They needn't, Prince argued. All they would lose was their ability to procreate, which was what they spent a good part of their lives avoiding anyhow. When the problem seemed to solve itself, why were they suddenly so desirous of holding on to it?

Whatever the cause in most other women, Prince had to admit that Rita Hallen at least had good reason. With her fading youth went her chance of achieving a permanent relationship with some other man. Men did not select wives in their forties on the basis of their competence in the operating room. Shipboard romances did not start with "And what do you do, Ms. Hallen?" "I am the best damned scrub nurse on any Ob-Gyn service in the country!"

Harvey Prince felt guilty about Rita. He feared her as well. For he could foresee that a highly emotional, menopausal woman might precipitate a public scandal that could threaten his career. In a sense, Rita Hallen had become a time bomb with deadly potential for him. He felt so trapped he dared not even hint at breaking off their relationship. It might trigger the very scandal he hoped to avoid.

All these thoughts went through his mind as he finished scrubbing. A young nurse stood by with sterile gown, powder, and gloves. He slipped his arms into the green gown and his hands into the thin surgical gloves. He looked about. Carlyle and Pierson were both ready.

"Let's take one last look at those X-rays and scans on that first case." Wearily, Prince led the way.

The films and the contrast studies had been mounted in the view boxes on the O.R. wall. Prince, Carlyle and Pierson studied them carefully. The evidence of cervical malignancy was strongly suggested. As was its spread. A full-blown case of fulminant recurrence with involvement of both bladder and rectum. Such widespread malignancy demanded a procedure as radical as a total pelvic exenteration.

But the bone scans were the final determinant. Since the spread had not yet reached the bone, the rest would be resectable. If bone had become involved, even an exenteration could accomplish nothing.

An exenteration, far more radical than a total hysterectomy, could take as long as seven or eight hours. It would be an exhausting procedure for a much younger surgeon. After his late night with Rita, then his wife's demands on him, he was a tired fifty-five-year-old surgeon at seven-fifteen this morning. He took one long last look at the films—and then it suddenly occurred to him: Damn it, why not? There has to be a first time.

So he turned to Carlyle. "What do you think? Are you up to it?"

Taken aback at such a sudden opportunity, Burt Carlyle hesitated before replying with great assurance, "I've been up to it since my second year of residency."

"Good!" Prince announced. "Pierson and I will assist. Unless you get into trouble. Then I'll take over."

"Of course," Burt answered, in his own mind banishing all possibility that he might fail.

Burton Carlyle approached the table with high confidence and gratification. This was the sign he had been hoping for. That Prince would demonstrate sufficient confidence in him to permit him to do one of the most intricate, involved, and lengthy of gynecological operations. He would have great news to tell LuAnne tonight.

The look in Rita Hallen's eyes when she saw Carlyle assume the position of operating surgeon was a direct question aimed at Prince. Her look seemed to demand, Are you really going to let a resident, even a very competent senior resident, do such a complicated procedure? You've never permitted that before. Other procedures, yes—but not this!

Harvey Prince read the rebuke in her eyes. He responded with an impatient look which ordered, Damn it, start passing!

With no further hesitancy, Rita Hallen reached across the table and slapped a scalpel into the gloved hand of Surgeon Burton Carlyle. With a look to the anesthetist for assurance that the patient was under and her condition was satisfactory, Carlyle made a long vertical incision in the soft belly, which had been painted a light shade of brown by two sterile solutions. It struck him that although the patient was white, the color of her belly now was not much different from LuAnne's.

Exenteration was an involved surgical procedure in use only since 1948. In the intervening years great improvements had been made not only in the technical aspects of the surgery itself, but in anesthetics, antibiotics, blood banking, and general care of the patient. So that a woman who once would have been doomed to death in months today had a better-than-fifty-percent chance of long-term survival.

Burt Carlyle began this life-preserving surgical procedure at seven-nineteen in the morning. He worked nimbly. Not so quickly as Prince, but swiftly enough to prove that he had all the skill and confidence required. Rita Hallen passed instruments to him in the proper order, anticipating his needs so that there was no hitch.

Craig Pierson and Harvey Prince assisted, with Craig doing the major portion. He admired the way Burt worked. He was an excellent surgeon. And cool. Very cool. Craig hoped that when his turn came to succeed Burt as Chief Resident he would be handed a few cases like this one, and he would acquit himself as well. That was one of the prerogatives of being Chief Resident: to get the unusual cases, the challenging ones, the cases that tested to the utmost your ability, skill, guts, and inventiveness.

Burt Carlyle's strong fingers were in the abdominal cavity now, palpating liver, kidneys, the entire bowel. He was sampling specimens to send to the path lab for immediate frozen section. He addressed himself to the para-aortic lymph-node area, removing suspicious nodes for additional frozen sections.

At ten past ten, one of the nurses on the O.R. team fed Carlyle sugar-enriched orange juice to supply the energy he needed to continue with the procedure. There was still a long way to go. The patient had been transfused to compensate for loss of blood. Another transfusion might be necessary and was ready.

Each report from the Path Lab dictated Carlyle's next step in the procedure. The node dissections in the para-aortic area had proved, fortunately, to be uninvolved. Carlyle turned his attention to the pelvic area now. The patient was transfused again. The anesthetist kept assuring Burt that the patient was responding well, despite almost seven hours on the table and the radical nature of the procedure.

It was after three o'clock in the afternoon when Carlyle started to close.

"Very good, Carlyle! Excellent!" Prince declared.

To himself, Prince observed drily, Good man. Damn good surgeon. Too bad the sonofabitch is black. Otherwise I'd love to have him in my office.

Burt Carlyle stepped away from the table, ripped off his bloody gloves, slipped out of his gown. His tan face was soaked with perspiration. The confidence he exhibited at the table had disguised the uncertainty that plagued him. Now that it was over and he had acquitted himself so well, he could afford to let down. He slipped onto a metal stool and breathed deeply and laboredly. His hands and arms ached. In the back of his neck there was a knot of tension radiating a pain that ran deep into his left shoulder.

Craig Pierson turned from the table to where Carlyle sat, exhausted, still sweating profusely. He leaned close enough to whisper, "Terrific! Old Goldfingers himself couldn't have done it better."

"Thanks, Craig," Carlyle said wearily. "Man, could I stand some food!"

"Call LuAnne first," Craig urged. "She'll be happy to know the old man chose you. And how well you did."

After a short break for a hurried sandwich, the team scrubbed again. This time Prince performed the hysterectomy, since the patient was the mayor's wife. When it was over, he debated doing the Horton case.

Should he make an attempt to get it in this afternoon? Hospital rules militated against starting any surgical procedure this late in the day unless it was an emergency. On the other hand, it should prove a relatively simple procedure. But he was tired. More tired than his relatively light day justified.

It must be Rita, he decided. Her obvious disapproval had put him under considerable pressure all through that exenteration. She was probably right, though. Word of this would surely get around the hospital by the end of the day. Any first, if it related to a man of Prince's eminence, was grist for the hospital gossip mill.

In addition to feeling unduly tired, Harvey Prince also had to consider the dinner party he had had Margaret arrange for this evening. It included Walter Deering, the hospital administrator, and several members of the Board of Trustees. From past experience, Prince knew how valuable it was to be on good terms with hospital trustees. Especially in an institution like State University Hospital, where the full-time men and the faculty of the medical school were always trying to put down private practitioners like himself, mainly out of jealousy of the huge sums of money he earned in contrast to their fixed, modest incomes.

He would have to be at his best this evening—fresh, ebullient, entertaining. For this reason, he was strongly tempted to put off the Horton case. But when he recalled how crowded his O.R. schedule was tomorrow (what he called a ten-thousand-dollar day), he decided to get the Horton case over with.

So he pretended great concern for her as he said, "The Horton girl's emotionally prepared for the operation. Let's not add to her worries by postponing. Let's do it now!"

At the same time, Prince decided to let Craig Pierson perform the exploratory. The lay public might not understand, but it was the way medicine, particularly surgery, was passed on from one generation to the next, from one pair of skilled hands to another.

Yes, it would be good experience for young Pierson, a weary Prince decided, allowing himself to feel magnanimous and righteous.

Cynthia Horton had been delivered to the prep room outside the O.R. and had already received atropine and Demerol as prescribed by her anesthetist. She was asleep when she was wheeled into the O.R. The anesthetist started an I.V. infusion to provide her with needed fluids and also to keep the vein open in the event she needed a blood transfusion later. Then, assuring himself that she was no longer conscious, he placed the mask over her face and began to administer the halothane.

Meanwhile the circulating nurse dipped a long forceps, with gauze pads affixed, into a solution of soapy provadine iodine. She proceeded to paint Cynthia Horton's body from her mid-thighs to the nipples of her young breasts, turning her white skin to brown. She applied a second prep solution, again covering the entire area, thighs to nipples.

Craig Pierson stepped up to the table, from the left side, to give utmost freedom and mobility to his right hand during surgery. He draped the patient's body with sterile green sheets so that only her abdomen was exposed. She had now become a square foot of brown-tinted flesh, which was the focus of attention of the entire surgical team—Craig Pierson, Prince, and Carlyle. On the other side of the table, Rita Hallen was ready to pass instruments across the patient's body.

Just before the operation began, Harvey Prince looked up at the large electric clock on the wall. Already four fifty-two. He would never make it home in time to greet his guests. But he could use that to advantage. Often when he had dallied too long at Rita Hallen's apartment, he would rush into the house, apologize to his guests, who were in the midst of dinner, and explain that some unforeseen emergency in the course of surgery had had first claim on his time and attention.

He would have to resort to that excuse again this evening.

Rita Hallen selected the scalpel from the long row of precise and gleaming instruments arranged on the sterile towel. She passed it to Craig Pierson.

He paused for an instant before making the first incision. In previous cases, the patient under his hand had always been an impersonal object. It was part of a surgeon's discipline never to permit emotions to affect judgment. Neither the surgeon's wishes nor his hopes, but only what he saw with his own eyes, felt with his own fingers, thought with his scientifically trained mind should determine his actions during surgery.

Craig wished now that he had not taken that history of Cynthia Horton, or learned that they shared the kinship of adoption. She was no longer merely a patient, the subject of a surgical procedure. She had become more. A kindred spirit. Almost a sister in the family of the unfamilied.

Perhaps he should have refused the opportunity to do this procedure. But he would have felt compelled to explain, and he had no desire to open that part of his life to anyone. As important, he did not wish to appear unwilling in Prince's presence. Prince was a power in the hospital, a skillful politician with great influence on appointments. And Craig was determined to succeed Burt Carlyle as Chief Resident.

Putting all those thoughts aside, Craig Pierson lowered the scalpel and made a fine-line transverse incision in the lower abdomen of young Cynthia Horton.

A vertical incision would have permitted easier access, examination, and sampling of portions of her upper abdomen if that proved necessary. But out of vanity for his reputation, Prince always insisted on transverse incisions for cosmetic reasons, so he could boast to his patients, "When I get done, you'll be able to wear a bikini and no scar will show."

Once her abdomen was open, the field kept clear of blood by suctioning and clamping, Craig's gloved hand reached into the open wound. He held out his right hand. Rita slapped an aspirating syringe into it. He drew up fluid from the peritoneal area and handed it to one of the assisting nurses to submit to the pathologist for cytologic examination. Evidences of malignancy might be found there.

Now began the careful examination by his gloved hands of the structures of the peritoneal cavity. He could feel no suspicious mass.

He reached deeper into the opening and carefully felt along the superior and inferior surfaces of the liver, seeking those subtle and treacherous little intrusions that would warn his hands of a dangerous finding. He carried out the same careful procedure on her diaphragm. Prince's eyes, peering across his mask, asked the question; Craig's eyes answered. No lesions. No indication of malignancy.

He proceeded to carry out the same careful search of viscera: large bowel, small bowel, no hint of metastatic disease. He examined the omentum. No sign of disease, but the approved procedure called for him to remove it nevertheless. He severed it from its attachment to the transverse colon. There was no evidence of disease between stomach and colon.

He began now to examine the retroperitoneal lymph nodes. An ovarian tumor, if it were malignant, could spread to those nodes. The affected ones would have to be excised. He palpated carefully the pelvic lymph nodes and then the para-aortic node areas. He proceeded to remove the anterior fat pad over the vena cava and aorta, which contained the lymph nodes.

He could come now to that area where there was the palpable mass. The right ovary. He elevated it into the field so he could see the mass as well as feel it through his tissue-thin gloves. He did not like the feel of it: hard and irregular. But one could not go by feel alone. It was, until identified specifically, only a mass. An intruding mass of some eight or nine centimeters.

He looked across at Prince, who availed himself of his right to examine the offending object. He studied it, felt it, then said, "Proceed!" But his eyes had rendered the verdict. Prince had no doubt that it was malignant.

Being a far younger man, Craig Pierson was less dogmatic in his assumptions. Or was it that he wanted to give this girl the benefit of every doubt? He must stop thinking about the girl and concentrate on that mass. He was allowing her to affect his judgment, if not his technique. He knew what he had to do now.

Unilateral right salpingo-oophorectomy was the technical term applied to the removal of that right ovary and the fallopian tube.

Emotionally, to a woman, part of her ability to conceive children went with it. Actually, the remaining ovary, if sound, would preserve her fertility. Even as he carefully excised the affected ovary and tube, Craig knew that with that removal his work for the day might not be over. Depending on the pathologist's findings, the girl under his hand might be at still greater risk.

With a sense of reluctance, he lifted the ovary in a surgical clamp, looked at it carefully before he finally, and almost reluctantly, consigned it to the specimen container. An orderly rushed it from the operating room to the Pathology Lab.

Aware of the possibilities, Craig had earlier checked and found that Dr. Sam Becker was on duty in the Path Lab. Becker was a good man. Some surgeons accused him of being too cautious about frozen sections, always wanting to hold off on his diagnoses until more definitive findings could be established in four or five days. Craig respected Becker's conservatism. He was not likely to be crowded by surgeons like Prince, who were eager to have immediate answers.

They would have to wait about fifteen minutes for the phone to ring with Becker's verdict. Meantime, Craig checked with the anesthesiologist about the girl's vital signs. All signs were stable. She was reacting well to the anesthetic. Why not? Aside from that damn nine-centimeter ovarian tumor, she was a perfectly healthy girl. Except for it, she would be getting a final fitting on her wedding dress this afternoon. With luck, she might still be doing that two weeks from today.

The procedure temporarily halted, someone turned on the music that could be piped into the O.R. when desired. Prince went to the phone. One of the nurses not required to scrub and remain sterile lifted the phone for him. He placed three calls. One to his office, to find out if any emergencies had developed during the day. One to his home to inform his wife that he would be late—a call which did not surprise her. One to his broker.

When he came away from the phone, he joined Craig and Burt, who were discussing the exenteration Carlyle had done earlier.

Prince interrupted. "You boys in the market?"

Carlyle admitted he held a modest amount of stock, mostly acquired through LuAnne's modeling fees. Craig had none.

"Too bad," Prince said. "Market's started up again. Nine points. Remember, boys: stocks, bonds, and tax-exempts. It's the only way out of this rat race."

Prince turned to Craig. "Listen, if you've got a few thousand salted away, don't leave it in a bank. Inflation will eat you up. Ten years from now, they'll pay you off in dollars worth less than your investment and interest combined. Take my advice. Hook on to some good, sound stocks with growth potential and ride them for the long pull."

Craig nodded, merely to avoid any further discussion. For he was thinking of what Becker might be discovering at this moment in the lab.

"I'll tell you, though," Prince reminded himself, "there's another possibility. The husband of a patient of mine—remember I did a hyst on a patient named Currie? Her husband is in real estate. He's thinking of putting up a shopping center and a group of low-income houses, garden apartments. He invited me in. One thing about real estate: God only made so much earth. And there're always going to be more people. So real estate has got to go up. If you want to put any money in, let me know. But soon."

Having dispensed all his financial advice for this particular day, Prince turned his attention to Carlyle. "How's the wife?"

"Oh, fine. Fine. Everything okay."

"Good. If she runs into any trouble again, I'd be glad to see her. Anytime."

"Thanks. Thanks very much," Carlyle said.

"Terrific job you did this morning. I know you boys on staff resent us attendings. But we don't resent you. We like to see you coming along. This morning I thought, Maybe I contributed just a little to the expert way that young man carried off that exenteration so beautifully. It made me feel good. Real good. Carlyle, one day soon we should have a talk. A good long talk."

Carlyle nodded. The two residents exchanged glances that confirmed what they had hoped. Prince might finally be going to select Carlyle.

The rest of the long wait went by with Prince speaking intensely to Rita Hallen, off in a corner of the O.R. Whatever the nature of the conversation, Prince rejoined the two residents appearing grim and angry. Neither Craig nor Burt Carlyle made any comment. But both of them knew that the friction between surgeon and scrub nurse had not to do with surgery.

Rita relieved her own hostilities by berating a young nurse over some minor infraction. She was so abusive that the girl ran weeping from the room. In such ways did Rita Hallen exert her domination over the O.R. staff, and at the same time vent her bitter frustrations. The hope she had had at thirty, when her affair with Harvey Prince began, that she could displace his older wife had gradually given way to the realization that now she had become the loser in the battle of age, being no longer thirty and no longer as desirable. Time had played an ironic trick on her, and there was no undoing it now.

The O.R. phone rang. Craig instinctively moved to it. But Harvey Prince took precedence. A nurse held the phone for him. It was Becker in the Pathology Lab.

"Sam?" Prince greeted.

"Yes, Harvey."

"Well?"

"I sampled five sections."

"And?"

"It's not easy to tell from a frozen section, Harvey. Not in this case."

"Bottom line, Sam, bottom line!" Prince insisted.

"I want to make it clear that I sampled one block of tissue for every two centimeters of diameter of that damned mass."

"I call that very adequate sampling. Now what's the verdict?" Prince persisted.

"I'd rather look at the permanent sections and give you a definitive report in four or five days," Becker tried to explain.

"Sam! I've got a patient open, on the table. I have to know!"

"Then I would say, of the three possibilities—benign, malignant, or borderline—this one is borderline."

"Is that all?" Prince asked, casting aspersions on Becker's failure to be more definitive.

"Borderline mucinous carcinoma of low malignant potential."

"Right," Prince accepted the pathologist's verdict, repeating, "Borderline mucinous carcinoma of low

105

malignant potential ... What do you think we ought to do?"

"The peritoneal fluid is not suspicious. I'll have the cytology report on that in a couple of days. Evidently the nodes are not involved," Becker said.

"I know that!" Prince responded impatiently. "I'm asking you what you think we should do now."

Becker was usually a mild-mannered man. Some people ascribed it to his being Jewish in a hospital that did not particularly favor Jews on staff. Others felt that Becker was soft-spoken and mild-mannered because of the nature of his specialty, having to pronounce life-and-death conclusions on many patients through the course of any given day. Still, Becker could be firm when a situation called for it.

"Harvey, I'm asked for therapeutic recommendations twenty times a day. Not having seen the patient, or all the clinical information, I am not qualified to give one. So don't press me for an answer!" Becker declared.

"But you do say it is carcinoma ..." Prince tried to pin him down.

"*A borderline mucinous carcinoma of low malignant potential*," Becker repeated very carefully. "And I still want that five days."

Prince turned away from the phone, allowing the nurse to hang up.

"What does Sam think?" Craig asked.

"Mucinous carcinoma of low malignant potential."

"Mucinous carcinoma ..." Craig repeated. Then he evaluated: "... of low malignant potential. Should we bivalve and wedge the other ovary?"

"No," Prince said decisively.

"Just to be on the safe side," Craig suggested.

"To *really* be on the 'safe' side," Prince said, "we'll do a complete cleanout."

106

"Bilateral oophorectomy? On a girl of only twenty-two?" Craig protested. He glanced beyond Prince at Carlyle, whose eyes supported Craig's challenge.

Harvey Prince turned and glared at Craig Pierson. He was not accustomed to having his decisions disputed, especially in an operating room before the entire surgical team.

At the same time he was considering, Wait five days for the definitive biopsy and then possibly have to go in again after that second ovary? His schedule was too crowded to allow for such luxury.

He made no mention of that, but said gruffly, "I've always done bilaterals in cases like this!"

"But the latest findings clearly militate against a bilateral—" Craig started to say.

Prince interrupted angrily, "Young man, are you questioning my judgment?" Then, in his most sarcastic tone, Prince delivered a scathing lecture.

"Dr. Pierson, I realize you young residents know everything there is to know about medicine and surgery. Like the academic and full-time men, you know so much more about it than we mere attending physicians and surgeons. After all, all we do is treat and cure patients. We do not engage in the marvelous research you fellows do. Nor do we go to all those wonderful and enlightening symposia at which you learn 'the latest findings.'

"Well, let an old hand at this business tell you a thing or two about ovarian carcinoma. Especially as it applies to the patient lying on that table. She is a young woman of twenty-two. True. But she has a malignancy in one ovary, and if you know anything at all about ovarian carcinoma you should know that in a large percentage of such cases there may be bilateral involvement. Now or later. Therefore, if you want this girl to have a decent chance of living out her normal life-span, you do a *bilateral* oophorectomy. *When in doubt, take it out.* Now proceed, *Doctor!*"

Craig Pierson did not move. Instead he challenged Prince. "This girl's about to get married! She's going to want to have children!"

"Then let her adopt them," Prince said simply. "Now, Doctor?"

"Sorry," Craig said.

"Do I understand you refuse to follow *my* orders in relation to *my* patient?" Prince demanded.

Slowly, and with considerable awareness of the possible drastic consequences, Craig said, "I still think it would be more advisable to close her up and wait five days for the more definitive Path report. Then, only if forced to, go in and take that other ovary."

With exquisite indulgence, Prince asked, "Is that your considered professional judgment, *Doctor?*"

"Yes," Craig said, softly but very firmly.

"Then get the hell out of my operating room!" Prince exploded.

"The schedule calls for me to assist here today," Craig said. "So I'll remain."

Prince glared at him, then assumed the position at the left side of the table. He held out his rubber-gloved hand. Rita Hallen hesitated. Burt Carlyle glanced across at Prince. For an instant, Craig thought his colleague would intervene and support him. But Carlyle said nothing. Rita Hallen passed a fresh sterile scalpel to Prince.

Prince ordered Carlyle to retract a bit wider. The surgeon reached into Cynthia Horton's abdominal cavity, presented her one remaining ovary, and proceeded to remove it, neatly and with excellent technique. He completed the procedure by removing the tube as well as her now useless uterus. He turned to Carlyle and ordered curtly, "Okay! Close!"

108

Prince turned and strode out of the O.R. Craig Pierson stared down at the small, inoffensive-appearing ovary that lay in the specimen container waiting to be delivered to the Pathology Lab. No need for haste now. The lab would have five days to perform the definitive pathological examination of both ovaries. Then they would know for certain.

One thing Craig Pierson knew for certain now. In a matter of minutes Cynthia Horton had been rendered sterile, infertile, for the remainder of her young life.

He stood by helpless, fuming, but silent, as he watched Carlyle's capable nimble fingers close up the patient. All instruments, pads, and other accessories to the procedure accounted for, Carlyle proceeded to repair the effects of surgery step by step, using the sterile staple machine to put the final clips into the incision that Craig had made when the procedure first started.

When Burt was finished, Craig ripped off his gown, mask, and gloves and started out of the O.R.

Chapter Nine

Attired as usual in a costly, custom-made gray flannel suit, tiny budding red rose in his lapel, Dr. Harvey Prince came down the corridor to Room 442. He knocked gently. Arthur Horton opened the door. Beyond Horton, Prince spied Barbara Horton sitting numbly in the large leather armchair. Her eyes betrayed that she had done all the crying she could do for the time being.

Prince smiled brightly. "Cheer up, Mother! It's over with. She's going to be fine. Fine!"

Barbara Horton started to say, "Thank God," but never enunciated the second word. Instead she began to weep in relief.

Horton, no less emotional but better able to conceal it after years of courtroom practice, asked, simply, "What did you find?"

Prince took on an air of compassionate but hopeful regret. "It was there, all right."

"Malignant?"

"Yes," Prince admitted, then quickly reassured them: "But we got it all. All! That girl owes her life to an alert, concerned doctor like Corbin. In these cases, catching it in time is the key. We could cure ninety-five percent of them if only we knew in time."

"You got it all? You're sure?" Horton pressed.

"Absolutely sure!" Prince declared.

"Thank God!" Horton said. "When can we see her?"

"She'll be in Recovery for at least eight hours. But she's good as new," Prince said. "Better, in fact!"

"Thank you, Doctor. Thank you very much," Horton said.

Barbara Horton came up out of her chair and kissed Prince on the cheek. "I can't say what's in my heart, so that will have to do."

"I am deeply touched and flattered," Prince said in a great display of humility as he reconsidered his fee. He had figured it to be two thousand dollars. It would be three thousand now.

As a last gallant gesture, he took the rose from his lapel and handed it to Mrs. Horton.

"Will the operation interfere with plans for the wedding?" she asked, becoming practical again now that all danger seemed past.

"When is she due to get married?"

110

"Four weeks," Horton said.

Prince smiled. "In four weeks all she'll have to remind her of this operation is an almost invisible scar and the relief of knowing that we saved her life."

As a seeming minor footnote, Prince added, "Oh, we'll have to put her on a regimen of estrogen. But that will only be a minor inconvenience."

"Estrogen?" Mrs. Horton asked, alarmed, "I read somewhere that can cause cancer!"

"In Cynthia's case, nothing to worry about, Mother," Prince assured her, smiling benignly.

He deliberately avoided explaining that since he had removed all her reproductive organs, Cynthia Horton was no longer susceptible to uterine cancer. And as to possible breast cancer, such hormonally induced disease was rarer than uterine cancer, and then developed only years after there had been prolonged use of such hormonal supplements.

Neither of the Hortons thought to pursue that, they were so thankful their daughter was safe once more.

In the dressing room up on the surgical floor, Craig Pierson removed the top of his pajamalike O.R. suit, twisted it into a tight bundle, and hurled it against the wall so that it fell not into the unsterile bin but onto the floor. He ripped off the green cotton pants and let them lie at his feet.

"Son of a bitch!" he exploded, laying out each syllable separately.

"Cool it," Burt Carlyle said, getting into his resident's whites. "Prince is the attending on the case. His was the final judgment."

"When you are faced with irreversible consequences, you don't remove both ovaries!" Craig shouted.

"Hold it down, Craig!" Carlyle cautioned.

"Hold it down? I ought to shout it from the house-tops! That sonofabitch left her sterile! Unable, ever, under any circumstances, to have children! She's only twenty-two! And about to get married!"

"That isn't the worst thing that can happen to a woman," Carlyle pointed out.

"It is, if it didn't have to happen!"

"It was a matter of judgment," Carlyle repeated. "His against yours."

"He's so damn busy doing hysterectomies at two thousand dollars per, so busy entertaining trustees, that he hasn't got time to keep up on the literature. He should know better than to do what he did!"

Carlyle smiled ironically. "You know what they say: that's why God made residents. To keep up on the latest developments because attendings don't have the time."

"Then why didn't he listen to me?"

"Because he's Harvey Prince and you're just a sec-ond-year resident who challenged him in front of the whole team. He wasn't going to let you get away with it," Carlyle said. "You know, LuAnne and I, we talk about you very often. She likes you. Respects you. But she doesn't think you have your head on straight. You always want to fight the system. Well, take it from people like LuAnne and me, who have spent a life-time fighting our way up the system. Go *with* it. Don't look for trouble. Finish your residency, go into prac-tice. Or be full time, if you prefer. But stop fighting. You're going to be one unhappy man. And you're going to make Kate one unhappy woman."

Craig stopped dressing to confront Burt. "Have Kate and LuAnne discussed me?"

"It's only natural," Carlyle said. "Girls of the same age talk about the same things: marriage, children."

112

"And what does Kate say?"

"Not much," Carlyle admitted. "As I get it, she's a quiet girl, solitary most times. She has a strong mind of her own. But I guess you know that."

Craig nodded. They finished dressing. The mention of Kate had diminished his hostility toward Prince. As they were leaving the locker room, Burt said, "Craig, about the Horton girl: Suppose she has to adopt her children instead of having them. Is that so bad? She's adopted. So are you. Would you trade your folks for other parents?"

"Of course not."

"So she'll have children. She just won't give birth to them."

"And about the other aftereffects?" Craig asked.

"Estrogen will take care of those," Burt Carlyle reassured him.

"Provided there are no complications," Craig said, his anger beginning to mount again.

Craig Pierson made his early-evening rounds to see how the patients under his care were progressing. The fifteen-year-old who had had the vaginoplasty was in good condition, and her chart reflected it. She would be out of the hospital in another few days. She would eventually be able to enjoy a normal sex life, though having children would always be beyond her. And she would want them one day.

Just as much as the woman in 403 who had had the tubal cauterization did *not* want them. Craig checked her out too. Her surgery of yesterday had gone off uneventfully and she would be going home in the morning, free forever of the burden of childbearing.

He stopped by to see the nineteen-year-old girl in 409. Young, blond, pretty, the kind people usually referred to as baby-faced. She too would never have children. She had been admitted with severe lower-abdominal pain which did not yield to high-dose intravenous antibiotics. Tests revealed the cause. The remedy was to go in and remove her ovaries, tubes, and other adnexal tissue which had been corroded by gonorrhea undetected too long before it was treated.

Examining her only served to renew Craig's fury about the Horton girl. She had done nothing to deserve her fate. He stopped at the nurses' station, ostensibly to glance at the charts of all his patients. But he reached first for Cynthia Horton's. He studied the last entry. Prince had made a note on the chart immediately after he came down from the O.R.:

Path report, malignant. Performed bilateral salpingo-oophorectomy as clearly indicated. No involvement of nodes, liver, diaphragm, omentum or other organs. Patient survived procedure well.

Plan: Hormonal treatment to begin on discharge. Dosage to be indicated later. Harvey Prince.

Prince had signed with his usual bold flourish.

Craig stared at the entry. He reached into his jacket pocket for the costly pen that Kate had given him on his last birthday—a big black pen with a large gold point for broad-stroke writing. She had laughed when she gave it to him, saying, "Doctors and pharmacists are impressed by boldly written charts and prescriptions. You be the boldest of the lot!"

He considered carefully what he would write, then proceeded to set down in large letters, *Path report was borderline mucinous carcinoma of low malignant potential. Advised closing up the patient to await definitive Path report in five days. And going in again only if report warranted it. Definitely opposed bilateral procedure on the basis of preliminary Path report.*

114

He underlined the last sentence. Then signed his name as boldly as Prince had signed his.

He knew when he slid the chart board back into the slot marked 442 that he had set in motion events that would not end with those few broad stokes of his pen.

Knowing that, he felt compelled to go up to the recovery room. He sought out Cynthia Horton. Her vital signs were good. She seemed to be sleeping peacefully. Her I.V., which contained a combination of fluids—sustenance and antibiotics—was functioning well. She was in good condition.

She opened her eyes for a fleeting moment, glimpsed him standing over her. Her eyes asked the question.

"You're fine," he said. "You're okay."

She smiled, closed her eyes, and reached out for his hand. The state they shared in common had created a bond between them. It made her feel safer, surer, that he was here. He wondered now, had Prince told her parents the condition in which his radical surgery had left the girl?

One day, and very soon, someone would have to tell the girl herself. This was not the time, nor was he, being only a resident and not her surgeon, the person authorized to tell her.

Once she drifted off, he gently set down her hand and slipped out of the recovery room.

The first question Kate asked when he arrived at her apartment was "Did Prince do her today?"

"The sonofabitch" was all he said before he drank half his bourbon in a single gulp.

"What happened?"

He told her in detail of the path report, his dispute with Prince. And what Prince had done.

"The sonofabitch," Kate agreed in breathy fury. "You'd think it was his God-given mission to go around sterilizing women. He does hysterectomies for a common cold! What did Burt say?"

"Not much."

"What do you mean, not much?"

"It was just between Prince and me." Then he confessed, "I saw Prince's entry on her chart. So I put mine in, in broad, impressive strokes. I want them to know. I want them all to know."

"Of course," Kate agreed, her blond head nodding firmly. But her psychiatrist's mind warned her that Prince was not a man to condone such an affront.

Later, to assuage Craig's anger about Prince, she enticed him into making love to her. After that, he seemed less hostile.

"Do you and LuAnne discuss me often?" he asked suddenly.

"Often?" Kate asked, puzzled.

"Burt said you and LuAnne talked about me."

"Of course. But nothing to become paranoid about. We talk about Burt too."

"Often?"

"About as often as we talk about you."

"What do you say?"

"We agree that he's ambitious, maybe a little too ambitious. He's trying to make up in one generation for two hundred years of deprivation."

"I mean, what do you say about *me?*" Craig demanded.

"I wonder, when are you going to grow up and stop being such an idealist?"

"Meaning?"

"Meaning that medicine, like everything else in this life, is carried on by human beings. And you can't

116

demand perfection of them. But most of all, it is too much to demand perfection of yourself."

"That's why I'm at the hospital," he replied. "To perfect my science—my art, if you wish. To learn how to do things so well that the patient is put at the least risk while being given the best chance of recovery. If I hadn't felt that way from the outset, I never would have studied medicine at all!"

"Very noble. But even that can be carried to extremes, darling."

"What does that mean, Doctor?" he asked a bit sarcastically. "Do you detect some neurosis at work here? Perhaps you'd like to call in the chief of your department on consultation on this most baffling case. We have here a strange young doctor. He has delusions. He thinks medicine should be practiced like what it is, the healing art. Not as something to do so you can pile up a list of high-quality stocks or tax-free bonds or choice real estate holdings. This deranged young man thinks that maybe we should give as much thought to our patients as we do to our stockbrokers. We should put him under restraint. Before he wrecks the whole system!"

Now it was Kate's turn to be offended. In a most professional tone she said, "We see this quite often. Unable to deal with his hostilities and guilts, the patient turns on the doctor and resorts to sarcasm. The brighter patients do that. The others often resort to aggressive conduct of other kinds."

"Thanks for the lecture," he said, pulling away to lie on his back, his hands clasped under his head.

"Darling, there's nothing wrong in striving for perfection. What is wrong is your reaction when you fail to achieve it. Or when some other doctor fails to achieve it."

117

"I know what you're going to say," he anticipated. "That missed diagnosis on the Collins girl. Every symptom she described had ulcer written all over it. It was a classic description."

"Except," Kate pointed out, "it turned out to be a metastatic abdominal carcinoma from her breast. So for days you went around whipping yourself emotionally for having missed it. You can't do that."

"I'll try not to," he responded, sarcastic again.

"You can't do it, because if you do, sooner or later you're going to have to give up medicine. You're only a physician, not a magician. With magicians every trick works perfectly. Unfortunately, doctors don't enjoy that kind of perfection."

"What do you want me to do? Call Prince now, in the middle of the night, and apologize to him? After all, I almost deprived him of his quota of mistakes for the week. I almost kept him from making another of his 'human' errors in judgment," Craig said bitterly.

"It would have been better," Kate said, "not to start a feud with Prince. In his judgment—and after all, he's her surgeon, not you—he decided a bilateral was called for."

"And I couldn't do it. It would be committing a crime. If you've seen as many women as I have who are desperate to conceive babies, you'd know."

"I see them too," Kate reminded. "The ones you Gyn men fail with often wind up with us."

"Then you know how that girl is going to feel when she finds out," Craig said. "I was trying to save her from that. After all, it's a hell of a way to enter into marriage. Which reminds me . . ."

"Don't," Kate warned. "I haven't made up my mind yet. For the next year and a half we are medical gypsies. Once we settle our professional lives, we can decide about us. And no, I do not believe in just living

118

together. I've dealt with too many cases like that at the hospital. That's like marriage, only with more problems built in."

"Burt and LuAnne's marriage seems good," he argued.

"Because she was willing to give up her career to become a wife and mother. That's her decision. I have to make my own. Besides, Burt knows what he wants to do, and he's going to do it."

"No question," Craig agreed. "I forgot to tell you. This morning Prince let him do a complete exenteration. Seven and a half hours, and he was terrific."

"Prince let him do an exenteration," Kate said thoughtfully.

"I know what you're thinking. Prince is going to ask Burt to come into his office."

"Fantastic break. He'd be making a hundred thousand a year in no time."

"And good-bye academic medicine," Craig said. "Not that I blame him. He's entitled, as they say."

He embraced her. She was good to the touch. Soft, warm, totally feminine. One would never suspect that she could be so professional and tough with him when the occasion demanded.

"Doctor, I love you," he said. "Do you ever have affairs with your patients?"

"Only in exceptional cases," she said, and she kissed him hungrily.

Chapter Ten

It was six-fifteen in the morning. Craig had not yet had breakfast, not even a cup of coffee; he was too busy making his early rounds. He had examined all charts to see if any changes of consequence had occurred in any patients during the night. There were no significant entries by the night resident.

But Craig did note that Cynthia Horton had been brought down from Recovery about midnight. He would stop in and see her last, so he could spend some time with her if she was awake.

Blinn joined him on his rounds, which went off uneventfully. He sent Blinn down to breakfast while he stopped by Room 442.

He eased the door open softly. Cynthia Horton was facing the window. She must be asleep, he thought. But in a weak voice she asked, "Who is it?"

"The doctor."

"Dr. Prince?" She tried to turn and face him. "Oh. Come in, Dr. Pierson. Please?"

He routinely took her pulse to see how she was reacting, emotionally as well as physically. He was rewarded with a steady, if weak beat. Not rapid, not too slow. He checked her I.V. bottle. The rate of drip seemed sufficient to combat the ileus that usually followed abdominal surgery. During that period of transitory paralysis of bowel function, the I.V. not only supplied nourishment, but, more important, body fluid as well. She should be over this post-op phase in twenty-four to forty-eight hours.

He examined the area of the surgery. There was no distension. No sign of complications. Throughout, she lay still and tense, scarcely breathing. When he finished, she dared to ask, "Nobody told me ..."

"Wasn't Prince by last night?" he asked, trying to discover what, if any, contact there had been between patient and surgeon after the operation.

"I don't know. I was asleep except that moment

120

when you came by," she said weakly. "What . . . what did they find?"

"Nothing too serious," Craig said, not wishing to alarm her.

"Was it . . . ?" she started to ask, and could not quite finish.

"Only borderline. And it's all been removed."

"All?" she asked, trying to raise herself and search his eyes when he responded.

He looked down into her young face, beautiful despite her black hair in disarray, with strands of it stuck to her damp white skin.

"It's very important to know exactly what he found," she said with solemn intensity. "I want to be honest with Pete. I don't want him marrying me and then have this happen again a year from now."

"The pathologist said it was a borderline mucinous carcinoma of low malignant potential."

"What does that mean?" she exacted, with anxious precision.

"It means there was a borderline cancer. . . ."

"I knew it," she said, "I knew it."

"Of *low* malignant potential. Which means that it was not invasive. We found no metastases. No affected nodes. No involvement of the liver, the omentum, or the surrounding tissue. None!"

"He took it all out—all? You're sure?"

"Oh, he took it all out," Craig said, a bit ironically. "I'm sure of that."

No need now to go into other possible dangers. Patients were always reassured by the lack of metastases, unaware that the deadly killer could also be transported through the body by the bloodstream, undetected. No need, either, to tell her now of Prince's decision to do a total hysterectomy. Or of the conse-

121

quences of such a radical removal in a woman so young.

She seemed reassured. "As long as they got it all."

"I don't think there's going to be need for chemotherapy. But Dr. Prince will have to decide about that."

"I hope there won't be," she said. Then, desperately, protested, "There can't be! I don't want him to see me that way!"

"What way?"

"People lose their hair." Unconsciously her hand went to her silky black hair. "When Senator Humphrey had his cancer, you could see the change in him. Each time you saw him on television, he became balder. His face grew thinner. He practically wasted away before your eyes."

She had become quite tense, was on the verge of tears.

"Cynthia, your case and the Senator's case are very different. His was inoperable. We caught yours early. Very early. So it's unwise to make any comparison at all. You can live a long and healthy life. I'm sure Dr. Prince will explain to Dr. Corbin. And Dr. Corbin will explain it all to you. And they will manage your case together, in consultation."

As he was leaving her room to go up to the O.R. and scrub, Cynthia asked once again, "You're absolutely sure they got it all?"

"They got it all," he said, responding to her specific question, careful not to breach his ethical obligation to the surgeon on the case.

He slunk down the corridor, feeling like a charlatan. He consoled himself by thinking, Kate would have wanted me to handle it that way. His beeper interrupted his haste to make the next elevator up to surgery. On his way to the phone, he pondered how Prince would greet him this morning after the confrontation of yesterday. Would Prince refuse to let him perform any surgery? Or would Prince attack him in his usual caustic style?

That was Prince's tactic when he was provoked and wished to punish a younger man. He would continually refer to him as "our bright young man." And, while he proceeded with his deft surgery, Prince would say, "Notice how our bright young man has suddenly developed nothing but thumbs. So awkward he can hardly hold the retractors properly. One of the great advances in the evolution of the species *Homo sapiens* was the development of the thumb. Making it possible to grasp. And opening the way to all the uses of the human hand which no other species can achieve. But our bright young man has carried evolution further, much further. He has developed *five* thumbs."

Craig was determined that if Prince used such demeaning tactics on him this morning, he would walk out.

He reached the phone and picked up his call.

"Pierson?" a deep masculine voice asked.

He recognized it as that of Ordway, Chief of the Ob-Gyn Department. Professor Clinton Ordway.

"Yes, sir."

"I wonder if you could drop by my office," Ordway said, trying to sound casual.

"I'm on my way up to the O.R.," Craig explained.

"It might be a good idea if you dropped by here first," Ordway suggested, in that way he had of giving a command without being overbearing.

"Of course. It's just that I'm scheduled to assist."

123

"That can wait," Ordway said in a more resolute voice.

Clinton Ordway was tall, florid, white-haired, imposing. He had been an excellent gynecologist. But in the past decade, once he became Chief of the department, he had gradually relinquished his contact with patients and devoted himself to his administrative duties. He had become skilled at fighting for budgets, recruiting new men, advancing research which enhanced the reputation of the entire hospital and, more specifically, of his department. He had become especially adept at dealing with trustees. His was the best-funded department in the hospital. In a time of stringent budgets, Ordway's was no small achievement.

The moment Craig arrived, he was shown into Ordway's office. The Chief was on his feet, ready to greet him, but a bit less amiably than usual. He gestured Craig to a chair in the conference area of his large office. Instead of joining him across the table, Ordway remained standing.

"Pierson, last evening I happened to be at a dinner in Harvey Prince's home. He took me aside and said that he did not intend to countenance insubordination from any second-year resident. Now, if you will, tell me exactly what happened."

Craig Pierson recounted the events in the O.R. When he had finished, Ordway remained thoughtful for a moment.

"You deemed your judgment superior to that of a man like Harvey Prince? A man who's done more of these procedures than you are likely to do in the next ten years?"

"If I may, sir . . .," Craig said, most circumspect now that he realized his conduct had already been judged

124

and condemned. "Dr. Prince is the most skillful surgeon I've ever scrubbed with. But he may be a little too busy to keep up."

"Keep up?" Ordway challenged, obviously resentful of the phrase.

"His decisions in the O.R. reflect the thinking of years ago. Several first-rate medical centers have recently reported excellent results in cases like this when they excise only the diseased ovary unless the permanent path report clearly indicates a reason to do a bilateral. That way there's at least a chance of preserving the woman's childbearing ability. That's all I was suggesting. Wait for the final Path report. And go back in only if clearly indicated."

"And be accused of doing unnecessary surgery?" Ordway asked. "You can't pick up a newspaper or watch T.V. without seeing the medical profession under attack for high costs, unnecessary surgery, and a lot of other nonsense!"

"Dr. Ordway," Craig responded, as respectfully as a resident can in differing with his Chief, "we had on the table a twenty-two-year-old girl, who is due to be married in four weeks. Prince's decision was made in a matter of minutes. But that girl will have to live with the consequences the rest of her life. I felt compelled to voice my opinion before the damage was done."

"Oh, so now it's 'damage'?" Ordway seized on Craig's word.

"The patient has been deprived of the most important function of her sex," Craig pointed out quietly.

"Pierson, before you go making any irresponsible charges, I think it would be wise for you to take a good look at Dr. Prince's record. We have a number of committees in this hospital who monitor the performance of our surgeons. Dr. Prince's operative mortality, his post-op complication rate are excellent. They compare

125

most favorably with figures of surgeons here and in other hospitals. So you can understand that I would accept his judgment over that of a mere second-year resident."

Craig Pierson felt a strong compulsion to dispute Ordway. But in the face of angry authority, he confined himself to a respectful "Yes, sir."

"Now, I'll try to find some way of patching up things with Prince. And it wouldn't do any harm if you apologized to him."

"Yes, sir."

"After all, Pierson, I wouldn't want Prince's feelings about you to become a factor when I have to designate my Chief Resident for next year," Ordway said, smiling.

It was phrased as a promise, but Craig recognized it for what it was, a very subtle threat.

At that moment, one of the phones on Ordway's desk rang.

"Nelly, I told you, no calls. . . . Oh, I see. Yes, yes, put him on." Ordway held his hand over the mouthpiece, "Prince. Maybe I can pave the way for your apology." He assumed a warm and hearty attitude as he greeted, "Good morning, Harve. Great party last—"

But it was quite evident from the abashed look on Ordway's face that he had been assaulted by Prince with a tirade which Ordway tried to interrupt several times, unsuccessfully. Finally he resigned himself to listening, while glaring at Craig. Ordway's face grew grimmer and grimmer.

"Yes, Harvey. Yes, I understand," Ordway finally said. "I'll deal with it. Don't worry."

Ordway hung up.

"Pierson, last night, did you make a note on the Horton girl's chart?"

126

"Yes, sir," Craig admitted.

"Before you did so, did you read the note Dr. Prince had made?"

"Yes, sir."

"And you thought it wise, prudent, to make your disagreement with Prince part of the patient's chart?"

"Not wise, or prudent. But necessary."

"I see," Ordway said, making no effort to disguise his fury. "Patients' charts are not a battleground on which the conflicts between doctors are fought! Disagreeing with Prince in front of the entire surgical team in the O.R. was foolish enough. But making that note . . ." His anger exceeded his ability to express it. "I'll see what I can do to repair the damage. But the first step, apologize to Prince!"

Craig Pierson strode down the corridor toward the Ob-Gyn wing. He thought of all the answers he might have made to Ordway. For example, when Ordway boasted of Prince's survival record, Craig now realized that he should have said, "If a surgeon does non-malignant hysterectomies, of course he's going to have a terrific cure rate. The patients were never in any danger in the first place!"

He was glad he hadn't said that. For if there was one post on which he had set his heart, it was to succeed Burt Carlyle as Chief Resident in his third year. Ordway, he recalled now, had made that subtle threat before Prince's call and the altercation about the conflicting notes on Cynthia's chart. After that call, Ordway was far more angry. Was it possible, Craig had to ask himself, that not only was the Chief Residency now in jeopardy: so was the remainder of his residency?

If it was, the alternative could be disastrous. Where could he go to complete his residency?

What good medical center would want a third-year resident who had done his first two years in some other institution? There would be the inevitable question: Why, after two years, did Dr. Craig Pierson decide to leave an excellent hospital like State University? Personality conflict? If so, it would be taken for granted that such a conflict was his fault.

He began to regret having made that bold, brave note on the Horton chart. To see how it looked in the cold light of a new day, he stopped at the floor desk, drew out the chart. He glanced down near the bottom of the page where he had written his note and signed it with such a hostile flourish.

His note was no longer there.

He studied the page. Prince's previous orders and his post-op report were all there. Only Craig's entry was missing. He fingered the page for a moment. Then, from the neatness of its appearance, he realized that Prince had removed the original page and written a new one, omitting Craig's protest.

He called Ordway at once. Ordway was neither surprised nor disturbed. "Yes, I know. And lucky for you. Prince decided to give you another chance. Damn decent of him. Any other man might have been vindictive."

Craig hung up, disturbed that a chart could be altered so arbitrarily. Yet he had to admit feeling relieved as well. His third year of residency did not seem so shaky now. It had been a close brush. But he had relearned a lesson he had forgotten.

In his first year of residency he had been advised by Wiley Fisher, an excellent young surgeon and Chief Resident at the time, "Pierson, if you want to get along with the attendings, remember that while you're better trained than they are, and better informed, the

128

trick is not to let *them* know that. Don't rub their noses in it. Be tactful. Never *tell* them. *Ask. Suggest.* And if anyone has to appear stupid, let it be you. Otherwise you won't get to scrub with the best men. You're here to learn. And when it comes to surgical technique, older men like Goldfingers have it all."

Craig entered Room 419 to find a patient whom Dr. Bell had admitted the night before.

"Mrs. Cates?"

The blond woman, who appeared to be in her late twenties or early thirties, was sitting up in bed. She wore a blue silk bed jacket to cover the plain white hospital gown underneath. She was attractive and obviously in good health. Nor did she evidence the same concern as most patients in Ob-Gyn. He glanced at her history. He noticed Blinn's signature at the bottom. This history was complete and detailed. Including the last note: "Dr. Bell has the patient scheduled for a tuboplasty tomorrow."

"Mrs. Cates, it's necessary for me to do a complete pelvic examination. I hope you don't mind."

"No," she said a bit reluctantly.

During the course of the examination, and to put her at ease, he asked, "What made you have a tubal ligation in the first place? A woman as young as you are."

"I just . . . decided, that's all. . . ."

His question had made her tense. He decided not to pursue it, but she volunteered: "I suppose you have a right to be curious."

"Not if it's going to cause you any embarrassment. . . ."

"I'm too damned intelligent to be embarrassed. At least, that's what I tell myself. I was part of the movement. What movement? Any movement. Women's

Lib. Planned Parenthood. Name it. I am a most pro-gressive, liberal, intelligent young woman. The kind the magazines would have you believe is the thing to be."

She was becoming a bit bitter now, more at herself than at the institutions she criticized.

"The small, compact, ever-loving nuclear family. Two children and that was all. Frank and I both de-cided on that. So instead of birth-control devices, each of which involved some risk or inconvenience, we de-cided, very intelligently, that I would have a tubal ligation. That way, if anything happened to me and Frank remarried, he could still have children with his new wife, if they chose.

"We had it so well planned. The only thing we didn't plan on was that Frank would pile up his Jaguar XKE against an abutment. And I would be the one who was left.

"Well, I've met a man who loves me. He loves my children, too. He wants to adopt them. But he would like children of his own, too. Children of *our* own," she amended. "I love him. And I understand how he feels. So I am going to do my damnedest to have his children. Do you think it's possible now?"

Her blue eyes were trying to exact his promise.

"Didn't you discuss that with Dr. Bell?" Craig asked.

"Yes."

"And didn't he tell you that in cases like this it is sometimes possible to reconstitute the fallopian tubes? But not always."

She was obviously disappointed, but said nothing.

"I've seen cases where it worked very well. Fertil-ity was completely restored," he said, seeking to give her some hope.

130

"The things we do . . . and in the name of intelligence . . .," she said sadly.

At the time Craig Pierson was completing his examination of Sylvia Cates, Dr. Clinton Ordway, who had closeted himself from interruptions ever since Craig had left his office, made a phone call.

"Dr. Becker, please!" In a matter of moments, he heard the familiar, soft voice. "Sam?"

"Yes, Clint, what can I do for you?"

"Did you do a biopsy on a patient named Horton late yesterday?"

"Frozen section. We'll have the paraffin block and the final report in four days," Becker informed him.

"What did that frozen section show?"

"Borderline mucinous carcinoma, low malignant potential."

"You reported that to Dr. Prince?"

"Of course."

"Tell me, Sam, do you recall what he said, if anything?"

"Well," Becker equivocated; he hated to become embroiled in such situations.

"Sam, it's important. I'd like to know."

"He asked what I would recommend. It happens all the time, Clint. On the close ones. The surgeon wants a lead. And I have to tell them, all I know is what that bit of tissue tells me. And a frozen section isn't always definitive," Becker said. "We miss them occasionally. None of us is perfect. So I never give advice to surgeons."

"Of course," Ordway said, about to hang up, when it occurred to him to ask another question. "Oh, Sam, the other ovary—did you examine that too?"

"Frozen section."

131

"And?"

"Absolutely clean, tumor-free."

Chapter Eleven

"It was necessary," Dr. Harvey Prince explained gravely. Barbara Horton sat in the big leather chair; her husband was balanced on the arm. Peter Tompkins stood at the foot of the bed. Cynthia, white-faced and stunned, sat up in bed, her violet eyes staring, unfocused.

"Necessary?" Barbara Horton asked, numbly.

"I take no chances with ovarian cancer. The first thing you ask when you feel one of those damned things is How far has it spread? Because if it has spread, even a little, it can be deadly."

He turned to Cynthia, smiled in a fatherly way. "My dear, I want you to know that it didn't spread at all. It was removed. Totally. To make sure, to be absolutely certain that you could live a long, healthy life, it was necessary to do what I just described. Now, you'll be up and out of bed tomorrow. You'll spend four or five days here, another two weeks recuperating at home, and then you'll be free to pursue all your other plans, including marrying this fine young man."

Prince smiled benignly, as if he had bestowed a gift upon the patient and was ready, if need be, to bless her marriage. Cynthia continued to stare, ignoring their eyes. "Explain it to me. Completely. What does it mean? How will it affect me?"

"Aside from not having children of your own, it won't affect you at all. You can get married and live a

132

perfectly normal life—better, in fact. We've removed the cause of most female troubles. And the inconvenience. No more periods. No more fears of unwanted pregnancy. Then when the time comes and you and your husband decide you'd like to have a family, you simply adopt."

Prince continued, "In fact, that way you can be sure of having healthy babies, without having to run the dangers and the difficulties of pregnancy. After some infants I've delivered, you should feel greatly relieved. I can't tell you how many times an anxious father has come to me and said, 'Doctor, can't they just let it die?' Because what has been delivered, while alive, is hardly a human being at all. Well, that can never happen to you. So, my dear, you can rest easy."

Far from reassured, Cynthia asked, "That's all? Those are the only aftereffects?"

"Of course, we'll have to assist nature a bit. But any aftereffects can be more than counteracted by hormonal supplements, estrogens. Used within limits, of course. We do it all the time. I'll get you started on a regimen in a few days."

"I see," Cynthia said. But it was quite evident that she was beyond seeing or understanding, and far from accepting.

Prince departed. Cynthia's mother breathed a soft "Thank God. I can tell you now, Cynthia darling, yesterday Ruth Hansen called. And she told me of a girl in her family. Nineteen. She had the same thing. But in her case it was too late. So you see, we're lucky. Very lucky."

She bent over Cynthia, kissed her on the cheek. "Everything's going to be all right."

But Cynthia sat up in her raised-back hospital bed and stared.

133

In a sudden and decisive attitude, she said, "I'd like to talk to Pete. Alone."

"Of course, darling," Horton acquiesced. He took his wife's hand, led her from the room.

They were alone. Cynthia Horton. Peter Tompkins. The moment the door whisked closed, he rushed to her side, embraced her, kissed her, seeking her mouth. She allowed him only her cheek. She was intent on having her say; kissing him would prevent that.

"Pete, darling," she began, "I want you to know that you're free to end it here and now. I will understand."

"Who said anything about ending it?" he protested.

She stubbornly continued, "You agreed to marry a whole, healthy girl. You're entitled to have a wife and children of your own. I won't hold you to any bargain that gives you less than that."

"I want *you*. The way you are," he insisted, embracing her again, pressing her head against his shoulder. "You have no idea what I've gone through the last four days. The first thing I thought, 'She'll never make it. I'm not lucky enough to have her. Somehow they'll find some way to take her away from me.' I've been afraid of that from the time we started going together. I said to myself, how can a homely dude like me be so lucky? What have I ever done to deserve a girl like her? I feel it every time we make love. When I watch you sleeping, I look down at you and say, 'All that beauty, and it's mine. What does she see in me? God knows, she could have done better. Much better.' "

Cynthia was weeping softly, pressing her wet face against his cheek.

"You won't ever have regrets?"

"Never!"

"When we have arguments—all couples do—will you ever throw it up to me?"

"I swear, never!" he responded, in complete honesty.

"I hope *I* don't," she said strangely.

"*You?* Why would *you*—"

"Because . . ." she started to say, but it was difficult; "because I feel like a . . . a cripple!"

"Don't ever say anything like that!"

"I'm not the same as I was, not the same . . .," she said emptily.

"I want you the way you are." He kissed her again, trying to stop the flow of her tears. "Love you the way you are. We're two very lucky people. It could have been worse. A hell of a lot worse. I'll settle for this, now and for all time!"

When he could not stanch her tears, he went out to find her mother.

"Talk to her, tell her," he implored. "She'll believe you. The wedding is still on. I insist on it! Everything is the same! Make her believe that!"

Barbara Horton wiped her daughter's eyes, brushed her lustrous black hair as she talked.

"Pete wants the wedding. If anything, he wants it even more now than he did before. I know what that's like. When you think you've lost something precious, you love it even more. Like the time you were driving home from college with Clare Owens and had that accident. For hours we couldn't get word about your condition. The police, the hospital, all they could tell us was that one girl was critically hurt, but they didn't know which one. Then we found it wasn't you. We loved you even more in that moment when we thought we might have lost you. So I know how Pete feels. In fact, this might bring you closer together. The

135

crises two people face either bring them closer or split them apart. You can feel happy and proud that Pete's the kind of man he is."

Cynthia gasped slightly, trying to recover. "What if the time comes and he wants children of our own . . . it's the least a man can expect from the woman he marries."

"You think your father loves me less because I didn't bear you? Who knows what we would have produced? A girl as pretty as you? I doubt that. A girl as fine as you? No one, not even a child of our own, could have pleased us more. You've been a delight to bring up, a joy to live with."

Barbara Horton kissed her daughter on the cheek and held her in a warm embrace. Pressed against her mother, Cynthia dared to say what had been tormenting her ever since Dr. Corbin had made his frightening discovery.

"Mommy . . . there's something I have to tell you. . . ."

Aware that it might be difficult for her daughter, she said, "It doesn't have to be now. Just rest and get some sleep."

"It has to be now." But Cynthia paused before she found herself able to say, "Pete and I, we've been having a relationship. Since my last year at college."

Cynthia expected a reaction of shock, or at least disapproval. But her mother said only a casual "And?"

"I thought you ought to know."

"What makes you think I didn't? Because you've been more discreet about it than some of your friends? I admired the way you lived the private part of your life privately. So if that's been troubling you, forget it. Now take a nap. You're still full of sedatives," her mother cautioned, loosening her embrace.

136

Cynthia insisted on being held. "Maybe it's more than that."

"More?" a puzzled Barbara Horton asked.

"Maybe my relationship with Pete was wrong, and this is punishment."

"God does not punish people for that. If He did, we'd all be punished. Including Daddy and me."

"You two?"

"Of course," Barbara admitted, then chuckled. "The funniest thing, and we still laugh over it to this day. We were both in school at the time. Dad in his second year of law school. I in my senior year at college. There came that time, I suppose every girl goes through it, when I skipped a period. What a time! Dad facing final exams in Real Property and Constitutional Law, and this on his mind. We were frantic. Four whole weeks. But then everything was normal again. Later, when we were married and I tried my darnedest to become pregnant and couldn't, we would laugh about those terrible four weeks and our needless worry.

"One day, my darling, you and Pete will look back on this and laugh. And as for having your own children, do you know a happier family than us?"

She kissed her daughter and slipped out of the room.

The demands of Craig's day had temporarily pushed the Horton case out of his mind. He had been summoned to care for an emergency involving a young woman brought in with a raging infection which had resulted from a self-induced abortion. He had assisted Dr. Winkler on three cases. He had performed two procedures himself. One a total hysterectomy on a forty-one-year-old woman whose fibroids,

137

though benign, were extremely uncomfortable because of their size. The other on a patient with a carcinoma in situ of the cervix, revealed by a Pap smear and confirmed by colposcopic examination and biopsy.

He came to the end of another tough, tiring day, and he felt it. The tension knot in his left shoulder was tighter and more painful than usual. He needed time off. He looked forward to dinner with Kate. He had called her twice. Both times she was dealing with emergency psychiatric admissions.

Just before he decided to ring her for the third time, his beeper paged him. He picked up the call at the nurses' station.

"Pierson," he reported in.

"One moment, Doctor," the operator said.

"Dr. Pierson?"

"Yes."

"Cynthia Horton."

"How are you feeling, Cynthia? Any pain? Any discomfort?"

"May I talk to you?"

"You're talking to me now."

"I mean . . ." She hesitated, "I mean, could you come to my room?"

"Something wrong?"

"No. I just want to talk."

"Be right there," he assured her, for he detected that her problem was less physical than emotional. He dialed Kate. This time she answered.

"God, what a day" was the first thing she said.

"I'm calling to tell you that I can't call to ask you out to dinner. Unless you want a late dinner."

"I've got my exercise class tonight," she started to explain, but he interrupted.

"Great. Wait dinner. I'll pick you up there."

"What's the emergency?"

"Who said there was an emergency?" he countered.

"It's in your voice."

"No emergency. Just the Horton girl. She wants to talk."

"What are you going to tell her?"

"Whatever she wants to know," he said firmly.

"Don't upset her, darling. She's not ready to face it yet," Kate warned. "If you need help, let me know."

"Okay, Mother," he said, as he often did when she assumed that he was incapable of dealing with the emotional problems of female patients.

She acknowledged the rebuke, not by apologizing but by saying, "It's enough we have a young emotional doctor to deal with; we don't want to compound that with an emotional patient too. Do we?"

" 'We' don't want to do anything but have a talk with a patient. And 'we' are quite capable of doing that without causing the doctor, the patient, or the hospital to collapse. Now may 'we' pick you up after exercise class?" he asked sarcastically.

"Of course," Kate said. "But if you can't make it, if the girl is more emotional than you suspect, just call and leave a message. I'll understand."

"Don't worry, I'll be there," he insisted, annoyed.

Psychiatrists always believed they had the original patent on understanding the moods, fears, and inner conflicts of patients. To be good, an Ob-Gyn man had to be medical doctor, surgeon and also psychiatrist.

Cynthia's door was slightly ajar. But he knocked before entering. He noticed at once that her dinner was still on the tray, untouched.

"Cynthia . . .," he opened the conversation pleasantly.

She did not respond, but stared at him, her violet eyes quite fixed and penetrating.

"You wanted to talk to me?"

"Close the door?"

"Of course," he said a bit warily.

She detected his reservation, for she hastened to explain, "Just on the chance that he's passing by."

"He?"

"Dr. Prince."

"Oh," he said, wondering if she had heard of his disagreement with Prince. If she had, how much could he reveal, bearing in mind Kate's warning about overburdening the girl so soon? "If there's something you want to discuss, Prince is really your doctor. I'm just a resident."

"There are things I have to know," she said. "Things I don't think Dr. Prince is telling me."

"Such as?" Craig asked cautiously.

"Well, in the first place, he's too pleasant. He smiles too much. If he had to do to me what he did, it can't be all that trivial, or the occasion for so damn much smiling."

"The surgery is over, the patient is doing well. Three months from now, yours might have been quite a different story. So every time we discover one this early and remove it completely, we feel lucky. That's a reason to smile." He hated himself for trying to explain away Prince's unctuously cheerful bedside manner.

"There's something Prince keeps passing over very lightly, smilingly, and I don't understand it."

"Ask him. Most patients are afraid if they ask the doctor too many questions he'll resent them. So they

140

don't ask, just go on worrying silently. No need. Medicine isn't practiced that way these days."

"Okay, then," she challenged quite directly. "*You* tell me."

"Anything," he offered.

"He talked about hormones, estrogens."

"Of course."

"I thought estrogens were for older women. Women in their forties, their fifties, women into their menopause."

"True," Craig said cautiously, realizing that Prince had never fully explained her situation to her and it might now become his duty to do so.

"I'm only twenty-two. Why would I need estrogens like some menopausal old woman?"

Craig hesitated. Should he explain and thus usurp Prince's duty and prerogative? And, if he decided to do so, could he explain it in a way least damaging emotionally? Kate was right. She had suspected the depth of the girl's disturbance. He resolved for himself his first question. If Prince had failed to be forthright and honest with his patient, he had forfeited his right. As to how Craig should tell the girl, now he wished Kate were here to do that.

"The ovaries which Dr. Prince found it necessary to remove not only have to do with the reproductive processes. They also manufacture the female hormones. When they are removed, the doctor has to make up for that by prescribing supplements. Estrogen."

"That's all?" Cynthia asked dubiously.

"That's all."

"It can't be that easy. Or that simple."

"But it is."

She was pensive for a moment, then said softly, as if to herself, "If only Prince didn't smile so much."

"I just told you the truth, and I'm not smiling," Craig said, then he broke into a small grin.

She tried to smile back. Instead, her violet eyes filled with tears which she was able to control. "I thought it was something horrible. Something he was holding back because it was too terrible to tell me."

To avoid responding to her declaration, he asked instead, "Have they got you out of bed yet?"

"No. Why?"

"I think you should be up on your feet. At least for a little walk around this room. Let's try it."

He held out his hands to her. She pushed back the coverlet. He was relieved to see she was wearing the white antiemboli stockings the hospital rules prescribed. She let her legs down carefully over the side of the bed and tried to rise to her feet. There was a moment of dizziness. He reached out to steady her. She righted herself and began to walk slowly across the room and back. He watched her. She had a young but womanly body. She would have had no trouble bearing children, he surmised sadly. She slowly walked the length of the room twice, looking to him for his approval.

"A few more times," he urged.

She continued walking.

"I'll write the orders on your chart. But even if the nurses fail to remind you, I want you up and walking at least half a dozen times a day."

"Why is walking so important?"

"It's just good to get the patient up on her feet as soon as possible."

He did not explain any further. It would do her no good to become privy to his real concern. The chances were excellent that he would never have to explain it to her at all.

When she had walked sufficiently, he gestured her

back to bed. Once she was comfortably settled, he said, "If you have any questions, don't hesitate. I don't want you worrying your pretty head over baseless fears. So any time of day or night, give me a call. If I can't handle your question by phone, I'll drop by as soon as I can. But you're not to worry. Understand?"

She nodded, smiling for the first time, her violet eyes expressing her appreciation.

"Good night."

"Good night, Doctor," she responded softly, closing her eyes and prepared to give in to the sedatives that had been administered to her.

At the door, he felt compelled to stop and caution, "If you feel any pain, especially in your legs or thighs, or notice any swelling, tell the nurse to get hold of me at once."

"All right," she said, half asleep, now that she had been reassured.

On his way past the nurses' station, he paused to look at her chart. Her vital signs had been checked and entered just before dinner. Normal. Her temperature was normal too.

He must remember to check her again in the morning.

Though the possibility of what he feared was small, if it did occur, the consequences would be drastic. He would not rest easy until she was past any possible danger.

Chapter Twelve

He had fully intended to leave the hospital at once so that he could pick up Kate on time. But his sense of

143

foreboding made him go instead to the Path Lab on the fifth floor. He caught Becker at the door, dressed and ready to leave.

"Sam, got a minute?"

"My wife's expecting me home. Family dinner," Becker apologized.

"Sam, make a minute. It's important," Craig insisted in a way that made Becker pause.

An experienced pathologist who had seen hundreds of interns and residents come and go, Sam Becker had his favorites, those few who, he could sense, would become the best and most dedicated doctors of the future. Polite and cooperative with all staff men, he was especially concerned and helpful with those rare ones. He liked to say they helped to improve the medical neighborhood.

Craig Pierson, alert, willing to learn, with exacting standards of performance, was one of Sam's favorites; what Sam termed a patient's doctor, not merely a mechanic. He had seen too many technicians and always lamented the fact that in financial terms they seemed the most successful. Sam had his own opinion of Prince, which he voiced to no one but his wife. Sam knew better than anyone else why Prince's record of "successful" operations was so good.

"Okay, Craig, what is it this time?"

The phrase "this time" irritated Craig. He knew he had a reputation with some attending surgeons and staff men for being an annoying stickler for detail. He had not thought that feeling was shared by Sam Becker. He hoped Sam was only reflecting the pressure to get home on time.

Sam took off his coat, tossed his hat toward a chair and saw it fall to the floor, as he asked, "Which case?"

"The Horton girl."

144

"Horton ... Horton ..." Sam tried to remember. "When you do as many biopsies a day as I do, it's hard to recall names."

"A case of Prince's. Bilateral salpingo-oophorectomy," Craig identified.

"Oh, that one," Sam said. "If I recall correctly, on frozen section it was borderline. It was confirmed later."

"That was the right ovary. I want to know about the left one."

"The left one," Sam Becker considered. "Yes, the left one. I'll look it up." Sam pretended to search his records, all the while saying to himself, Damn it, I wish he hadn't asked me. I know what I'll have to say. Then I know what he'll say. So for his sake, I wish he hadn't asked. Sam found the record.

"Well, Sam?" Craig prodded.

"The left ovary was clean. No sign of tumor," Sam admitted.

"The arrogant sonofabitch!" Craig reacted exactly as Sam had anticipated.

"I've got to go," Sam reminded him, to avoid a lengthy discussion.

"Yeah. Sure. Thanks, Sam."

They stepped into the corridor. Craig asked, "Sam, you're going to present this at the Path Conference tomorrow, aren't you?"

"Another ovarian carcinoma, another bilateral." Sam tried to pass it off.

"Sam, this is not just 'another'!" Craig said angrily. "This is a young girl. Who might live fifty more years with the mistake of a doctor who should have known better!"

"Let's get out of here. I don't want to be seen discussing this with you in a corridor."

They were walking along the quiet, dark street that led away from the hospital.

"What I say now, kid, I do not want repeated. If it is, I will deny it. Understand?"

"Understand," Craig agreed.

"You're agitated about the Horton case. I am agitated about hundreds of Prince's cases. They say he's very skillful with a scalpel. That he does a better, quicker hysterectomy than any other surgeon in the city. He should, the bastard, he does so many. Needless ones. Sometimes I think he calls his accountant and asks, 'How much do I need to make my quota for the year!' Then the next ten women who come in are automatically diagnosed as needing hysterectomies."

"Don't you ever say anything?" Craig demanded.

"A pathologist is not a policeman; he is a researcher, who is called upon to deliver an opinion. He renders that opinion. But he does not decide on the therapy. Any discussion as to whether what was done was right or wrong is up to the staff. To other surgeons. To the Chief of the department."

"Ordway . . ." Craig considered.

Becker tried to justify the man. "Ordway's job is to keep the Ob-Gyn department running. And he does. It's a damn good department, too. Better than most I know of."

"It's his job to be a policeman," Craig reminded him.

"But not *yours*," Sam Becker said, finally coming to the point he wanted to make.

"It's got to be someone's," Craig protested, "and if Ordway doesn't choose—"

"Craig, I'm old enough to be your father. So I think I'm in a position to give you advice. This is not your battle. Don't fight it. Because you can't win it. All that can happen is that you'll endanger your career, possibly even destroy it, and nothing will change."

"Something has to change!" Craig insisted.

"Craig, my boy, who won out? The *Titanic* or the iceberg? You're up against a medical iceberg. A medical windmill. And you are Don Quixote. The big difference is this: Don Quixote was an old man at the end of his life. You're a young man at the beginning of your career. Don't ruin it. Because we need doctors like you. Doctors who care. Whose minds are on the condition of the patients, not the condition of the stock market. For *your* sake, I would prefer not to discuss this case at the Path Conference," Becker said.

They had reached Becker's modest apartment house only a few blocks from the hospital.

"Discuss it, Sam!" Craig urged.

"I would rather not."

"Discuss it," Craig insisted.

"Think about it overnight," Becker advised in a sober, fatherly way.

"If you won't introduce the case, I'll ask for it!" Craig said.

Becker finally relented. "I'll bring those slides to the conference. But think about what I said. Think about all the patients you'll be abandoning to men like Prince if you get yourself kicked out."

As Sam Becker watched Craig walking determinedly down the dark street, he was tempted to call out, "Boy, listen to me! It's too late! The butcher has done his work. That girl's an empty shell. At only twenty-two. But it's too late . . . too late . . ."

Kate had been waiting for more than an hour. But there were no recriminations. She had expected he would be late. She knew the Horton girl was in trouble. Serious emotional trouble. It would have taken more than a brief visit to reassure her.

Usually when they met, Craig embraced Kate and kissed her full on the mouth before she had a chance to say a word. This time, because she deduced from the weary set of his posture, from the angry look on his face, that he needed her, she kissed *him* full on the mouth, before he could say a word.

"Let's get something to eat," he suggested dutifully. "You must be starved."

"I've got something home. Cold chicken. I roasted it last evening, then got too involved in the new literature to eat. Fascinating stuff. The literature, not the chicken." She attempted a joke to change his mood. She failed.

She mixed him a drink. "A psychiatrist can always tell by the way the patient enters the office whether he has big troubles or only little ones. And tonight my patient has big trouble, very big trouble. Talk!"

He related his conversation with Sam Becker.

"Sam's a good man," she said. "A very honest human being. If you got into a jam, he'd stand by you."

"I know that. So I thought, is that why he's urging me not to press this? Because it will put him on the spot?"

"Craig, darling, instead of trying to find selfish motives, grant Sam the courtesy of believing him. Because he's right. You get a reputation for being a troublemaker, you'll never become Chief Resident. Or even a senior resident. They might force you to resign."

"So you agree with Sam."

"If I thought you could keep quiet about this and live with yourself, I'd say Sam is right. But some men

148

were never meant to live those lives of quiet desperation you read about. You're one of them. You'd eat yourself up. So go on, do what you have to do. I'll be with you all the way."

She kissed his bristly cheek, whispering. "You'd better go shave while I set out supper. No man with such a stubbly face is going to make love to me tonight."

Dinner and the white wine were long gone. Love was over too. She had sensed the tension in him throughout. She was glad that he was now relaxed and lying by her side, breathing more gently.

"What were you thinking about?" Kate asked, turning on her side to run her fingers across his smooth cheek, down to his strong, craggy chin.

"The possibilities. . . ."

"You're still free to change your mind," she observed without urging any course.

"I meant Cynthia's possibilities."

"Prince'll put her on estrogen. She'll get married. You said the other day her fiancé insists on it. And then she'll adopt a child or two or three or a dozen."

"What's bugging me is, what happens if they *can't* put her on estrogen?"

"What are you talking about?" Kate asked, rising on her elbow to look down at him.

"What if, because of some complication, estrogen is contraindicated?"

"But if she can't have estrogen . . .," Kate began to protest, but stopped quite abruptly.

"Exactly," Craig said. "She'd have a premature menopause. And everything that goes with it. Flushes. Aging effects on her skin. On her vagina. Possible pain and bleeding on intercourse. What kind

149

of marriage and sex life could those two have under such conditions? Prince hasn't just removed her ovaries, he's exposed her to terrible possibilities."

Kate felt the resurgence of his anger and decided not to let him know she shared it.

"The chances of her developing post-op complications are small," she consoled.

"No post-op patient is immune from a thrombophlebitis. That's why we put antiemboli stockings on them. That's why I had her out of bed and walking this evening. If we're lucky, yes, she'll get through it all right. But for some days, she'll be at risk. At great risk."

"You didn't tell her?"

"Of course not," Craig assured her. "Though she did look at me a bit strangely when I insisted she get out of bed and walk."

Kate was silent for a time, meditative.

"What, Katie?"

"When I interned at Parkside, we had a case of a girl with premature menopause. No psychiatrist there could treat her. Not even the Chief."

"What happened?"

"She signed herself out against advice. Two weeks later she committed suicide."

Chapter Thirteen

Interns, residents, and staff physicians were gathering for the weekly Pathology Conference. Some had brought cups of coffee with them and were standing about, leisurely discussing patients or social matters. Some rushed in, interrupting other duties in an effort to be prompt. Professor Ordway was a martinet about the presence of all Ob-Gyn surgeons at such meetings. The staff men and women respected his orders. Attending physicians, whose practice took them outside the hospital, made a sincere effort to show up when convenient. For there was always the inherent threat that if they became too lax, their privileges at the hospital might be canceled. And an affiliation with the State University Hospital was a valuable asset to the reputation of any physician or surgeon.

The only man who seemed exempt from attending Ob-Gyn Path Conferences was Harvey Prince. In his case, even Ordway made an exception. Between Prince's office practice and his demanding surgery, it was unreasonable to expect his attendance on any regular basis. Besides, Ordway was unable to insist, since Prince was a power in the Ob-Gyn department, being a social and business intimate of a number of members of the Board of Trustees.

Therefore it was no surprise to Craig Pierson or Burt Carlyle to discover that Prince was not in attendance today.

Ordway seemed in a particularly irascible mood as he gave Dr. Sam Becker a signal to open the conference. The room was darkened. Becker sat beside the slide projector so that he could use the light that bled from it to refer to his notes.

His first set of slides involved a case of carcinoma of the cervix. The patient was a woman of twenty-eight.

Her history followed the classic characteristics of such cancers, including early sexual activity and a positive history of venereal disease. On the basis of the high incidence of cervical carcinoma in prostitutes

151

and the very low incidence in nuns, it was presumed there was some causal relationship in promiscuous sexual activity. The etiology, it was assumed, might be a virus passed on in the same way as venereal disease.

Becker had completed his presentation of the case. The staff gynecologist who had treated the patient outlined the course he followed. Since she was beyond surgical resection, she was to receive radiation therapy. Her prognosis was very guarded.

Regretfully, he concluded, "This is not only a classic cervical carcinoma. It is also a classic case of neglect. If she had exercised one tenth the concern for her health that she did for finding lovers, this would have been picked up by any doctor. She'd have had an excellent chance for recovery."

Becker presented three more cases, projecting the pathology slides, calling attention to the affected tissue. He enlarged the diseased cells and held the varicolored slides in focus on the screen while the surgeons involved described patient, symptoms, signs, diagnosis, and treatment.

"It's getting late," Ordway reminded the meeting, indicating that though there was more material, the conference had run longer than anticipated, conflicting with the demands for the doctors on the wards and in the O.R.s and Emergency.

As the men started to rise, Sam Becker said, "There's only one more case."

In view of the extensive gossip that had spread through Ob-Gyn service concerning the conflict between Prince and Craig Pierson, Ordway realized that he would only be compounding the problem by deliberately censoring discussion now.

"As long as it's only one more case," Ordway conceded to Becker. "And if it won't take too long."

Becker presented the slides of Cynthia Horton's biopsies. In his usual thorough manner he pointed out the sections he had sampled.

At this stage of a Path Conference it was customary for the surgeon involved to describe the procedure he had employed and his reasoning. Instead, Ordway announced, "Since the surgeon in charge of the case is not present, we should postpone any discussion. I'm sure Dr. Prince will be here next time."

He rose abruptly from his chair, his usual signal that the conference was over. Someone close to the door snapped on the lights.

Despite that part of him which warned against it, Craig Pierson blurted out, "I assisted at that operation! In fact, I removed the ovarian tumor. I would like to report on the case now, since there's no guarantee that Dr. Prince will be here 'next time' or the time after that."

Ordway glared at Craig. Becker's eyes pleaded with him. Burt Carlyle's barely noticeable shake of the head tried to dissuade him. Still, determined, Craig would not relent. Finally, since the rest of the staff was aware of the conflict involved in this particular case, Ordway felt forced to yield.

"All right, Pierson, if it won't take too long. We all have heavy schedules."

"The slides, please!" Craig said to Sam Becker.

The room dark again, Becker projected the slides of the diseased ovary in the same order as before, pointing out the same affected areas.

"Dr. Becker, do you have the slides on the other ovary removed from the same patient?"

Realizing that Craig could not be dissuaded, Becker inserted those slides and was forced to point out the absence of any finding of tumor cells.

"Dr. Becker," Craig persisted, "wouldn't it have

153

been possible to arrive at the same conclusion—that the left was clean—if the surgeon had not removed but had bivalved that ovary and presented you with a wedged sample?"

The formality of Craig's address to Sam Becker suddenly transformed the meeting from an informal professional exchange of information into an inquisitorial proceeding. More aware of that than any other physician in the room, Becker decided, for Craig's sake, to sidestep the issue.

"That," Becker said, "is a decision to be made by a surgeon, not a pathologist."

Ordway seized the moment to dismiss the entire episode lightly. "Pierson has just given us a perfect illustration of the practice of medicine with the aid of that infallible diagnostic tool known as the hindsight scan."

There was some laughter from the interns. Those residents who had scrubbed with Prince did not laugh. But neither did they come to Craig's defense.

Craig expected that at least Burt Carlyle might speak up and point out that in this case it was not hindsight. But Burt remained silent.

Ordway ended the meeting. "I understand the patient is recovering very nicely. She has an excellent chance for a long-term survival from a form of carcinoma that is among the most deadly. Now I think we'd best get back to our respective jobs."

Craig Pierson and Burt Carlyle were striding down the corridor. The tense atmosphere of the conference room still engulfed both men. Guilt made Burt Carlyle break the silence.

"Christ, Craig, what were you trying to accomplish? You lost that battle the moment Prince decided to do a bilateral."

"There'll be other battles, other wars. We can't just lie down and play dead for big shots like Prince. He was wrong. Wrong!"

Craig became aware that passersby were turning to stare at him.

"Just tell me one thing," Burt said in an angry whisper. "What good is it going to do the Horton girl to prove Prince was wrong? Or is it a macho thing with you? You are going to prove that you are smarter than Old Goldfingers. If that's what you have in mind, I'd pick a smaller target. And a different case."

Craig turned to confront Carlyle. "You didn't agree with Prince. I could see it in your eyes!"

"I don't agree with lots of things I see in surgery," Carlyle said. "But I don't have to make a public issue of them. All I say to myself is, Learn from their mistakes. Who does a greater number or variety of cases than Prince? So from whom can you learn most? Even from his mistakes? Prince!"

Because Burt felt himself becoming loud enough to attract attention, he seized Craig by the arm and pulled him into a utility room. Once they were alone and unobserved, Burt said, "Craig, follow Ordway's advice. Go to Prince. Apologize. Before he kicks you off his scrub team."

When Craig did not relent, Burt pointed out, "You'll never get a chance to assist on as many interesting cases with any other man. It would be the same as missing your second year of residency. And I can tell you, the second year is crucial. You learn to do all the procedures that you'll be capable of doing on your own as a senior resident. And you do it under an experienced man like Prince.

"Craig, I know you're steamed. Teed off. But take it from someone who has two hundred years of ancestry in biting your tongue, this is a time to do just that. Bite your tongue. Swallow your pride; go to Prince and apologize."

"And who apologizes to the girl in 442?" Craig asked bitterly.

Burt lost his patience. "Don't be a goddamned fool! The most important thing I learned in my internship in general surgery was never to allow any one patient to become that important. Never let any one case, any one mistake, your own or someone else's, loom that large. Go to Prince. Apologize. Stay on his scrub team. For your own sake."

Chapter Fourteen

The young black woman looked up from the examining table at Dr. Craig Pierson. Her eyes were large with fear; she was obviously tense. When he proceeded to examine her, she grew more so. It was clear to him that she had not submitted herself to a doctor's examination very often. While he proceeded with his bimanual he encouraged her to talk.

"What made you decide to come in? Did your own doctor send you in?"

"I don't have no own doctor."

"You just got the idea yourself?" he asked, pressing gently on her abdomen to make quite sure that there was no symptom she was keeping from him. Her stomach was soft, resilient to his touch, revealing no suspicious masses.

"My sister-in-law," the woman admitted, with a sense of guilt that caused Craig to become suspicious.

156

"What did she say?"

"She said, These times a man not knowing one day to the next if'n he's going to have a job, it's not good to have too many children. She said, Better to have few and give them more, than to have many and give them not enough."

"Your sister-in-law said that?"

"She smart. She been to college. She's a teacher. She says it's too late for us. But it is only the beginning for the children. So give them every chance. And the best way is to have few."

"How many do you have?" Craig asked, continuing with his examination.

"Five," she admitted.

"Ages?"

"Nine, seven, six, three, and two. The seven and three are the boys," the young woman said.

"These days, five is quite a number. So you and your husband decided . . ."

The woman tensed under his touch, betraying her secret.

"Are you here without telling him?"

Her wide eyes revealed that he had guessed the source of her tension.

"Have you ever discussed having this done?" he asked gently, not wishing to add to her conflict.

"No," she admitted.

"Why not?"

" 'Cause I think he would say no," she admitted. "So my sister-in-law and me, we talked it over and she said, go on and do it, then it don't matter what he says, it's done."

"So you think he would object?" Craig asked.

"I think he would not like me to have any operation. Imagine if I should die, and leave him alone with five

157

little ones, and him trying to scratch out a living while having to care for them. . . . It's too much, too much," she said wearily. She added wistfully, "And he loves me. He wouldn't want nothing to happen to me. So he'd say, Don't go looking for trouble, and he'd say no."

"Well, let me put your mind at ease about one thing. It isn't dangerous. We make a very small incision right about there," he said, indicating the spot on her naked abdomen. "We go in with a scope and seal off your fallopian tubes, and that's all there is to it. You'll be home the next day."

"That's all?" she asked, her eyes begging for reassurance.

"That's all," he promised. "That's not to say we guarantee nothing will go wrong. But in this operation it rarely ever does."

With considerable determination she said, "Then do it! Do it and get it over with!"

"Mrs. Harrison, are you quite sure you want to do this without letting your husband know?"

Her eyes filled with tears, but she did not cry.

"He's going to take it badly. He might think I'm saying he's not man enough to make do for me and the children. I don't want to hurt him."

"Can't his sister talk to him?"

"They don't talk very easy. He being a laboring man who never got past the first year of high school. And she so educated. He always feels . . . not good enough. So whatever she says, he's bound to say no."

"Well," Craig said, "if you sign a consent form we can do the procedure. But I would suggest you let him know first."

"If he agrees, will you be the one to do it?"

"Me or one of the other residents. They're all good men," Craig said.

158

"I'd feel better if you did it," she said cautiously.

He smiled. "You've never seen me operate; how do you know? I might be the worst doctor here."

"I don't think so," she said.

"Why not?"

"Because you take time. The other doctors who see the clinic patients, they're always in a hurry. They seem angry. 'S if unless you got some real bad sickness they don't want to be bothered."

Though she did not phrase it well, he knew what she was trying to say. He had the same complaint himself. Interns and residents, seeking unusual and complicated cases for the experience they might gain, tended to be brusque with those patients who presented minor routine illnesses and complaints. To them the clinic was a practice field, not a place to care for patients whose illnesses, though commonplace to physicians and surgeons, were quite real, worrisome, and many times overwhelming to simple people.

"I'll try to do it myself. If not, it'll be Dr. Carlyle or Dr. Bernstein. Both good men. But talk it over with your husband. Even if he doesn't agree, at least he'll know. He won't feel you've done it behind his back. Okay?"

She was pensive for a moment, then smiled faintly and agreed, "Okay."

"When you come back, ask for me. Dr. Pierson. And I'll do it if I can. Or I'll make sure you get into the hands of a very good man."

"Thank you, Doctor."

He pulled back the curtain of the cubicle and was starting for the next one when his beeper sounded insistently.

"Craig?"

He was startled. It was his mother. Quite upset, but

159

as apologetic as she usually was those rare times when she had dared interrupt him at the hospital.

"Mom? What is it? What's wrong?"

"It's Dad."

"What? Heart attack? I keep telling him to slow down—"

"No, nothing like that," she interrupted.

"Then what?"

"Tony Ciardo had this bad back and he couldn't show up—"

"Mom, what about Dad?" he asked impatiently.

"I'm trying to tell you. Tony hasn't been able to work the last week. So Dad's been doing the work himself. Yesterday afternoon he was cutting the dead branches off this tall pine on the Henderson property and he . . . he fell . . ."

"Did you call a doctor? What did he say?"

"They took him right to the hospital."

"It was that bad?"

"We don't know. They didn't finish all the tests."

"Which hospital? What's the doctor's name?" Craig asked.

"Good Samaritan. And I don't know his name," his mother said. She added apologetically, "Sorry to bother you, son. I know how busy you are. But I'm frightened. Very frightened." With that last word she almost began to weep.

"Mom, take it easy. It might be nothing. I'll get hold of the doctor and find out."

"Call me soon as you know?" she pleaded.

"Of course. Maybe I can work it out so I'll come back home for a few days. I've got some time off coming," he said, in his mind canceling a short weekend Kate and he had decided on to see the fall foliage out in the country.

160

He had examined and made decisions and recommendations on eight clinic patients before his call to Good Samaritan finally reached the right doctor there.

"Dr. Halloran? Dr. Pierson, State University Hospital."

The hospital's reputation always served to impress other physicians.

"I understand you admitted my father yesterday afternoon. William Pierson. Accidental fall from a tree."

"Oh, yes, he did mention he had a son who was a doctor. Very proud of it, too. We admitted him for observation."

"And?"

"So far we find a concussion. And a comminuted fracture of the right elbow. We're doing more testing, though. Possibly even a brain scan. But that's purely defensive. To make sure it's nothing more than a concussion."

"Maybe I ought to be there."

"If you can make it, it wouldn't hurt."

"You don't like the prognosis," Craig concluded.

"A man his age climbing trees. Lopping off branches. Of course he won't be able to do that anymore. His right arm is going to be virtually immobile. He won't believe me. So perhaps it would be a good idea for you to be here."

"Okay. I'll work it out somehow," Craig promised.

He had called Kate. He had tracked down Ordway in a meeting with Walter Deering, the Hospital Administrator. Ordway was quick to grant him four days off. Burt Carlyle would juggle the schedule to cover for him. Privately, Ordway was relieved to have Craig away from the hospital for a time. The repercussions of the issue he had created at the Pathology Conference still lingered. Word had filtered back to Prince, who was furious. By the time Craig returned, the Horton girl would be released and the whole affair should have blown over. Prince was too valuable to the Department to antagonize. Aside from this one issue, Craig Pierson was too good a resident to lose. Ordway looked upon his family emergency as a fortuitous event.

Craig took a taxi from the airport directly to Good Samaritan, and without calling his mother. Halloran would be completely frank with him alone, but might shade the facts in the presence of an anxious wife.

Halloran turned out to be a resident, like himself a second-year man. He was short, stocky, blond, and with blue eyes that were quick and suspicious. His first remark was a question, not a statement.

"Pierson, what's a man with a history of coronary disease doing climbing trees and going through the exertion of sawing off thick limbs?"

"Coronary disease?" Craig asked, startled.

"Take a look at his chart, at his cardiogram. I had one taken. Just on a hunch."

Halloran spread out the E.K.G. tape. "There, and there, and there. Very clear evidence of a coronary episode. Didn't you know?"

"Of course not."

"A man seventy-one, with a history like this, and then that fall..." Halloran shook his head sadly. "He's got to quit."

"He wouldn't know how," Craig said.

"I know," Halloran agreed. "Had the same trouble with my dad. They work so hard all their lives provid-

162

ing for their children, the habit gets deeply ingrained. They think they have to go on providing for the rest of their lives. Just in case one of the kids doesn't make it. My father produced one son who is a doctor, as you can see. One is a lawyer, on the legal staff of an insurance company. And another is a stockbroker who does handsomely. And yet he couldn't taper off. He went on 'providing.' Until he had a second coronary. And that was it. Worked right down to the last day of his life. You don't want that to happen to your dad, do you?"

"Of course not."

"Then lay the law down," Halloran advised.

"Where is he?"

"Sixth floor. Semiprivate."

It was a small bare room, with hardly enough space for anyone to pass between the two beds. His father was fixed in a ninety-degree posterior splint, elevated, and in ice packs. His shock of gray hair was a disheveled mass that hung down covering his right eye. He had a two-day growth of white, stubbly beard.

When he saw Craig in the doorway, he seemed to rise up in bed, in surprise. Only the splint inhibited him from getting out of bed to greet him.

"Craig . . . Craig . . .," he said, his eyes filmed over with gratitude and pride. He called to the wizened man in the bed opposite. "This is my son I was telling you about. The doctor." He turned to Craig. "What are you doing here? You should be back there at the hospital taking care of all those women."

"What happened, Dad?"

"Oh, this." He glanced disparagingly at his splint. "Nothing. It was a mistake to tell them my son was a doctor. They started doing all kinds of tests, taking

163

care of me like I got hurt real bad. They made such a fuss I was sorry I said a word."

"Dad . . .," Craig interrupted. "Dad, why didn't you tell me you had a heart attack before?"

"Who said—" the old man started to protest.

"I saw it. On the E.K.G."

"Oh, that. That's . . . listen . . . that's over with. . . . I mean . . ." He tried to diminish it but could not.

The little man in the opposite bed improvised, "My doctor says, Go for a walk. Five times a day, get out of bed and go for a walk." He slipped out of bed. When Craig offered to help him with his robe, he declined politely, saying, "Therapy. They say I got to do for myself as much as I can."

Once he had left the room, Craig's father said in a grim whisper, "Cancer. His wife told me. He ain't got but a few weeks." Bill Pierson said compassionately. "Too bad. Very nice man. We talk a lot. About things. Life. What it's been. What it might have been. I think he knows. He don't let on to his wife. But a man don't talk that way unless he knows."

"Now, Dad, what about you?"

"Soon as this arm heals I'll be good as new."

"I mean about the coronary. When? How? Did you tell Mom?"

"Nothing happened. I swear nothing happened," Bill Pierson protested.

"You didn't feel sick at all?"

"I had a little indigestion. So I stayed home from work for a few days. But that's no heart attack."

"Damn it, Dad, I've told you a thousand times, if you feel bad, no matter what you think, let me know. I'm the doctor, not you."

"Ah, a women's doctor," his father said deprecatingly.

164

"Dad!" Craig said, calling him to account.

"Okay, next time I'll call," his father grudgingly consented.

"We're going to make sure there is no next time." Craig was taking command.

"What does that mean?"

"It means no more work. Sell the business. Give it away. But no more, Dad. Understand—no more working!"

"Look, Tony's come back. And I've got some high school kids lined up for after-school work. It'll be easy. Easy!" the man protested.

"You've worked all your life. Since you were twelve. It's time to stop."

"What'll I do?" the old man lamented.

"Don't worry. I'll take care of Mom and you. Things are pretty good now and can only get better. So don't worry."

"All my life I've been on my own. Now to be a burden to my son . . . that's some way for a man to end his days, being a burden."

"You're not a burden, Dad. I'll be happy to do it, proud to do it."

"From the earliest days I said, I want to give this boy everything I never had. For myself, I want nothing except the satisfaction of knowing he had every chance. But now . . . Look, you don't owe me a thing! Nothing! Whatever I did was because *I* wanted to do it. I got more satisfaction out of it than you did. You should have seen the look in Dr. Halloran's eyes, the way it changed when I said to him, 'My son is a doctor too.' It gave me"—he fumbled for the word—"it gave me importance in his eyes. I was somebody. All because of you, son. So you don't owe me a thing. Whatever I did for you, it's marked Paid in Full!"

165

The old man was trembling, and the tears in his eyes spilled over, though he tried to hold them back.

Craig embraced him. "Dad . . . Dad, don't cry. It's all right. I understand."

"Your mother—did you tell her?"

"Not yet."

"Then don't make it sound like I failed her. That's the one thing I never wanted—to fail her, to fail you. Because, to tell the truth, the business isn't worth anything. I can't sell it. I tried. My customers, there are not so many anymore. And the ones I have, I guess they continue just to be nice to me. That's why I had to . . ." He hesitated before admitting, "Tony didn't get sick. I just couldn't afford to pay him anymore. So I had to do the work myself."

"Damn it, Dad, why didn't you tell me? There are things more important than pride!" Craig exploded.

"Like what?" his father asked, brushing the tears from his eyes. "Maybe kids of today feel that way. But to my generation, without pride a man was nothing, nothing."

"Of course, Dad," Craig said softly.

"So when you tell your mother . . ."

"I understand. Now rest—take it easy. And give this a chance to heal."

"Are you leaving today?" he asked hesitantly, not wishing to appear to make demands on his son.

"No, I've arranged for a few days off."

"Good . . . Good . . ." His father was reassured. "I'll feel better knowing you're here. Your mother'll feel better. I think of her alone in that empty house—especially these days, when a woman isn't safe even behind locked doors. I worry about her."

"She'll be okay, Dad. I'll talk to her. Maybe it's time

you both moved south. A warmer climate; a nice, safe, protected condominium," he suggested, wondering where he could get the money for such a luxury.

It had been almost a year since Craig had last come back to the modest two-story frame house where he had lived most of his life. It was distinguished by the tasteful and abundant shrubbery that set it off from the other equally modest homes on the block. The walk had been redone—the same walk he had biked along on his way to and from grade school and high school. He almost expected to find his bike propped up against the porch where he had usually left it. It was not there, because his father had given it to a young boy down the street for helping him during the summer rush.

He walked up the path, up onto the porch, where the boards still creaked in all the same places. Before he could open the door, his mother was there. She flung her arms around him and held on tightly. He felt a tremor go through her body. The tears she had fought against on the phone were flowing freely now.

"He's okay, Mom. He's doing fine."

"Thank God," she said, releasing him. "You know, when doctors at a hospital tell you that, you don't believe them. . . ." She realized what she had said and smiled. "Maybe I shouldn't say that now. . . ."

"Say it, Mom. Say it, because a lot of times it's true." He smiled to make her feel better.

"Well, what did they say?" she asked anxiously. "Will he be all right?"

"He'll be all right," Craig promised, realizing that he was now himself indulging in one of those half-truths doctors resort to. "But he won't be able to work anymore. He has a comminuted fracture . . . he broke his elbow. So he can't use his right arm the way he used to, can't bend it."

"Did you tell him?" she asked, a worried look beginning to crease her thin face.

Not having seen her in almost a year, he could realize now how much she had aged. "I told him."

"What did he say?"

"He didn't like it."

"But what did he say? Will he do it? Retire?"

"He has to," Craig insisted.

"You know . . . that thing about Tony having a bad back. I didn't believe that. I think he thought he could do it all himself and save the money. Business hasn't been so good lately."

"He told me."

"It must have been painful for him. He had such dreams. In years gone by he would promise me that one day, when you were through medical school and he didn't have all those bills to pay, the business could run by itself. Tony and one other man. We could live comfortably, take long trips and vacations. But in the last five or six years things have got worse. It's been a struggle, a struggle."

She did not say it, but it was clear it had been a great hardship for them to see him through school. These two people whom he might never have known if some social-service person in the adoption agency had shuffled through his papers and decided that he should belong to some other couple. These two had given him the most and the best of their lives.

Impulsively, he put his arms around his mother and held her very close, her head pressing against his shoulder, which she barely reached. He could not say it; she would not permit it. But she knew what he felt, and she was deeply touched.

168

"Mom, did you know he had a heart attack?"

"No," she responded, leaning back from Craig and looking up into his eyes fearfully. "Is that why he fell off the tree?"

"Before that. Months ago."

"He never told me. Once . . . once he complained of a bad upset stomach . . . he was in bed for a few days . . .," she recalled.

"That was the time."

"Heart attack . . .," she whispered breathlessly; the thought frightened her as much as if it had just occurred. "He can't go back to work. No matter what he says, he can't go back!" she resolved.

"He's not going back; he knows that now," Craig said.

"But what will—"

He interrupted. "You'll sell the house. And the business. There must be some value still in the business. Maybe Tony will take it on by himself and pay you out each week. And you'll move down south."

"You're going to take your father away from the seasons?" she asked. "He loves the seasons."

"It'll be better for him down there."

"And the . . . the money?"

"I'll take care of the money," Craig assured her.

"That he won't permit. He has always said to me, That boy owes us nothing. He has repaid us a hundred times over. He has an office to open, and those things cost money, lots of money. . . ."

"If I stay in academic medicine or become a full-time man, I won't have those expenses. So don't worry about it. It'll work out. The main thing, you have to convince him that going south is best."

"Will we get to see you, son?"

"Of course," Craig promised. "Another year, once

I'm through with my residency, I'll have lots more time. Lots!"

The phone rang, and as it did, she remembered. "Oh, I forgot. A girl called. She said her name was Kate something."

"Lindstrom?" Craig asked.

"That's it," Anna Pierson said.

He answered the phone.

"Craig?"

"Yes, Kate?"

"How is he?"

Craig reported what he had found and decided.

"Then it's not all so serious. Good. Good!" Kate sounded relieved. "I was worried. When are you coming back?"

The question alerted Craig. Kate was too self-sufficient to become so concerned about his return after only a day.

"Why? What is it?"

She hesitated, giving him added reason for concern.

"Kate?" he demanded.

"Prince. He heard about the Path Conference. He considers it a personal attack on his reputation at a time when he was not there to defend himself."

"If he gave up golf on Wednesdays, he'd be at the Path Conferences as he should be!" Craig accused.

"That's not the point. He resents you. And he's teed off enough to do something about it."

"Like what?" Craig asked, less belligerent and more concerned now.

"I don't know. But the air around here is not good. Not good at all. So as soon as things at home permit, come back. Come back, Craig?" She sounded as if she were almost pleading.

Chapter Fifteen

Harvey Prince had completed a long, profitable day in the operating room. He had done seven cases, two of them complicated. He had not even had time for lunch between cases, but had had the nurses feed him sweetened orange juice for quick and sustained energy. He had been silent through most of the day, not his usual loquacious self. He did not joke with the residents, or make suggestive remarks to the young student nurses, which most times he did to conceal his relationship with Rita Hallen. He never fooled anyone. But he always carried on his transparent little charade of flirting with the younger nurses.

Except on this day. For he had arranged a meeting with Clinton Ordway in the office of Walter Deering, Hospital Administrator. The meeting had been set for five o'clock to accommodate Prince's crowded schedule. At four forty-five, midway through the fourth hysterectomy he had done this day, Prince turned to Burt Carlyle and said curtly, "Close!" He briskly walked out of the O.R.

He had showered, dressed in one of his gray flannel suits, with a costly crimson-and-gold Macclesfield cravat, a gift from a grateful patient. He affixed the budding red rose in his lapel. When he had brought his white moustache to the proper tilt, Harvey Prince was ready.

He rode down in the elevator, rehearsing how he

would open the meeting. By the time he opened Deering's door, he was ready. A bit late, as he intended to be, and assuming a high degree of indignation, Harvey Prince was prepared to make his demand.

His first words were preceded by a sign of weariness. "It's been a rugged day, gentlemen. A very rugged day. A man should not have to go through such a day and then be troubled by meetings such as this."

Used to Prince's theatrics, both Deering and Ordway said nothing to contradict him. In truth, wielding the power he did, Prince had summoned them to this meeting and they were resigned, though not eager, to listen.

"However," Prince began, launching into the attack he had prepared, "this is an urgent matter. Mind you, I don't raise this question on my own behalf. After all, what difference does it make to me or my career if some pompous young resident, carried away by his own importance, decides to attack me?

"It's this hospital I'm concerned about! If we get a reputation for permitting insubordinate residents to attack other doctors, we run some grave risks. First, we are not going to attract or hold good attending physicians and surgeons. Eleven years ago when I came to the city, I chose this hospital because of its reputation. Other doctors will come after me, and will make their choice on the basis of the same criteria. Reputation. As a finely run, responsible institution. If you lose that reputation, the good men will go to other hospitals. And there are some excellent ones in this city. I've had offers from them to move over. But I am a man of strong loyalty. I'll remain here, just as long as you make it possible for me to remain."

Once Prince had made his threat, he became a bit

more relaxed. "Mind you, no one doctor is that important. I could have a coronary in the O.R. tomorrow and this hospital would still continue to function. Some other man would come up to take my place. Perhaps not with so large a practice.

"The bigger question is this: if you permit residents to carry on such open criticism as happened in the Pathology Conference the other day, and that gets back to patients, you are opening the door to a tidal wave of malpractice suits. Things are bad enough, what with greedy lawyers seeking opportunities to pounce on dissatisfied patients. Hand them such a weapon as another doctor's opinion that something was done that harmed a patient—my God, what a field day those shysters would have! And what a hell of a time we'd have defending ourselves against suits like that. To say nothing of what it would do to the hospital's malpractice premiums!"

Both Ordway and Deering nodded in grim agreement.

"Well, the best way to put an end to this is simply to put an end to it," Prince suggested. "Being a surgeon, I approach every problem the same way. If there is a diseased part, remove it. When in doubt, cut it out!"

"Exactly what are you suggesting, Harve?" Deering asked, for they were golfing partners as well as friends.

"Get that arrogant young sonofabitch to resign!" Prince said, no longer making any pretense at reasonableness. "And if he won't, fire him!"

Ordway sought to temporize: "Perhaps there's some other way."

"What other way?" Prince demanded angrily.

"Well, if you feel so strongly about this, why not

173

refuse to have him scrub with you?" Ordway improvised, thinking if he would keep Pierson out of Prince's way his hostility might eventually subside. "I could have Carlyle arrange the residents' schedule to accomplish that."

"I do not want Pierson to have any contact at all with any of my patients!" Prince declared.

"Even that could be arranged," Ordway agreed quickly, thinking it would satisfy Prince's need for vengeance.

"I don't know," Prince said, pretending to equivocate. "It would leave him free to do the same thing to other surgeons. These young bastards who think they know the best and latest in medicine are just dying to show up men like me. That's what I like about Carlyle. He knows his place. He has respect for experience. He's willing to watch and listen and learn. Not like Pierson. Too bad Carlyle's black."

"Harvey," Ordway interposed, "aren't you condemning Pierson on the basis of a single case? He's never been insubordinate before."

"If it happened once, it can happen again. We can't let him get away with it," Prince insisted.

When neither Ordway nor Deering picked up the cue, Prince continued: "As I was saying to Gus Wankel on Sunday when we were climbing up to the ninth tee, I said, 'Gus, as a trustee, you ought to look into things at the hospital. Not just go to Board meetings, listen to a lot of dull reports and vote. Get to know the place firsthand.' "

Prince did not say whether he had discussed the Pierson matter with Wankel. But he had made clear that his social relationship with several trustees gave great weight to any suggestion he made. Both Ordway's job as Chief and Deering's as Administrator depended on the favor of the trustees.

174

"Harve, I give you my word, we'll discuss it and take some steps. Pierson won't get away with this," Deering promised.

There was a note in Craig Pierson's box when he returned to the city. It was a cryptic message from Clinton Ordway: *See me!* Craig shoved the message into his pocket and went to the nearest phone. He had the operator try Kate on her beeper. She did not answer. Undoubtedly she was in a session with one of her clinic patients.

He had no trouble reaching Ordway, who broke out of a meeting to see him. The Chief ushered him into a small side room.

"Pierson, this has become most serious!" Ordway began, setting a grim tone for the meeting. "When you openly disagreed with Prince in the O.R., I gave you my best advice: apologize. You chose to ignore that. A bad mistake. To make matters worse, before the entire staff you openly questioned Prince's judgment in the Path Conference.

"Well, it got back to him, as I suspected it would. So now it comes down to this: he wants me to secure your resignation."

Craig stared hard at Ordway.

"I think Deering and I were able to satisfy him with something less. You are not to be assigned to scrub with him ever again. And he does not want you to have contact with any of his patients at any time, for any reason!"

Craig did not reply at once. But he realized, as did Ordway, that this decision excluded him from a great number of patients on the Ob-Gyn service.

"The way I have arranged things," Ordway suggested, seeking to minimize the blow, "I'll have Carlyle assign you more heavily to the wards and Gyn emergency for the rest of the year. You can still scrub with Fraley and Bell and some of the other men," he added, referring to two of the younger surgeons, from neither of whom Craig was likely to learn a great deal.

He realized Ordway was trying to let him down as easily as he could, and he appreciated the Chief's concern. But at the same time, without saying it, Ordway was making it clear that not only was it now out of the question that Craig might become Chief Resident; it had become highly questionable that there was much value in his staying on to become a senior resident.

"Pierson, because I respect you, I want to give you some good advice. Let us say, for the sake of argument, that you were right and Prince was wrong. Let us say that not only were you right but you could prove it. Think of the harm you might be doing that girl by making a cause of this thing."

"What more can I do to her after what Prince did?" Craig demanded.

"If this dispute between you and Prince gets back to her, put yourself in her position. Deprived of ever bearing any children through an avoidable error in judgment. That would be far worse for her than if she were in this condition because it was *un*avoidable. Think about it."

Craig did not respond at once.

Ordway suggested very gingerly, "You might ask Dr. Lindstrom about the possible effect on the girl." Ordway did not wish to make a point of Craig's relationship with Kate, though he was quite aware of it.

"And think of the reaction of other doctors. Which surgeon wants a smart-ass young resident looking over his shoulder second-guessing his every move? Who wants a man around today who tomorrow might be willing to testify against him in a malpractice suit? You may be destroying your entire career even before it gets started."

Ordway paused to allow his warning to sink in. "Personally, I think, with Prince, deep down, it's a matter of vanity. So, massage his ego a little. It may still not be too late to apologize. Of course he'll gloat, spread it around the hospital. But that's exactly what will mollify him. Try it. It might work. After all, you can still learn a lot of surgery from him," Ordway advised sincerely.

Craig had called Kate. She promised to meet him for a cup of coffee in the hospital cafeteria. It gave him time to consider what Ordway had said. A strange man, Ordway. You always had the feeling that behind that outer shell of the firm but understanding administrator was a surgeon who would rather not be Chief at all.

The most significant point Ordway had made was the irrefutable fact that it would do Cynthia Horton no good to create an issue now.

By the time Kate arrived, his mind had been made up. He rose to greet her, kissed her—more than a casual kiss. In times of stress he knew how much he needed her. She knew it too, could tell from the way he held her.

"Kate, darling, whatever we've talked about in the past about us. About you wanting to put off marriage or my insisting on it. Well, things have changed. Now *I* want to put it off."

"Put it off?" she echoed, taken aback.

"This is a hell of a place to tell you. I'm sorry. Meet me later?" he asked.

"No, tell me now," she said. Her blue eyes were

moist, but otherwise she was in complete control of herself.

"The trip home gave me a chance to think. . . ."

"About us."

"And other things."

She wished she could resist, but she had to ask, "It wasn't anyone back there? Some girl you used to be in love with?"

"It's . . . it's Prince. It's what happens if I can't stay on to complete my residency. It's the next two or three years."

"Your folks? Now that your dad can't work any longer?"

"That's part of it," he admitted. "I owe them too much."

"So you've decided to apologize to Prince?" she guessed.

"The alternative would be to leave here. Resign. The reason? On the surface very valid. I had to go south because of a family health problem. But where does a man go to finish his residency? Hospitals ask questions. Ordway's right: what hospital is going to want a resident who'll be looking over the shoulders of attendings watching for their mistakes, their malpractices?"

Kate said nothing. She just stared at him. It was enough.

He exploded suddenly: "Let's get out of here! I feel like a prisoner talking to his lawyer in a jail cell!"

They left the hospital grounds, walked down by the river. The day was cool, the sky blue, except for great billows of white clouds—friendly clouds.

She did not prod him to talk. When he was ready, he would say it.

He turned from staring across the river to look into

178

her blue eyes. "Kate ... darling ... you have no idea what it did to me to see Dad lying there, imprisoned in that damned splint. A man who's been free and independent all his life. An active man. Now he'll be a captive of enforced retirement. The least I can do is relieve him of financial worries."

Kate stared back at him. "And you think I wouldn't understand or be willing to share in it?"

"My obligations are mine, not yours."

"Because you 'owe' him."

"Both of them," Craig corrected.

"Craig," she said firmly, "what makes you think that what they did for you was any different from what my folks did for me?"

"Yours had to. Mine didn't. I oftentimes wonder, what would have happened to me if they hadn't taken me? Would I have lived out my life in orphanages, institutions of one kind or other? What would I be now if it hadn't been for them? I have no right to jeopardize everything they worked for, sacrificed for."

"So you want out?" she asked simply.

"I don't want to be held to promises, or plans, or dreams. I want to untangle my life at the hospital."

"Meaning apologize to Prince," she called him to account.

"I have to," he admitted.

"And you want me to say, Go on, Craig, you're free. Go set things right and one day when you're all straightened out, come back. And I will be waiting."

"Damn it, Kate, I'm trying to say, Turn me loose. Let me go. Forget me. For your own sake."

"I can't," she said. He stared at her. She stared back, and smiled faintly. "Funny. Until today I might have. Until today I kept feeling, *I* want time to work out my own career problems. *I* want to be free. But from the moment you asked, I suddenly realized how it would be without you. And I don't want that. Don't ask me to wait, but I will. Don't make commitments. I don't need them. But I'm sorry, I can't let you go.

"And as for your folks, and how you feel about them. If my dad had an accident and had to give up the farm, I'd do the same thing you're going to do. Not because I 'owe' him. But because I love him. It's the same with you. They loved you—that's why they did all they did for you. You love them, so you want to do all you can for them. That's all there is. Why can't you let yourself believe that?"

He took her in his arms and held her close. He pressed his face against hers. He inhaled the fragrance of her and found himself suddenly thinking, How nice, how feminine, that she is not in a specialty that makes her reek of the operating room or the experimental lab. It made him chuckle.

When she asked, "Craig?" seeking an explanation, he only shook his head and kissed her.

They walked back up a long, steep hill toward the hospital, holding hands, not caring that passersby stared at two adults in white residents' uniforms walking so unashamedly in love.

As they approached the hospital, he said, "I came here today to tell you I wanted to be free. Now I'm more committed than ever."

It was her turn to laugh. "In my specialty, the word 'committed' has a different meaning."

They arrived at the tall red brick building which housed the Emergency Rooms and the wards. She looked up into his dark, craggy face.

"How are you going to tell Prince?"

"The simplest way. Just call him, ask to see him, and say, 'I've thought it over; there was a difference of opinion. You've had far more experience than I, so your judgment must have been better. My way might have necessitated a second operation. A second risk,' " he kept improvising. Finally he gave up, saying, "I'll find some way."

She stood on tiptoe and kissed him on the cheek. "Craig, however you decide to say it, first make sure it's something you want to say."

He looked at her questioningly, then admitted, "It won't be easy."

"And don't give yourself any more excuses. Don't do it for them. Or for me. Whatever you do, do it for Craig Pierson. Because you're a man with a troublesome conscience. That's what I love about you."

Chapter Sixteen

He called the O.R. and found that Prince had a heavy schedule today. An exenteration and three hysterectomies. A better-than-ten-thousand-dollar day. Craig felt a sudden surge of envy because Burt would probably do the exenteration, that complex surgical procedure Craig always looked forward to doing once he became Chief Resident. Now, unless he could patch things up with Prince, he would never realize that opportunity.

Of course, his apology would only be the beginning. He was sure that however he phrased it, Prince would have his own version of it around the locker room, the O.R.s, and the entire hospital before he was content to forgive him, if he ever did forgive him.

While waiting for Prince to come down from the O.R., he passed the time by examining the patients' charts to learn what changes had taken place in his three-day absence.

The woman on whom he had done the procedure to reconstitute her fallopian tubes seemed to be progressing well. He made a mental note to recommend her discharge in forty-eight hours if her signs continued stable. Whether the operation had succeeded they would discover only later, if she was able to conceive.

Two older women, both troubled with postmenopausal bleeding, on whom he had done D.&C.s to rule out endometrial carcinoma, had sufficiently recovered to have gone home two days ago. But with Medicare and health plans paying the bills, they had both decided to take advantage of what they considered their right, and still remained in the hospital. It relieved them of the drudgery of their home lives and allowed them to rest under fairly pleasant conditions.

That had become a problem in recent years in many hospitals. Utilization Committees complained of it. Beds intended for the truly sick were being occupied by the self-indulgent. It was a waste of good usable space and of personnel as well.

When Craig suggested to the first of the women that she should get out of bed and walk about a bit, she demurred, saying, "You're looking to get rid of me, Doctor."

The second woman, in her mid-seventies, said only, "Sonny, after you've scrubbed and vacuumed as many floors as I have, a week in bed is a wonderful thing." She was a night cleaning woman in a large office building. This hospital stay, under a union health plan, had been her first true vacation in more than twenty years.

He smiled when she called him Sonny, but he felt quite sad that the most enjoyable experience of her latter years should be a stay in the hospital.

He was on his way down the corridor to check on another post-op patient when his beeper arrested him.

The operator had a message for him. "The patient in 442 would like to have you come by and see her. Soon, if you can."

He hung up, determined to ignore the message. Until he had straightened things out with Prince, he had better not look in on any of his patients. Cynthia Horton was in excellent hands if Burt Carlyle had been overseeing her post-op care.

But Craig did consult her chart. She had been taken off I.V. once her post-op ileus had passed, and she had been on solid foods for the past few days, since this was her seventh day. Her signs were normal and stable. There seemed no reason to antagonize Prince further by stopping by, even to chat with her.

He was proceeding to another patient's room when his beeper sounded again. He used the phone at the nurses' station.

"Dr. Pierson?"

He recognized Cynthia's voice at once. "Yes. What can I do for you?" he asked, prepared to give some plausible excuse to avoid her.

"I haven't seen you for three whole days."

"I've been away. Family business."

"Serious?" she asked, sounding truly concerned.

"My father had an accident. But he's okay now."

"Oh, I'm glad." She hesitated. Then: "Doctor, could you come by and see me? Just for a minute?"

"I'm rather busy right now," he improvised.

"Just for a minute?" she pleaded.

He never liked to ignore a patient's emotional plea. It was sometimes of greater consequence in her recovery than her physical condition, especially with Ob-Gyn patients.

"If there's something you want to ask, perhaps I could tell you over the phone."

"Remember the last day you were in to see me? You made me get out of bed and walk. And you examined me closely. Especially my thighs."

"Yes, I remember."

"Well, there's something now about my right thigh that *is* different."

A patient often develops such delusions when she dwells too long on any suspect part of her body.

"Exactly *how* is it different, Miss Horton?"

"You used to call me Cynthia," she said, sounding rejected.

To himself he said, God, she's not going to try to seduce me to test whether she's lost her feminine appeal! Women do that with their Ob-Gyn men from time to time, mistaking pure professionalism for a lack of masculine interest.

But aloud he said, "Of course, Cynthia. Now, *Cynthia,* what seems to be different about your right thigh?"

He was prepared to listen to some imagined change. He was startled to hear her say, "It burns."

"Burns?"

"Feels very warm. It's never felt that way before."

"Warm?" he considered, cautious, trying to avoid some of the inevitable speculations that word invited. "Did the nurse take your temperature this morning?"

"Yes."

"What time?"

"About six-fifteen. Right after I woke."

"Okay," he said. "Don't worry about it. I'll . . . I'll call you back."

184

He hung up, turned to Veronica Ryan, chief floor nurse.

"Ronnie, go into 442 and get me a temp."

Ryan stared back, aware of Prince's orders forbidding Craig to see any of his patients.

"Ronnie! Do it! It's important!" Craig ordered.

He waited an anxious five minutes before Ryan returned.

"Well?"

"A hundred point nine."

"Rectal," he assumed.

"By mouth," Ryan corrected.

"By mouth?" he questioned, startled.

"Shall we put her back on antibiotic I.V.?" Ryan asked. "I can't do that without an order from Dr. Prince. Or from Carlyle."

"If I thought it was an infection, I'd authorize it myself," he said. "This may be more—a hell of a lot more."

With sudden determination, he asked, "Ronnie, do me a favor. Call up to the O.R. Find out how long Prince and Burt will be busy."

When she hesitated, he explained, "I'd rather not make that call."

She understood. When she hung up, she informed him, "They're closing up one hysterectomy and have two more to go."

That would mean two or three hours at least. Short a time as that might seem, it could have long-lasting, possibly even fatal consequences. He decided, To hell with Prince's prohibition.

He went into 442. He threw back the coverlet on Cynthia Horton's bed and began a careful examination of her legs and thighs. He drew down her antiemboli stockings, pressed and searched for any swellings

185

in her legs. He pressed gently along the entire length of both her thighs. He detected a swelling on her right thigh, at the place where she complained of feeling the burning sensation. A burning sensation was not the classic sign of what he suspected, but it could not be ruled out. He flexed her right feet upward. She reacted involuntarily in pain. A positive Homan. That, and the slight swelling, reinforced his suspicion of a femoral thrombophlebitis. There was only one way to make absolutely sure.

He went out to see Ryan. "Get Miss Horton onto a gurney and up to X-ray. I'll call ahead and arrange for a venogram."

The look on Veronica Ryan's face demanded an explanation.

"Prince's up in the O.R. Someone has to do something *stat*. I'll take the consequences. Get her up there!"

By the time Cynthia Horton was wheeled into the room that Craig had arranged in X-ray, Dr. Romano, the radiologist, was ready with the proper instruments and materials. Reassuring her that this would be a painless procedure, he filled a large hypodermic with the dye. He located her femoral vein and carefully and gently injected the dye. Then he ordered the X-ray technician to proceed.

She took the number and type of films Craig ordered. Cynthia Horton lay on the table, submitting herself to the procedure, very rigid throughout. Her eyes sought Craig's at every opportunity, pleading for an explanation he could not supply without turning her curiosity to terror.

He had an orderly return Cynthia to Ryan's care. But he waited in X-ray for the films to be developed.

186

The technician mounted them in the view box in the viewing room. In a moment, Dr. Romano came in to join Craig. Together they moved slowly along the line of films, staring, pointing. Romano took a red marking crayon out of his pocket and drew a large warning circle around a dark shadow on one plate.

"There it is," Romano said.

"Thrombus."

"No question."

"I'd better start her on an anticoagulant immediately," Craig said gravely.

"Absolutely," said Romano, reinforcing his decision. "Unless you want to risk a pulmonary embolus."

"There are other risks, too," Craig said thoughtfully, "but we'll face those later, when we have to."

Within ten minutes Craig Pierson had given Cynthia Horton her first injection of heparin. On her chart he wrote out and underlined specific instructions as to how large a dose and how often it was to be administered to the young woman. Also, he ordered that she was not to be released from the hospital for ten days. That done, he proceeded with his other duties. But he was constantly nagged by the possible complications of what he had discovered. For the time being, all he could do, all any physician could do, was wait and hope the patient would respond.

It was late afternoon when Barbara Horton came to visit her daughter. This time she had brought with her not a fresh bed jacket, but a small overnight case in preparation for Cynthia's release, which Dr. Carlyle had said would be tomorrow. She inquired at the desk what time she might call for her daughter. The nurse on duty there, who had replaced Veronica Ryan during her dinner break, reached for the chart, found

Craig's new orders. "I'm sorry, Mrs. Horton, but your daughter is not due to be released for ten days."

"But I was told only yesterday by that very nice black doctor . . . I don't remember his name . . ."

"Dr. Carlyle?" the nurse suggested.

"Yes," Barbara Horton said. "He told me himself, yesterday afternoon, that she could go home tomorrow."

"I'm sorry; all I know is what Dr. Craig wrote in her chart."

"Well, we'll see about that!" Mrs. Horton said sharply.

Not wishing to alarm her daughter, she called from the pay phone in the visitors' room. Indignant, she told her husband what she had discovered. Though he was preparing a witness for trial the next morning, he promised to take steps at once. He called his senior partner, Bruce Miller, who was Chairman of the hospital's Board. Miller called Walter Deering, who called Dr. Ordway.

Ordway himself came down to the Ob-Gyn floor to examine the Horton chart. When he saw Craig's boldly written, underlined plan for treatment, he picked up the phone at once.

"Dr. Pierson, please!"

Craig was in Emergency, examining a young woman who was in intense pain. He discovered the cause quickly. Ectopic pregnancy. He ordered the woman admitted and scheduled for surgery at once. That done, he answered his beeper.

"Pierson?" Ordway demanded.

"Yes."

"May I see you at once?"

"In your office?"

"On the floor!" Ordway corrected.

188

"Damn it, Craig," Ordway exploded, "until you apologized, you were specifically forbidden to have anything to do with Prince's patients! I thought I made that quite clear!"

"Yes, sir, you did."

"And now this!" Ordway said, slapping his hand violently against the chart. "Without consulting the doctor on the case. That's unethical! Highly unethical! And the only way I find out about it is through a call from a trustee! You pick the damnedest way to do things!"

"Dr. Prince is up in the O.R. I didn't think it wise to disturb them there. It was quite clear what had to be done. So I did it."

"You had no authority to do it!"

"As a resident on the service, whom the patient has requested to see, I felt I did have authority. In any event, there was no matter of judgment involved. Not when a patient is running the risk of a pulmonary embolus."

Ordway could not dispute that, so he only grumbled, "You should have called some other resident, some staff physician. Anyone."

"Anyone but me," Craig suggested.

"Yes, exactly!" Ordway said, already preparing himself to face an irate Prince.

"The patient asked for me" was all Craig could say in his own defense.

"That may be a justification in your mind, but I wouldn't mention it to Prince. It will only enrage him even more," Ordway cautioned. "Well, it's done," he said finally. "I'll do what I can to protect you."

"Thanks," Craig said, a slight tinge of sarcasm in his voice.

189

Ordway detected it, his face flushed in momentary anger. "Pierson, I'm trying to make a doctor out of you despite yourself. Remember that."

"Of course. Sorry." This time Craig was sincere.

By the time Dr. Harvey Prince finished his last procedure for the day, it was past six o'clock. And though he had permitted Burt Carlyle to do the last two hysterectomies while he merely assisted, he was quite tired. He consoled himself, Thank God tomorrow is Wednesday. No surgery. A golfing date with his broker, who had come up with a new tax-shelter idea that he would explain thoroughly during the eighteen holes and over drinks later. In fact, Prince felt, he could use a drink right now. He kept a bottle of twelve-year-old Scotch in his locker for just such afternoons. Today, instead of one shot, he took two.

He was getting out of his scrub suit when the message reached him. Would he come down to the floor as soon as possible? The message was from Walter Deering. Prince dressed a bit more hurriedly than usual, but did not forget the budding red rose for his lapel. When he reached the floor, both Deering and Ordway were waiting for him. Deering took him aside and explained Board Chairman Miller's interest in the Horton girl and the sudden reversal of orders for her discharge.

"Who the hell gave orders like that?" Prince exploded indignantly.

Deering looked to Ordway, whose burden it now became. As gingerly as he could, he explained about Craig Pierson.

"That young bastard?" Prince questioned fiercely. "I expressly forbade him to go near her! I want to see him. Right now!"

"He's not here," Ordway said.

190

"Are you sure?"

"Quite sure," Ordway said, for he had ordered Craig not to be present when Prince discovered what had happened. "The girl's mother, father, and fiancé are waiting in her room. And they're very upset."

"I don't blame them," Prince said belligerently. "I'll talk to them at once."

Quietly, Ordway warned, "I'd have a look at her chart before you do." Prince glared at him. But Ordway persisted, "I would."

When Prince arrived at the desk, he found Burt Carlyle examining the chart.

"Well?" Prince demanded.

"They just brought it up."

"What?"

"The report from X-ray. Her venogram."

Impatiently, Prince ripped the chart out of Carlyle's hands and stared at it. But he handed it back much more slowly and soberly.

"A girl so young with a thrombosis . . ." was all he said. Both doctors knew how grave the consequences could be.

"You never detected any sign when you examined her early this morning?" Prince asked.

"Nothing. But a hidden thrombus is not uncommon. In fact, that's the most dangerous kind."

"Thank you, 'Doctor,' " Prince said acidly. "Thank you for the instruction."

Prince started down the corridor toward room 442. Burt Carlyle watched him go, thinking, I'll take his crap only as long as I have to. But one day I'll unseat that bastard. Till then, I'm going to smile and be nice to the man. And maybe we'll both wind up in the same tax shelter someday.

In his brisk walk from the desk to Room 442, Dr. Harvey Prince prepared himself to confront the Hortons and the girl's fiancé. By the time he opened the door, he was in full command of his own feelings, putting forth his best and most encouraging manner.

"Well, good evening! I'm glad you're all here. I rushed down from the O.R. as soon as I heard. It seems we have a bit of a problem here. Nothing to get excited about, I assure you."

"Cynthia was scheduled to go home tomorrow," Arthur Horton complained. "Suddenly, this afternoon, they say they want to keep her another ten days."

"And the wedding's only three weeks away," his wife added.

"Now, Mother, you just sit down and relax. And you too, my dear." He smiled at Cynthia, for he noticed that the girl was extremely nervous. "Perhaps we might lower your bed a bit." He proceeded to press the button that gently let Cynthia Horton slide down into a more comfortable position.

"Now, then," he began, "we have here a slight complication that is not unusual after a surgical procedure. While it is not alarming, we always treat it as if it were, because we want to be absolutely sure that we have taken every precaution. We'd rather be safe than sorry. If it means keeping the patient for another ten days, so what? Your hospital plan pays for it anyhow.

"Actually it's good this came to light this afternoon instead of tomorrow afternoon, when it might have gone undetected and the results could have been dangerous. This way, we've been warned, and we've taken steps to alleviate the condition."

Mrs. Horton was reassured; her husband was not. A trial lawyer, he was not easily comforted by mere words. He had examined too many lying witnesses, prepared too many of them, to be easily misled. Prince detected suspicion in Horton's eyes. He felt called upon to continue.

192

"Mr. Horton, what we are dealing with here is a simple postoperative thrombophlebitis. It is a clot that has formed in the pelvic femoral vein in the thigh. The treatment is simple. We give the patient heparin several times a day and the clot gradually resolves. To be absolutely safe, we do that for ten days. So while we don't like to delay discharging our lovely patient, I'm sure we now all understand why it has to be done this way," Prince concluded.

Mrs. Horton, relieved, smiled at Cynthia, who made a weak attempt to smile back. Prince felt that he had accomplished his purpose. If Horton was still concerned, and if the young fiancé was not particularly happy, Prince discounted that. He was sure he had regained the patient's confidence.

"So get a good night's sleep, my dear. And we'll keep close watch on you until this temporary inconvenience is over."

He smiled at Cynthia, then eased his way to the door, where he stopped and asked, "Am I at least going to be invited to the wedding?"

Without waiting for an answer, he left. Outside the door, he gave a sigh of relief. It had gone off more uneventfully than he had anticipated. But he did need another drink, and soon.

Chapter Seventeen

Shortly after Dr. Prince left Room 442, Arthur Horton excused himself. He went to the pay phone in the visitors' lounge, carefully closed the door, and dialed the number of the hospital.

"Dr. Craig Pierson," he demanded.

"One moment, please," the operator sang out in her usual pleasant but hurried delivery.

It took much longer than a moment before she reported, just as pleasantly, "I'm sorry, but Dr. Pierson does not seem to be in the hospital at this time."

"Can you tell me where I can reach him?" Horton asked urgently.

"I'm afraid we're not allowed to give out that information," the operator informed him, annoyance beginning to replace her cheerful tone.

"This is an emergency. I must get in touch with Dr. Pierson at once!" Horton insisted.

"I'm sorry, but I cannot help you," she replied curtly. "If you leave a number, I'll try to have him call back."

Horton considered that for a moment, then hung up. He called his senior partner, Bruce Miller, at home. Miller asked for the number of the phone in the booth, and instructed Horton to remain there. Within seven minutes, the booth phone rang. It was Walter Deering, Hospital Administrator. He informed Horton that Dr. Pierson would be calling him very soon.

Arthur Horton and Craig Pierson met in the hospital coffee shop. Horton deliberately chose a table in the most remote corner.

"Dr. Pierson, my daughter tells me that when you discovered her condition you became acutely concerned. You rushed her up to X-ray. You administered some drug to combat her thrombosis."

"Heparin," Craig explained. "It's mandatory in a condition like hers."

"So I understand," Horton said. "But Dr. Prince was in to see us. He tried to make light of the whole thing. Too light. Now, I know you fellows have your professional ethics. Just as we lawyers have ours. I

194

don't want you to get into trouble with your superiors. So I won't invite you to comment on Dr. Prince's conduct.

"But we had a case in the office a few years back. And it involved malpractice." Horton hastened to assure him, "Don't worry, I'm not thinking of suing anybody. I'm only interested in protecting my daughter. In the case we had, the thrombosis developed into something else."

"An embolism?" Craig asked.

"Yes. It shot to the patient's lung and proved instantly fatal. I want to know, in plain, simple terms: is that a possibility in Cynthia's case?"

"In any patient with a thrombosis, that's always a possibility. That's why we put them on heparin as soon as we discover it."

Horton nodded his head sadly. "Then Prince's attempt to pass this off as a slight complication was really dishonest. . . ." Horton shook his head. "No, I said I wouldn't ask you to comment on him." He was silent for a time. "So it's very serious," Horton said, trying to accept the facts of his daughter's condition.

"*Can* be serious," Craig corrected, to ease the man's obvious distress.

"How long before we know?"

"They'll keep her on heparin for ten days. They should know in that time."

Horton nodded gravely. "Doctor, she has complete confidence in you. I can tell by the way she talks about you. There's a rapport, a respect, an affinity. . . ."

"There is. We're both adopted."

"Dr. Pierson, because of how she feels about you, and because you're honest with her, and with me, I want you to take over the management of her case as long as she's in the hospital."

"I can't do that."

"Dr. Prince?"

"Ethics."

"Can you at least look in on her? See to it that she's getting the right care?"

"She's Dr. Prince's patient. He's forbidden me to see her," Craig admitted simply. "But I give you my word, if I see something wrong I'll figure out some way to do something about it."

"Thank you," Horton said, greatly relieved.

Craig was greatly relieved too when the older man ended their talk by saying, "I must get back upstairs. They'll wonder what's happened to me."

It was past midnight. Kate was serving coffee and trying to ease his conscience.

"Horton didn't ask," she said, "so you didn't have to tell him."

"That's a cop-out," Craig said, angry not with her but with himself. "The man wanted the truth. I gave him half-truths, empty assurances."

"Craig, darling," Kate said, in the voice she used when she was more mother than lover, "we psychiatrists face that situation more frequently than you do. I often deal with a patient about whom I know the whole truth but I don't force him to face it. I let him grow into a gradual recognition of it. Until he's finally able to cope with it. And in a way, the patient does the same with me.

"He only admits as much as he feels he can cope with. But gradually, if I succeed, it all comes out. When he can handle it. It's the same with Horton. What if you had told him the whole truth tonight?"

"I could have destroyed him," Craig admitted. "Still, I should have said, 'Mr. Horton, instead of worrying about what will happen to your daughter if she has a fatal pulmonary embolus, worry about what might happen to her if she *doesn't!*" Craig said bitterly.

Grimly, Kate agreed: "After a thrombophlebitis, she can't have estrogen without risking another thrombus. And without some estrogen replacement . . ."

"Say it! Loud and clear, my darling Kate. With both ovaries removed and no estrogen, what will she become?"

"A menopausal old woman at the age of twenty-two," Kate admitted softly.

"We might have consoled her by saying if she can't have natural children she can adopt. But what do we say to her when her first flush comes on? And then it keeps on happening? And what of all the other consequences? What do you say to a girl of twenty-two?

"Now, Kate, because you love me and want to console me, you will tell me that I am not responsible for that. That I tried to stop Prince. But I did *not* stop him. That girl is lying in her bed thinking I saved her life by discovering her thrombosis. Her father may think that I'm honest and noble. But the fact is, I have been deceiving them both!

"Well, I may not be able to help her any longer. But I am going to try to help those who come after her!"

Clinton Ordway sat back in his large, comfortable desk chair and stared at Craig Pierson, pondering the startling request the resident had just made. To deny it would be an evasion; more simply put, an official cover-up. To grant it would put young Pierson at considerable risk. Either course was distasteful to Ordway. But the issue had been presented in such strong terms by this headstrong young man that Ordway felt he had to respond.

"I won't deny your request. But before I grant it, I

want you to think carefully of what this can mean to your future."

"I've thought about it," Craig said.

"Overnight? Frankly, if I were staking my entire future on such an action, I'd think about it a good deal longer. Prince is a man with enormous clout. Not just in this hospital. But with the American College of Surgeons. And District Board of the College of Obstetricians and Gynecologists. When you apply, he could manage to have you rejected by both. That could be the end of your career in academic medicine. You might have to go into private practice whether you want to or not."

"I've thought about it," Craig said. "The more I think about it, the stronger my feeling becomes."

Ordway nodded sadly. "Well, if you insist, I'll see that the case is presented at Grand Rounds. Carlyle is chairing the next session. I'll notify him."

As Craig reached the door, Ordway called out, as if it were a just-remembered courtesy, "Oh, by the way, how's your father?"

"Recuperating. But his elbow was shattered. He'll have minimum mobility in his right arm."

"Sorry," Ordway said. "But then I guess he's at retirement age now anyhow."

"He won't be able to work any longer, that's certain."

"Will that throw much of a financial burden onto you?" Ordway asked.

"Yes," Craig admitted.

Ordway shook his head sympathetically. "Too bad. Especially to come at a time like this."

In that moment, Craig suddenly realized that in an adroit manner Ordway was threatening him. Sensitive to the look of resentment in Craig's eyes, Ordway quickly said, "I meant at a time when you're betwixt and between. Not yet eligible to practice, and too early to get a full-time man's salary. It'll be a hardship, I'm afraid."

Ordway was relieved that Craig left without responding to his clumsy threat. He summoned his secretary and dictated a note to Carlyle adding one more case to Grand Rounds, day after tomorrow.

Chapter Eighteen

The auditorium was beginning to fill up. There was a much larger turnout than usual for this session of Ob-Gyn Grand Rounds. Somehow, word had got around. Men and women in the Department—residents, staff, attendings, interns, even some nurses—were present.

The air boiled with the contentious atmosphere of a college town on the day of a traditional football game. Staff men had gathered to see an attending surgeon attacked. The attendings had come to watch an impertinent young resident get his ears pinned back and were eager to join in the pinning.

Too obviously absent from the meeting was Dr. Harvey Prince. He had chosen not to dignify Craig Pierson's attack. His interests would be better represented by his colleagues. Since he had no operating schedule on this day, Prince chose to spend the afternoon with Rita Hallen. At the moment Burt Carlyle was prepared to announce the first case, Harvey Prince was making love to Rita, who had, of late, been complaining of neglect. He was not a man without conscience. Besides, it pleased him at his age to be able to satisfy two women on a continuous basis.

Doctors were still streaming into the auditorium when Burt Carlyle announced the first case. Since Grand Rounds drew doctors away from their other duties, such meetings had to start and end promptly.

The first case was one in which a surgeon, under the unexpected exigencies of an operation that threatened to go sour, had improvised a new surgical technique. Today he came to the stage, described the original case, exhibited slides, detailed his new technique. Then he answered the questions of other surgeons who were interested in adopting it. The surgeon also informed them that he had prepared a paper which had been accepted by the *Journal of Obstetrics,* so that complete detail would be available soon to the entire profession. But, he offered, if any of the men would like to scrub with him and observe, he would be delighted to have them.

Thus this first case fulfilled the prime purpose of Grand Rounds, sharing new and important information for the enlightenment of colleagues and students.

The second case had a less fortunate outcome. It concerned a missed diagnosis which had had a tragic result despite radiotherapy, chemotherapy, and immunotherapy. Had the diagnosis been made at the time of the patient's first examination, surgery might have intervened to avoid a mortality.

The third case involved the use of colposcopy as a means of localizing an abnormal area on the cervical surface. A diagnostic procedure used successfully in Europe, it had only recently come into widespread use in this country. The presentation at Grand Rounds was done by a gynecologist who was interested in having this sophisticated method adopted by all Gyn specialists at State University Hospital.

200

Interesting though they were, all three cases proved only a prologue to the case most of them had gathered to hear. Burt Carlyle, attired in spotless resident's whites, always meticulous, as if to give the lie to racist slurs, now rose to present the fourth case. His black eyes glanced over the top of his reading glasses as he stared down at Craig, seated in the first row. They seemed to ask, Are you sure you want to go through with this? Craig stared back defiantly. Burt Carlyle had no choice but to announce, "Next is a case involving a bilateral salpingo-oophorectomy which will be presented by Dr. Pierson."

Since only the medical and surgical facts were important, the participants in the case were not specifically identified—neither patient nor surgeon. But all those in the large auditorium knew. They were aware, too, of the confrontation that had taken place in the O.R. on the day of surgery.

As soon as Craig rose to present the case, a clear division was discernible in the room. The older men all seemed to coalesce in their hostility toward Craig. The younger men sided with him, though among his supporters there were many who felt he was foolhardy.

Craig made a simple presentation of the history of Cynthia Horton's case, from her first checkup through the surgery, and then raised the question as to the proper surgical procedure.

Spofford West was a short, portly, dignified man, and most energetic despite the fact that he was in his sixties and had a busy operating-room schedule second only to Prince's. Though most people considered them competitors, in this instance they had a common interest. West came down the aisle to face his colleagues while delivering his opinion.

"I think we're confronted here with a classic case of

twenty-twenty hindsight. An affliction which, I notice, is confined mainly to the young. When I was an intern and a resident, we spent our time trying to learn from older, more experienced men. These days, it seems, the main purpose of residents is to instruct their superiors. Especially through the use of an unfailing medical instrument known as the retrospectoscope."

The older men expressed their agreement in laughter, encouraging West to continue.

"Now, those of us who have been around for more than a few years know that in as many as fifty percent of the cases where you have one ovarian tumor, you're likely to have bilateral involvement. Therefore, where there is any question at all, a bilateral is clearly indicated!"

He received support from a number of men who commented, "Right!" "Absolutely!"

"Dr. West," Craig began, quite respectfully, "we were dealing here with a young woman of childbearing age."

"Unfortunate!" West shot back. "But in a mucinous cystadenocarcinoma—"

Craig interrupted to point out, "You left out the term *borderline!*"

West rode over Craig's correction.

"In a mucinous cystadenocarcinoma, conservative surgery is not advisable. Never has been!"

"Until recent findings," Craig argued.

West glared at him as he said, "That second ovary would have had to be removed sooner or later. Or haven't you learned that yet?" the older doctor demanded sarcastically.

Craig felt a rush of blood to his cheeks, from both anger and embarrassment.

Burt Carlyle intervened, "Gentlemen, and ladies, it is getting late. We all have our schedules."

"Just a minute!" Craig exploded. "I think Dr. West's last remark demands an answer, because it defines the question very clearly. That question seems to be, *who* has learned *what* and *when*. Well, residents with their 'easy' schedules, which usually only require about a twenty-hour day, seem to have more time to follow the latest literature than attendings who do four or five hours of surgery a day and then leave their patients to the care of those same residents.

"If some surgeons would take time off between rounds of golf, or other *affairs,* they might read up on the latest work being done in this field. Recent reports from several of the most reputable hospitals in the country prove that the appropriate treatment for this type of tumor would have been *unilateral* salpingo-oophorectomy. Then *after* the woman's childbearing years were over, for *preventive* purposes, the second ovary could be removed, because of the potential for bilateral development."

West smiled indulgently. "You young fellows are so proud to be ahead of the parade that you'd subject your patients to any newfangled theory that comes along."

"Not any more than you old fellows would keep inflicting the same *old* crimes on your patients," Craig shot back in rejoinder.

The moment the word "crimes" had passed his lips, Craig realized he had blundered. The silence that followed his outburst confirmed his fear.

Burt Carlyle tried to diminish the effect of the moment by immediately intervening. "It's twenty past one. We all have heavy schedules. With your permission, I'll close this session. . . ."

West interrupted and renewed his attack on Craig.

"Young man, in my entire career I have never heard any doctor classify an accepted surgical practice as a crime! What if six months from now, or two years from now, that second ovary became malignant and possibly fatal? What was done in this case was the most effective preventive measure to take. Only inexperience makes you disagree, young man!"

West's face was flushed; behind his spectacles, the sweat of fierce indignation had begun to glisten.

Still Craig persisted, "As far as preventive measures are concerned, if we did a hysterectomy on every thirteen-year-old girl, we'd wipe out uterine cancer in one generation. But at what price?

"I've always been taught that the basic principle in medicine or surgery is to cure the patient with a minimum of functional impairment. In this case, the therapy deprives this patient of ever functioning as a normal childbearing woman. Indeed, the effects may be more drastic than that."

West glared at Craig Pierson, then broke into a small contemptuous smile. He turned abruptly and left the hall. There was considerable hostile whispering among the older men, who drifted out of the auditorium in small groups. The younger men lingered, in a show of solidarity with Craig. But they said nothing. It would have been politically unwise.

Among the older men, only Sam Becker lingered. He made his way down the aisle to Craig's side.

Sam was irascible and annoyed. "So you had to be the smart kid on the block. You made your point. Idiot! Why do you think this meeting was packed with attending surgeons, but the one surgeon involved was conspicuously absent? They set you up. Prince does not appear, so you can't accuse him of speaking out of personal interest. He leaves that to 'disinterested,' 'neutral' members of the medical community. But who was here? West. Who is the Chairman of the

County Board of the American College of Surgeons. And Maxwell, who is the man in this district appointed by the American College of Obstetricians and Gynecologists to interview applicants for admission. Do you think either of them will forget that you used the word 'crimes' today? What do you think will happen when you come up for admission to those two organizations?

"And what do you think is going to happen to any future appointment you might seek if you're not a fellow of the A.C.S. or A.C.O.G.? Even if you go into private practice in some remote part of the country and the time comes when a G.P. has to refer one of his patients to an Ob-Gyn man. He hauls down his *Directory of Medical Specialists* and looks up Ob-Gyn men in his area. And he finds Pierson, Craig. He reads a nice list of school affiliations, and your association here as a resident. But suspiciously absent is any affiliation with the two most prestigious organizations in your field. What is he going to say to himself? This young man must have done something that caused him to be rejected. He does not bear the stamp of approval. So that G.P. will search out some other Ob-Gyn man.

"All this you created with the unfortunate use of that one damned word. What you did today you won't be able to undo in a lifetime," Becker concluded sadly, shaking his head.

"Sam, what would you have wanted me to do?"

"I guess . . ." Sam Becker said sadly, ". . . be a coward like the rest of us. I'm sorry, kid."

He patted Craig on the shoulder in a gesture of fatherly concern and affection.

Craig started out of the auditorium. He saw Kate, standing at the head of the aisle. She was conferring with Burt Carlyle, who was reporting the detail of the meeting.

"I tried to get here on time," Kate apologized. "But we had an emergency admission. A psychotic who had just murdered his wife and child, then tried to kill himself but failed."

"I suppose Burt told you."

"I had to," Burt admitted. "What did Becker say?"

"Just about what you'd expect."

"Damn it, Craig, I tried to shut you up," Burt said, angry with himself as well. "Didn't you see me glare at you when I said time was pressing. What the hell did you think I meant? But once you used the word 'crimes' . . ."

Kate interceded, "Craig, *did* you say 'crimes'?"

He nodded, admitting, "Okay. That was ill-advised."

"Is 'ill-advised' a euphemism for fatal?" Burt Carlyle asked bitterly. "Damn it, Craig, you don't change minds by attacking the people you want to convince! You couldn't have said anything worse!"

Kate's eyes warned Burt she wanted to be alone with Craig.

"Look, I have to make up tomorrow's schedule," Burt said. "See you later."

"Shall we get some coffee?" Kate suggested.

"Why not? There's hardly a problem in this world that cannot be solved by having some coffee," Craig said bitterly.

Kate stared into his eyes and said in a low, firm voice, "You're not going to get away with that, Craig!"

When she called him Craig in that particularly severe tone, he knew she was deeply angry with him.

"You're not going to use me as a whipping boy to assuage your own guilt. I'll give you sympathy be-

206

cause you need it. And understanding because you deserve it. You did try to do something constructive. And you failed. But don't take it out on me!"

He loved her most when he could have resented her most. She was honest and tough with him, as she was with herself.

"I'm sorry," he said, softly.

"Coffee?"

"Coffee," he agreed.

While Craig and Kate were reliving the entire disastrous meeting and seeking some means of averting the consequences, Dr. West was on the phone to Harvey Prince.

"Harv?"

"Yes, Spoff? How did it go?"

"Better than I hoped," West gloated. "He not only attacked you, he attacked every attending there. He's a stubborn young man. Which is good. We won't have any trouble with him anymore."

"Was Ordway there?"

"No," West said.

"He was ducking the meeting," Prince concluded.

"He wants to be in a hands-off position in case there's trouble. Well, there is going to be trouble," West anticipated eagerly.

"Good," Prince agreed. "Let's get rid of him once and for all."

"It shouldn't take much now to make him resign," West agreed.

"Resign, hell! I want him fired!" Prince ordered. "I want on his record that he was kicked out!"

"Harv, he's arrogant, but he's still young. Let's not destroy him. Resignation will be bad enough."

Prince thought for a moment, then relented. "Okay,

just get rid of the bastard. And keep me out of it. I don't want to be involved."

"I'll handle it diplomatically, don't worry."

West placed a call to Clinton Ordway. Ordway was not in. West was content to wait. Delay would only work in their favor. By the time he met with Ordway, the Chief would have had complaints from a dozen other attendings. The case against Craig Pierson would be so convincing that resignation would seem like lenient punishment.

Chapter Nineteen

Craig Pierson stopped at the nurses' station to peruse the charts of those patients to whom he still had access. He found no significant changes. Those who were post-op were doing well; no unexpected fevers, hence no infections. He would stop by and see each of them before the afternoon was over.

Instead of considering it a luxury to have so much time to himself, he felt lonely and excluded. He missed the excitement of being pressured every hour of the day, from early before-breakfast rounds, to surgery, back to rounds, to calls from Emergency. It was a ceaseless grind, which every resident griped about—but enjoyed.

He had finished with his patients' charts, but could not resist stealing a look at Cynthia's. Despite the fact that Ryan, the charge nurse, was staring at him, he deliberately selected her chart, glanced at the top page, saw that she was still on the same dose of heparin he had ordered. He discovered there had been a second venogram. The thrombus had not resolved. An embolism to the lung or heart was still a fatal possibility.

His beeper summoned him. An Ob-Gyn resident was needed in Emergency Admitting. The operator informed him that Dr. Carlyle had been called but had not yet arrived. The Medical Resident in Emergency had then asked for Dr. Pierson.

As Craig strode down the corridor through the usual noisy crowd in the Outpatient Medical Clinic, he became aware of a shrill, hysterical voice. At first he could distinguish no identifiable words. But as he approached the far end of the corridor, he could hear, quite distinctly, a young woman's panic-stricken voice.

"Get him out of here! I don't want him to touch me! If he comes near me I'll kill him!" The words ended in an outburst of hysterical sobbing.

Craig raced the rest of the way. He burst into the E.R. and discovered that Burt Carlyle had preceded him. But Burt was not close to the patient who lay on the examining table curled up in the fetal position. Her face was hidden from his view, but he saw bloodstains on her torn clothes.

Two uniformed policemen waited in a corner. Both appeared uncomfortable and speechless. One of them gestured a futile apology to Burt Carlyle, whose eyes were grim and hurt. He motioned to Craig to take over.

Craig moved to the table. Gently he reached out to turn the girl on her back so that he could make an examination. The presence of the police, the condition of the girl's clothes, the bloodstains told him all he had to know. The Social Service worker, with the note pad, confirmed it. This patient was a rape victim, brought in for immediate examination for legal purposes.

At the touch of his hand, the girl turned on him, crying out, "I don't want any black sonofabitch to touch me. *He* was black. The one who did it! They're all the same. Get your hands off me! Get them off!" she screamed.

Craig glanced at Burt Carlyle, gave him a look which ordered, Get out, I'll handle this. Carlyle did not move; he seemed intent on experiencing the entire painful episode.

Craig forcibly seized the girl by the shoulders and turned her about. Though she resisted violently, he forced her to look into his face, when she realized it was not Carlyle but a white doctor, she gradually relented, gave up struggling, and was content to lie still and sob, tears flowing down both sides of her face.

Craig drew a white screen around the table to shield the girl while he made his examination and dictated his findings. There was no doubt of forcible and painful entry. He took some smears to determine if there was any trace of semen or sperm.

By the time he completed his examination, he had ascertained that she had suffered a tear that would require surgical repair. She had a superficial laceration on the side of her head. She was, most of all, in a state of shock and hysteria.

He stepped out from behind the screen to ask the officers if they needed any further statement from her for police records. Since they did not, Craig injected the patient with a strong dose of Valium. He ordered her put on a gurney and taken up to the Ob-Gyn floor, where he would indicate a plan of treatment.

When he looked around, he discovered that Burt Carlyle was gone. He found him in the doctors' station on the floor. Carlyle sat in an old squeaky swivel chair, facing the wall, silent and brooding.

"Sorry, Burt," Craig began, "but—"

"But what?" Carlyle demanded, venting on Craig the anger he had been unable to direct at the hostile girl. "Because she was raped by a black man, suddenly all blacks are rapists."

"The girl was hysterical. She didn't know what she was saying."

"She knew enough to know she didn't want a black doctor to touch her!" Burt shouted back.

Craig slammed the door closed so that Burt's angry voice would not travel the entire length of the floor.

"Okay now, Burt. You want to let it out, let it out on me. I'm white too. A girl is seized, beaten up, overpowered, brutally invaded in the worst act that can be committed on a woman. Do you expect her to be rational? A black man did it, ergo, Don't let another black man touch me. That's all it was. Don't let it mean any more than that."

"So that's all it was?" Burt challenged vehemently. "Well, Mr. White Man, answer me just one question. Have you ever heard a white woman who was raped by a white man scream, 'Get me a black doctor'? Answer me that!"

Craig respected Burt too highly to lie or dissemble. The phone rang. Burt chose not to answer it. Craig did.

"Pierson."

"Doctor," the floor nurse informed him, "the patient in 442 would like to see you if you're free." She had relayed the information in too formal and detached a manner. Evidently gossip about the encounter in Grand Rounds had got around quickly. The nurse chose not to become embroiled in the Prince–Pierson controversy.

"What seems to be the trouble with the patient?" Craig asked, adopting the nurse's aloof and antiseptic attitude.

"She claims to be having a fever; insists she has."

"Did you take her temperature?" Craig asked.

"Ninety-eight six," the nurse informed him crisply.

"And still she claims to be having a fever?"

"She insists on seeing you. What shall I tell her?"

"I'll drop by as soon as I can."

He hung up. He turned back to Carlyle, who was facing away again.

"Each time . . .," Burt began, then seemed to deliberately abandon what he had started to say. "From case to case you make a little headway. Until there are days when you can convince yourself that it doesn't matter. Patients accept you for what you are. A doctor. Then something like that happens and you're back to square one. You're the black kid everyone thought was dirty, dishonest, and worthless. You're no better than the man who raped her."

"You going to tell LuAnne?"

"Sometimes I do, sometimes I don't. After all, it's like telling her that's what our kids will be going through. I don't like to keep reminding her."

"By the time they're growing up, it'll change," Craig consoled him.

"I doubt it." To bury his own feelings, he asked, "What was that call?"

"442," Craig said.

"Running another fever? That's all we need now," Burt said.

"No fever. Just thinks she has one."

Burt Carlyle slowly swung his chair around to confront Craig. "Jesus, not that!"

"Could be," Craig said. "She asked to see me."

"It would be better if I saw her," Burt volunteered.

"She asked to see me," Craig insisted.

Burt shrugged.

Craig smiled. "And not because I'm white."

Burt looked up at him and finally smiled back. But Craig could tell from Burt's eyes that the hurt would burn a long time.

Far down the corridor Craig could see Mrs. Horton waiting just outside 442. He knew the look. The patient's family waylaying the doctor to question him out of the patient's hearing.

"Doctor," Mrs. Horton began, "she's running a bad fever. Could it have to do with the phlebitis in her leg? Is it getting worse?"

"As far as we know, that's resolving. Not as quickly as we would like, but it is resolving," Craig said.

"Does that mean there can't be an embolism?" she asked.

"We never know until it's all cleared up, Mrs. Horton," he said very matter-of-factly. "That's why we treat it as cautiously as we do."

She nodded, appreciating his frankness. She tried to convince herself the prognosis was hopeful. "Well, at least the fever isn't caused by that. What could it be? An infection?"

"She doesn't have a fever."

"She complains of being very hot. She breaks into sweats. Like she used to when she was a little girl with a high fever," Mrs. Horton explained. "It comes on just like that. Sometimes it lasts for minutes. Sometimes for an hour or more."

213

"How long has it been going on?" he asked.

"Two days now. I've called Dr. Prince, but he's in his office so rarely."

"Yes, he's busy—very busy," Craig said in a noncommittal way.

"Please, have a look. But don't say anything that will upset her. If you have anything to say, say it to me," Mrs. Horton urged.

Craig never liked being drawn into conspiracies against patients. Even by members of the patient's family.

"Mrs. Horton, your daughter is not a child any longer. She's twenty-two. An adult. If there's anything to say, it should be said to her."

"May I be there when you examine her? I'd like to know what you think," the woman pleaded.

Craig hesitated. It would be difficult enough to speak frankly to the girl alone. The tendency to react emotionally would be greatly intensified if her mother were present. Yet Cynthia would need someone to comfort her. If, indeed, any comfort could be found in this situation.

"Of course," he said. "Come in."

Cynthia Horton was sitting up in bed. Her pretty face was clean of any cosmetics. Her black hair had been tied back in a red ribbon. Yet wisps of it had worked themselves free and adhered to the sides of her damp cheeks. She was pale, much paler than she had been on admission. And thin. He had recalled that on her chart a nurse had noted that she did not eat well, sometimes sending her trays back untouched. That, he knew, was a mental condition, not physical. It severely limited the manner in which he had intended to handle the situation.

Before he could say a word, she asked petulantly, "Did you get my message?"

214

"I came as soon as I could."

"Didn't they tell you?"

"They said you complained of a fever."

"Then they took my temperature and they lied to me," she accused.

He recognized a frequent syndrome among patients whose course of treatment and recovery had gone differently than predicted. The time always came when they began to suspect that everyone was in a conspiracy against them.

"Cynthia, they did not lie to you."

"The nurse said my temperature was normal."

"It is."

She shook her head in impatient frustrated denial, avoiding him by staring out the window.

"Cynthia?" her mother pleaded in an effort to make her more reasonable.

"Why don't we take your temperature now and I'll let you see for yourself," Craig suggested, selecting a mouth thermometer from his pocket. He shook it down. "Under the tongue, please?"

Throughout the three-minute wait which seemed an eternity, Mrs. Horton tried to engage Craig in a silent conspiracy by eye. As if to apologize, Believe me, she isn't like this at all. Just make her well and she'll be herself again.

Craig concealed his own fears. When the three minutes were up, he reached for the thermometer, glanced at it, handed it back.

"See for yourself."

Cynthia took the tiny glass instrument, rotated it until she could find the straight silver line.

"What does it say?" he asked.

"Ninety-eight and something," she said. "That's not exactly normal, is it?"

"Couldn't be more normal," he said.

"Then why do I get those hot spells, those terrible sweats?" she asked.

"Do you get them often?" Craig asked, wondering if Prince or one of his associates had prepared her in any way.

"More by night than by day," she said. "But sometimes almost every three or four hours. When I get them, it feels like I'm burning up."

"Have you told Dr. Prince about this?"

"He hasn't been by in two days now."

"And his associates?"

"One of them comes by every morning," Cynthia explained. "But they never stop long enough to answer any questions."

Craig debated with himself how much he could or should reveal to this girl who was not his patient. Finally he said, "It's not a fever. So we have no reason to suspect any infection. The thrombophlebitis is resolving."

Everything he was saying was true. Yet it was all evasion. He hated himself for doing it. But even if he told the girl the blunt truth, it would not change by one iota the course of her condition, or the treatment.

There was no treatment. It was Prince's responsibility to tell her that.

Even while Craig spoke to her, he could see a deep-red flush rise into her throat and up into her cheeks. Pale before, they now became a deep red. Perspiration began to glisten on her forehead and her face. It trickled slowly down her neck, losing itself between her young breasts.

"That's it," the girl whispered. "That's the way it happens. Open the window! Turn on the air conditioner."

He lifted the window high, letting the fresh air

216

flood the room. Cynthia threw back the light coverlet as if to drink in all the cool air she could, to soothe her flushed and burning body.

All the while, Mrs. Horton stared at Craig, her eyes demanding some answer, some explanation. But how does one explain to a twenty-two-year-old girl that she is in the midst of a menopausal flush? That in a biological sense, she is as old as or even older than her mother? How?

In some cases, such symptoms could be tempered if the physician had prepared his patient. Obviously Prince had not attempted to do so. So the girl was struggling to combat symptoms that were not only distressing, but mystifying as well.

Craig decided there was only one way to handle the situation. If Prince would not, he would. The patient's health and safety superseded any fine points of medical ethics.

"Mrs. Horton, would you step outside for a few minutes?" he asked.

"If you're going to examine her, I'd like to remain. After all, she is my daughter," Mrs. Horton persisted.

"I'm only going to talk to her. Everything I say to her I will say to you later. But for now I would like to be alone with her."

Mrs. Horton stared at Craig, then at her daughter, but seemed unmoved until Cynthia asked, "Mom, please?"

Hospital doors have a way of easing closed as if they were whispering secrets. This door sounded more that way than any Craig could remember. It seemed to set the tone for what must now take place.

"Cynthia . . .," he began, "there are some consequences of the kind of surgery . . ."

With no word, no warning, the girl began to weep.

217

She made no sound. But the tears streamed down her face, staining her pillow. She made no effort to wipe them away.

"Cynthia?" Craig asked gently. "Why are you crying? Do you have pain?"

She shook her head.

"Then why?"

"I don't know," she admitted. "I lie awake at night and cry . . . and I don't know why. It's never happened to me before. I ask myself why, but I don't know, I just cry."

"How long has that been going on?"

"The last three days. Nights, mainly. I don't think I dare cry during the day."

"Why not?"

"I'm afraid. The last few days, all the time, I'm afraid."

"Afraid Pete will leave you?" Craig suggested.

"No. He's been terrific through it all. I'm not afraid of any special thing. Sometimes I think maybe I'm afraid of dying. That they didn't get the whole thing out. But I say, No, not if they promised me it's out. So I ask myself, Then why am I crying? I never used to cry like this. Now, at night, or when I'm alone, I just cry," she said pitifully.

"Could it be because you've been in the hospital longer than you anticipated?"

"I don't think so."

"Not even when you feel you should be out shopping for your trousseau? Seeing to the last-minute plans for the wedding? Shopping for furniture?" he asked.

"I knew all that would come," she said. "Waiting even made it more exciting. Like waiting for Christmas morning when you're a child. But the last few

218

days, I'm just afraid. So I cry. Tell me—honestly, now—*has* anything changed? Did the lab find something they haven't told me about?" She searched his eyes seeking a truthful answer.

"No."

"Something's changed. I feel it; I know it," the girl said plaintively, beginning to weep again.

How, Craig asked himself, how do you render into the least painful language the fact that this girl is suffering all the depressive symptoms of premature menopause due to surgical castration, with even more symptoms to come? And do you tell her how avoidable it all was? No, not that part of it. But the unalterable, unavoidable facts must be revealed to her by someone. That she trusted him, sent for him, in her difficulty, imposed that obligation on him.

"Cynthia, what you are undergoing now is not mysterious. These are quite usual symptoms for certain conditions. The depression, the nervousness, the feeling of unexplained fear, the hot spells. Once a woman's ovaries are removed, those are usual and natural consequences," Craig explained.

"But what do you do about it? There must be something . . .," the girl insisted.

"Usually we prescribe an estrogen supplement," Craig said.

"But I'm not 'usual.' Why?" she asked.

"Because of what happened to your vein you can't have estrogen. Without it, you're going to be subject to these symptoms. But they are not dangerous," he tried to reassure her.

He had not dared to mention the other possible concomitants of her condition. This would be enough for her to digest for the time being.

"It's not dangerous . . .," she evaluated. "Will it

219

ever go away? Being afraid. Crying that I can't control. Can't understand."

"Yes, eventually it will go away."

She seemed to accept his answer. She nodded—small, uncertain movements of her head. Her pretty face was most thoughtful.

"If you say so, Dr. Pierson, I believe you," she agreed finally. It seemed to stanch the flow of her tears. She wiped her eyes with the palms of her hands. She could even manage a flicker of a smile.

His hand was on the stainless steel doorknob when she asked, "Those hot spells . . . are they the same as hot flushes you hear older women talk about?"

He turned slowly before he said, "Yes, Cynthia. All your symptoms are the same as those that older women complain about."

"You mean that I . . . I'm like they are . . . I'm having . . ." She could not bring herself to use the only word that applied. Finally, she did say it. "I'm having menopause . . . like a woman twenty-five years older than I am? Is that what you're trying to tell me?"

"You are having what we term premature menopause," Craig said as gently as he could.

Her tears began again. This time she buried her face in her pillow, ashamed to face him or anyone. She had taken upon herself the guilt for her condition. For a girl who had to live her life as an adopted child, with all the uncertainties that entailed, she had not the inner resources to cope with her present tragedy. He knew he could not comfort her now.

He stepped outside the door, explained as briefly and succinctly as he could to Mrs. Horton, then went down the hall to the nurses' station to write out an order for Valium, five mg, Q.I.D.

He picked up the phone and dialed Kate's extension.

"Kate . . . when you have a chance . . . see the Horton girl."

"What happened?" Kate asked.

"I had to tell her," Craig said.

"Everything?" Kate asked.

"Everything except the possible vaginal complications," he admitted.

"Yes, that had better wait until she's absorbed this," Kate agreed. "I'll look in on her."

Chapter Twenty .

Kate Lindstrom changed from her white hospital suit into the simple dress she had worn to the hospital early that morning. She preferred to approach Cynthia Horton as one young woman to another, sensing that by now the patient had become disenchanted with all physicians.

As Kate approached 442 she discovered Barbara Horton outside the door, damp handkerchief in hand, distraught look on her face. Mrs. Horton challenged her: "Who are you? A friend of Cynthie's? I should warn you—"

"Dr. Pierson asked me to look in on her. I'm a psychiatrist," Kate explained.

"Psychiatrist," Mrs. Horton said bitterly. "So it's gotten worse. They won't let her leave here alive!" she exploded in a tortured whisper.

"Mrs. Horton, you're not helping."

"Each day it gets worse! It was going to be a trivial operation. Most likely it was nothing, they said. But it *was* something. And after that, with her leg, it grew worse. And now, this . . ."

"Mrs. Horton, please . . ."

"I should be in there with her," the mother explained. "But what can I say? What can anyone say? She needs me. And for the first time in her life I can't help her."

"Let me see what I can do."

Kate pushed the door open quietly. She had expected to find Cynthia in tears. Instead the girl lay perfectly still, straight and stiff, like a marble sculpture of the deceased atop a medieval stone crypt. She did not acknowledge Kate's presence. Her eyes were closed. Her face a mask.

"Cynthia . . ." Kate spoke softly. The girl did not respond. "Dr. Pierson told me." Still the girl did not respond. "I thought if we talked about it, it might help."

The girl remained rigid and silent. Kate detected that this might be the first stage of a severe depression which would add still further complications to what had already become a most dangerous case.

Kate had spent many nights reading up on the psychological aspects of cancer patients. Their psychiatric problems were unique, their prognosis in most cases very bad, their mental outlook usually far worse than that of other patients.

This was especially true of the younger ones, who were obsessed by the injustice of their situation. They had always assumed illness and dying were only for the aging. Especially did those young people feel that way who had enjoyed a relatively healthy childhood. To be suddenly confronted with serious illness, to have to contemplate the thought of death was a shock of such magnitude that severe depression often resulted.

In some cases, there was a far worse aspect. To the young, worse than dying was surviving in mutilated

condition. Especially so if the mutilated parts concerned their sexuality.

A young woman on the brink of marriage, who had
yet to bear a child, could look upon such an operation
as total destruction, exceeding in its devastation even
death. Always the cry was the same; expressed or silent, it was a tortured protest; so much to live for, so
much, and now all gone. Gone.

Aware of the tendency of most patients to blame
themselves for their disease, Kate hoped to coax Cynthia into talking. "I know how you feel. But it's not
true."

As Kate had hoped, she had evoked a puzzled reaction. The girl did not open her eyes, but half-turned
in the direction of Kate's voice. An involuntary response, but a response nevertheless.

"Most patients' first reaction is to blame themselves. They feel they must have done something
wrong to have earned this disease. It's true that in
some cases, a very small percentage, we can attribute
cause and effect, such as in smoking and lung cancer.
But in most cases we don't know the cause. In your
case, we certainly don't know.

"We do know one thing. It's nothing as mystical as
punishment for sins of omission or commission. There
is nothing you failed to do that could have brought
this on. Nor anything you *did* do that brought it on."

Kate paused, to give Cynthia a chance to react. Silence seemed to have a compelling effect. Cynthia
turned away and, without opening her eyes, began to
speak in a low monotone. Though her feelings were
intense, her voice had a flat, distant, clinical sound
that made Kate more uneasy than she had been when
the girl was silent. She had seen too many depres-
sives; she knew the signs too well.

"The patient," Cynthia began, referring to herself

most disturbingly in the third person, "the patient *did*
do something that brought it on."

"Yes?" Kate prodded.

"I hadn't wanted to, but everyone did, so I did. No,
actually, I did want to. But I knew that I shouldn't. If
I didn't love Pete, if I didn't feel he loved me, I
wouldn't have let it happen. But we planned to get
married—always, from the earliest days. . . ."

Her disjointed effort to deal with her sexual relationship was nothing new to Kate. She had confronted
that many times in cases in which one dealt with the
consequences of sexual permissiveness. It was difficult for young girls in these times, caught between the
values with which they had been brought up and the
pressures of their own generation. She let Cynthia
continue.

"I think that when the time came to punish 'the
patient,' they said, Let us take away from her the parts
of her body which she used to commit those sins."

"Who are 'they,' Cynthia?"

"I don't know," the girl said vaguely. "What I can't
understand is, Why *this* patient? Why *this* girl?" she
amended. "Why this one girl—why?"

"Do you think God sits up there someplace and
looks down at this earth and says, We will make an
example of one girl? This one girl, Cynthia Horton? Is
that what you think?"

Kate did not expect an answer. "No, this is not
something you caused, or you could have prevented.
It was something that happened. Something the doctors discovered and had to cope with."

She did not dare delve into the extent of the operation.

"So you can't blame yourself. The main thing is
you're free of the disease now. They'll check you up

every six months, to make sure. But as far as anyone can tell, you are clean. Remember that."

Cynthia did not appear encouraged.

"The thing to do now is get over this complication, which I understand is beginning to resolve. And to look forward to the rest of your life, which can be long and . . ." The need for honesty made Kate qualify, "relatively healthy."

"It can't be," Cynthia said.

"You may feel that way now, but I assure you a few months from now . . ."

Though the girl said not a word in dispute, Kate became silent. For she could see the flush rise up from Cynthia's chest. The girl broke into a profuse sweat. She rolled her head back and forth on the wrinkled pillow, wiping away the sweat with her bare palms. Finally she buried her damp face in the pillow.

A natural phenomenon over which neither patient nor psychiatrist had any control. Kate could only wait for it to pass. Tempted to dry the girl's face, Kate resisted, since it might make their relationship personal rather than professional.

The flush had subsided.

"How long will those go on?" Cynthia asked. "All my life?"

"In some cases a few months, in other cases a few years." Kate was encouraged that the girl had made some connection with her future life.

Somehow the intervention of the physical manifestation of her condition created a more intimate feeling between the two young women. Cynthia spoke more freely, no longer needing to refer to herself in the third person.

"When I said 'they' before, I didn't mean God. I don't know what I meant. Except there's this fear I have when things are going either too well or too badly. If things go too well, I'm afraid 'they' will do something to spoil it. Like now. Getting married to Pete was everything I ever dreamed of. 'They' wouldn't let it happen. When things go bad, very bad, as they have now, 'they' did it. Always it is 'they.' 'They' were responsible for my being born. For my being abandoned."

"Were 'they' also responsible for your being given to the Hortons, who seem to be two extremely loving people?" Kate asked.

"But how much nicer it would have been to be theirs: *really* theirs. And not have that shadow follow me. That other mother. Somehow I feel she is one of 'them.' She never wanted to have me. But because I insisted on being born, she's going to punish me for the rest of my life."

The girl asked suddenly, "Do you think I'm going insane?"

"I think you're going through all the reactions we expect from patients who've been told they had cancer."

"I know that my thoughts about her and 'them' make no sense. Yet I can't shake them," Cynthia said. "Sometimes they wake me at night," she confided. "I am dreaming of Pete and suddenly he disappears, but she is there, hating me, accusing me. The strange thing is I can never remember in the morning what she looked like. She has no face. Only eyes. Eyes."

The girl turned away, "If I am going mad, tell me. So it won't come as such a surprise. I've had too many surprises in the past few weeks."

There was little that Kate could say to comfort her, and if there had been, she would have withheld it to encourage the girl to talk. Open expression of her fears and thoughts would have a therapeutic effect.

226

"Those dreams in which Pete disappears and my other mother replaces him ... you know about dreams; that's your profession to know ... does that mean he's going to leave me? Not that I would blame him," she quickly added.

"Since it's your dream, not Pete's, it's not an expression of his intentions but of your fears. You're afraid he might leave you now. Has anything happened?"

"He comes here every evening. He stays till I fall asleep. He talks on, making plans for our wedding, our home, as if nothing had happened. He talks about adopting children. About how much better it would be. How we can be sure of perfect babies every time. I lie here and listen, praying all the while that I won't have one of those flushes. I don't want him to see me this way."

"What could happen if he did?"

"I don't know, except he might become frightened and run away, leave me—forever."

"Like your other mother?"

"I guess," Cynthia conceded. Then she confessed softly, "It's terrible of me. My mother is out there worried sick about me, trying to do anything she can to make me better, but all I can think about is the other one, the one who deserted me. God, what a way to repay them for the love they gave me!"

"I'm sure they understand," Kate said. "So there's no need to invent guilts for yourself."

"I don't know ... I don't know ...," Cynthia said hopelessly. "Sometimes I wish ..." But she did not complete the thought.

"Wish what?" Kate asked gently.

"That thing in my leg ... I understand that can break off and send bits to the lungs or the heart ... and that would be the end of it. Sometimes I wish it would!"

"Do you feel that way now?" Kate asked.

"No, not now," the girl said. "Would you come see me again in a day or two?"

"If you'd like."

"Please? You're the only one I can talk to without worrying about your feelings. I don't want to hurt Pete, or my parents. And if they heard me talk this way . . ."

"I'll drop by. And if you want to talk when I'm not here, call me."

"Can I ask you something now?"

"Of course."

"You and Dr. Pierson . . ."

"Yes?" Kate asked.

"Will you get married?"

"There are career matters to settle first."

"Get married! Soon!" the girl urged. "Before anything happens."

Kate hurried down the corridor of the Ob-Gyn floor. She thought she had caught a glimpse of Craig going into one of the wards. But she discovered it was another resident. She went back to her own office in Psychiatric and made a note for herself, since she had not wanted to make an entry in the patient's chart.

She had a premonition that at some time in the future she might be called up to report her findings.

Craig Pierson had just emerged from the O.R., where he had assisted one of the full-time surgeons in a complicated hysterectomy in which the disease had spread extensively. It appeared so hopeless there was a strong temptation to close up the patient and let the disease take its course. But the surgeon did not feel justified and had decided on an exenteration, which had taken seven and a quarter hours. He had permitted Craig to do a part of the procedure and had complimented him on his technique.

It had been a tough afternoon, but worthwhile. Especially since his surgical time had been cut down so sharply by Prince's prohibition. Craig shed his O.R. suit, washed up, and got back into his whites. He made his final end-of-day rounds of patients, saving his visit to 442 for last, since he knew he might be there for some time.

Cynthia Horton was alone. Her father had come by to take her mother out to a quick dinner. They would be returning soon. Pete was not there. A meeting out of town, he had called to say. Craig was relieved to note that she seemed less depressed than she had been during the afternoon.

"She's a beautiful girl," Cynthia said.

"Dr. Lindstrom?"

"Lovely blond hair. And honest blue eyes. Have you ever noticed, people with blue eyes don't find it so easy to lie as people with brown or black eyes."

"Matter of fact, I hadn't," Craig said smiling.

"You're going to get married, I understand," Cynthia observed.

"Were you the patient or the doctor? You got more out of her than I ever did."

"We talked. She's very nice. Friendly. Open. I like her," Cynthia said. "I wish I could believe her completely."

"Don't you?"

"Right after she left, the fears started again. And I get this feeling they'll never end."

"They will. Though while it's going on, you do get this feeling that it'll never end."

Her parents returned, so Craig felt safe leaving her.

As he released the door, expecting it to hiss closed behind him, he was alerted by the fact that it did not. He turned. He was facing Mr. Horton.

"Doctor, do you have a minute?"

"Of course."

"An office—a private office?"

"Come along."

Craig closed the door of the residents' office to ensure privacy. Horton did not make any preambles, but asked directly, "Doctor, what would happen to her if Pete were to decide . . . well, if he changed his mind about marrying her?"

"He's not the only eligible young man in the world," Craig said, hating himself for the evasion. But then, he did not hold himself out to be a psychiatrist or a marriage counselor.

"He might be, for her," Horton said gravely. "After all, she is what one must consider damaged. Another man wouldn't understand. With Pete, at least, they were in love before this happened. But starting fresh, with another man, I don't think she can . . . she's too sensitive . . . too timid . . . and this has only made things worse."

"Aren't we worrying about something that may never arise?" Craig asked.

"I wish I could be sure," Horton said.

"Why? Did anything happen?"

"I thought we'd take Pete out to dinner this evening as long as he was going to be here."

"Cynthia said he had to go out of town on business."

"That's what I told her," Horton said. "The truth is, he is not out of town. He simply avoided coming here this evening."

"I see."

"That's why my question—What will happen to her if he decides to bow out now?" Horton asked grimly.

"She's going through a time of natural depression. She needs someone to comfort her, to see her through. I had hoped, expected, he would."

"So had I," Horton said. "Well, we'll wait and see," he said in a disturbed and comfortless way.

Craig turned away, assuming that the unsatisfactory interview was over. Horton made him turn back sharply when he asked, "Doctor, what is osteoporosis?"

Craig stared, searching Horton's eyes to see whether he was asking for information or testing Craig's honesty.

"Osteoporosis," Craig explained, "is a loss of density in the bones. The mineral content of the matrix is lost and the bones become 'soft.' Why do you ask?"

"What causes that?" Horton asked.

"A number of things can cause it," Craig answered guardedly.

"Such as removing a woman's ovaries?" Horton pressed.

"Yes. Where did you find out about osteoporosis?" Craig asked.

"I've been doing some reading. I don't understand a lot of it, but I get enough," the man said sadly. "Enough."

Horton was thoughtful. Then he said, "Can't let them know . . . can't."

He did not explain further, but asked, "Doctor, I'm an attorney, used to dealing with other people's intimate problems. I respect confidences. So if I promise to take no steps, you can trust me."

"I trust you," Craig said, though he was puzzled.

"If you tell me, I will not tell Cynthia. I will not even tell her mother. They've both gone through enough. But for myself, and as a guide to how to treat them, I must now know the whole truth. What is the

231

total extent of the damage that has been done to my daughter?"

Craig's first and immediate inclination was to refuse to answer. These were medical issues, to be settled among doctors, and not with laymen who, intelligent and sophisticated though they might be, were not in a position to evaluate or react professionally to an unfortunate set of facts. But Horton's direct question made him decide this was a time to speak out.

"Mr. Horton, what I tell you is confidential. For Cynthia's sake. She is in quite fragile emotional and mental condition. I don't know how much more she can absorb. So handle this information as you would highly radioactive material."

Horton nodded, accepting Craig's warning with the degree of gravity Craig intended.

"The consequences of your daughter's present condition will be far-reaching. Infertility is only one. She can always adopt. But her situation is more discouraging than that. As a natural consequence of her condition, she will not only be deprived of being a mother; it is possible that she might not be able to function as a wife in the normal way."

"What do you mean?"

"It is most natural for young husbands and wives to have regular, frequent sexual intercourse. With her condition, and deprived of estrogen, the vagina can eventually lose elasticity, become thickened, hence easily traumatized, causing great pain and frequent bleeding. This might possibly rule out enjoyable or satisfactory intercourse. If that happened it might jeopardize the chances of a happy marriage."

"If she doesn't have her marriage to look forward to ..." Horton did not dare pursue his speculation. "Do you think Pete knows?"

"I'd have no way of learning that."

"I wonder if that's why he didn't come to the hospital tonight," Horton considered. "We'll have to find some way of preparing her. Otherwise, I don't know what will happen to her . . . I just don't know. . . ."

Suddenly Horton exploded in hateful, vengeful whisper: "That bastard Prince . . . Someone ought to do something. . . . To destroy a girl's life that way . . ."

Craig did not answer. To have given vent to his own feelings would only have enraged Horton even more.

Chapter Twenty-One

It was just past two o'clock in the morning. Harvey Prince had been in a deep sleep, aided by a strong sedative, which he sometimes took to ensure a restful night before a long day in surgery. He had not stirred, not even when his wife nudged him several times to interrupt his snoring. She had finally taken refuge in one of the guest bedrooms.

It was most unusual for the phone to ring during the night in the Prince home. He always left instructions that any emergency calls should be directed to his younger men.

This night, however, the phone did ring. Very insistently. Since his wife was in the guest bedroom, which did not have an extension, she could not protect him from the call. The ringing was so prolonged that it finally roused him. He groped for the phone, thinking, Damn it, not Rita! Twice before she had done that. But not in recent years. Yet now, when she was approaching menopause, with all the insecurities that that invoked, it might well be she. Fortunately, Harvey Prince realized, his wife was not in the room.

"Yes?" he said hoarsely into the phone.

"You bloody sonofabitch, I ought to kill you!" a man shouted. He was obviously drunk.

"Who is this?" Prince demanded, fully awake and alert now.

"Who is this? The man whose daughter you destroyed! You never told us what would happen, never warned us ... you just cut her open and destroyed her ... destroyed her!"

"Who is this?" Prince demanded, furious now.

"How many young women have you destroyed lately, that you don't even know? Want to run down the list?"

Something in the man's voice became familiar. Prince asked cautiously, "Horton, is this you?"

"Who else? You bastard! I ought to kill you."

Without replying, Harvey Prince slammed down the receiver. He consulted his watch, decided that it was too late to take another sleeping pill without impairing his reactions in the O.R. He had to trust that he might fall asleep again without any aid. After an hour of tossing and turning, he went down to the bar and poured himself a large shot of brandy. He took it back to bed and sipped it slowly. Brandy usually induced sleep in him. But before he went off, he had time to analyze that phone call in detail. Horton was drunk. True. His drunkenness was obviously occasioned by his daughter's condition. As far as Prince knew, there had been no radical change in the last forty-eight hours. Her thrombophlebitis was responding. The danger of a pulmonary embolism had diminished. What could the man be raving about? Unless,

234

of course, the complete nature of his daughter's prognosis had been explained to him. And if it had, who would most likely have done that?

Just before he went off to sleep, Prince decided that he would see Ordway first thing in the morning.

"Clint, this is no longer a suggestion, it is an order," Harvey Prince said. "Pierson has got to be fired!"

"It's very serious business firing someone from a hospital staff. If we offered him the opportunity of resigning—"

"I was willing to settle for that before. But not now!" Prince interrupted fiercely. "I want him fired. I want it on his record. I am going to teach that meddling young bastard a lesson!"

Ordway had seen Prince in these rages before. Sometimes it was over an O.R. nurse who had offended him, or a careless resident; but always after a few days had passed, and Prince had had a chance to cool down, the issue resolved itself through sheer inertia. But Ordway had to admit he had never seen Prince quite so vehement before.

"Harv, in the first place, we don't know if Pierson told Horton anything. That's only a suspicion on your part," Ordway pointed out in a moderating tone.

"Who else could it be? Not one of my boys. Not Carlyle. He thinks he has a chance to come into my office. He wouldn't jeopardize that. It can only be Pierson! I want him fired! Fired!"

Ordway glanced at the clock on his desk. "Harv, aren't you supposed to be scrubbing right now?"

"Yes," Prince admitted, "so this will give you an idea how serious I think it is. That I'm down here now when I should be up in the O.R.!"

He turned and departed the office abruptly. Clinton

235

Ordway leaned back in his swivel chair, yearning for the old days, when he had practiced surgery and did not have to referee the eternal war between attending physicians and staff.

Reluctantly, he lifted his phone. "Get Dr. Pierson."

Craig Pierson was involved in a bimanual examination of a patient brought into Emergency with severe cyclic pain secondary to endometriosis. He had concluded that surgery was necessary and should not be postponed. Though his beeper was insistent, he did not honor it until he had first assigned the patient to the ward and written out orders for a complete workup and to prep her for surgery at once.

By that time, an irate Clinton Ordway appeared in Emergency. With a single, sharp gesture he ordered Craig into the utility room and slammed the door shut.

"Did you say anything to Arthur Horton that could have caused him to get drunk and call Prince in the middle of the night and threaten him?" Ordway demanded.

"Horton wanted to know the full truth about his daughter's condition. I felt it was time someone was honest with him."

"Are you implying that we haven't been honest?"

Conscious of the fact that he risked antagonizing a man who had actually tried to befriend him, Craig said, "No one had told the patient or her parents all the consequences. Someone had to."

"So you appointed yourself that someone," Ordway said unhappily. "Damn it, Craig, there are ethics!"

"What's ethical about keeping the truth from a patient?"

"That's not what I mean, and you know it!" Ordway fired back. "Ethics! The way one doctor treats with

236

another. The obligation not to interfere in the manner in which a doctor takes care of his patient."

"What about the ethics that protect patients?" Craig asked.

"Hell, man! I'm trying to save your neck and you're making it most difficult!" Ordway exploded.

"Once Horton asked about osteoporosis, I thought I might as well tell him everything. How could I know he would get drunk and make a wild phone call in the middle of the night?" Craig said, then added, "Though if it had been my twenty-two-year-old daughter who had been needlessly castrated, I might have done—"

Ordway interrupted angrily, "Never say that! Not in here. Not out there. Not anywhere!"

"Say what?" Craig challenged.

"Words like 'needlessly.' And 'castrated.' Don't you realize you're setting up Prince and this hospital for a malpractice suit?" Ordway warned. "God, I hope you didn't say anything to Horton about needless castration."

"Of course not."

"You're sure you didn't say anything like that? After all, Horton's an attorney. That's all we need—another big malpractice case. Our premiums are high enough as it is." Ordway was silent and contemplative for a time. "Look, stay out of Prince's way! And stay out of that damn room! Give this thing a chance to cool."

Once that afternoon, between cases, Harvey Prince called Clinton Ordway. Fortunately, Ordway was not in. Prince left a message: "What have you done about Pierson?"

The next day, Prince called twice. The second time, Ordway could not avoid the call.

"Clint? Did you interrogate Pierson?"

"Yes."

"Was he the one who talked to Horton?" Prince demanded.

"Yes. He talked to Horton."

"Then I expect you will do what you have to," Prince said crisply. He hung up before Ordway could argue or refuse.

Ordway realized that this time, different from all previous times, Prince was determined enough not to give up. Still, he tried to convince himself, if he could stall for a few days . . .

For the next three days, though Cynthia Horton had called for him several times, Craig Pierson avoided going to her room. He asked Burt to cover for him. Once, when Burt was up in the O.R. with Prince, Craig sent young Blinn to see what she wanted. She wanted to see Dr. Pierson. Still, Craig refused. He was not only endangering his own career; he was putting Ordway in a most difficult situation. Ordway had been a helpful ally in more than one instance when things could have gotten pretty tense. Every resident made his share of mistakes, had his share of run-ins with attendings, needed protection during the vital learning days of his first year or two. Ordway had been most understanding. He was entitled to have his situation respected.

But the most persuasive reason was that there was nothing he, or anyone, could do for the patient. All Craig could offer her would be soporific lies. And they might prove damaging. The best that could happen to her now was gradual acceptance, slow adjustment to her condition. In her case, unfortunately, the best and the worst were not far different.

He waited around one evening until the time for Horton's usual visit. He met him at the elevator and guided him to the residents' office.

Before Craig could question him, the penitent father confessed, "I'm sorry. After what you told me, I ...I had to get drunk. But I haven't told anyone. Not Cynthia. Not her mother. No one! I give you my word."

The man began to weep. Craig said to himself, Christ, no! Don't do this to me. I can't take a man weeping. I'll never be able to take it.

But out of consideration for the man's sensitivities, Craig said nothing. Gradually Horton recovered. "Sorry," he said. "I don't have any chance to let go. During the day I'm in court. At night I don't dare tell Barbara what I know. I just have to go around holding it in."

"I understand," Craig said gently.

"There's no way?" Horton asked. "You mean, in all of medical science, everything they know, everything they've discovered, there's nothing ..."

"Some conditions are irreversible and untreatable."

Horton took a handkerchief out of his breast pocket, wiped away the dampness from his eyes. "I'd better go in and see her now. She expects me, waits for me. There's a little-girl look in her eyes that says, Now that Daddy's here it'll be better. She has such trust, it destroys me. Destroys me."

Horton was on his way to the door when Craig asked, "The young man ... her fiancé ..."

"Pete?"

"Yes. Has he been here in the last three days?"

"Only once," Horton said.

"Has she said anything?"

"No. But I think she's beginning to suspect," Horton admitted sadly.

"He could be very supportive right now," Craig advised.

"What can I say to him? What can I tell him without lying?" Horton asked.

There was no good answer.

It was past three. In his sleep, Craig turned to Kate, embraced her. They had remained that way for the past hour. He needed her on this night, more than on most. They had talked at length about what he might have to do if Prince had his way. They talked of what she might do, too. Though she had not said it, he sensed that her professional drive demanded that she remain at State University Hospital, or some other equally large and important hospital. If he were fired, or even allowed the courtesy of resigning, his options would be limited. There were always opportunities for an Ob-Gyn man in a small-town hospital, or in some small medical group away from large metropolitan hospitals. That would mean no research at all, and limited surgery. He would be forced to refer complicated cases to other men in larger cities, men who might not be as capable as he, but who had the facilities. Whereas he had only his skill, which would diminish from lack of use.

They had fallen asleep after making love again. She remained awake longer, thinking, They are going to destroy him. I can see it now. He appears so tough and rugged, with that strong face and that angular jaw. Physically he may be tough, rugged. Inwardly he is extremely sensitive. Women sense that about him, which is why he is such a good Ob-Gyn man. But the same sensitivity that makes him a trusted doctor to his patients is what will allow the system to destroy him. He cannot abide injustice in medicine. He cannot accept anything short of the most meticulous care for each patient.

At three-thirty, her phone rang with the persistent urgency that only early-morning calls inflict. She broke from his arms to answer it.

"Lindstrom," she announced instinctively, though she was momentarily lost.

"Sorry to bother you at this hour," the operator apologized, quite self-consciously. "But is Dr. Pierson there?"

Had Kate been more awake, she would have been outraged at this intrusion on her privacy.

"Why? What is it?"

Across her mind flashed the sudden thought that Prince, in his desire to embarrass and demean Craig, had decided to exploit their relationship.

The operator dispelled that suspicion. "It's most urgent we talk to him. There's an emergency."

"What about the night resident?" Kate asked in a whisper, trying not to disturb Craig.

"This concerns a patient named Horton, Cynthia Horton. They feel he's the only one who can talk to her."

"Talk to her? Now? At three-thirty?" Kate asked, no longer trying to whisper. Craig stirred and was beginning to come awake.

The operator said crisply, "One moment, I'll put the floor nurse on."

The floor nurse took over. "Dr. Pierson?"

"One moment," Kate said, handing the phone to Craig.

"Pierson. Yes?" Craig said.

"Cynthia Horton is threatening to jump from her

fourth-floor window. And nobody can talk her out of it!"

"Christ!" Craig exploded. For a moment he was silent. Then he said, "Keep her talking. I'll be there as soon as I can!"

Chapter Twenty-Two

They dressed hurriedly. Within seventeen minutes they were at the hospital. The elevator did not seem to rise fast enough. Craig bolted between the doors while they were still opening. He raced down the dimly lit, hushed corridor. It was only when he approached 442 that he could hear subdued but fearful whispers.

The nurse's aide who was standing guard at the door said, "Thank God you're here. It's pretty bad."

He opened the door cautiously. Any sudden move or change in conditions might precipitate the one thing that must be avoided at all costs. Cynthia must not be startled into fulfilling her compulsion. Inside the room, Craig found the night resident and the chief floor nurse talking softly but continuously, trying to maintain a tenuous but vital contact with the unfortunate girl who was perched in the open window. Both resident and nurse were tremendously relieved to see Craig.

"Take over," the resident whispered. "We haven't been able to do a damn thing. Can't even get close enough to get some sedative into her."

Craig motioned the nurse away and moved toward

242

the window himself. Cynthia, who had once appeared so young and beautiful, now presented a caricature of herself. Her inner torment, created by her sense of nothingness, had distorted her features even as it had distorted her mind. She was a frail fragment of the girl he had interviewed her first day in the hospital.

He was shocked at how much she had changed in just the few days since he had seen her last. He wondered what could have done it. That could be determined later, and only if she could be dissuaded from this precipitate compulsion toward self-destruction. That was up to him now.

"Cynthia . . .," he began softly.

At the sound of her name, she edged further out the window.

"Cynthia. It's me. Dr. Pierson."

For an instant she dared turn back to see him. But it did not diminish her compulsion to destroy the self she now had begun to hate.

"Cynthia, if this is what you want to do, I can't stop you. All I ask is the chance to talk to you," he pleaded.

She would not face him. However, neither did she make any further menacing moves. She stared into the black night. He watched her frail body breathing in short, convulsive, spasmodic gasps. Each muscle of her body was a taut rope. She was in the critical phases of a deep, possibly fatal depression.

"You can talk to me, Cynthia—you know that. Because we share something none of the others do. We know what it means, don't we? To be cast off, put out, deserted, rejected. Isn't that true?"

With these words he had hoped to make her relent somewhat, or face him so that he could make eye contact with her. He failed. He glanced at Kate, who urged him on with a single sharp nod.

243

"Cynthia," he tried again, "no matter how you feel about yourself, you have to think of others. Your mother and dad. Who love you so much. And who would have to live out their lives remembering what you do now. How do you think they'll feel? Asking themselves every day, Where did we fail her? What did we do that we shouldn't have? Or fail to do that we should have? That's a terrible guilt to put on two people who love you so much."

He edged slightly closer to her, to test whether he had any effect on her. She edged farther out the window. He drew back, not wishing to exert any more pressure on her than he had to. Now he became aware that below them, cars were beginning to roll into the courtyard. He knew they must be police cars, rescue cars. He hoped desperately they would do nothing to disturb her. Fortunately, she seemed oblivious of them.

"Cynthia"—he sought another avenue of approach—"you and I know what it means to be left, deserted. Yet that's what you want to do now, to your mother, your father. Desert them. They've given you so much. Is this all you have to leave them? This memory?"

Slowly she turned back to stare at him.

"Everybody . . .," she said in a strange and strained voice; "everybody who touches me . . . whom I touch . . . everybody is doomed . . . doomed."

Now that she had responded to him, he tried to keep her talking. "Everybody? Who?"

"Mommy. Daddy." Craig noticed that she had reverted to her childhood designations for them. "Everybody. It's a curse I carry around. A disease I was born with. This is the only way to end the disease, to free them all. Mommy. Daddy. Pete. All!"

244

"Free them?" Craig asked, more sharply now. "How free will they be tomorrow if you do this to-night? How free will they be a year from now? When they keep staring at your pictures desperately wishing they could bring you back. To tell you how much they love you. You'll be destroying their lives too."

He was becoming more apprehensive of the sounds and movements below the window. He hoped they would not precipitate some rash move on her part.

"A curse . . . a curse . . .," Cynthia repeated aim-lessly, staring out into the night, remote from him again.

He had to keep talking, to maintain that contact, fragile as it was.

"Cynthia . . . remember how we talked once about finding your other mother?"

That seemed to evoke an involuntary response from her. She had ceased her jerky, spasmodic breathing for an instant.

"If you do this now, you'll never have a chance to discover who she was. All your life you've wondered. Well, give yourself a chance to find out. I'll help you. I'll show you how it's done."

She glanced back, her look betraying doubt as to whether to trust him or not.

"I will," he promised.

She seemed to be considering that when suddenly from below a powerful burst of searchlight lit up the window and the entire room. The sudden flash of light terrified her. She started, unbalancing herself in the open window. Craig lunged forward and grasped for her, barely able to seize her arms. She was out of the window, hanging precariously from his desperate but uncertain grip. For a moment she struggled. Then she went limp. Straining desperately, bit by bit, he gradually increased his hold on her until he had both his arms around her frail body. Carefully, slowly, he lifted her back through the window. All the while the bright searchlight held them in its beam.

He placed her limp, moist body on the bed. He covered her, and without looking to the nurse he ordered a hypodermic and a strong dose of Valium. Now he became aware of the trickle of sweat that slowly made its way down his chest. He realized how cold and damp he was around the neck, where his collar was drenched. On his back his shirt clung to him. His face dripped with perspiration so profusely that it hung in a large drop at the end of his nose.

He slumped into a chair. Kate wiped his face dry. The nurse returned, administered the sedative, and left.

"We have to begin intensive treatment with her," Kate said. "Else it's bound to recur. In fact, we should move her to Psychiatric. She's more than a surgical case now."

"Wonder what triggered it?" Craig pondered, exhausted.

"She's had a lot of time to brood. And one hell of a lot to brood about," Kate said.

"Look, you go back home and get some sleep. I'll wait with her."

"I'd rather stay," Kate insisted.

"Okay. Then curl up in that easy chair and get some rest," he urged. "She'll be asleep for hours. I hope."

He went to Cynthia's side, found her pulse. The sedative had slowed it somewhat, but it was still far more rapid than normal, reflecting the degree of her mental torment. Her breathing was shallow, and occasionally her arm twitched.

As he turned away from the bed, his gaze suddenly focused on a crumpled ball of paper on the floor just

246

under the night table. It did not have the limp shape-lessness of a piece of discarded tissue. Curious, he reached for it, flattened it out.

It was a note which began, *Darling, darling Cynthia* ... He glanced down at the bottom of the page. It was signed *Pete*. In view of the events of the past hour, he felt authorized to read it.

Darling, darling Cynthia ... *I know how you must feel about my not having come to see you every night this week. It's not that I love you less. But I need time to think.*

We've always been honest with each other. I think honesty now is more important than ever. So I don't want to lie to you, or pretend, which is the same thing. I want to get my head straight and then be completely open with you.

It didn't matter to me too much about not having our own children. We can always adopt. And if we're lucky, we'll get a girl just like you. And maybe a boy or two as well. So I don't want you to worry about that.

It's the other part. Our love has always meant more to me than just sex. Yet we can't deny that sex has been part of it. And now, with what the doctors say, and my own doctor agrees with them, I have to ask myself, Can I cope with a marriage that offers less? It's not that I love you less, it's that I doubt myself. And I have to find out.

I'll always love you. But I need time, time. All my love. Pete.

Craig stared at the letter, then without a word passed it to Kate. She read it hastily. She looked across Cynthia's bed at Craig.

"God, didn't he know what he was doing?"

247

"I guess he assumed she'd been told."

Kate shook her head sadly. "She'd have had to find out one day soon. But not like this. And not from the man she loves. No matter how kind he tried to be, or how loyal—to find out in this way. No mystery now why she tried it."

"People joke about how doctors bury their mistakes. They never mention the patients who live out lives of frustration, pain, and tragedy."

Kate did not answer.

"Damn it," Craig resolved, "I'll see to it that Goldfingers doesn't make any more 'mistakes.'"

There was a rustle of whispers outside the door. It swung open. The night floor nurse was being backed into the room by two anxious parents, Barbara and Arthur Horton.

"She's fine! The emergency is over," the nurse tried to assure them. "We only called because we thought we might need you."

"We came as fast as we could," Horton explained, "but living out in the suburbs, it took some time. Now that we're here, we insist on seeing her."

Craig intervened. "Come in, come in," he said. "Just be quiet. Please?"

Both parents stood at the foot of the bed and stared at Cynthia until they were reassured that she was asleep and safe.

"What happened?" Arthur Horton asked.

Craig handed him the letter. Horton scanned it hastily, passed it to his wife.

"He shouldn't have . . ." was all Barbara Horton could say before she broke into tears. "We were going to tell her. In time. In a way that wouldn't hurt her more than necessary. But this . . . no wonder she became hysterical."

248

"Worse," Craig said in simple honesty.

"Worse?" Horton challenged. "What could be worse ..." But he realized without being told. "God, no. That girl ... that little girl who loved life so much ... I don't believe it. There must be some mistake. You must have misinterpreted what she said."

"Mr. Horton," Kate intervened, "there is no possible way to misinterpret a girl poised in an open window threatening to jump."

"No!" Barbara Horton blurted out, then dropped away to a futile whisper. "No ... she couldn't ... she didn't ... didn't ...."

"I'm glad you weren't here. It wasn't a very nice thing to see," Kate said.

Horton moved to Cynthia's side, took her hand, patted it gently, then pressed it alongside his cheek, while he threatened, "I'll kill him ... I'll kill him ...."

"The boy was frightened," his wife pleaded. "He had no way of knowing."

"Prince," Horton corrected. "I'll kill him! I swear to God, for what he's done to her, I'll ... I'll ...." He broke off, set his daughter's hand down gently, and turned to face Craig. The man's eyes were moist as he said pitifully, "I'm not a violent man. I wouldn't know how to go about killing anyone."

He sank into a chair, staring toward the bed. His wife moved to his side, but could only whisper, "Arthur ... oh, Arthur, what are we going to do?"

He shook his head hopelessly.

To ease their suffering, Craig suggested, "There's nothing you can do here. Why don't you just go back home? I assure you she's perfectly safe."

"We'll stay till morning. When she wakes, the first thing I want her to see is us," Arthur Horton said.

Craig nodded. He and Kate left the two anxious parents with their daughter. He stopped at the desk to instruct the charge nurse, "Send two blankets into 442. Maybe they can get some sleep."

The elevator door opened onto the deserted main floor. Only one person was waiting to go up. Peter Tompkins. A glance affirmed that he had dressed hastily and rushed to the hospital as soon as the Hortons had called.

"How is she?" he demanded, breathless.

"She's all right now," Craig assured him.

"What happened?"

"Your note," Kate said frankly. "That was not the way she should have found out."

"You mean she didn't know? No one told her? I assumed . . ." He broke off, speechless.

"You assumed wrong," Kate pointed out.

"Oh, God," Peter Tompkins said. He sank down onto the wooden bench near the elevators. "What the hell have I done to her? I was only trying to be honest. We've always been open with each other. We've always . . ." He couldn't finish.

"Sometimes it's kinder not to be too honest too soon," Kate pointed out.

Craig felt compelled to intervene. "Exactly what did you mean in your note about what your doctor 'told' you?"

"About what happens to a young woman in Cynthia's present condition. How it makes sex impossible," the tormented young man explained.

"Did he say 'happens' or 'might' happen?" Craig demanded.

"I don't exactly remember," he admitted.

"And did he use the word 'impossible'? Or don't you 'exactly remember' that either?" Craig asked furiously. "That's the trouble when a little knowledge gets into the hands of laymen! Then because you panicked, she panicked."

"I'm sorry if I misunderstood, very sorry," young Tompkins said. "Can I go up and see her? Can I try to explain?"

"She's sleeping," Craig said.

"I'd like to see her. Just look at her. Would it be all right?" He addressed his plea to Kate.

"I wouldn't," Kate warned. "If she did wake, seeing you would only increase her guilt."

"Then what can I do?" the distraught young man asked.

"I'd do a great deal of thinking before I did anything more, if I were you," Kate said sharply.

It was dawn when Craig and Kate stepped outside the hospital. Far to the east, the sky was beginning to brighten. They stood in the cool morning air, breathing deeply. There was no need to say anything. No need for her to ask, or for him to explain.

He said simply, "Okay. Today I will do it."

Chapter Twenty-Three

The Morbidity and Mortality Review was always convened around a table in the large conference room on the main floor of the hospital. Though Clinton Ordway was lenient about attending surgeons' failing to appear at Grand Rounds, he was most insistent that they be present at M.&M. conferences, since those actions

251

and decisions of surgeons which had led to serious complications or death were discussed by their colleagues. If for no other reason than to defend or explain his procedures, every attending surgeon appeared, unless he was involved in emergency surgery.

Though an M.&M. conference pretended to be a self-policing review, a man's colleagues were more apt to justify than to censure his errors of judgment or performance. So such meetings had become a formality every hospital staff pursued, most times to lend the aura, if not the fact, of self-examination to their work.

Ordway waited impatiently as the older men straggled in one by one, each pleading an excessively busy schedule. Once all were assembled, Ordway called the meeting to order.

He glanced at his agenda. The first case involved a twenty-six-year-old woman who was late in delivering. The obstetrician had decided on a cesarian. During the course of the operation she had died on the table from an anaphylactic reaction to the anesthetic, to which she proved highly allergic. The surgeon, a reputable and active doctor with a large practice, was most regretful about the error. He protested that he was not accusing anyone, but he did confess, "Imagine how I felt—the patient going into shock right under my hand. I took it for granted the anesthetist had checked her out for allergies. I had no idea . . . no idea at all. When it was too late—well, what could I do? It was tragic. Tragic!"

Having disclaimed his own responsibility, he could appear not only distressed and innocent, but victimized as well. The anesthetist, who had slipped into the meeting after the case was announced, spoke up from the end of the table.

"I think it should be pointed out," he began, "that

there was nothing in the patient's chart to indicate the existence of any allergy. The intern who took her history should have been more careful. After all, by the time I had a chance to question her she was under preliminary sedation. . . ."

One of the older surgeons interrupted, "You mean you didn't see her the day before the procedure?"

"It was only decided the morning of operation that she was going to have a caesarian. And with her chart before me, there seemed no need. After all, a young woman of twenty-six, no cardiac or pulmonary history, no record of allergy. I had to assume that the intern who saw her on admission had done a proper workup."

"Who was the intern?"

Ordway consulted the file. "Blinn. Willis Blinn."

Instinctively, Burt Carlyle and Craig Pierson exchanged glances. Carlyle's face betrayed an angry flush.

From down the table, one doctor was heard to comment, "Oh, Blinn. One of those. What can you expect?"

To avoid a bitter and painful confrontation, Craig anticipated and cut off Carlyle's reaction.

"I don't wish to make any defense of Blinn. Because I didn't witness the interview. But it seems to me that there were at least two other opportunities to elicit the facts. One was in the office of the obstetrician who had obviously been taking care of the patient during her pregnancy."

The obstetrician interrupted, "She had no history of any allergies, as far as we could determine!"

Craig continued, "And the second was the morning of the operation. Despite the fact that it was an emergency, there was nothing about the woman's condition that would have been affected by a delay of half an hour or even an hour."

The anesthetist edged forward. Ignoring Craig, he explained to the rest of the group, "I wish someone would explain to our young friend that I was just off another case for Dr. Wilhelm when I was called in on this one. I had a crowded schedule that morning. The best I could do was prepare her for anesthesia on the basis of what information I had. When these young fellows have been out in practice for a while, they'll realize the pressures that mount up. Besides, if a man can't trust the patient's history, well, it's a sad day. A very sad day."

"Believe me, I sympathize with you," one of the older, gray-haired men volunteered. "I don't know what medicine's coming to. These days you have to bite your tongue and watch things disintegrate. The way things are going, something like this was bound to happen."

He deliberately avoided staring at Burt Carlyle, which only pointed up his meaning all the more.

"Thank God, I won't have to put up with this sort of thing much longer. I'll be glad to retire before the whole damn system goes to hell. But it's what they want," he concluded bitterly.

Burt Carlyle leaned forward so that he could stare down the long conference table at the surgeon, "Doctor, let me ask you—"

But Craig interrupted, "I'd like to say a word about Blinn. He's young. He's black. And he's nervous. Because he knows that before he walks into any ward or private room he's going to be treated like an orderly, not a doctor. He needs to be encouraged. He's damn willing, and the first one to recognize his own shortcomings. I think he's going to be a good doctor one day, if we give him a chance."

At the same time, Craig cast a restraining glance at Burt Carlyle, whose cheeks darkened and whose black eyes were fiercely hostile.

The old doctor assumed an indulgent smile as he addressed Craig. "Sonny, let me tell you something. When I went to medical school, even very capable students had trouble getting in. And some Jews, with excellent records, never made it at all. Unless they went to school in Germany or Italy. But these days, we go looking for the unqualified. They don't have to know a goddamn thing. They only have to be members of a minority and schools roll out the red carpet for them.

"Now, I've seen that young fellow Blinn. He's a nice kid. And he does try hard. Which is exactly the point. Hard as he tries, he isn't good enough. There's only one important fact in this case: Blinn never took a proper history. Now we're trying to place the blame on an innocent surgeon and an anesthetist whose only crime was believing the patient's chart."

With the gravity of a judge, and his age to support him, the old surgeon concluded, "I say surgery has come to a sorry pass when doctors are going to be blamed for that!"

Having found an ally, the surgeon involved in the case intoned self-righteously, "It's the price patients are going to have to pay for this tidal wave of unqualified doctors we're turning out. Like turning cancer cells loose in the bloodstream. Who knows how far they will spread? And how fatal they will eventually prove to the system?

"It's a black plague. A new black plague—that's the best you can say for it. If you will excuse the expression," the surgeon concluded.

In the rear of the room, someone chuckled. Burt Carlyle turned angrily to confront him. "Whoever the hell you are, I would like to compare records with you! High school, college, med school! Any records you want! Pick them!"

Ordway took over to calm Burt. "Carlyle, there was nothing personal intended. Everyone knows your record. The fact that I selected you to be Chief Resident certainly demonstrates how I feel about you. It was an unfortunate comment. Which I am sure no one in this room subscribes to."

But no other doctor spoke up to apologize for it.

"Now, then, the next case," Ordway announced, to change the subject.

Craig Pierson noted, as he always did in M.&M. conferences, that by one means or another the doctors on the case had adroitly managed to avoid any guilt for an unnecessary death. What should have been an astringent procedure of self-judgment had become a pretentious means of absolution. No matter what Blinn might have done, or not done, two older, more experienced doctors had goofed, blown it. There was no other way to say it. So a twenty-six-year-old woman had died, giving birth to an infant who came into this world without a mother. And the doctors responsible pointed the finger at a young black intern and thus acquitted themselves.

The second case concerned an exenteration during which the patient, having been on the table for five and a half hours, had required several blood transfusions. The patient had accepted the first two without any adverse reaction. But after the third transfusion the patient had reacted violently. Though the procedure was carried through to a successful conclusion, the patient had suffered renal failure and died within thirty-six hours.

The obvious cause: an infusion of incompatible blood.

His face red with anger, the surgeon complained, "Damn it! I'm more outraged about this case than the patient's husband! When I send down to the bank for Type A blood and I am assured that I am getting Type A blood, I should get Type A blood!

"As soon as I left the O.R. I went down to the bank myself. And what did I discover? Two pints of blood had been sent to two different O.R.s. One Type A, one Type B. It's clearly marked on the record. The Type A was for my patient. No question. But the orderly who brought them up to the floor made a *little* mistake," the surgeon accused bitterly. "He just delivered the wrong blood to the wrong operating room! That's all. A little slipup. A little fatal slipup! Because once that B blood was infused into my patient, there was nothing anyone could do. Shock, renal failure were unavoidable. Because of one lousy mistake by one orderly whose mind was probably on whether he should go out on strike or not!"

The surgeon concluded by looking around the table to solicit support from his colleagues.

"I've noticed the same thing," one of the other attending surgeons spoke up. "With all due respect, Clint"—he cast an approving look at Ordway—"you do run a fine department. But the level of efficiency of hospital employees these days is mighty low. You can't trust any of them."

"Then why do you?" Burt Carlyle called out accusingly.

The surgeon glared at Carlyle. "If we can't depend on the hospital personnel, we'll be spending all our time doing the work of menials. When a man sends for Type A blood he has a right to expect Type A blood. And if he can't, well . . ." the man ended up hopelessly. "These days . . ."

"Why *do* you?" Carlyle persisted.

"Why do I *what*?" the surgeon shouted back, exasperated.

"You said you couldn't trust hospital personnel these days. Yet an orderly brings a pint of blood into the O.R., the wrong type, and neither you nor the anesthetist checks before transfusing it. There were two professionals who could have prevented this unnecessary death, yet neither of them did!"

"It's not my job," the surgeon retorted angrily.

"We never expected we'd need a third transfusion, so the blood was late getting up there," the anesthetist declared defensively. "With the patient's pressure falling rapidly, there wasn't much time."

"Not even time enough to look at the label on the bottle and check it against the patient's type?" Carlyle shot back.

Craig tried to warn him quiet with a pleading look. For he knew what the outcome had to be.

"You have to trust somebody," the surgeon declared. "When you go into practice you'll find that out, 'Doctor.'"

Burt glared at him because of the derogatory use of the title. Whereupon the surgeon smiled smugly. "The orderly involved turned out to be white. So you needn't become so upset, 'Doctor.'"

Ordway intervened swiftly: "Gentlemen, Morbidity and Mortality Conferences are not held to air personal or group grudges. But to discover why patients suffer needless or avoidable morbid or fatal consequences. So that those mistakes are not repeated.

"I will not stand for personality attacks, or racial slurs. Or anything else that gets in the way of the practice of good medicine and good surgery."

Several more cases were heard. In each instance, the doctor involved presented his explanation of how

the avoidable death had occurred, always without any
fault or complicity on his part. Where a doctor had
obviously made an erroneous diagnosis or prescribed
the wrong therapy, always there were symptoms,
signs, and circumstances which seemed to substantiate his erroneous conclusion. And there was at least
one physician present who defended him by pointing
out how logical his incorrect conclusion appeared to
be.

Two more cases were heard. Two more avoidable
deaths were discussed. Two more doctors were exon-
erated by their colleagues.

Surely, now, Craig thought, Ordway must introduce
the Horton case. Instead, Ordway glanced down at his
agenda and announced quietly, "That brings today's
conference to a close." He flipped his folder shut.

"There *is* another case," Craig reminded him.

"We've reviewed all the mortality cases," Ordway
announced. "Today's session is adjourned."

"What about the Horton case?" Craig persisted.

"Horton?" Ordway echoed, as if the name were unfamiliar.

"I don't wish to use names, but I'm forced to. The
case of Cynthia Horton. A patient of Dr. Prince's."

"Oh, that case," Ordway pretended to be reminded.
"It was removed from the agenda."

"Why?" Craig demanded.

Burt Carlyle tried to silence him with a sharp, forbidding glare. But Craig demanded of Ordway,
"Why? After all, this is a Morbidity and Mortality Conference. And I would say that in her case morbidity is
certainly a marked result."

"Because of the pressure of time, we've confined
ourselves to mortality cases today. Besides, as I understand it, the patient's been removed to Psychiatric.

Obviously she's one of those patients emotionally unequipped to deal with the fact of her malignancy. God knows, I can't blame her. At her age. However, this meeting is closed."

Craig leaped up, ready to accuse Ordway of deliberately censoring the discussion.

Burt Carlyle intervened. In a low, forceful whisper he said, "Don't! Did you hear me, Craig? Don't say another word!"

Craig glared at his colleague, their eyes locked on each other's like fixed laser beams. Craig's eyes accused, You're joining them. You're protecting Prince. After what he did.

Burt's eyes remained firm and unapologetic in the face of Craig's accusation. It was Craig who finally relented. Ordway gave a signal to the other physicians and surgeons, who began to depart.

There were only two men left. Burt Carlyle. And Craig Pierson.

"Say it!" Burt dared.

"What would you expect me to say?" Craig asked, which in its way was the most painful accusation of all.

"Come to the house tonight," Burt suggested. "I want to talk to you."

"What would we have to talk about, Burt?" Craig asked, indicating the immensity of his disappointment.

"One hell of a lot!" Burt Carlyle said angrily. "Seven o'clock. LuAnne'll make dinner. Bring Kate if she's off duty. Okay?"

Craig finally nodded.

Throughout cocktails and dinner, stilted conversation was deliberately directed at avoiding open conflict. LuAnne kept up a steady chatter about her childbirth classes.

"Of course, why black women need classes in birthing I'll never know. For generations now, people have accused us of breeding too much. Now they give us classes in how to." LuAnne laughed. "I think the answer is, Go out in the fields, pick cotton, and let it just happen naturally." But no one joined in her laughter.

Burt decided to confront the issue head-on. "Okay, Craig! Let's have it! Everything you didn't say this afternoon. Accuse me. Get it off your chest."

"Just tell me one thing," Craig demanded. "Did you and Ordway have it arranged between you?"

"You expect me to deny that. I won't. Yes, we damn well did have it arranged between us!"

"That's what I thought."

"But that still doesn't answer the question, *why*. Why did I conspire with Ordway to bury this case? What was the first thing that flashed into your mind? Say it!"

"Prince. You didn't want to jeopardize your possibility of joining his office."

"Of course," Burt said. "In fact," he confessed reluctantly, "it was the first thing that entered my mind, too. When you glared at me, the disappointment so fierce in your eyes, I asked myself, Why did I do it? Was it because Ordway had said, We've got to keep Craig from taking a step that might destroy his career? Or was it Prince?

"It's no secret. That's the goal I've had in mind from the first time I assisted him in the O.R. I worship that man's technique. So he does more hysterectomies than any three other surgeons combined. All I have to do is learn from him. When my turn comes to take over, I won't do any unnecessary ones, but I'll do the necessary ones magnificently."

Burt paused before admitting, "And make a fortune in the process. My wife, my kids are going to have the best of everything! I don't want any hand up, any head start, any special treatment. The best affirmative action for a black man is his own affirmative action. I learned that from my grandmother, while my mother was off taking care of other women's homes, other women's children."

He was silent for an instant before he admitted in an anguished whisper, "Maybe that's one reason why I did it. There was another. That arrogant bastard who made that remark about a new black plague. Because some unqualified minorities have been taken into the medical system, every black doctor must be branded inept, bungling, dangerous to his patients.

"I don't want to be faced with that accusation for the rest of my life!" Burt exploded, rising angrily.

Burt began to pace, speaking in a low voice. "I know you won't believe this. But I swear to God, there was another reason. Ordway's reason. Times when you think he's siding with Prince, he's actually protecting you."

"Fat chance!" Craig scoffed.

"Craig!" Kate insisted that he give Burt a hearing.

"Ordway's subject to pressures too. Trustees. Budgets. After all, it's men like Prince who keep the service going.

"Why are Prince's admissions always made on Fridays for surgery next Monday or Tuesday or Wednesday? Prince'll say it gives the staff a chance to do a proper workup on the patient. But you know the labs are virtually shut down over the weekend. There's no chance to do a workup. Not till Monday. So the patient lolls around, at a hundred seventy-five dollars a day, or more.

"Nothing is done. But the hospital picks up another five hundred dollars. Then at the end of surgery, who keeps patients on for an extra two or three days? Our good friend Harvey Prince. Why? Because that means another five hundred dollars a bed per week for every bed Prince has occupied. Is it any wonder that Prince has more beds reserved for him than any other attending in Ob-Gyn? He's a gold mine not only to himself but to the hospital."

With each fact Burt pointed out, Craig's fury kept mounting. "And that's the man you're defending?"

"*You* are the man I'm defending! Because for all those reasons, Goldfingers has muscle in that hospital. Muscle enough to have you kicked out. That's why Ordway bypassed the Horton case. That's how he induced me to cooperate. But now . . ."

Burt turned to stare down at Craig. "Now, I have to ask myself the question you asked me. Was it really you I was concerned about? Or myself? Craig, don't ever make me answer that question. Because I don't know."

Out of respect for the tormented man's feelings, Craig did not reply.

"Craig, if you feel betrayed, I don't blame you. My grandmother wouldn't blame you either. She always used to say to me, 'You ain't got no more claim to respect than the claim you make on yourself. Ain't nobody going to pass a law that'll make you a man. You got to do that by yourself.' "

Sadly, Burt concluded, "If you feel I let you down, for whatever reason, I'm sorry. I did what I thought was right. Especially after Ordway told me that now Prince insists you be fired!"

It was midnight when Kate and Craig left the Carlyle apartment. It was long past two o'clock in the morning when Craig and Kate sat over cold coffee in her dinette still pondering what Burt Carlyle had said.

"Fired," Craig repeated. Without saying it, he was considering all the consequences of that word. "If it weren't for my dad, I'd say to hell with Prince. Let 'em fire me! I don't give a damn!"

"But there *is* your dad," Kate pointed out. "What are you going to do about it?"

"I don't know," he confessed. "I don't know."

They had both been silent for a time before Craig asked, "How is Cynthia getting along?"

"She'll be a long-drawn-out case. A girl twenty-two is not going to become adjusted to what happened to her, not for a long time. If ever."

"It shouldn't have happened; it never should have happened," Craig repeated doggedly.

"But it did."

"He won't get away with it," Craig threatened.

"It seems he already has," Kate said grimly.

Chapter Twenty-Four

"Damn it, Craig! You're using up the patience of your best friends!" Ordway exploded. "No! I will not put that case back on the M.&M. agenda!"

The Chief hesitated, considering whether to reveal what he had in mind. Finally, he said, "Craig, the pressures have been building up. Now the other attendings think you're going too far in the classic war between academics and practitioners. So I've been thinking that perhaps I ought to rotate you."

"Rotate?"

"I suggest we exchange you with one of the second-year residents at City Hospital. A three-month rotation. It wouldn't do any harm for you to learn how Ob-Gyn departments in other hospitals function. So I've been in contact with Leverit over at City. He's amenable."

"Why? Do they have a troublemaker over there they want to get rid of?" Craig demanded.

"I'm not trying to get rid of you!" Ordway replied furiously. "I'm trying to keep you out of Prince's way for a few months. So he'll cool down."

"Old Goldfingers," Craig remarked bitterly.

"I know how you feel," Ordway commiserated, in a gentler, more conciliatory tone. "Don't forget I was young once. Imbued with great ideals. Until I found out that in medicine, as in any other profession, ideals must give way to reality."

When Craig responded with a hostile look, Ordway pointed out, "You're not just antagonizing Prince: it's the entire profession. We're under attack constantly. The government, lawyers with their malpractice suits, the news media with their exposés.

"Because of all that, we physicians have become what you might call a highly sensitized body. You know from your knowledge of immunology what happens when a sensitized body is invaded. The immune system mobilizes all the body's resources against the invader. In this case, *you* are the invader, the enemy. Don't expect any help from other doctors. They'll be too busy defending the profession."

Craig's silence encouraged Ordway to feel that he had finally made an impression on the angry young man. But his relief was to prove short-lived.

"Dr. Ordway, if we don't clean up our own mess, then the government will do it for us, or the media will, or the lawyers will. We have to stop covering up for our incompetents and our frauds. We have to adhere to our own ethics. Or someone else will make sure that we do."

Ordway nodded—not in assent, but in regret.

"One thing about being young, Craig: all difficult questions seem so simple. A few surgeons are less than ethical; therefore, drum them out. Simple, isn't it? But at the same time you slander every hospital they're associated with, you disgrace every physician in that same specialty, you attack the entire profession."

Ordway paused before confessing, "I know what I'm talking about. Before I came here to State University, I was at another hospital. We had an attending surgeon very much like . . ."

He broke off before naming Prince, and began again. "We had a man about whose cases our Tissue Committee too frequently reported, 'lack of pathology demonstrated' or 'no valid indication for surgery.' It became embarrassing, dangerous. We decided to revoke his hospital privileges. His lawyers threatened us with a libel lawsuit. In the end, we were powerless to do anything but permit him to resign gracefully so that he could affiliate with another hospital."

"And the patients he treated after that?" Craig demanded.

"We weren't concerned with anything except protecting our own hospital. Those are the realities, my boy. If we were to take any steps against Prince, you

266

can imagine the pressure, legal and political, that he could mount."

Furious with the impotence to which Ordway had just confessed, Craig could still feel compassion for the older doctor.

"Craig, I know how you feel. I feel the same way. I've watched frauds with polished bedside manners succeed. I've seen fine doctors, with only the patients' interests at heart, fail financially and die unhonored because they were better doctors than they were businessmen or politicians. So early in the game, I decided I couldn't be the keeper of any conscience but my own. If I could come through a day and feel that I had done well and honestly by my patients, that would be enough. So I shut my eyes to what other men did.

"Then, for some reason that I can only ascribe to sheer vanity, I made it my ambition to become Chief of the Service. I told myself, If I become Chief, I will improve and upgrade the care we give our patients. I've tried. But I don't know if I've succeeded. And what have I done to myself? Become a politician of sorts. I've had to be. After all, our budgets come from the state. That means we need clout in the capitol. To make it possible to get the latest equipment. The excellent facilities that attract young men of ability like Carlyle, like you.

"That's why, every once in a while, you find me shepherding a group of state senators through the department. Showing off what we have, and what we do. Pointing out what we need to do more. But that's only part of the game. It takes behind-the-scenes maneuvering. That dinner at Harvey Prince's home a few weeks ago was as much for my benefit as for his. He had invited the mayor, a political leader, and three state senators. We had a most elegant dinner. Margaret is a splendid hostess. After dinner, we spent a very constructive hour in Harvey's den. I think our budget for next year will be increased, even though other state departments will be cut down.

"Now, the point is this. Of the five men there, four of them were husbands of women that Harvey had operated on. Grateful patients. The invitations were extended by Mrs. Prince to the other women. The men attended because their wives wanted them to. And because Prince wanted them to.

"You can't deny the man's power. So I can't deny him when he says he wants you to resign."

"Resign?" Craig challenged pointedly.

Ordway realized that he had been caught in a euphemism. "Did Burt Carlyle tell you?"

"He told me."

"Okay, then. I don't have to be diplomatic. Prince wants you fired. I want you rotated. Take your choice."

Craig remained silent.

"You don't have to decide right this minute. Think about it. Then come back tomorrow and tell me you agree to be rotated."

Craig nodded soberly. He started for the door, stopped suddenly. "I don't have to think about it."

"Good!" Ordway said, considerably relieved.

"I want to be fired!"

"Fired?" Ordway's face flushed in both anger and frustration. "I won't accept that answer! Think of what it'll mean to your career, to your ability to provide for your folks. Your opportunity to practice medicine in some first-rate institution. Think about that!"

"You really mean think about it, then give you the answer you want. My answer is, I want to be fired! Now, fire me!"

268

"What if I refuse?"

"I'll tell Prince you refused," Craig shot back.

"Damn it, you're deliberately looking to wreck your career!"

"No, I just want to be fired," Craig said firmly.

Frustrated beyond enduring, Ordway exploded, "All right, Pierson. You are fired! Now, get out!"

"May I have that in writing?" Craig asked coolly.

"You certainly can!" Ordway said. He pressed down the key of his intercom and ordered, "Nelly, come in! And bring your book!"

Unaccustomed to such brusque orders, Nelly Burnham nervously entered the room, took her accustomed place, book open, ready to take shorthand.

Ordway swung his swivel chair around so that he faced Craig while he dictated.

"Craig Pierson, M.D., Department of Obstetrics and Gynecology, State University Hospital. Dear Dr. Pierson: In consequence of recent events, the details of which I need not cite in this letter, but which reflect an uncooperative and obstructive attitude on your part, and which disrupt the harmonious working of this Department, it is my duty to inform you that your employment is hereby terminated.

"You have two weeks in which to wind up your affairs and, if possible, find yourself a place in some other institution which may prove more suitable to your ambitions and personality."

He glared at Craig. "There! Does that satisfy you?"

"Yes," Craig said with unruffled deliberation. "Yes, that's fine."

He left. Ordway looked to Nelly Burnham, who had been his secretary during all the years he had been Chief. She was obviously puzzled, but too disciplined to inquire.

"He's the most frustrating young man!" Ordway exploded "I just wish . . . I just wish he weren't such a promising young surgeon. That'll be all, Nelly."

Once she had left the room, Ordway picked up his private phone and dialed a number he knew well.

"Dr. Prince, please," Ordway said crisply. "Ordway calling."

In moments, the familiar voice was on the line.

"Yes, Clint?"

"I wanted you to be the first to know. I just fired Pierson."

"Good! Teach the young bastard a lesson!" Prince said with great satisfaction.

Kate Lindstrom glanced at the letter. A single glance was all it took. She looked up at Craig.

"You had to do it, didn't you?"

Feeling accused, Craig replied, "It was either this or run away and hide. Call it rotation or resignation, it was running and hiding. Oh, don't think it was easy. I tried to persuade myself not to do this. I said, You can't buck the system. Not now. Later, perhaps, when I've gotten entrenched somewhere."

"Craig," she tried to interrupt.

"Before you say anything, Kate, hear me out. So I asked, Where am I going to get entrenched? In some small town no one ever heard of? Taking care of post-menopausal women who don't need a doctor but only someone to talk to? From such a position of 'entrenched strength' I am going to do what I can't do now? I'd never let myself get away with that.

"I also tried to buy myself off by saying, I have my folks to think about. I owe them so much. And I do. But I can't run out on what I believe. I had to make a stand, and I did. It won't be easy, but it beats slinking away into the nothingness of a useless practice which

270

is only a means of making money. Hell, that isn't medicine, that's business. And grubby business at that.

"Either *I'm* right about the way medicine should be practiced or *Prince* is. And if he is, then I don't belong in medicine. Here. Or anywhere."

"And how do you find out who's right?" Kate asked.

"By staying right here and demanding a hearing."

"Hearing? Before a group of doctors, every one of whom will look on you as a radical, an upstart, a young Turk who wants to rock their very comfortable, very remunerative boat? What chance do you think you'd have?"

"Somehow, someone has to recognize the truth!" Craig persisted.

"Of course," Kate said in a whisper.

"Kate, darling, I know what this can do to my career, and to our lives. But this isn't your war. If it hadn't been for me, you wouldn't be involved now. You can still back out."

"But it is for you and I am involved. Don't you think I've been doing my own thinking? Ever since the night of Cynthia. Ever since I watched you try to talk her back from that window. I realized that in a way you were contemplating the same thing she tried to do. To cop out by going south to some place you don't know, where you'd rot for lack of teaching, research, and the demand for expert surgery. For you, that would have been professional suicide. You had to do this."

"Then you're not angry?" Craig asked, studying her lovely, intent face.

"Angry? I blame myself," she confessed.

"What for?"

"For encouraging you to be what you are," Kate said.

She embraced him.

"It isn't only Cynthia," he said. "It's all the other young women after her who come under Prince's skillful, willful hands."

"I know," she agreed compassionately.

"There's still time to decide, Kate, what do you want? A hero? Or a husband?"

"Not a hero. Just a husband who won't spend the rest of his life feeling that he failed . . ."

Now she could not hold back her tears, for they both knew what lay ahead.

Within the day, Craig Pierson, using the hunt-and-peck system, managed to type out an official response to Ordway's letter of dismissal. It ended with a single simple paragraph:

> I AM, THEREFORE, DEMANDING AN OFFICIAL HEAR-
> ING TO DETERMINE WHETHER MY CONDUCT JUSTIFIES
> THE ACTION TAKEN BY THIS HOSPITAL IN DISCHARGING
> ME IN THE MIDST OF MY SECOND YEAR OF RESIDENCY.

The letter was delivered by hand to Ordway's office. Within fifteen minutes of its receipt, Craig Pierson's beeper summoned him to the phone.

"Dr. Pierson, Dr. Ordway would like to see you in his office at once!" Nelly Burnham ordered crisply.

"I'm sorry, but I'm doing a cutdown on a patient. An intern failed to insert an I.V."

"He said at once!" she reminded him officiously.

"As soon as I can."

Within ten minutes, Craig Pierson presented himself in Ordway's waiting room. Nelly Burnham greeted him quite formally.

"I will tell him you are here."

When Craig opened the door of Ordway's office, he

discovered Deering, the Hospital Administrator, seated across the room, his attitude one of hostile preparedness.

Ordway began straightaway. "Deering and I have discussed your letter. We do not think your request for a hearing is justified. We feel we have sufficient grounds for your discharge. And I think you'd find that most of the men in the department feel the same. Therefore, we are rejecting your request."

Deering nodded grimly, supporting Ordway's stand.

"You've taken a step that seriously affects my career," Craig said. "I'm entitled to have that passed on by other physicians after a complete presentation of the facts."

"*We* know the facts, and *we* have decided," Deering interposed. "That's final!"

Craig turned to Ordway. "You've spent a great deal of time explaining the effect this would have on my career. Don't tell me that suddenly the effect is trivial and doesn't justify a hearing."

Ordway flushed slightly, while Deering became more hostile. "Pierson, we have neither the time nor the manpower to conduct such a hearing. Even if we did, put yourself in the position of the men who'll sit in judgment. Older men, busy men who may feel forced to volunteer but who'll resent your wasting their valuable time. Even if they tried to be fair-minded, they'd grow bored and resentful with a long hearing.

"I never said it had to be a long hearing," Craig pointed out.

"I'm sure Harvey Prince will put in a strong defense."

The look that passed between Ordway and Deering

confirmed for Craig Pierson that his letter had already been discussed with Goldfingers.

Deering resumed the offensive. "You got yourself into this mess despite good advice. Don't compound it by asking for official condemnation of your obstructive conduct and thus deprive yourself of all chance of getting another post."

"I think what Walter has in mind," Ordway interceded, "is that we might work out a good letter of recommendation that might ease the way for you at some other institution."

"You fire me, then you give me a letter of recommendation?" Craig smiled at the irony. "No, I think I'd rather have the hearing, if you don't mind."

"But we *do* mind," Deering said angrily.

"Then you don't leave me any alternative," Craig said.

"What does that mean?" Deering asked, sitting up even more stiffly.

"I'll have to go into court and sue."

"On what ground?" Deering demanded, rising up to confront Craig eye to eye.

"My reputation has been damaged."

"Let me warn you now, you bring lawyers into this and we'll plow you under! This hospital has one of the best law firms in the city on retainer. If it's a case of matching legal talent, or dollars, you don't stand a chance!"

Craig nodded at the inevitability of Deering's threat.

"We'll let you know about a hearing," Deering said sharply.

After Craig Pierson left the office, both Deering and Ordway were silent until the Administrator asked, "You think he meant it? That he'll sue if we turn down this request?"

274

"I never suspected he'd go *this* far, but he did," Ordway pointed out.

"When you're that young you can be idealistic and unreasonable," Deering said.

"I know one thing: it gets tougher as you get older," Ordway said regretfully.

Deering glanced at him suspiciously. "You're not on his side, are you?"

"Of course not," Ordway was quick to reply.

"Well, I'll talk to Harvey Prince and see what he wants to do."

"You said he was opposed to a hearing," Ordway reminded him.

"That was before there was a threat of a public lawsuit."

"Maybe we should consult our counsel first."

"I already have," Deering admitted. "They were quite sensitive to the possibility of a lawsuit. And they don't like it. Not only the publicity, but the consequences. They don't think there's much chance we'll lose. But if we do, the way juries are acting these days, it could be for a sizable sum. And then there's one other possible consequence. The Hortons might sue for malpractice."

"Well, then?"

"I'm afraid we'll have to let Pierson have his hearing," Deering concluded.

"How do we go about it?" Ordway asked. "This department's never had such a hearing before."

"Our counsel says it can be done either of two ways. Before our own Medical Board, or we can assemble a panel of experts from the State Specialty Board," Deering volunteered at once, betraying how intensively he had investigated the subject.

"Our own Medical Board . . ." Ordway appeared to consider soberly. He did not reveal to Deering that he

275

was actually thinking the hospital Medical Board, composed of older men, zealous in protecting the hospital's reputation, and themselves, from any scandal, would turn such a hearing into a drumhead court-martial. Their judgment would be swift and rendered with such finality that Pierson's termination would be viewed with the same surgical effect as when one excised a cancerous tumor. At any cost, Ordway felt he must avoid submitting Craig's fate to the hospital's own Medical Board.

So he asked Deering, "To give every appearance of being fair and unprejudiced, wouldn't it look better if the decision was made by an independent entity like a panel of outside experts?"

"Good point, Clint," Deering said. "I'll discuss it with the lawyers right away."

"Meantime, I'll compose a list of able, experienced men who might serve."

"Excellent," Deering said, and left Ordway's office.

Alone, Clinton Ordway picked up his *Directory of Medical Specialists.* Exasperating as young Pierson could be, Ordway felt he was at least entitled to a fair hearing. So he settled down with the volume from which he might assemble a list of possible judges for the hearing.

While Ordway was so engaged, Walter Deering was on the phone from his own office. He thought the matter of sufficient importance to interrupt Harvey Prince in surgery.

"Harve? Walter."

"Yes?"

"There's going to be a hearing."

"The Medical Board?"

"Ordway suggested, and our counsel agrees, it

276

should be an independent board of experts. Would seem more impartial, and have more weight. So Ordway's making up a list of possibles."

"Good idea."

"Any suggestions?" Deering asked.

"Show me the list the moment you get it," Harvey Prince said cryptically, not wishing the nurse who held the phone for him to be privy to the exact nature of the conversation.

Clinton Ordway studied the list of Ob-Gyn specialists who were members of the Board of Governors of the District College of Obstetricians and Gynecologists. He knew them all, by reputation or personally, having met most of them at various seminars and meetings.

He evaluated the dozen most likely names, admitting to himself that unfortunately by age, status, and other indices, all were men who would likely favor Prince.

Chief among the candidates was Joseph Simmons, Chairman of the Board of Governors. A well-established surgeon, past middle age, he was renowned for his resistance to the changeover from independent attending practitioners to hospitals that were staffed by full-time men. One of the diehards of the old system, Simmons would surely condemn any young upstart resident who had the audacity to disagree with an attending surgeon. Still, Simmons was Chairman. One could not bypass him without creating a good deal of suspicion, if not resentment.

Ordway felt forced to go through the formality of asking Simmons to preside, hoping that the surgeon's backlog of cases would prevent him from serving. That would give Ordway a free hand in inviting other men. Surely out of the twelve men on the Board of Governors there must be three who, if they were not entirely impartial, would at least be understanding in their judgment of a young man like Craig Pierson.

The question in Ordway's mind became one of strategy. How to present the subject to Simmons in such a way as to ensure his refusal. He considered writing a long letter stating the situation in such complicated terms as to put Simmons under the impression the hearing would consume a number of days and be a serious interruption in his heavy schedule. Ordway made several attempts to draft such a letter, but gave up, realizing that the less of this matter he committed to paper, the better. No one had any way of knowing how far this case might be pursued. Counsel for the hospital had already warned Deering that an appeal to the courts from such a hearing was possible.

So Ordway decided that once he had cleared his list with Deering, he would call Simmons and handle the matter informally, by phone.

Deering had returned the list, with the approval of the attorneys, who agreed that Simmons was the first man who had to be invited.

Ordway deliberately chose to make his call to Simmons at a time when he was likely to catch the surgeon during his O.R. schedule. Caught at such a moment, he was bound to refuse.

Joseph Simmons was a tall man, with the frame of an athlete. His florid face was the result of a touch of high blood pressure, plus a spartan devotion to physical exercise which included jogging and weekends of golf. When his own internist warned him against his tendency to overdo in face of his blood pressure, Simmons, the patient, would only laugh and say, "You

278

sonofabitch, I'll outlive you by ten years! I'll be one of your pallbearers!"

Simmons was equally dogmatic about and intolerant of change. There were days when he confessed to his closest professional intimates, "I hope to go out at the operating table. But before all these damned new-fangled government rules and regulations ruin the practice of surgery. Full-time surgeons are nothing but hired hands. It's disgraceful. Thank God, I can retire anytime I want to. And I will, before I let any of these young squirts crowd me."

He treated the residents and interns at General Hospital as his enemies. He never tired of telling them how when he first became an intern he had received only thirty dollars a month and board. He had been forced to be suitably and neatly attired at all times. In his day, no young man would dare appear in the O.R. sporting a beard. As for women residents in surgery, unheard of! They didn't have the strength, the sheer manual strength necessary to do surgery. These days...he would say...these days...and then leave his sentences unfinished for lack of sufficiently strong invective to convey his resentment.

Knowing Simmons' propensity for swift, negative decisions, Ordway placed the call, identified himself to the operator, and succeeded in overcoming her protests about not disturbing Dr. Simmons in surgery.

Simmons was at the table having just completed the removal of a cervical cancer and was about to close up the patient when the O.R. phone rang insistently.

"Who the hell is that?" Simmons demanded. He turned to an assisting nurse, and had to bend a bit when he commanded, "Wipe!" She wiped his damp, florid face with a gauze pad. The phone rang several more times.

"Somebody answer the damned thing!" Simmons called out angrily.

One of the unsterile nurses lifted the phone.

"It's for you, Doctor."

"If it's my office, tell them it can wait. If it's Admitting, I'll need three more beds tomorrow. And my regular O.R. schedule for the rest of the week." With that, Simmons turned back to the table.

"It's a Dr. Ordway."

"Ordway? Okay," Simmons agreed grudgingly. He turned to one of the residents and ordered, "Close her up, Junior. And don't leave your monogram on the sutures."

Simmons strode to the phone, bent so that the short nurse could hold it to his ear, and barked, "Yes, Ordway?"

Encouraged by the impatience in Simmons' voice, Ordway began a long, involved, deliberately obfuscating explanation of the nature of the call. He was halfway through when Simmons interrupted.

"I'll be glad to chair that hearing! What day do you plan to have it?"

Taken aback by such a prompt and eager acceptance, Ordway tried to warn, "It might take several days. Perhaps as long as a week."

"That's okay!" Simmons agreed vigorously. "Be glad to do it."

"Good, good," Ordway said with little enthusiasm. "I'll try to round up two other men of equal standing. . . ."

"I'll save you the trouble!" Simmons interrupted. "I'll select two men from the Board of Governors."

Ordway had no alternative but to agree. "Of course. I was going to confine my choices to the Board."

"I'll get back to you with the names. And also a date we all agree would be best."

280

"Yes, of course," Ordway agreed. "You understand the nature of the hearing sufficiently to explain it to them?"

"Harvey Prince briefed me on the situation. I got the whole picture," Simmons confided vengefully.

Chapter Twenty-Five

Clinton Ordway had called Kate Lindstrom to suggest a meeting. Rather than make such a meeting the subject for hospital gossip by being seen together in the staff cafeteria, Ordway suggested the small restaurant around the corner. There, over coffee, which neither of them touched, Ordway explained the situation, summing it up by saying, "with Simmons, Kearney, and Fein on the panel, it won't be a hearing, it'll be a lynching."

"I know," Kate admitted.

"Then do something!"

"What?"

"Talk him out of it!"

"I can't," Kate said simply.

"Can't? Or won't?" Ordway asked.

"Both. I *won't* because he's old-fashioned about one thing. Integrity. He believes in it. I won't rob him of that. And I *can't*, because I don't think I would succeed."

"Then warn him he's not only going up against Prince. But against three men who look on themselves as the last defenders of a citadel called private practice. They're pledged to beat off the onslaught of the younger generation or die in the attempt. Harvey

Prince couldn't have picked three men who would favor him more."

"I know," Kate said, thoughtful, frightened, yet quiet and contained. "I'll do what I can."

Kate Lindstrom spent the rest of the afternoon dealing with psychiatric outpatients who presented their pitiful problems to her.

From moment to moment she found herself barely listening to their complaints as her mind kept dwelling on her own. If it were not for their dependence on her, she would have fled the clinic and found some quiet place to confront her own difficulties.

Her last patient, a young woman who was being treated as part of a rehabilitation program for child-abusing parents, stopped in the midst of reciting her experiences of the past week to stare at Kate. "Doctor, are you listening to me?"

"Yes, yes, of course." Kate was too quick to assure her.

"I thought . . . I don't know . . . it was like you was off somewhere else . . . like you felt that there was no use listening, that you can't help me, that no one can . . ." The young woman started to weep, tears coursing down her thin, pale cheeks.

"You've made a great deal of progress in the past six weeks. You're coming along fine. Just fine!" Kate insisted, angry that she had permitted a personal problem to rob this unfortunate young woman of help she desperately needed.

"I didn't do anything to Janie this week . . . I swear, I never touched her. There was times . . . times . . ." The woman faltered.

"Say it," Kate coaxed gently.

"Times I felt I might . . . times I . . . I . . ."

"Times you wanted to?" Kate asked.

"Yes," the woman admitted. "But I didn't, I didn't!" she said, a bit proud. "So it is getting better, isn't it? Isn't it, Doctor?"

"Yes, it's getting better," Kate reassured her.

The day was over finally. Kate Lindstrom completed her notes on the patients she had seen. Then, instead of getting out of her lab coat and into her street clothes, she went up to the Psychiatric Wing. She strode down the corridor past rooms with locked doors, past patients who wandered aimlessly up and down the corridors, dressed in robes and wearing slippers, the uniform of that army of invalids of long occupation.

She found room 317. The door was partly open. She knocked nevertheless.

"Yes?" a young, anxious voice called out.

"Dr. Lindstrom. May I come in?"

"Oh, please."

Cynthia Horton was sitting in a big leather armchair, dressed not in her robe, but in a plaid skirt and a cherry-red cashmere sweater. The bright cashmere set off her shining black hair. It was most encouraging to Kate, until she fixed on Cynthia's eyes. The tension was still there. And signs of much crying. She rose to greet Kate.

"Beautiful skirt," Kate said. "And I love that color on you."

"I wanted to look bright for them. Cheerful," Cynthia confessed. "I've given them so much pain."

"Then your dad'll be here, too?"

"Mom's picking him up at court. They'll be by as soon as they've had dinner. Dad never eats when he's on trial. He spends his lunch recess going over notes he's made on the morning's testimony." Suddenly Cynthia realized, "Why did you ask about Dad?"

"I have to talk to him."

"About Dr. Pierson," Cynthia concluded.

"Yes."

"Is there trouble? Is it about me?" Cynthia asked.

Not wishing to add to her burdens, Kate said, "It's a personal matter. Ask your dad to call me. I'll wait in the residents' office."

"Soon as he gets here," Cynthia promised. "Do you really like this color on me?"

"Yes."

"It was Pete's favorite color," Cynthia said.

Kate noticed that she spoke of her fiancé in the past tense.

Cynthia realized it too.

"I keep waiting . . . for him to come back, to say something," Cynthia confessed.

"Give him time to get adjusted," Kate tried to encourage, concealing her own doubts.

"You think he will?" Cynthia asked. "Get adjusted?" Then she confessed, "The last time he was here I had a flush. I tried to conceal it, but I couldn't. I just couldn't. Do you think it scared him?"

"Possibly," Kate said. "But he'll get over it, I'm sure."

"I don't want him to just get over it. And I don't want him to come back out of pity. Or because he's afraid of what people might say. I only want him back if he wants me," she said staunchly. But beneath her protest, Kate could detect Cynthia's strong need to have him back on any basis.

More than an hour later, Arthur Horton sought out Kate Lindstrom in the Psychiatric residents' office.

"When Cynthia told me, I suspected it would take more than a phone call. What is it, Doctor?"

284

She told him of the impending hearing. Arthur Horton nodded gravely and advised, "He can demand legal representation at such a hearing. And I'd be most willing to serve. At no fee, I might add. As a personal as well as a professional duty."

"Then may I talk to Craig and tell him?"

"By all means."

"Thank you; thank you very much."

"Now you tell me something," Horton said.

"Anything."

"Cynthia?" was all he asked.

"She's making progress. But I think it will depend to a large degree on what Pete finally decides," Kate admitted.

"If he deserts her, there's liable to be another 'episode'? Is that it?"

"It happened once before" was all Kate would say.

Horton nodded gravely. "Tell your young man to get in touch with me."

"This is a conflict between doctors," Craig exploded. "It ought to be settled by doctors. I don't want outsiders involved!"

"But Ordway says it's a stacked panel," Kate protested.

"I never expected anything else," Craig said. "I'll convince them or I'll lose. I can't be any worse off than I am now!"

His unusual outburst warned Kate that more was involved in his reaction than deciding whether to have counsel represent him.

"Craig? Darling?" she coaxed gently.

Her tone defused his anger. He admitted, "I called the hospital to check on Dad. Hypostatic pneumonia. One of the complications with orthopedic patients

285

who have to be immobilized. They've got him on antibiotics."

"How does it look?"

"They won't know for forty-eight hours. I ought to be there."

"Then go."

"Now, with that hearing coming up?"

"You go! I'll attend to everything here," Kate said.

"Talk to Horton. Thank him. But explain."

"Of course."

When she called Horton, the lawyer warned, "Foolish. He precipitated this by being emotional. He's going to be even more emotional at that hearing."

"I know," Kate admitted, "but he insists this is a matter for doctors to decide."

"Tell him if he needs advice, I'll be available at all times."

"Is there any advice you can give me now?" Kate asked.

"If you can't find weaknesses in your adversary's case, look for ways to impeach his witnesses," Horton advised sagely.

Kate was silent as she relfected on that.

"By the way, when you need my help on the appeal . . ."

"You think we'll have to appeal?" Kate asked.

"With a panel like that, Pierson'll lose," Horton predicted.

Harvey Prince was savoring the excellent brandy of which he kept a plentiful supply at Rita Hallen's apartment. In accordance with their long-established and discreet habit, they had had dinner in a small Italian restaurant where Prince was well known and his identity carefully guarded by the proprietor. They had returned to Rita's place, as they had so many times in past years. Some brandy, some hospital gossip, then the inevitable sexual encounter.

This night Rita appeared even more on edge than she had been recently. She refused to take any brandy, but stared at his glass as he emptied it sip by sip. Resenting her impatience, he deliberately took more time with his brandy.

When she could bear it no longer, she demanded, "Is it going to take all night for you to finish that goddamned drink?"

"Rita . . . Rita, darling," he comforted, "I'm sorry. I was enjoying it, and enjoying looking at you."

He put his arms around her, kissed her—a quick, virtually antiseptic kiss, which did not escape her notice.

"Don't do me any favors!" she exploded viciously.

"Darling, what is it? What's wrong?" he asked, prepared to listen to another of her frequent demands for marriage. He was unprepared for her answer.

"That was a stupid thing you did," she accused.

"What?"

"That hearing!"

"I didn't ask for it. That young bastard Pierson did."

"You could have stopped it."

"It's the best way to get rid of him. And make sure he's shut up forever."

"*After* the damage is done," Rita pointed out.

"Damage?" Prince asked, chuckling. "With Simmons, Kearney, and Fein he hasn't got a chance. Clever move on Simmons' part. A nice balanced panel. A WASP, a Catholic, and a Jew. Too bad they didn't expand the panel by one member and find a black. These days every group has to be represented. Otherwise the Supreme Court might say it's illegal."

Harvey Prince laughed, raised his brandy glass, and downed the last of the pungent liquor in one final swallow. He embraced Rita once more, but her rigidity warned him.

"Rita?"

"What about the side effects?"

"What side effects?" he asked, irritated now.

"Who was in the O.R. when you made the decision to do a bilateral?"

"The whole crew. Why?"

"Who was closest to the table—who heard the conversation between you and Pierson? Who is most likely to be called to testify?"

"Carlyle, you..." he had started to enumerate, when the cause of her concern suddenly became clear to him. "You mean, what happens if you're called to testify?"

"Yes!"

"Just tell the truth. The lab report. The disagreement. My decision," Prince said. "I wouldn't ask you to do anything else."

"What if Pierson asks about *us*?"

Prince hesitated a moment. "Oh, I see what you mean."

"What better way for him to try to break down my testimony than to ask questions about *us*?"

"Men like Simmons, Kearney, and Fein are not going to be influenced by gossip. They'll only want to hear the medical facts involved."

"*They* won't be influenced," Rita agreed. "But the word will get around. After all, this hearing will attract a lot of attention. Then what happens?"

"It'll be forgotten the day after the hearing is over," Prince said glibly. But he was beginning to appreciate the validity of Rita's fear. Also the opportunity it presented him to be free of her and what had become an onerous involvement.

288

As if she read his mind, Rita Hallen turned away. In a moment he could tell from the tremor of her shoulders that she was weeping. Guilt made him comfort her. He embraced her and pressed her head against his chest.

"Rita . . . darling . . . please . . ."

"It'll become a public scandal. And then . . ." she sobbed.

"And then things will go back to being exactly what they've always been." He led her toward the bedroom. She went willingly. Not because she believed him but because she desperately felt she had to.

After, in the darkness, when she had fetched him another brandy, he lay on his back, sipping it and talking freely. "I don't think Pierson would dare question you. After all there's that resident in Psychiatric, the girl he's practically living with. I'm sure he wouldn't want that to come out."

Because she had been sexually satisfied and was grateful, Rita burrowed closer to his naked body and agreed, "I'm sure he wouldn't."

"Come to think of it," Prince said, "that might be very interesting."

"What?"

"I'm going to have a look at that Horton chart. If I remember correctly, that Lindstrom girl was involved at an early stage of the Horton case. It might be a hell of an idea to call *her* to testify. Could serve two purposes. Use her testimony in some way. And very subtly remind Pierson that if he mentions *us*, I'll mention *them*. Yes, first thing tomorrow I'll get my hands on that chart."

His sudden inspiration so delighted him that he felt inspired to make love to Rita a second time in the same evening—most unusual in recent years. Though this time it was quite mechanical, and his thoughts were elsewhere. He must get possession of that chart. His testimony must take advantage of every possible fact revealed by it. He must be prepared to explain any damaging entries. He was delighted now that he had earlier removed the page that contained Pierson's defiant and disputatious entry about his decision in the O.R.

One thing more he must do. Rita's fear about gossip did not disturb him. But there was one potential witness of greater consequence who did. Burt Carlyle.

As he was dressing to go home, Prince said suddenly, "I'll have a talk with Carlyle."

"Don't forget they're friends. Pierson and Carlyle."

"I know. But Carlyle's a bright, ambitious young man. He knows that friendship won't buy you a cup of coffee in these times."

"Don't do anything without talking it over with your lawyer first," she advised.

"Lawyer? Hell, you don't think I'm going to make that young bastard the emotional underdog by walking in with a lawyer while he comes in alone?" Harvey Prince smiled. "Don't worry, baby, when it comes to handling himself on his feet, your Harvey is as good as they come.

"You haven't seen bedside manner until you see me in action on Monday!" he anticipated.

Chapter Twenty-Six

The next morning when he arrived at the hospital, Harvey Prince went directly to the Psychiatric floor and examined the chart of Cynthia Horton. Making what seemed a plausible excuse to the charge nurse, he borrowed the chart for several hours.

In kind, the chart nurse pretended to be unmindful of Prince's unusual action. She waited until Dr. Kate Lindstrom came on duty and reported to her.

When the chart was returned later that afternoon, Kate sat down alone in the residents' room and studied it carefully, entry by entry. Aside from the single page that had earlier been replaced to delete Craig's dissenting opinion, nothing in the entire long and complicated chart appeared to have been changed or tampered with in any way. She wondered to what purpose Harvey Prince meant to put the chart.

Meanwhile, Kate had an investigation of her own to pursue. Somehow that became more urgent now that Prince had resorted to this strange tactic.

Dr. Craig Pierson raced up the steps of Good Samaritan Hospital and into the elevator. At the third floor, he hurried to the semiprivate room where he had last visited his father. The second bed was occupied; his father's bed was crisply made up but empty.

"Where is he? What happened?" Craig demanded of the other patient.

"They came and took him last night."

"Took him? What do you mean? Where?" Without waiting for a reply, Craig raced down the corridor to the desk. "Mr. Pierson—where is he?"

"They moved him up to I.C.U. last night," the charge nurse said.

"Why? Did he have another coronary?" Craig demanded.

"I don't know. I wasn't on duty. I.C.U.'s up on the seventh floor."

Impatient with hospital elevators, which always

seemed the slowest in the world, Craig raced up four flights of stairs, found the directional arrow to I.C.U., and slowed only when he approached the glass wall that sealed off that unit from the rest of the noisy floor. Out of concern for the other patients, he entered softly and asked in a whisper, "Mr. Pierson?"

A young bearded cardiac resident said, "Room nine."

"What's he here for?" Craig asked. When the resident resented his question, he explained, "I'm his son and a physician."

The resident now became cooperative. "His orthopod figured with his cardiac history, and now with pneumonia, he'd be better off up here where we can monitor him constantly."

"How's he doing?"

"So far so good," the resident assured him easily.

But when Craig stared into his eyes, the resident limited his assurance: ". . . considering the state of his condition."

"Dad?" Craig asked softly. Bill Pierson's eyes opened, closed, then opened again suddenly.

"They shouldn't have bothered you, son," he said weakly.

Craig spoke to his father, but kept glancing at the monitor behind his bed, watching the blips dance across the screen. They were as slow and tired as his father's heart must be. He slipped into the chair alongside the bed, took his father's hand. It was thin, cold, blue-veined, mottled with brown spots which age had tattooed there.

"What are they doing to me?"

"Just precautionary, Dad. They want to make sure nothing happens," Craig assured.

292

"I thought . . ." But Bill Pierson did not continue for fear of recalling once more the illness he had concealed years ago.

"No, Dad, it's not another coronary," Craig reassured him. "So just rest, relax, let the antibiotics go to work on that pneumonia."

Content to lie there, his hand held in the affectionate grasp of his son, Bill Pierson felt at peace and secure. In a while, without opening his eyes, he said, "Remarkable what they do these days. My father was forty-two when he died from a heart attack. Here I am seventy-one, and still going strong. Well, maybe not so strong. But still going. Because of young men like you. Makes me proud, son, that I had a little hand in it. Seen your mother?"

"I came here straight from the airport."

"Call her. Tell her you're here." The old man chuckled. "Soon as she wipes her eyes, she'll go right into the kitchen and start cooking. And you better be ready to eat. A lot. You hear me, son?"

"I know, Dad."

"Go call her!" he insisted.

Craig went to the pay phone just outside I.C.U., a phone from which many sad calls had been made in the eight years since the unit had been set up.

"Hello?" his mother responded, in a voice that seemed to expect bad news.

"Mom?"

"Craig? Son? Where are you?"

"At the hospital with Dad."

"What happened?" she demanded, her voice rising in pitch and concern.

"Nothing. Just thought I'd come take a look," Craig said. "He's fine, fine."

"Thank God. I was so worried . . ."

293

"I'll check with the doctors, then come out to the house."

"I'd better come in. They only let me see him twice a day. Once before lunch. And for a short time before dinner," his mother said.

"I'll be here, waiting. I love you, Mom."

"I know, I know," she said, but sadly.

He was about to hang up when there was a flurry of activity outside the phone booth. Several doctors and nurses raced toward I.C.U. He followed them. When he passed beyond the glass wall, he could see them converge on the cubicle where his father lay.

He recognized their efforts, the equipment, the hushed excitement. He raced to the door to hear the resident say, "Okay!" A technician activated the two paddles that had been placed on his father's chest and back. The body heaved. But there was no other response. Again the resident gave the command. A second jolt did not shock his father's heart into beating again. The line on the monitor remained flat, the sound an ominous monotone of warning. The third jolt of electricity accomplished nothing.

Craig pushed aside the emergency crew and the equipment and began to apply tremendous manual resuscitation. He worked until his sweat dropped off his face onto his father's bare chest. In a while, exhausted, and acknowledging the fact of death, he slumped on his father's body and wept. The resident cleared the room, permitting Craig to be alone with his father's lifeless body.

For a whole day and night he tried to reach Kate. She was not at the hospital, not at her apartment. He called her home in Wisconsin. She was not there. Nor did her mother know where she might be.

294

He was puzzled, and distressed. She had never met his father, but he had told her so much about him that he was sure she would want to be at the funeral.

He called Ordway to explain that he could not return in time for the start of the hearing. Ordway was sympathetic, but could not avoid mentioning that a delay would only infuriate the panel, all three of them extremely busy surgeons who had rearranged their schedules to be free on Monday.

The funeral was a small affair, under the guidance of the mortician who had been one of his dad's customers in years gone by. Friends came, including some Craig had not seen since high school days.

From them he learned how inordinately proud his father had been, how he had bragged about him. The man he had considered so silent during his lifetime, so incapable of expressing his feelings had obviously been far less secretive when it came to sharing his pride with friends and neighbors. The things one learns when it is too late.

Craig asked the minister not to deliver too long or too flowery a eulogy. His father had been a simple man and would have disapproved. The minister spoke briefly and honestly of a man who had devoted his life to making things grow. Green fields, trees, shrubs, hedges, and one son who had grown to manhood to honor his father.

His mother wept silently throughout. At the cemetery, when the coffin began to sink into the fresh brown earth, she faltered and Craig had to support her. Otherwise she comported herself with dignity. Craig knew his father would have been pleased with her quiet acceptance of his death. He would not have wanted a fuss made over him.

Neighbors had prepared for their return from the

cemetery with food, hot coffee, and sufficient people to keep the house from seeming large and empty.

Neighbors, friends, and some of Dad's old customers spent a few warm hours telling and retelling events in his life. Of trees he had saved, and others that he had had to cut down with great regret. They told how he had come out on unexpectedly bitter-cold nights to save shrubs and plants from an untimely freeze.

Mostly they talked of how he had felt about Craig. Craig had been a much greater part of his father's life than even he had suspected.

It was late, and the mourners were gone, when the phone rang.

"Craig?" It was Kate.

"Darling, where've you been? I've been looking all over for you."

"I know. My mother called. What's wrong?"

He told her.

"Oh," she said in a breathless voice that expressed her surprise and her sorrow. "Shall I come? Would it help?"

"I'd love you to meet Mother. But I have to get back. In time for the hearing."

"I'll come anyway," she said, "even if it's only for a few hours."

He went to the small airport to meet her. It was close to midnight when the two-engined plane appeared from out of the low-hanging clouds. Its beams pierced the night to seek out the runway. It touched down with a rasp.

In minutes Kate was in his arms. He knew now how much he had always needed her.

When the two women met, without a word they embraced each other as though they were old friends. Then his mother held Kate off and stared into her face. "I always knew when my Craig chose a girl she would be lovely and beautiful and fine. And you are. I always used to say, 'Dad, when Craig . . .' "

She turned away, wiping her eyes.

Over coffee, his mother asked Kate many questions about herself, her family, her early life. Soon they were exchanging anecdotes and memories. Mother was telling Kate stories about Craig's boyhood, virtually from the time he had been placed in her arms as a tiny stranger. She recalled the time she had first told Craig he was adopted. And of the fights he had had with other kids who were not and who taunted him.

She told of the time he had come home from school with one eye bruised and the other cut over the eyelid. He had been in a fight with two kids who had tried to force him to admit that his mother and father weren't his real parents. He had kept insisting they were the best parents in the world. He had been a stubborn boy, his mother said.

And was still stubborn, Kate reflected. Probably always will be.

His mother had gone up to bed. Kate and Craig remained in the parlor.

"You never told me: where were you for almost two days?" he asked.

"Chasing rainbows," she said ironically.

"What does that mean?"

"Horton advised if you can't attack the case, attack the witnesses. Find some weakness. So I went looking."

"For what?" Craig demanded.

"I was able to get a look at Prince's file in Personnel."

"Why?"

"It kept bugging me. Why, eleven years ago, would a man like Prince leave an excellent hospital and a city where he'd built up a large practice? At a time when he should be reaching the peak of his career, why would he make such a change?"

"What did you find out?"

"I searched his entire file. Everything clean. In fact, his letters of recommendation are so laudatory they're almost embarrassing."

"It didn't take a whole day to go through his file," Craig said.

"I decided to go back to his old hospital and do some checking."

"And?"

"Those letters of recommendation are genuine. I spoke to two men who signed them."

"That shouldn't be any surprise. We know he's a terrific surgeon."

"Still"—Kate hated to abandon her suspicion—"I was so sure. A man like Prince to up and leave a profitable, secure situation? Some doctors leave because of personal friction in a hospital. Or scandal in their personal lives. Or the health demands of a wife or a child. Or because they favor a milder climate or less pressure. None of that applies to Prince. So why?"

Her psychiatrically oriented mind would not permit her to be satisfied with less than a motive that made sense.

When Kate Lindstrom returned to her office in the Psychiatric Wing, she found an accumulation of messages from patients as well as other doctors on staff. There were also three messages from Peter Tompkins,

Cynthia Horton's fiancé. Erstwhile fiancé, Kate reminded herself grimly. She was strongly tempted not to return his calls. But precisely because she was, she made it her first order of business.

The agitated young man desperately pleaded that Kate see him at once. She could find room for him only at the end of her already crowded day.

"You've got to help me!" were his first words when he confronted Kate Lindstrom in one of the private consultation rooms.

"Exactly what kind of help do you want?"

"It was bad enough before . . ." he started to say.

"Just how bad *was* it?" Kate prodded, to make him confront his own situation more realistically.

Tompkins stared at Kate resentfully. He started to pace, exhibiting not only his torment, but also his need to avoid looking at her as he confessed.

"It was the way things kept growing worse. At first the operation was to be a minor procedure. Yes, they hinted it might possibly develop into something serious. But not that serious. Suddenly, they'd destroyed any chance of our having kids of our own. I could live with that. But then her thrombosis. And everything that flowed from that. Including . . ."

"What it might possibly do to the sexual part of your lives?"

"Yes . . .," Tompkins started to say. "Then once she tried to commit suicide, I had to ask myself, What am I getting into? What if that happened again?"

"Are you sure that's really what troubles you?" Kate asked. Tompkins turned on her to argue, but she continued firmly, "Or is it your own guilt at having precipitated her attempt?"

"I had no way of knowing she hadn't been told!" he defended himself angrily.

"Of course not. Still, it was your note that did it, so

you feel guilty. Is that what you came here to discuss with me—how to deal with your guilt?"

"It's more than that," Tompkins confessed. "I love her, Dr. Lindstrom. I really love her. It's the future I don't know about. Myself. I'm going to need help to find out if I can make our marriage work. Since you know the case so intimately, I want your help."

"That may not be possible," Kate warned.

"Why can't you help me?"

"Mr. Tompkins, sit down." When he hesitated, Kate commanded, "I said, sit down!" Once he had, she continued, "Listen to me very carefully."

He nodded cautiously.

"Cynthia Horton is my patient now. For her to have continued trust in me, I have to be completely honest with her. Before I could treat you, I would have to get her permission."

"I'm sure she'd say yes," he responded quickly.

"Even that is not the point. She loves you. She wants your continued love. Of course she'd agree. The question I have to resolve for myself is this: would my asking her for permission raise such hopes in her that if your treatment didn't work out, she would become so depressed that there might be—"

"Another attempt?" Tompkins anticipated.

"There might be very damaging consequences. I think she's groping her way to a recovery. I don't want to do anything to upset that. So I don't want to ask her just now."

"Then when?" he asked impatiently.

"That will depend on you," Kate said. "You're frightened, and have every right to be. You're confronting a very difficult challenge. In her condition, sex is certainly not impossible, but it might become difficult. Marriage under those circumstances can only

300

succeed if there's understanding, love, patience, un-usual consideration—"

"But you did say it's possible it could succeed," Tompkins interrupted, seeking reassurance.

"There are no quick or easy answers. That's why I don't want you to make any rash promises or resolves. Out of guilt or any other impulse. Think about it. Then if you come back and say you're willing to work at it, hard and earnestly, I'll ask Cynthia for permission to treat you. But I don't want to raise any false hopes in her. Do you understand?" Kate demanded.

Tompkins sat still and silent. Finally, he nodded gravely.

"Call me if you decide you can do it. Don't bother, if you can't," Kate said most professionally. "Until that time, we'll both go on the basis that we have never had this conversation."

On the Friday afternoon before the Monday on which the hearing was to commence, Harvey Prince was completing his sixth case in the O.R. It had been a routine day. Aside from one woman who suffered momentary cardiac arrest in the midst of a hysterectomy, but who had been revived, it had been a day like most others for him. What he had roughly estimated to be an eight-thousand-dollar day.

He permitted Burt Carlyle to finish and close the last patient while Prince himself stripped off his surgical gloves and went to the phone to check his office, call his broker to find out how the market was doing.

Burt was finishing by the time Prince returned to the table.

"Burt, you in a rush?"

"No. Why? What's wrong?" the black resident

asked self-consciously, assuming Prince was criticizing his technique.

"Oh, nothing like that," Prince smiled. "Just thought if you had a little time we might go out and have a drink. It's been a long day. And there's something I want to talk to you about."

"Let me check the floor. If there are no problems, I'm free as the breeze."

"I'll be in the cocktail lounge across the street," Harvey Prince said amiably.

Within half an hour, Burt Carlyle found Harvey Prince nursing a Scotch on the rocks, from the special twenty-year-old blend the bar stocked only for him. Once Burt had been served, Prince began:

"Burt, you and I should've had this talk months ago. But things have been so hectic I haven't had a chance. Practice is growing faster than I can handle. And I can't turn them away. Believe me, it isn't the money. After all, beyond a certain point it's hardly worth my while to take on any more cases, federal and state taxes being what they are. But I have to. Out of regard for those women who come seeking help. They're always recommended by someone—a doctor you know, or a friend, or another grateful patient. I'd have to be pretty coldhearted to turn them away. As I said, things are hectic. Have been. And I guess always will be. So I've been meaning to talk to you but never found the chance."

Prince took another sip of the smooth, icy liquor, savoring the taste of it.

"Burt, I've been watching you for a long time now. I liked the way you did that exenteration on your own some weeks ago. Marvelous. Skillful. Sure. You knew exactly what you were doing every moment. I wouldn't hesitate to entrust any patient of mine to you. So I've thought about it very carefully, and I have come to a decision. I would like you to come into my office as soon as you finish your residency."

Burt Carlyle hoped that his eagerness was not too transparent. Cool, he cautioned himself: play it cool. He must have succeeded, for Prince, anticipating an objection, went on to urge:

"I know what you're thinking: this would remove you from academic medicine. And to that I say, So what? Suppose you stay in academic medicine, become full time. What can you expect? Thirty-five thousand your first year. Small, piddling raises after that until you reach the munificent annual income of fifty thousand a year, sixty?

"My boy, I will guarantee you seventy-five thousand dollars a year to start. After that, write your own ticket. Because I don't expect to practice forever. The time will come when you and the other two men in my office will take over. And there's enough gravy for all of you. I'd say, conservatively, within five years you'll be making a hundred and fifty thousand a year, maybe more!"

Prince chuckled. "So much for academic medicine." He turned more grave now. "There's one other thing, Burt, that you should consider. Power. Leverage with the Board of Trustees. I want to be clear about this. Now I am talking to you as a black man. With the kind of power you'd have working out of my office, you could do a lot for your race.

"You wouldn't be like Reverend Hathaway. He's on the Board only because the Trustees felt they needed a black figurehead to appease the community. He sits there. He listens. Always makes some benign pronouncement or other. But he has no input. Sometimes I think he ought to just make a benediction and leave, for all the good his presence does on the Board.

"But you would have power. There's no reason why

303

you should be the only black resident on Ob-Gyn. There should be more. There can be, if you play your cards right. For that reason alone you ought to think seriously about my offer. Take the weekend to consider it. Talk it over with that lovely wife of yours. Seventy-five thousand a year to start. Think about it. And let me know by Monday."

Harvey Prince was signing the tab when he pretended to suddenly recall, "Oh, I forgot. You can't talk to me on Monday. I'll be busy with that damn hearing. But I'll want your answer as soon as that's over."

Harvey Prince felt satisfied that he had handled the matter most adroitly. He had no doubt at all that Carlyle, ambitious as he was, had got the message. Prince's offer was clearly dependent on what developed during the hearings.

Chapter Twenty-Seven

The hearing In the Matter of the Termination of Dr. Craig Pierson was held in the luxurious boardroom of State University Hospital. It was a long room, with paneled walls of linenfold oak and a polished table of a single majestic plank of Honduran mahogany fifty-four feet in length, and wide enough for the three presiding surgeons to sit abreast at the end of the table.

Simmons sat in the middle, since he was the chairman of the District Board of Governors. On his left sat Dr. James Kearney of Misericordia Hospital, stolid and grim, as usual. On Simmons' right sat Dr. Myron Fein of Mount Zion, a small man, almost tiny, who seemed pleasant and affable. But those who had worked with Fein in the O.R. knew him to be a man of violent rages when the slightest detail went wrong.

Clinton Ordway and Administrator Deering were present to protect the hospital's interests in the event institutional practices came into question during the hearing. It had been suggested that the hospital be represented by an attorney. But since none of the parties had chosen legal counsel, the Board of Trustees had voted against it. Gus Wankel, a close friend of Harvey Prince's, cast the deciding vote, since Prince wanted the hearing to be as private as possible.

The stenotypist, a drably dressed young woman who wore black-framed glasses and whose face revealed only a bored expression, set up her machine and was ready. Simmons, Kearney, and Fein were ready. Sitting on his side of the table, Craig Pierson was ready. Only the place opposite him was empty. The chair designated for Harvey Prince.

Simmons was growing impatient when the door was flung open. Prince entered in great haste.

"Sorry, gentlemen! Very sorry! Emergency. Ectopic! And a hell of a lot further gone than it should be. But she's in good hands. And now, I'm all yours."

He took his place across from Craig.

"Good morning, Pierson," he said in a pleasant and condescending manner.

"Good morning," Craig responded, trying to adhere to Arthur Horton's advice: "Don't let your inner feelings govern your outward attitude. If this becomes a matter of personal hostility, you'll ruin your case."

Prince must have received similar advice from his attorney, but was better able to execute it, for he said, "I understand you've had a serious loss in your family. Terribly sorry."

305

"Thank you," Craig said, wishing his opponent were less pleasant and ingratiating.

"Now, then," Simmons said as he opened the hearing. "As I understand it, we are here because Dr. . . ." Unfamiliar with the name, he had to consult his notes. "Dr. Craig Pierson has been dismissed during the second year of his residency. The causes are insubordination, personality conflicts with attending surgeons, unethical interference in the cases of other surgeons. Upon being dismissed, Dr. Pierson requested a hearing by way of appeal. This hospital, in the interest of fairness, decided to convene such a hearing."

Simmons cleared his throat slightly. "Now, as presiding officer of this panel, I wish to set down some simple rules. We are here to get at the truth. So anything I deem necessary to discover the truth will be allowed. Everything else will be ruled out. We'd like to accomplish this hearing in the swiftest and fairest way possible.

"In short, let's hear both sides. But with dispatch! We have no time for indulgence of either party. One more thing: the decision of this Board will be final and binding on all parties.

"Dr. Pierson, anything you wish to say at the outset?" Simmons inquired suddenly.

In accordance with Horton's instructions, Craig replied, "Since I've been dismissed, I consider myself accused of some wrongdoing. Therefore I would like to hear testimony as to the specific charges before I say anything."

Simmons appeared annoyed with Craig's reply. But Fein smiled. "It seems we have here what we used to call, in the Army, a barracks lawyer. Someone who is not an attorney but intends to act like one."

Simmons turned his attention to Harvey Prince. "Doctor?"

"Are we going to abide by the formality of swearing witnesses?"

"Since this is an official hearing," Simmons declared, "I assume we must. Would you like to be sworn, Doctor?"

"Not yet. But I would like a witness to be sworn."

"Oh, you have a witness waiting?" Simmons asked.

"I have several witnesses."

"The first one, then," Simmons said briskly, to get things moving.

With a smile of smug conceit, Harvey Prince said, "My first witness is Dr. Craig Pierson."

Taken by surprise, Craig flushed in anger, glared at Prince, and turned to Simmons. "I don't choose to testify at this stage of the proceedings, since there has been no testimony against me."

Simmons lowered his glasses and stared over them at Craig as he pronounced, "Since we're not abiding by any stringent legal procedure, I think you should testify, Doctor!" Without waiting for Craig's acquiescence, Simmons instructed the stenotypist, "Administer the usual legal oath!"

Once she had, she nodded to Simmons, who in turn addressed Prince: "Proceed, Doctor."

Prince leaned forward on the table, staring across at Craig as he asked, "Dr. Pierson, in view of the fact that this entire series of events began with a surgical procedure, would you explain to the panel what happened in the O.R. that day?"

"A patient, twenty-two years of age, was presented for an exploratory laparotomy. I scrubbed with Dr. Prince. In fact, I performed the oophorectomy on the right side. It was sent up to the Path Lab for a frozen section. The report came back, borderline mucinous carcinoma of low malignant potential.

"Whereupon Dr. Prince ordered me to remove the left ovary as well."

"And what did *you* do?" Prince interposed quickly.

"I refused."

Kearney took the opportunity to mutter, "We've got some young men like that at Misericordia too."

In a voice that was edged with disapproval, Fein asked, "Young man, you mean to tell us that the surgeon in charge of the case decided on a procedure and you refused to carry it out?"

"There was a good reason—"

"You'll have your turn, Doctor!" Simmons interjected. "Right now, Dr. Prince is submitting his testimony." He turned to Prince. "What happened after that?"

"I completed the procedure myself."

Kearney nodded, endorsing Prince's action.

Lest Kearney prejudge the situation, Craig insisted, "I would like to explain my actions in the O.R."

"Dr. Pierson, no one on this panel intends to deprive you of your chance to defend yourself. But you were the one who asked that Dr. Prince submit his case first. So we will proceed. Dr. Prince?"

"My second witness is Dr. Clinton Ordway."

Ordway glanced at Deering, seeking a cue, for he had not expected to be called. Deering indicated he had to submit, if only to protect the interests of the hospital. Ordway took the oath from the stenotypist.

Prince asked, "Dr. Ordway, would you tell the panel if Dr. Pierson was actually dismissed."

"He was."

"Wasn't he first offered the chance to *resign?*" Prince pursued.

"Yes," Ordway admitted.

"In fact, Doctor, isn't it true that you and I conferred

a number of times to try to keep him out of harm's way? That we agreed to have him removed from my scrub team and we relieved him of any postoperative care of my patients specifically to avoid any further friction?"

"Yes," Ordway had to agree.

"Isn't it also true that Pierson *asked* to be dismissed?"

"It's a technicality, whether a man is asked to resign or is dismissed."

"I want it clear. He was offered the chance to resign, refused, and demanded to be fired. Right or wrong?"

"Right," Ordway was forced to concede.

"So he could demand this hearing," Prince concluded, driving the point home.

"I wouldn't know," Ordway said, in a last effort to shield Craig.

Prince turned to Craig. "Surely Dr. Pierson can tell us, if he would?"

Craig considered avoiding an answer, then decided, and announced firmly, "Yes. That was my reason."

"So you see"—Prince turned to the panel—"we're all here, at great inconvenience and expense of both time and money, to satisfy the capricious whim of this arrogant young man. Whose real purpose escapes me."

With hardly a breath's pause, Prince accused, "Unless he's here to carry out a personal vendetta against *me!*"

"This is a purely professional matter!" Craig shot back.

Prince ignored Craig's explosion and turned back to Ordway. "Tell this panel, Doctor: Didn't this young man criticize my decision during the Pathology Conference?" Ordway hesitated. Prince insisted, "Dr. Ordway, surely you remember?"

Finally Ordway had to confess. "Dr. Pierson did make some critical remarks during the Path Conference."

"Did he also insist on having this case discussed at Grand Rounds? Again critical of my decision?"

"Yes."

"And did he also attempt to have it discussed at the Morbidity and Mortality Conference?"

"It was not discussed," Ordway pointed out.

"The important fact is, this young man tried to have it discussed!" Prince pointed out. Then he turned to the panel, "So, gentlemen, you can see that there's a pattern here of personal vengeance."

Prince shook his head, as if regretful over the entire sad affair. "I don't have to tell you men the continual conflict that goes on between attendings like us and staff men. Judging by the jealousy on the part of young men on their way up, you'd think we got where we are by sheer luck. These days young doctors want to go right to the top without the long, tough climb we had to endure."

Prince continued regretfully, "I dread to think what surgical practice will descend to after we're gone. We're the last of a dying breed, gentlemen. The last of the independent individuals who raised the practice of surgery from a science to an art. Because those who come after us will be safely ensconced in institutions as full-time staff men. Salaried employees. Hired hands. There'll be no incentive to achieve greatness, because there will be no rewards for greatness. I think we've seen the last of the great surgeons," he said sadly, having made the three panel members not only his colleagues but, with himself, the beleaguered defenders of a professional way of life which had been bountiful to all of them.

Craig interrupted, "Dr. Prince, are you testifying, or is Dr. Ordway testifying?"

Prince turned on him. "Young man, I'll continue until the chairman of this hearing asks me not to!" With that he turned to Simmons, who rendered a small nod of permission to continue.

"As I was about to say," Prince resumed, with the air of an aggrieved victim, "for reasons that will become quite apparent later, from the mouth of another witness, this young man resents me. He has embarked on a campaign of professional vilification against me."

"That's not true!" Craig shot back.

"And the result is this hearing. Gentlemen, I must apologize to you for this whole regrettable episode."

Fein agreed compassionately: "I know how you feel, Dr. Prince, when a man with your record has to justify himself. It's the fate of our generation, I suppose, to be accused, vilified, and forced to defend ourselves."

"You'll appreciate that even more," Prince said, "when you've examined the rest of the record in this case. He reached under the table for his attaché case and produced a thick copy of a patient's chart. He slapped it down on the conference table with dramatic impact.

"This," he announced, "is a Xerox of Cynthia Horton's chart. It contains all the facts in her case. Signs and symptoms. Diagnosis. Day-to-day condition of the patient. Surgical procedure. Postoperative plan. Complications, if any. You gentlemen are free to consult it." He pushed the fat document toward Simmons.

"Before you gentlemen examine that chart, I want

to warn you. One entry has been removed!" Craig charged.

Simmons looked to Prince. "Doctor, has this chart been tampered with in any way?"

"Of course it has," Prince conceded, far too readily, to Craig's surprise.

"Under what circumstances?" Kearney asked, leaning forward for the first time.

"After surgery, I came down onto the floor and wrote up what I had done. And also my notes for the post-op plan. Thereafter, Dr. Pierson wrote on the same page—with quite a flourish, I might add—his complete disagreement with my decision. And his own recommendation for the manner in which he thought surgery should have been carried out."

Prince smiled, giving every appearance of being regretful. "At the time, never suspecting the extent of this young man's vendetta against me, I dismissed it as a rude, impulsive, immature act. And most unwise. So, to protect him from charges of insubordination— solely for his sake—I removed that page and rewrote my entry. You will find it here. It is the one page that is shorter than all the rest. In view of what's happened since, I regret having done that. I wish it were there now so you men could see it for yourselves. The most impudent, insubordinate note I've ever seen in any patient's chart."

Craig looked to Ordway to respond. But the chief was already under Administrator Deering's forbidding glare.

Craig slowly sank back in his chair, realizing that Prince had turned an outright forgery into a strong argument in his own behalf. Prince was as shrewd a tactician as he was a surgeon.

"But, gentlemen, the chart you have before you is incomplete in other important aspects too. I needn't tell you how often the patient's attitude affects the nature and the outcome of her treatment.

"We're in a specialty in which we deal not only with the patient's body but her emotions as well. That was more true in this case than most. To appreciate the pressures on me in this case I must ask you to be indulgent so I can give you a more complete view of this patient than is in the written record.

"Dr. Simmons, would you turn to the very first page and see who it was who took the history of Cynthia Horton on her admission to the hospital?"

Simmons leafed through the chart to find the page designated GYNECOLOGIC HISTORY. "It's signed by Dr. Pierson."

"Gentlemen, I don't know the procedure in your hospitals, but surely you don't have a second-year resident take a history in a routine gynecological case."

Myron Fein observed, "Interns—that's always the job of interns."

"And yet here we have a second-year resident taking such a history. Strange, isn't it?" Prince asked, intriguing the panel to pursue the question.

Fein turned to Craig. "Doctor, that's a logical question. I hope you have an equally logical answer."

"An intern, a man named Blinn, had gone in to take her history. But he didn't succeed."

"You don't have to be a genius to take a history," Fein remarked intolerantly.

"The patient was extremely tense and unresponsive," Craig explained. "In a way, you might say she was in shock. Emotional shock. After all, she was only twenty-two, looking forward to getting married in four weeks. And suddenly she found herself in a hospital facing an exploratory. With all the possibilities that threatens."

Kearney leaned forward. "Doctor Pierson, would

you say she was more tense and emotional than the situation justified?"

"She has a personal history which colored her outlook on life."

"And that is?" Kearney persisted.

"When I asked about the incidence of carcinoma among her close female relatives, she confessed she had no knowledge of her natural family. You see, she was adopted."

"Still, you succeeded in getting a history on her, whereas the intern did not," Fein remarked.

"She trusted me because we have something in common. You see, I too am adopted. So she felt able to confide in me rather freely."

Fein was satisfied with Craig's answer. Simmons was not.

"Doctor, you said she confided in you rather freely. What did she confide; what did she say?"

"It's highly personal and of no relevance to his hearing," Craig demurred.

"You might be suspected of withholding important evidence," Simmons threatened.

Considering the alternative for a moment, Craig acquiesced. "She felt—has felt, from her earliest years—that she has been the victim of fate. That she had been cast out. That destiny would prevent her from enjoying the good life that other young women she knew were privileged to have."

Prince intervened: "Dr. Pierson, would you say she was obsessed with dying at a very young age?"

"I wouldn't say obsessed."

"Deeply concerned, then?" Prince insisted.

"Yes; yes, she was," Craig was forced to concede.

Having established that point, Prince addressed the panel. "Now, gentlemen, I wish you would consult

314

her chart and see under what conditions she finally signed the consent form."

Simmons flipped through lab reports, C.B.C.s, X-rays, scans until he found the signed consent form and the note that accompanied it.

"Who is Dr. K. Lindstrom?" Simmons asked.

Prince said, "A psychiatric resident on staff here."

"A psychiatric resident?" Fein asked, startled. "To get a consent form signed?"

"Is he available for questioning?" Simmons asked.

"She," Prince corrected, then added quickly, "I think she must be asked to appear."

"Then we'll take a recess and resume when Dr. Lindstrom appears. See that she's here within fifteen minutes!"

Chapter Twenty-Eight

During the recess, Harvey Prince was too obvious about isolating himself from the panel to give the impression that he did not know them well, had not sat with them on numerous committees over the years. He studiously referred to his notes, of which he had a thick folder. On occasion, when it seemed his notes demanded he refer to Cynthia Horton's chart, he would slip down to the end of the hearing table and riffle through the pages seeking a particular entry.

Meanwhile, Craig Pierson sat immobile, making every effort not to surrender to the panic that had begun to overtake him. He had never before been involved in a legal action. To suddenly face three men who had the absolute power to determine his professional destiny was a new and terrifying experience. They were no longer doctors but judges. Three men, obviously set against him, who could decide whether he would be fired in disgrace or be permitted to remain with his reputation intact. He had begun to regret having demanded a hearing.

And Kate? Craig had deliberately not involved her, had even forbidden her to be present, not wanting to jeopardize her professional career. Now Prince had summoned her. What could he ask her? How would she respond? Of course she would be loyal to Craig, but would that in itself discredit her defense of him?

Craig was pondering those possibilities when Kate arrived, in her white lab coat, an eager look on her lovely face. She made straight for Craig, sank into the chair beside him, took his hand, leaned close, and whispered, "I haven't been able to do any work for worrying about you, darling. I'm glad you finally sent for me."

"I didn't send for you," he whispered.

"Then who?"

"Goldfingers."

"What does he want?"

"Something to do with Cynthia's signing the consent form."

Before Kate could respond, Simmons was rapping on the shiny mahogany table, calling the hearing to order.

"Dr. Prince, you wished this witness to appear?"

"Indeed I did." He smiled across the table at Kate. "Good morning, Doctor."

"Good morning," Kate said, wary and tense.

"Dr. Lindstrom, a question has come up about an entry in a patient's chart. I thought you could enlighten the panel."

316

"I'll do my best," Kate said, tightening her grip on Craig's hand under the table.

"Good," Prince said. "A consent form for surgery is usually secured by the surgeon or a resident on the service. But in this one case, it seems the consent form was secured from the patient by you, a psychiatrist. Would you explain why?"

Kate glanced at Craig, then stared across the table at Prince. He smiled at her so paternally that she knew she was being entrapped.

Simmons nudged: "Dr. Lindstrom?"

"Yes, of course," Kate began. "The patient was unusually apprehensive. She refused to sign the consent form when it was presented to her by the resident—"

Prince interrupted, "*Which* resident?"

"Dr. Pierson," Kate admitted. "So he sent for me, thinking I might reassure her and persuade her to sign. Which I did. That's all that happened."

"That's all?" Prince repeated sarcastically, casting doubt on her choice of words. "Surely there must be more. For example, what did you say to her? What did she say to you?"

"That is privileged, between patient and psychiatrist," Kate responded.

"We're all doctors in this room. Except Mr. Deering. And we'll exclude him if you wish. But I think we're entitled to know what was said in this most unusual circumstance. I've been informed that even in a courtroom you'd have to testify to what was said before you were able to get this consent form signed."

Once Simmons had had Deering leave the room, he instructed Kate, "Doctor, we are all physicians here. The confidentiality that binds you binds us. You are ordered to speak fully."

Having no alternative, Kate began, "I found the pa-

317

tient to be tense. Quite suspicious of all doctors. In fact, she even accused Dr. Prince of doing many unnecessary surgical procedures."

"I resent that!" Prince interrupted angrily.

"I was asked to relate fully what happened during my conversation with the patient," Kate explained sweetly. "I pointed out that in her case all the doctors involved were only trying to save her life. That she had this unfounded fear because she had been deserted in infancy. And she feared that at some crucial moment in the operating room she might be deserted again. . . . It's not unusual for a patient to be extremely anxious when facing exploratory surgery. She was more extreme than normal."

Fein leaned forward, staring at Kate. "Doctor, how did her anxiety manifest itself?"

"She talked of things in the past tense. Her impending marriage, for example. She seemed to have given up hope. I considered that extremely dangerous. When a cancer patient acquiesces in the disease, her chances of recovery or survival drop sharply. We've made studies of that."

"Dr. Lindstrom," Kearney interjected, "would you say that the patient was so seriously disturbed that she had given up on her own survival?"

"The logical end of her fears—her thwarted marriage, the findings she anticipated during surgery— her whole outlook was so fatalistic that one could assume she had accepted death as a likely outcome."

"I see," Kearney said, attaching great significance to Kate's answer.

She felt compelled to elucidate. "You Ob-Gyn men know better than anyone that whatever threatens a woman's sexuality is to her a small death. This patient felt that more than most. Perhaps it was her youth. Compounded by the fact of her adoption."

318

"The point is," Prince resumed his questioning, "she was most apprehensive. I believe you said, more apprehensive than is normal. Is that right, Dr. Lindstrom?"

"Yes; yes, I would say so," Kate admitted.

"And this was *before* any surgery had been performed," Prince pointed out.

"Fear of an impending event can be more threatening to a patient than reality," Kate responded.

"Tell me, Dr. Lindstrom, at the time you saw her, would you say that her overriding concern was survival?"

"Isn't that everyone's fear in time of crisis or danger?" Kate countered.

"I agree with that," Prince said quickly, "because I myself had come to the same conclusion about that girl."

Prince turned slightly to address the panel. "I needn't tell you, gentlemen, that the night before any operative procedure a surgeon thinks about the total patient. Not merely the body that is presented for surgery. Or that area of human flesh which is exposed by the drapes. But a total human being. A wife, a lover, a mother. And in those hours of contemplation on the eve of surgery, a doctor must ask himself, What can I do to best benefit that total patient whom tomorrow morning I must probe for the hard facts that will determine her life or death?"

Prince paused, and Craig realized that this was a well-rehearsed speech. He was sorely tempted to remark that whatever Prince had thought the night before, it was more likely what to tell his broker the next morning. But to avoid antagonizing the panel, who also had brokers, investments, and business concerns, Craig remained silent.

Prince continued, "That night before I operated on

the Horton girl I promised myself, whatever it was humanly possible to do to assure her a long life, I would do. If it's possible for a surgeon to be overdetermined about saving human life then, yes, I suppose I was overdetermined in her case because of her desperate fear of dying so young.

"All that mattered to me was to save that poor, tormented girl's life. So I could come down from the O.R. and say to her, My dear, don't worry, we got it all. You're going to be fine, fine. For the very reasons Dr. Lindstrom has so clearly set forth. Thank you, Dr. Lindstrom."

But Craig intervened. "I believe I have a right to question witnesses."

Simmons nodded.

Prince smiled. "Dr. Simmons, because of the highly personal relationship between Dr. Pierson and Dr. Lindstrom, which I deliberately chose not to mention before, I'd feel better if they were not sitting so close during the questioning."

Prince had made his point about their affair without seeming ungallant.

Kate slipped from the chair alongside Craig to one quite far removed. She glared across at Prince. "Better?"

"Better," Prince replied, smiling. "Now, then . . ."—and he made a gesture which indicated that Craig was free to question Kate.

"Dr. Lindstrom," Craig began in a formal tone, "during your talk with the patient, before she signed the consent form, was it only her concern about survival that troubled her?"

"She was afraid the operation would destroy her chances of getting married."

"Was her wedding all arranged?" Craig asked.

320

"It was to have taken place four weeks later."

"Did the patient say anything about any other fears she may have had?" Craig asked.

"Because of her adoption, she had looked forward to having children of her own. Children who would grow up free of the uncertainties that tormented her," Kate replied.

"So that her ability to bear children was a matter of great importance to her?"

"Very much so," Kate said.

"If you were a surgeon faced with such a patient, would it have been an important concern to you to preserve her childbearing ability, if at all possible?"

Before Kate could answer, Prince interrupted: "Dr. Lindstrom is not a surgeon. Therefore she should not be allowed to answer any question that begins, 'If you were a surgeon'!"

Fein smiled broadly and agreed, "Absolutely right, Prince! You want my opinion? I never give a hoot in hell for psychiatric testimony. You know what we say in my circle: a pyschiatrist is a Jewish doctor who can't stand the sight of blood!" He laughed, and Simmons joined him. Even dour Kearney permitted himself a suppressed chuckle.

Simmons recovered to say, "This is a question involving surgery, so only surgeons are qualified to express opinions. Any more questions, Dr. Pierson?"

Craig looked at Kate, saw in her moist eyes her self-reproach. She felt she had failed and damaged his case.

"No more questions," Craig said grimly.

"Dr. Prince?"

"Yes. One more question. Dr. Lindstrom, could the patient have borne her own children if she were dead?"

"Of course not."

"So that saving her life was the first and most important thing. All else had to be sacrificed to achieve that. Am I right?"

Prince smugly awaited Kate's answer. It turned out not to be the answer he had expected.

"Dr. Prince, I haven't once heard you mention the possibility that both her life *and* her childbearing ability might have been preserved."

Prince's face flushed in anger. The attitude at the end of the table changed slightly. Simmons and Fein were no longer amused. Their faces now reflected disapproval. Kearney's thin, forbidding face seemed to be screwed a few notches tighter.

Prince could not permit her challenge to go unanswered. "Since Dr. Lindstrom was not present, did not receive the pathologist's report, or have to make the decision, I don't think she's qualified to have any opinion on that. Though, obviously, Dr. Pierson and Dr. Lindstrom, being so close personally, have had a great deal of time to discuss this case. Otherwise, I don't know any basis on which she could even suggest such a possibility."

Kate Lindstrom reacted in a flush of fury. She paused to crystallize her response. Then, speaking directly to the stenotypist, she said, "Dr. Prince keeps hinting at my relationship with Dr. Pierson. There is no need to hint. We are lovers. We have been for more than a year. We will continue to be. And if things work out, we will be married. As soon as this is over!"

Her announcement came as a surprise not only to Prince, but to Craig as well. It was the first firm declaration he had been able to extract from her. But she had not finished.

"Now, the question is, feeling the way I do about

him, would I come here and lie for him? I would like to. But I can't. Because I am not given to lying. So I admit, yes, the patient was unduly fearful about dying. Which permits Dr. Prince to hide behind it and say that it affected his decision. But there was more, much more. And that was, as much as living, she wanted to be mother to her own children. To make up for all the doubts she had been forced to suffer in her own life.

"Now, you gentlemen may say, saving her life was paramount. One surgeon who was there tells me that both her life and her fertility could have been preserved. Either because I love him or because I know him to be a man of integrity, I choose to believe him!"

Kate was tense to the point of tears, but she managed to control them. The three panel members were all made suddenly self-conscious by her outburst. It was Kearney who observed drily, "I think we've heard enough from this witness."

Simmons resumed charge of the hearing. "If there are no further questions . . ."

Prince did not respond. Simmons gestured to Kate that she was free to depart. Instead, she moved back to Craig's side.

"I'd feel better being here," she said softly. She took Craig's hand again, determined to remain. While Craig was comforted by her presence, he realized that now the fate of two young physicians depended on the outcome of this hearing.

Under the pressure of time, Simmons urged, "Dr. Prince, if you have any further facts to present . . ."

"A question has been opened up here that I think calls for an answer. But I'll have to call other witnesses. So if it suits the panel, I'd like to put this over until tomorrow morning."

A whispered conference among the three panel

323

members followed. Simmons turned to face Prince. "Doctor, since we do have some time left and we want to keep these proceedings as brief as possible, is there any more material in the patient's chart that we might cover today?"

"There certainly is."

"If you could enlighten us," Simmons invited.

"I can indeed. Because therein lies the real reason I asked that Dr. Pierson be dismissed!"

"Please explain," Simmons urged.

"Once the frozen section revealed a carcinoma, I felt I had no choice but to do a bilateral. I say, better safe than sorry. When in doubt, take it out."

"That was the point at which Dr. Pierson refused to complete the surgery?" Fein asked pointedly.

"Not only refused. But proceeded to argue with me," Prince replied indignantly. "My plan at the time was, Save the girl's life. Make sure she is absolutely free of disease. Then put her on a regimen of estrogens to avoid the aftereffects."

Both Fein and Kearney nodded, affirming Prince's plan.

"Of course, at that time no one had any way of foreseeing the unfortunate morbidity that would follow surgery. I did not expect a girl of twenty-two to have a thrombosis. But once that happened, naturally I was prevented from prescribing estrogen, not without inviting another and possibly fatal thrombosis."

The panel members concurred.

"Now, this is where we run into the consequences of Dr. Pierson's highly unprofessional conduct."

Craig half-rose from his chair as he protested, "To disagree with a surgeon is not unprofessional conduct!"

"To talk too freely to the patient's family *is!*" Prince

shot back heatedly. He turned to the panel. "You won't find it in there, because it's not part of a patient's medical experience. But I want you to know what this young bastard did!"

To protect Prince, Simmons cautioned, "Doctor, I don't think we need that phrase on the record." To the stenotypist Simmons said, "Eliminate that word and in place of it say 'young man.' "

Taking his cue from Simmons, Prince continued in a more temperate tone: "This young man went to the father of the patient and told him that he considered my surgery too radical. That I had castrated that young woman when it was totally unnecessary. He so enraged and misled that man that in the middle of the night, drunk and abusive, he called me. He accused me of all sorts of crimes against his daughter. It was nerve-shattering. Not the kind of attack a surgeon of my standing should be forced to endure. It was one of the worst experiences of my entire professional life. For that alone, Pierson deserved to be dismissed!" Prince glared across the table at Craig.

"Yet that's not the worst of it," Prince continued, his momentum increasing with his rage. "You will find there, in that chart, the events that led to that patient being transferred to Psychiatric. One evening, without any symptoms, as far as I or any resident could discern, she made an attempt on her own life!"

All three panel members instinctively reached for Cynthia's chart to confirm Prince's statement. As presiding member, Simmons had priority. Then he passed the chart on to Kearney, who finally passed it over to Fein. Prince waited until they had confirmed his statement.

"It's significant that when that crisis occurred, the night charge nurse sent for Dr. Pierson. Why Pierson and not me? Why Pierson and not Carlyle, who is Chief Resident? Only one reason: the closeness of this particular patient and this particular doctor."

Prince paused for a moment and smiled cynically. "Now, one might say, Pierson did prevent her from jumping, and thus he emerges the hero. However, I ask you to consider this: Pierson admits having told her father of her condition. I suggest Pierson was also the one who told that girl of her condition. Cruelly. Bluntly. Without any preparation. Pierson precipitated her panic; Pierson caused her to make this attempt on her own life!"

Craig moved to leap from his chair, but Kate restrained him with a strong grip on his arm. Sensing that he had scored strongly, Prince was determined to press his victory.

"We have here a psychiatrist who had contact with the patient before the event, and after," Prince continued, staring across the table at Kate. "I suggest it's reasonable to ask her if, in view of the patient's general psychiatric condition, such word about her future condition might not have thrown her into a deep depression which resulted in this attempt." He invited benignly, "Doctor?" When Kate hesitated, Prince urged,"In the interest of enlightening the panel?"

Kate paused before answering, seeking some way to phrase her reply that would be truthful yet least damaging.

Simmons finally forced her hand. "Doctor, your failure to answer might be misinterpreted."

"The patient was unusually tense. For reasons that have already been cited here. The fact that she had been brutally castrated—"

Fein interrupted angrily, "Doctor, we asked for

326

your psychiatric evaluation of the patient's state of mind! We'll decide whether surgery was proper or not!"

"The fact of her condition, when brought home to her, could have deepened her depression. That, in conjunction with her other problems, might have precipitated a suicidal episode."

"Thank you," Prince said, in mock gallantry. "Mind you, gentlemen, the girl was not Pierson's patient. He had been ordered not to have any contact with her. Yet somehow he got this information to her, with the unfortunate but inevitable result. If that isn't insubordination, carried to a dangerous degree, then I don't know what the term means. But worse, he is not only insubordinate, he is dangerous."

Kearney looked grimly at Craig. "Dr. Pierson, did you have contact with the patient after being specifically ordered by the surgeon in charge of her case not to?"

Craig was forced to admit, "She kept asking for me. I tried to avoid her. But she insisted, since my staying away only made her more anxious. I felt I had to see her."

"And did you tell her the prognosis of her condition in view of her thrombosis?" Kearney pursued.

"I did not," Craig said.

"Yet she seems to have discovered it."

"From a note sent to her by her fiancé," Craig explained.

"And where did *he* acquire that knowledge?" Kearney persisted.

"He told me that he had discussed her case with his own physician."

Suddenly Kearney accused, "Then you've also had conversations about the patient with him?"

"Yes. But nothing improper or unethical," Craig insisted.

Kearney nodded skeptically, making a tasting motion of his thin, bluish lips before he said, "But you do agree that her full knowledge of her condition, obtained through that note, caused her to make an attempt on her life?"

"I have to assume so," Craig had to concede.

Kearney did not comment except to make a small grunt that gave the appearance of grave disapproval.

At that point, Simmons announced, "We are obviously not going to finish today. We will resume at ten tomorrow morning."

Chapter Twenty-Nine

"Plowed him under!" Harvey Prince exulted to Rita Hallen. He refilled his glass, slowly rotating the brandy as he inhaled its fragrance. He took a sip, savored the taste of it before letting it warm its way down his throat.

Rita listened expectantly. Moments of triumph always had an aphrodisiac effect on him. When he succeeded in some difficult and challenging surgery, or delivered a lecture to an important group of his colleagues, or was awarded some honor, he was at his most amorous. He made love like a lion, she used to say to him afterward. Tonight promised to be such a night.

She was not disappointed.

After it was over, she heard him mutter, "I'll destroy him, destroy that bastard. . . ."

"Harvey, what'll they do to him?"

"Vote to affirm his firing. Make sure he never gets on the staff of any decent hospital again!"

"He's a bright young man," Rita suggested cautiously. "I've had plenty of chance to observe him in the O.R. Excellent technique."

"Too bad he never learned the technique of minding his own business. In every medical school they ought to have a class called Respect for Your Elders. Teach those young squirts to listen, learn, and keep their mouths shut. We can't have doctors criticizing doctors!"

Irritated by Rita's indirect plea for leniency, he continued, "Don't worry, honey, at the end I'll make a nice speech about how he's young, has to learn, and not to be too hard on him."

"And then what?"

"They'll uphold his getting fired, and kick him out!" Prince said, laughing. His laughter was cut short when he remembered. "Damn it, that reminds me, meant to call Carlyle. What time is it?"

"Just past ten."

"Not too late," Prince decided, slipping down to the rumpled bed and reaching for the phone.

"Burt? . . . Oh, sorry to disturb you, Mrs. Carlyle. Burt there? Dr. Prince." Before she could put down the phone, he continued, "By the way, Mrs. Carlyle, Mrs. Prince . . . Margaret . . . will be calling you one of these days to have lunch. She likes to know the wives of the young men in my office. Now put Burt on."

He waited a moment, but it was long enough for him to detect the look of disapproval on Rita's face. He must remember never to mention his wife in her presence. Rita had always fantasized that one day she would have the privilege of taking the young wives to lunch as Mrs. Prince.

"Burt? What's your schedule tomorrow?" Prince listened, greeting each duty with an "I see." Or an "Uh-huh." Or "Right, right."

When Carlyle had concluded, Prince said, "The reason I wanted to know is that in all likelihood we're going to have to call you to testify tomorrow morning."

Rita could not hear, but was keenly aware that Carlyle asked to be excused from a duty that would put him in direct conflict with a close friend. Prince listened, his face betraying a growing intolerance. "Burt, like it or not, you are involved. If my reputation is on the line, and you're coming into my office, then, in a way, your reputation can be affected too. After all, it's not as if you're asked to lie about what happened. Forget about me, forget about our future association. In the interest of truth, I thought you'd want to say what happened that day."

Prince's voice, which had been so affable and reasonable at the outset, had become impatient and dictatorial.

"I know it isn't easy for you, Pierson being a friend. But you only have to say what happened! We got a lab report that the first ovary was malignant. I ordered him to take out the second ovary, and he not only refused but had the audacity to argue. Naturally, I had no choice but to finish the case myself. Now, that's what happened, isn't it?"

Prince waited for Carlyle's assent.

"Well, then, I don't see that you have any choice about testifying," Prince argued. "Unless, of course, I've misjudged you. I'd hate to think I've been wrong about you, Burt."

He had not used the words, but his meaning was quite clear.

330

"Of course, they may also ask you about Pierson being forbidden to talk to the girl and ignoring my instructions. Or anything else you know about the case. Just be truthful, Burt. I'm not trying to hurt Pierson. But I can't let this challenge to my reputation go unanswered. One day when you take over my practice, you'll know how I feel."

Harvey Prince listened, nodded, and said, "Good, Burt. Good. See you tomorrow."

"What did Prince want?" LuAnne asked.

"He wants me to testify."

"Will you?"

He closed off any discussion: "It's late. You should get your rest. And I have to be in the O.R. to scrub by seven."

He turned off the light and slipped back into bed. He slid his arm about her and drew her close, nuzzling his face into that delicate curve formed by her neck and her shoulder.

She had said nothing. But he could sense the tension in her. He wondered, was it a characteristic of all women, or just black women, like his mother and his grandmother? When their men were down, put upon, unable to fight back, was there always that silence which pretended not to rebuke them? Yet it was the most accusatory rebuke of all. He could recall long silent suppers, when something had gone wrong for his father, when he had had to bite his tongue and suffer some injustice without fighting back. His mother never said a word. But their supper was soured by the silence of shame.

He knew she would not say it. He had to.

"He as much as said that if I didn't testify he would have to reconsider his offer," Burt said, expecting it would evoke some response. When it didn't, he finally admitted, "I want that spot in his office, Lu. I played it smart. Knew how to bide my time. When to flatter him. When to do some showy bit of surgery to impress him. Two and a half years of doing everything right, and now . . . now . . ." He trailed off.

"Tell me what you'll say to them. I want to be sure in my own mind that you're being honest."

"Do you think I'd lie?" he asked indignantly.

" 'Two and a half years,' " she quoted back to him. "A man dreaming of one ambition for that long might not even know he's lying."

"You make it sound that it's myself I'm thinking of," he exploded angrily. "It's you! It's *him!*"—which was the way he always referred to their unborn baby. "I want to send him to the best schools, make him the smartest black kid who ever lived! This is my way of making sure!"

"Why do you speak of my child," LuAnne said, "as if he's going to be a soldier in some war you're fighting? If that's the reason you want a child, it's the one reason I *don't* want one!" Tears welled up and start down her chiseled face. "We've got to stop using our children to work off our own hostilities!"

"I'm sorry, darling, sorry. . . ." Burt tried to comfort her.

She sobbed a bit; then between sobs, she asked, "Call me Mama?"

"Mama?" he asked, puzzled.

"Call me Mama, like a black man calls the woman he loves. Stop striving to be more white than any white man. You be you. So I can be me. And our children can be themselves."

"All right, Mama," he said, softly. Then he admitted, "There's only one question . . . one question they might ask that I don't want to answer."

"What question?"

"If I were the surgeon in charge, and I had to decide whether to do a bilateral on that girl, what would *I* have done?"

"What, Burt? Tell me."

"On a girl twenty-two . . . under those conditions . . . *never!*"

"Then Craig was right."

"Of course he was," Burt Carlyle said. "I just hope they don't ask me."

After Harvey Prince hung up the phone on Burt Carlyle, he was silent for a time before he said, "I didn't expect any resistance from that black sonofabitch. But he came around in the end. Ambition is a wonderful lubricant."

Prince laughed and held out his brandy glass demanding a refill. Rita poured him an unusually large shot. In a victorious mood, he drank two stiff slugs. With Rita and Burt Carlyle, the only two witnesses of consequence were now under his control.

That confidence and the brandy had a synergistic effect. He leaned back expansively, holding the glass up to the light of the bedside lamp to study its golden color.

Suddenly he said something that caused Rita Hallen to tense and listen carefully.

"They're not going to do it to me again," Prince declared determinedly. "They're not!"

"Not going to do *what?*"

"Doesn't matter now," he said, seeking to terminate the conversation. He put aside his glass, enfolded Rita in his arms. Before long he was making love to her again. This time he was unusually aggressive, almost furious. It was the strangest lovemaking that had ever occurred between them. More violent, yet less passionate.

It caused her to probe. "Darling, what did you mean before . . . 'they won't do it again'? Who are 'they'?"

"Wasn't any 'they,' " he replied impatiently. "One man. One young man—jealous, resentful. Who the hell ever heard of practicing medicine or surgery by statistics?"

He rolled onto his side, snatched his brandy glass, and drained it. "That's right!" he exploded suddenly. "Statistics! Because I was more successful than all the other men at the hospital, he accused me of doing unnecessary surgery. I laughed him off. But he kept gathering figures.

"Nobody paid any attention to him. Until he began spouting his damned statistics. He didn't dare name me; I'd have sued him for every cent he had. But he kept calling me an 'eminently successful surgeon,' a 'surgeon of great reputation.' 'The most successful surgeon in the eastern part of the state.' Pretty soon it became clear who he was referring to. Me!"

He held out his glass. Rita reached for the decanter on the floor beside the bed. "Just because I did four times as many hysterectomies as any other man in the whole county does not mean they were unnecessary! After all, I had the largest practice; naturally I did the most hysterectomies. But that's not the way they saw it. Of course, they were all Ob-Gyn men. Competitors. Greedy, like vultures waiting to pounce on my practice if they could drive me out.

"Margaret said, 'To hell with them, why fight them? You can do as well anywhere you go.' I'll say one thing for Margaret: she was loyal. Throughout the whole thing, she stuck by me. Even offered me all the jewelry I'd bought her so I could afford to come here and set up practice again."

334

He smiled. "Silly girl had no idea of my investments. I needed her jewelry like the Arabs need another oil well. The important thing is, she offered. That's why, Rita, darling, I can't ever . . ."

He realized, a moment too late, that in his alcoholically expansive mood he had revealed far more than he intended about the reassuring lies he had been telling Rita all these years. He lay perfectly still, attempting to detect if she had understood fully the import of what he had almost admitted.

Stunned, Rita had momentarily stopped breathing. What pained her almost as much as his long-practiced deception was her own sad realization that, in truth, she had actually been a collaborator in his deceit by choosing to believe it.

But she knew, too, that if she confronted him with it, by bitter accusations or tears, it must mean the end of things between them. She had neither the courage nor the strength for that now.

When she resumed breathing, she made every effort to conceal her pain and her anger by remarking, "So that's why you came here eleven years ago?"

Once assured that she would not make a tearful issue of his unfortunate slip, he was quick to admit, "That's why."

"Funny," Rita said. "When you first joined the hospital, everyone was so impressed. You, coming from such a fine hospital in the East, with such recommendations and praise from your colleagues there."

"Those letters, all that 'praise'? Only written to get me to leave without making a public stink. For my sake? Oh, no. They were protecting themselves. Their hospital. After all, if I made a public scandal, patients might start saying, 'If Prince has been doing that for nine years, what about the rest of the men on that staff? What are they getting away with?' So to get rid of me in a nice, quiet way, they gave me all those magnificent letters."

He chuckled. "In a way, you could say they blackmailed me with praise. 'Be a nice boy and go quietly and we'll say only nice things about you.'"

Then, with angry determination, he added, "Well, they're not going to do that to me again! At fifty-five a man can't pull up stakes and start up again somewhere else. So I am going to destroy that arrogant young bastard!"

He snorted in amusement. "Come to think of it, he probably *is* a bastard. Pierson. I mean a real, honest-to-God bastard. Did you know he's adopted? Came out in the hearing today." He laughed again.

After a long moment of silence, Rita asked, "Isn't there any way out of this without destroying him?"

"He picked this fight. Let him know how it feels to lose!" Prince said fiercely. In anger, he snatched at his costly diamond-encrusted wristwatch, which he always placed on the bedside table before making love. It was just past midnight.

"I'd better go. She waits up for me," he complained, attempting to give the impression that returning home was an onerous duty and hoping thereby to offset his unfortunate confession of moments ago.

He had gone. Rita Hallen sat before her mirror, brushing her long black hair, studying her face. Without deceiving herself, she could feel reassured that she was not unattractive. But neither was she young. Of all nights, this was not one for self-deception. For Harvey Prince had opened up not one wound, but two. Deep wounds. Of the kind she could not heal by revealing them to others.

One went back to that time when her fiancé had died suddenly of that overdose. It had been under-

336

standable to the Hospital Administrator that she would need a six-month leave of absence to recover from the tragic event. He did not know, nor did anyone, that she was three months pregnant at the time. More aware than most women of the potential dangers of the only kind of abortion available in those days, she had chosen to bear her child.

She gave him up for adoption. Lost all trace of him. And though tremendously and, at times, painfully curious, she had never made any effort to find him again. So somewhere in this land, there was a young man, now nineteen years of age, probably living with the nagging knowledge that he was an adopted child. People might refer to him in the same vicious, derisive way in which Prince had referred to Craig Pierson.

In defense of her unknown son, and the man who had fathered him, Rita Hallen bitterly resented Prince's coarse epithet. It served to rekindle in her all her fantasies of what the boy must look like—so much like his unfortunate father, who had been quite handsome.

Only when she neared the end of her brushing did she dare to dwell on Harvey's words: "That's why, Rita, darling, I can't ever . . ."

Alone now, she could muster all the things she should have said at that moment. Silently she accused, Liar! Cheat! Fraud! You unmitigated sonofabitch! All these years, inventing lies and excuses, to go along with your empty promises! I hate you! I've always hated you! I've always . . .

The tears started down her cheeks as she had to confess, I've always known, and always chose to believe you. Why, tonight, when you said that terrible thing, why didn't I turn on you and say, Get out! Out of my bed! Out of my house! Out of my life?

And because she knew why, Rita Hallen sat before

her mirror and wept. She hated him more than she had ever hated anyone. Until she realized you couldn't hate anyone that much without having loved him.

She fell asleep, as she so often did, alone, in tears, and aided by the remainder of his brandy.

For the record, witness Burton Carlyle recited his educational background up to and including his present status as Chief Resident in Ob-Gyn at State University Hospital.

Satisfied with Burt's credentials, Simmons turned the hearing over to Harvey Prince.

"Doctor," Prince began, "would you tell the panel what took place in the O.R. the afternoon that a patient, Cynthia Horton, was operated on?"

Meticulously avoiding any opinion, Burt Carlyle recited the facts, including the wait for Becker's Path report, Prince's decision on a bilateral oophorectomy, and Craig's refusal to perform the procedure.

"Doctor, that same morning in the O.R., did I permit you to do a rather complicated operation?" Prince asked.

Puzzled at the import of Prince's question, Burt answered nevertheless, "I performed an exenteration. Under your direction, of course."

"Have I always been considerate about making sure that younger men, second- and third-year residents, have a reasonable opportunity to do procedures that will help train them?"

"Yes, I would say that."

"Let me put it another way. Have you ever had reason to complain that while scrubbing with me you haven't had your fair share of surgery to do?"

"No, no reason to complain."

338

"Did you do as much surgery in your second year of residency as in your third?"

"Of course not."

"And why not?"

"Third-year men are expected to do more. It's their last chance to get experience before they go out into practice, or go on surgical staff," Burt replied.

"Now, isn't it true that some second-year men, eager and ambitious, sometimes feel that they're being deprived of the opportunity to do the more involved types of surgery?"

"I guess so," Burt admitted. "I felt that way when I was a second-year man."

"As did we all," Harvey Prince agreed, smiling at the panel. "In fact, that's the one thing about surgery that never changes. Griping second-year residents. They can't wait till they get to be third-year residents and have their pick of ward and emergency cases. They seek ever-wider fields to conquer," Prince said a bit sarcastically. "And our friend Pierson, here, was no different, was he? I mean, you two being friends, you must have heard him gripe about not being given enough chances to do more surgery?"

"As you said, we all feel that way in our second year," Burt agreed.

"Now, that morning, I permitted you to do an exenteration. You have said so?"

"Yes," Burt agreed cautiously, wondering where Prince was attempting to lead him.

"But Pierson was only permitted to do a routine exploratory laparotomy and unilateral oophorectomy."

"Yes."

"Have you ever heard Pierson express the opinion that he felt he was confident that he could do more complicated surgery—say, an exenteration?"

"If a surgeon hasn't got confidence, he ought not to approach the table," Burt said, thinking to defend Craig since he now had the opportunity.

"Is there such a thing as having *too* much confidence?" Prince asked suddenly.

"I don't know what too much confidence means," Burt said.

Prince chuckled, turned to the three older men on the panel. "Spoken like a third-year resident. Full of piss and vinegar." He made an aside to the stenotypist: "Take out those last words. Someone might misunderstand." He turned back to Burt. "What I mean, Dr. Carlyle, is this: might a man feel equipped to do cases in his second year that are beyond his ability and experience?"

"Dr. Pierson and I have scrubbed together many, many times on ward cases. His technique is excellent."

"His technique is not in question," Harvey Prince said a bit sharply. "Only his overreaching ambition. This young surgeon, feeling he was being denied opportunity for experience, could have resented the man he felt was depriving him. And thus he could have decided to disagree with him, and make serious and outrageous charges against him. Such as Dr. Pierson has made against me!"

Burt Carlyle hesitated to answer.

Prince pressed, "You do admit he felt deprived of opportunity?"

"There was nothing personal in that," the young black resident tried to explain.

"Stop beating around the bush, Doctor," Prince said, giving the appearance of anger and frustration, though inwardly he felt the examination was going well. Carlyle's attempt to defend Pierson was so ob-

340

vious as to achieve the opposite purpose. "Doctor, let's lay it on the table. Had you ever heard Pierson make uncomplimentary remarks about me *before* the Horton case?"

Carlyle stole a glance at Craig and Kate, then paused to phrase his reply most carefully.

But Prince did not give him that opportunity. He asked pointedly, "Doctor, have you ever heard Pierson refer to me as Goldfingers?"

"Well, that's a fairly common . . ." Burt stopped, his tan cheeks unable to conceal the blush of embarrassment that was building there.

Smiling benignly, Prince coaxed, "It's no secret. It's a fairly common expression among interns and residents when they refer to me."

Prince turned in the direction of the panel. "The price of success, I expect. Doctor, may we assume that Pierson used that designation for me?"

Burt Carlyle nodded. The stenotypist observed drily, "I'll need a verbal answer."

"We may assume so," Burt admitted.

"Exactly what did it mean?" Prince continued to press.

"Goldfingers . . .," Burt began to explain, "has several meanings. First, it's a tribute to your technique. All the younger men admire your deftness and skill. The comparatively short time your patients remain open and under anesthesia means less risk."

"And the other meaning?" Prince persisted.

"I suppose it's a reflection on the number of cases you do. . . ."

"And the fees I charge?"

"I suppose so."

"Don't be hesitant about it. I neither feel sensitive nor apologetic. The laborer is worthy of his hire, as the Gospels say. So, as far as young men like Pierson are concerned, Goldfingers can be a term of criticism—derision, if you will."

"I wouldn't single out Pierson," Burt said defensively.

"Okay, Doctor, let's not single out Pierson. But let's not exclude him, either," Prince said. "The point is, Pierson resented me. 'Goldfingers' wouldn't let him do the kind of surgery he felt entitled to do. That's what it comes down to. And it was especially marked that afternoon of the Horton case, because that very morning I had chosen you, not him, to do the exenteration."

"I wouldn't say he was resentful that day," Burt pointed out.

"We'll let the panel decide that," Prince said, making the most of appearing to be fair-minded about the matter. "Thank you, Doctor."

Burt Carlyle was tremendously relieved. Especially when Craig, realizing the pressure and the conflict the black resident was undergoing, sacrificed the opportunity to question him.

Burt was about to rise from his chair when Simmons leaned in, drummed his fingers on the table, then said, "One moment, Doctor."

Burt slipped back into his chair, his momentary sense of relief suddenly dispelled. Simmons, Fein, and Kearney turned their chairs about to huddle and exchange whispered comments and opinions.

Simmons nodded to his colleagues. He turned his attention back to Burt. "Doctor, leaving aside prevalent attitudes, and speaking solely of Dr. Pierson's relationship with Dr. Prince, can you tell us, *was* there a feeling of hostility—"

"No, sir," Burt said, anticipating the question. "Pierson did not—"

342

"I haven't finished yet," Simmons interrupted curtly. "Speaking of Dr. Pierson, and only of Dr. Pierson, was there any hostility *or* resentment *or* jealousy on the part of Pierson toward Dr. Prince?"

Burt hesitated. Then: "No hostility. No resentment. Perhaps a little jealousy, but it would be natural for a young man coming up to feel, One day I'd like to be in that class. But rather than hostility, I'd say it was a form of admiration."

Unimpressed with the answer, Simmons suddenly asked, "Dr. Carlyle, is Pierson a friend of yours?"

"Yes, sir."

"Did Pierson ever say anything to you about the coincidence between his background and the patient's?"

"You mean about them both being adopted as children?"

"Yes."

"He mentioned it, but only in passing to explain why he was able to take a history that an intern like Blinn could not."

"Did he have any feelings about that?" Simmons asked.

"Blinn is one of those affirmative-action babies. I don't hold any brief with them myself," Burt said, his own sensitivities coming to the surface now that the black intern's name had entered the testimony.

"I wasn't referring to him, Doctor," Simmons corrected, while a look passed between him and Fein that took note of Carlyle's sensitivity to the subject of race. "All I meant was, did Dr. Pierson seem to be unduly interested in, or solicitous of, the patient because of this common bond they shared?"

"I wouldn't say so."

"Had Pierson ever before refused to carry out a surgical procedure that Dr. Prince decided on?"

"No, sir."

"Just this one case?" Simmons pursued.

"As far as I know," Burt said.

Now Fein assumed the role of inquisitor. "Doctor, bearing in mind that the man is a friend of yours, and you don't want to get him into any more trouble than he is already in, tell me one thing. Isn't it possible that in this particular instance, a combination of emotional forces made Dr. Pierson do what he did that day? By combination of forces, I mean his resentment of Dr. Prince, *plus* his special feeling for that girl. Isn't that possible?"

"I . . . I don't think so. . . ."

"Doctor, would you operate on a patient who was related to you, or with whom you had some special affinity?"

"I would prefer not," Burt admitted.

"Then isn't it possible that Pierson, having a special affinity for that patient, might, in a roundabout way, have been doing the same thing? Namely, refusing to continue to operate on a patient with whom he felt emotionally involved?" Fein suggested.

Because it promised a way out for Craig, Burt was relieved to agree.

"Yes, it is possible. Unfortunately, his refusal that day came out in a way that made it seem like insubordination. I don't think he meant it to be."

Fein smiled. "If that was so, Doctor, how do you explain Pierson's continued personal vendetta against Dr. Prince? During the Path Conference, Grand Rounds, and the Morbidity and Mortality Conference?"

Burt Carlyle blushed, but could not answer.

Fein turned to Simmons and Kearney. "I just wanted to see how close a friend of Dr. Pierson's he is."

344

Prince sat back, unsmiling. Inwardly he felt that Carlyle not only had helped to prove his case, but at the same time, under Fein's questioning, had proved himself to be a witness biased toward Pierson.

Simmons asked, "Doctor, is there anything else you'd like to add to your statement?"

Burt Carlyle hesitated and finally said, "No, sir."

"Then we thank you very much. You're excused."

Burt Carlyle rose and swiftly left the room without glancing at Craig Pierson or Kate Lindstrom.

Chapter Thirty

The remainder of the morning was given over to hearing the testimony and examining the slides of Chief Pathologist Sam Becker. At the end of his presentation and once the lights were turned on, Kearney asked, "Doctor, when Prince asked your opinion on what surgical procedure was indicated by your findings, how did you respond?"

"That I am a pathologist, equipped to examine tissue and report findings. I am *not* equipped to, nor would I ever presume to, advise surgeons on surgery."

Kearney nodded grimly. It was obvious he himself had had that same dispute with pathologists many times.

Just before he excused Becker, Simmons asked Craig, "Do you have any questions, Doctor?"

"Just one. Dr. Becker, when you sectioned Cynthia Horton's second ovary, what did you find?"

"It was clean—absolutely healthy," Becker replied, and felt that his entire testimony was justified by that one answer. Without even a glance at Prince, he started to rise.

Before he was up from his chair, Prince asked, "Dr. Becker, do you know the incidence of eventual involvement of the second ovary once one has been found to be malignant?"

"Very high."

"How high?"

"I've seen estimates that go as high as fifty percent," Becker admitted.

"So that since there was a finding here of a mucinous carcinoma, though only borderline, it was good practice to remove that second ovary in order to save that girl's life."

"Are you asking a question or making a statement?" Becker countered.

"It's a question in the form of a statement," Prince challenged.

"If you require some answer from me, I can only say I found that second ovary to be perfectly healthy," Becker reiterated.

Fein intervened. "Doctor, let's not beat around the bush. If it had been up to you, would you have removed that second ovary?"

"It wasn't up to me, thank God. I don't like to make decisions like that. Maybe that's why I'm a pathologist, not a surgeon."

Becker was excused. Simmons decided to take a break for lunch. Kearney and Fein went out to eat. Simmons lingered. As Craig and Kate headed for the door, Simmons called out, "Pierson!"

"Yes, sir?"

"Got a minute?" Simmons asked.

"The way things stand, time is about the only thing I do have."

346

"I'd like to talk to you. *Alone.*"

Kate's look indicated clearly she would rather not leave. Simmons' eyes warned that she had better.

Once alone with Craig, Simmons said, "Son, what I'm about to say is off the record, as the lawyers say. I've made it a point to acquaint myself with your *curriculum vitae.* Your record is excellent. I think you could turn out to be one hell of a surgeon. So I wouldn't want you to ruin a promising career.

"We're dealing with a matter of judgment. Your judgment against Prince's. I'll be frank with you. I think that Kearney or Fein or I would have made the same decision Prince made. So we're not going to condemn Prince. Which leaves us the other alternative: to confirm your dismissal. Now, I don't want that to happen. But you're not giving us any choice."

Simmons paused, hoping that Craig would recant, but he did not reply.

"If you're harboring any thoughts about an appeal to the courts, forget it! No judge is going to decide a question that surgeons disagree about. So think it over during the lunch break. If you come to me later and say you want to square things, I think I could work it out so that you leave here quietly with a fistful of good recommendations. Think on it. And let me know."

Craig stared at Dr. Simmons. "What are you offering me—the chance to do a little medical plea bargaining?"

Simmons flushed in anger. He obviously did not approve of Craig's figure of speech. "I was only trying to give you every chance."

"If I wanted 'every chance,' I wouldn't have carried the matter this far."

"No, I guess not," Simmons agreed sadly. He made

347

one last effort to persuade Craig. "You can't do that patient any good!"

"No. But there'll be other patients. And somebody had to stop him sooner or later."

Simmons shook his head sadly. "Just remember, I tried to warn you."

The hearing reconvened. Kate had not reappeared, nor was there any message from her. From the disapproving attitude that prevailed at the head of the table, Craig knew that Simmons had reported to the other two members both his offer and Craig's rejection. All three seemed grimly impatient. Fein and Kearney continued to make notes on the yellow pads before them. Simmons did not. Instead, he drew from his portfolio a sheaf of typed pages which he placed before him with a calculating air of anticipation.

He directed the stenotypist, "We're back in official session." He turned to Prince. "Doctor, did you have anything further to say, or any other witnesses to present?"

"I'm quite satisfied with the opportunity you've been kind enough to afford me," Prince said graciously.

"Well, then, Dr. Pierson, do you have any witnesses you wish to present in your own behalf?"

"No witnesses, sir. But I do have certain scientific papers I'd like to present to the panel, papers which prove the desirability of unilateral oophorectomy in cases such as this." He offered to the panel reprints of articles from several obstetrical and gynecological journals.

Being nearest to Craig, Fein accepted them, hastily glanced at the titles and the summaries stating the conclusions of each paper. "I've read all these before," Fein said, dismissing them. He handed them to

Simmons, who glanced at them and passed them to Kearney.

"Is this the sum and substance of your case, Doctor?" Simmons asked.

"That. And a statement I would like to make," Craig responded.

"Before you make any statements, we have some questions we would like to ask you," Simmons said.

He picked up the typed pages he had before him. Craig realized now that Simmons had come to the hearing prepared to ask a series of specific questions. Or had those questions been prepared for him by someone else? By Harvey Prince, perhaps. He had no doubt now that he was confronted by a sly, subtle conspiracy masquerading as an impartial hearing purporting to be in search of scientific truth, but actually intended to protect Prince and the profession from exposure and scandal.

Yet he had no choice but to endure their questions and defend himself as well as he could.

"Doctor, how many oophorectomies have you scrubbed for in your entire career as an intern and resident?" Simmons began.

His sarcastic emphasis on the words "entire career" did not escape Craig.

"I've never kept records, but if I had to make an estimate, I'd say ninety, a hundred," Craig responded.

"Ninety, a hundred," Simmons repeated, belittling Craig's experience. "Would you venture a guess as to how many of those were benign?"

"More than half," Craig responded, concerned as to where Simmons' questions were leading.

"Now, as to those which the Path Lab reported as being malignant on frozen section, how many resulted in bilateral ovarian excisions?"

"I don't know."

"Make an estimate. All? Most? Half? Few? None?" Simmons demanded sharply.

"I . . . I would say . . . most," Craig had to admit.

"So that a decision to do a bilateral is not unusual," Simmons asked, capping his series of questions.

"No, I suppose not."

"Yet that's what you're accusing Dr. Prince of doing," Simmons said, like a vindictive prosecutor. He glanced to his two colleagues with an air of intolerance.

"There is a difference!" Craig interjected.

"Is there?" Simmons asked, more in argument than in inquiry.

"The cases I've witnessed were, in the main, women in their forties and fifties. Past childbearing age," Craig pointed out. "The loss of both ovaries was neither serious nor damaging."

"And in the long run far, far safer, you will agree?" Fein interposed.

Craig hesitated, realizing the question was a trap. But finally he had to admit, "Under those circumstances, yes, safer. But those were not women of twenty-two, and about to marry, as was the patient in this case."

Kearney brought his hand down on the table in a blow that punctuated the discussion. "Damn it, I've heard that argument for the last time!" he declared intolerantly. He glanced at Simmons. "Sorry, but I want that statement on the record, just as I said it!" He turned back to Craig. "Young man, let me set you straight on one thing. No doctor is more protective than I am of the sanctity of childbearing. I'm a Catholic. I not only have never done an elective abortion in my whole career, I won't allow them to be done in my hospital! But when sterilizing a woman is the way to save her life, I say sterilize!"

350

"Even a young woman of twenty-two who hasn't yet had a chance to bear a child?" Craig fought back, aware that he was shouting, but unable to control it.

Kearney shook his head slowly but impatiently. "Did it ever occur to you, Doctor, that a young woman of twenty-two has more time left to live than a woman of fifty, and should be protected *more*, not *less*?"

"Only two things occurred to me at the time," Craig responded. "A girl of twenty-two was on the table. The Path report said, borderline mucinous carcinoma in one ovary—*borderline!* The second fact was that there was no palpable finding of any mass in her other ovary. Those two facts added together said only one thing to me: *Caution. Give her a chance!* A chance to do what every woman is born to do, bear children! That's a precious right. It belongs to her!"

For the first time during the entire proceeding, Kearney smiled. It was a thin, bloodless smile, and quite sardonic. "Young man, when you've seen the number of women who come to me begging for hysterectomies for the sole purpose of sterility, you wouldn't think so highly of that 'precious' right!"

"In this particular case, there was a special reason for this patient to want to have her own children."

"Doctor," Simmons responded acerbically, "we are surgeons. Not fairy godmothers, in whose power it is to grant the patient's every wish. We have to make choices. Hard choices. As in this case."

Craig exploded impatiently, "Damn it, in this case the choice was not between life and the ability to bear children! Her life was not endangered at that point. The tumor was *in situ,* completely contained. It was removed. From that point on, we had every obligation to wait and see. And not to commit irreversible damage before we were sure!"

Kearney exploded with some vehemence, "I say a surgeon's prime obligation is to protect life. All else comes second. And I must also say I am not in the habit of being lectured to by a young man who hasn't even finished his residency!"

Clinton Ordway, who had been silently rooting for Craig throughout the hearing, realized that the young resident had now so antagonized his judges that he had destroyed any chance he might have had of presenting his case.

Kearney underscored that as he turned to Simmons and gestured hopelessly, indicating he saw little reason to proceed with the hearing. But Simmons still had unasked questions before him. He was determined to complete the job for the record.

"Tell me, Dr. Pierson: during the disagreement in the O.R., did you suggest that you wedge the second ovary instead of removing it?"

"Yes, I did," Craig admitted.

"And your reason?"

"It was preferable to removing it, and with it the patient's last chance to bear children," Craig responded.

"Doctor, don't you know that wedging an ovary, taking samples from it for biopsy, has a tendency to reduce the reproductive ability of that ovary?"

"Yes, of course."

"If you were so concerned about preserving the patient's reproductive capacity, why did you suggest wedging?"

"Reduced capacity to bear children is still preferable to total, complete, and final loss of fertility. Which, as I said, was most precious to this particular patient."

Simmons pursued him. "Tell me, Doctor, is it the surgeon's job to make his decisions based on psychiatric findings, or on surgical findings, pathological findings?"

352

"Of course on pathological findings," Craig agreed angrily. "But in this case the Path findings did *not* point to a bilateral!"

He was shouting again, too emotionally involved to make the best presentation of his own case. Arthur Horton had been right. He needed a calmer, cooler mind than his own to defend him properly. But it was too late for that. In his own way, he too had made an irreversible decision. Destroying his own career.

Fein, who had sat quietly through the entire angry exchange among Craig, Kearney, and Simmons, asked thoughtfully, "Doctor, you keep talking about 'this particular patient'—by which I assume you mean her early history."

"Yes," Craig admitted.

"Now, I understand why you'd be sensitive to that, considering your own past. But what I would like to know is this: Suppose the choice had been up to her, not up to Dr. Prince? In your opinion, 'this particular patient,' faced with the choice of dying or giving up forever the right to have children, what would she have chosen?"

Craig was a long time thoughtful before he was able to answer. For though he detected no hostility in Fein's manner, he was aware of the danger inherent in his question.

"It is my honest opinion," Craig said, "if all the facts had been explained to her, and she had the capacity to understand them, if she knew what is contained in those scientific papers, she would have opted to take the risk, bear her children, and then resubmit to surgery."

"Even if you explained to her the statistics on ovarian carcinoma?" Fein asked. "The most fatal of all female cancers?"

353

"I only know one thing," Craig responded. "When she did have the choice, between what she is now and dying, she tried to die."

There was a sudden hush in the large room. For a moment none of the three inquisitors chose to ask any further questions. Finally Simmons asked, "Doctor, explain that phrase, 'what she is now.' "

"A twenty-two-year-old menopausal woman deprived of the supplementary benefits of estrogen, which might have given her a chance at a normal existence," Craig said.

"Are you blaming Dr. Prince for her thrombosis?" Simmons asked.

"Only for the avoidable irreversibility of her condition," Craig said gravely, staring across the table at Prince.

Simmons referred to the questions in his notes before asking, "Doctor, assume this case had not been complicated by a thrombosis and the consequent contraindication of estrogen. Assume the operative procedure had been carried out exactly as it was. The patient had a normal recovery. Was placed on a regimen of estrogen. Proceeded to get married and live a fairly normal life thereafter. Would we all be here today?"

Craig had to concede, "Possibly not."

"*Possibly?*" Simmons followed swiftly.

"*Probably* not," Craig agreed. "Once the patient was no longer in the hospital, once she had resumed her life, damaged as she was—"

"I resent that word!" Prince shouted angrily across the table.

Simmons intervened to assure Prince that his rights would be very well protected. "Please, Dr. Prince." He turned his attention back to Craig. "You were saying, 'once the patient had resumed her life . . .' "

354

"I'd have been troubled by what had been done to her. But like most doctors, once the patient was out of my care I would gradually have tended to forget. I don't justify that. I only admit it's what happens. Under the pressures of a resident's day-to-day life, I guess I would eventually have wiped out the memory."

Simmons nodded. "Tell me this, Dr. Pierson: at the time the decision was made to perform a bilateral oophorectomy, did you point out to Dr. Prince what could result if the patient later suffered a thrombosis?"

"No," Craig admitted.

"Why not, if you seem so exercised about it now?" Simmons asked.

"Because at the time . . . at the time . . ." Craig repeated, and found himself entrapped.

"Isn't it because at the time no one could have predicted that a girl of twenty-two, in seeming good health, would have suffered a thrombosis?"

"A thrombosis is always a postsurgical possibility. Else why do we put antiemboli stockings on all bedridden patients?" Craig asked.

"A good point. But what would you estimate that possibility to be? Fifty percent, forty, thirty?"

"I'd say about ten percent," Craig conceded.

"Or even less, possibly?" Simmons challenged.

"Possibly."

"Now, Doctor, once one ovary is found to be malignant, what are the chances of the second one being malignant or becoming malignant at some later time if allowed to remain in the patient?"

"Depending on the length of time—say, years—as much as fifty percent," Craig was forced to grant.

"Aha," Simmons exclaimed, as if he had achieved a breakthrough. "So what is at the crux of this issue, as I understand it, is the following: Dr. Prince, at a vital

355

point in the procedure, had to decide between two eventualities. A possible thrombosis, with a less-than-ten-percent chance of occurring. And the spread of a malignancy which had almost a fifty-percent chance of occurring. He chose the odds that favored the patient. You disagreed with him. And that's why we're all here now."

"That's a grossly unfair statement!" Craig protested.

Simmons overrode him. "I'm not finished. Doctor!" Once he had silenced Craig, he continued, "You yourself admitted that if the thrombosis had not occurred and the patient was put on estrogen, you probably would have forgotten the whole thing. So actually you've been trying to defend your own insubordinate conduct by condemning Dr. Prince for events that took place *after* he made his decision.

"Medicine and surgery couldn't be practiced at all if each of us were judged by events that happened *after* we had done our job reasonably, cautiously, and capably."

Simmons looked to his colleagues to enlist their support and agreement.

Craig bolted up from his chair, leaned across the table at his three judges. "God damn it, you won't get away with this!"

"Doctor . . ." Simmons tried to override him. This time Craig would not be silenced.

"You may be very shrewd, Dr. Simmons. You may trap me with clever questions. But that does not mean you're right. Or that Prince was right!

"Oh, yes, if the choice had been between the possibility of the spread of cancer on the one hand and a thrombosis on the other, then by all means do what Prince did! But what Prince refused to admit, or even discuss, was the third possibility! The best possibility for that patient!"

356

Craig reached across and seized the papers he had earlier submitted as part of his case. "The procedure described in these new studies! The conservative alternative. Remove what is dangerous. But by all means preserve what is healthy and life-giving.

"We'd never castrate a man without serious thought to the consequences. But when it comes to women, either out of callousness or sheer habit, we are far more reckless."

Craig turned on Prince. "A doctor's obligation is to give the patient every chance to live a normal life. Damn it, if what we do to a patient is such that when she discovers it she wants to commit suicide, then we have a great deal to answer for! And instead of sitting around this table . . ."

Craig turned now from accusing Prince to glare at his judges.

"Instead of sitting around this table using percentages to conceal the issue, instead of doctors helping doctors to conceal their own mistakes, we should sit as judges of each other, and of ourselves. We will all make mistakes. But the way to prevent future mistakes is not to cover up today's mistakes. Dig them out! Judge them! And vow never to repeat them! But that can't be, if older men like you do what you've just done to me."

Craig felt the cold sweat trickle down his lean cheek. He could feel the clinging touch on his back where his shirt was wet through. He realized that his leg was trembling from tension. His hands were clenching and unclenching, as they sometimes did after an especially long and intense surgical procedure. It required all his effort to retain control and continue.

"You men may console yourselves with the transparent excuse that Dr. Prince saved that girl's life. I

357

say at the point where he made his decision, that girl's life was *not* in danger. You may hide behind the excuse that what Prince did has been done for half a century now. Is accepted practice. I say the latest findings prove him wrong! And he should have known that, unless he's too busy doing surgery to keep up with it. He violated the one ancient rule that should govern all physicians and surgeons. Administer the most helpful therapy with the least harmful effect on the patient.

"*The* patient. In the day-to-day pressure of our work, every patient begins to look like every other patient. Suddenly they become a group—patients. And we find ourselves treating them according to general rules. We must remember that each of our patients is a special, singular human being. A woman. With a life to be lived. Unless we treat them that way, unless we leave them better off than they were before, perhaps we have no right to touch them at all!"

Kearney challenged sharply, "Are you saying that Dr. Prince would have been better advised not to do any surgery at all?"

Craig glared at Prince. "Surgery? Of course. Butchery? No!"

All three panel members—Simmons, Kearney, and Fein—glared fiercely at Craig on the use of that word. But far from being silenced, he was outraged as he continued, "And the rest of you are equally guilty! You have made our science a professional's game, with the ethics of whores! A medical Mafia, with the same code of honor! *Silence!* We do not inform on one another. We do not reveal our mistakes and trespasses. As if, as conspirators, we had taken a blood oath against the rest of the human race who are called patients! I say it is time that stopped. It is time . . ."

Craig did not conclude his attack but slowly sank back down into his chair, covering his damp face with his hands and trying to wipe away the sweat. There was an awesome stillness in the room.

Finally Simmons cleared his throat and announced hoarsely, "After that outburst, I think we're all entitled to a recess."

Craig left the room swiftly. Prince lingered, to exchange some words with the panel. But by their attitude, they made it clear they wished time alone for discussion.

Once the room was cleared, Fein spoke up first. "Too bad. Fine young man. Dedicated. Bright."

"Not bright enough to keep his mouth shut. Using a word like 'butchery.' We have to protect the profession from scandalous accusations," Simmons said. Kearney nodded in agreement.

"Of course," Fein finally agreed. "I suppose we have to vote now."

"There are no other witnesses."

"How do we do this?" Fein asked.

Self-consciously, Simmons admitted, "This is the first time I've presided over such a panel. It would seem to me proper to announce our decision orally. Then each of us confirms it in writing."

"Then let's do it," Fein agreed, but could not avoid adding, "I'll always wonder what would have happened to that patient if Prince *had* adopted Pierson's recommendation."

The other two did not respond.

Out in the corridor, Harvey Prince and Craig Pierson waited. They did not speak. There was no need. Prince was confident of victory. Craig had already accepted defeat. He desperately wished Kate were here, if only to make disaster seem a little less painful. He tried to call from the public booth. Kate did not respond to her beeper. She had evidently left the hospital complex. He went back to wait outside the door for the inevitable decision.

Inside the boardroom, Simmons was saying, "Let's get it over with."

A bit hesitantly, Fein interposed, "May I make one suggestion? That we word our decision in such a way as not to hurt that young man too much."

"We've got to uphold his dismissal," Simmons declared. "If we don't, we'll be attacking Prince, a man with an excellent reputation."

"I know," Fein agreed, "but Pierson's too good a young man to lose, or disillusion. I wish there were some way . . ."

"He refused to resign when given the choice," Kearney reminded him.

"Yes," Fein admitted. "Still . . ." But he had no concrete suggestion to make, so he finally relented, nodding in agreement with his colleagues.

To console him, Simmons pointed out, "He created the issue, Myron. He provoked this hearing. We were only called in to decide it."

Prince returned to the hearing room. Craig followed within moments. They took their places on opposite sides of the long polished mahogany table. Simmons waited in grave silence until Ordway and Deering returned. Craig could tell from the ominous silence that his future had already been determined.

Simmons adjusted his thick-framed glasses and very somberly declared, "On the basis of all the testimony we've heard, we have come to our decision. Rather than keep everyone in suspense pending formal noti-

360

fication, we wish to declare it now. It is the unanimous consensus of this panel that Dr. Craig Pierson has indeed been guilty of unprofessional conduct as charged. He was insubordinate in the operating room. He was insubordinate, highly unprofessional, and unethical in interfering in the postoperative care of a patient whom he had expressly been forbidden to see by the patient's surgeon.

"This not only was a breach of ethics, but proved a dangerous practice which led to the emotional complications that occurred in this case. We have therefore come to the conclusion that Dr. Craig Pierson's dismissal by State University Hospital is justified, and we affirm that action."

Clinton Ordway could not help glancing compassionately at Craig Pierson, who stared straight ahead—seeing nothing, but realizing full well what Simmons' words meant for the rest of his career in medicine.

After Simmons' pronouncement there was a moment of silence until Prince said briskly, "I thank you gentlemen for your time and patience. And for your decision."

As Prince was rising from the table, there was a sharp knock at the door. Welcoming the intrusion as a final punctuation to distasteful events, Simmons called out, "Yes? Come in!"

The door opened slowly. His white resident's outfit accenting his tan face, Burt Carlyle peered into the room.

"May I?"

"This hearing is over," Simmons announced.

Carlyle interrupted, "There's something I feel compelled to say."

"It's too late."

361

Burt Carlyle could glean the truth from the look on Craig's face.

"Maybe . . . maybe I can still change your minds."

Simmons betrayed his impatience. "You had your chance to testify, Doctor."

"Not really," Carlyle disputed.

Prince glared at Burt Carlyle—a hostile warning of the consequences. He spoke to the panel. "I know what's been going on. During the recess, Dr. Pierson made a phone call from the booth. Obviously this is the result. Some foolish last-minute attempt to influence this panel!"

"I'm not here because anyone called me," Carlyle protested; "I'm here because I choose to be. For my sake, if no one else's! And I insist on being heard!"

"The matter is closed," Simmons repeated.

Despite Ordway's desperate signal to Carlyle to be silent, the black Chief Resident insisted, "It is not closed as far as I'm concerned. There was one question none of you men asked. But you should have asked. And I mean to answer it. To satisfy myself, if no one else."

"It won't change anything," Simmons warned.

"I don't give a damn!" Burt Carlyle shouted. Accusingly, he advanced toward the panel. "Why didn't any of you ask, 'Dr. Carlyle, you were the only other surgeon who scrubbed on that case. You were there when the Path report came back. You heard the discussion. What would *you* have done under the circumstances?' I think that's a fair question, an honest question for you to ask. And it is still is. So I think it deserves an honest answer."

Craig called out, "Burt, no! It won't do any good!"

But Burt Carlyle continued: "And the honest answer is, I would have made the same decision as Dr. Pierson. Give that girl every chance to bear children.

I would not have deprived her of that by an arbitrary decision by one man who at the moment was more interested in the hospital brass he was entertaining that evening, and in the new tax shelter his broker had just told him about, and whether his crowded operating schedule would be inconvenienced by a second operation."

The look that passed between Harvey Prince and Burt Carlyle made it clear that the young black resident had forfeited all chance of joining Prince's prosperous office.

Their backs to the rest of the room, the judges conferred in whispers. When they swung about, Simmons asked, "Dr. Carlyle, during your original testimony, you made no mention of joining in the argument between Prince and Pierson. Did you?"

"No, sir."

"You said nothing at that time?" Simmons pursued.

"No, sir," Carlyle was forced to admit.

"It strikes us as very strange, then. You now come here with such strong feelings on the matter, but at the time, when you could have had some influence, you said not one single word." Simmons shook his head dubiously.

"There was a reason," the black resident said.

"What reason?" Fein asked, aware of the resident's painful uneasiness.

"At the time . . .," Burt Carlyle said, "especially after Dr. Prince had allowed me to do a total exenteration and had been so laudatory about my work, I nurtured the hope that he was testing me and that as a result he would ask me to join him in his office."

"And did he?"

"Eventually, yes," Burt Carlyle admitted. "At ten o'clock last night."

Again there was a whispered conference among the

three judges. Simmons swung about to announce their conclusion.

"Despite your brave, if foolhardy, attempt to support your friend, we find nothing in your new statement to alter our decision. But we thank you for coming forward. . . ."

Burt Carlyle turned and started slowly for the door.

Damn fool, Craig Pierson kept saying to himself; damn fool, to endanger himself for me. He must have known it was hopeless.

"I think we can safely close this hearing at this time," Simmons said. The other two panel members nodded.

Chapter Thirty-One

Dr. Kate Lindstrom sat in the modest waiting room of Dr. Leonard Stiehl while the gynecologist consulted with the last of his patients. She had not informed his receptionist-nurse of her mission, permitting her to assume that she was here as a new patient. To further that impression, she had given the nurse routine, first-visit information. With the exception of withholding from her the fact that she was a physician and psychiatrist.

While she waited, Kate fingered a note that showed the wear and tear of five hours of continual folding and unfolding. In a woman's handwriting, it stated: *Suggest you investigate Dr. Prince's previous background. Especially young doctors on service prior to his resigning.* The note was unsigned. It had arrived with Kate's usual interoffice hospital mail, but instead of the usual interoffice envelope, this envelope was blank, with no identification of the sender.

It could be a hoax, Kate had feared. But at the time she left the hearing, Craig's situation was so precarious that desperation had forced her to pursue even this blind lead. It had not been easy tracking down Dr. Stiehl. It had required a visit to Prince's previous hospital, where she had questioned the Chief of the Ob-Gyn Service, Dr. Charles Angelo. Angelo's reaction had been one of annoyed impatience.

"Weren't you here some days ago? Asking similar questions?" he had demanded.

"Yes."

"Then what brings you back?" Angelo asked. "And please be quick about it; I'm very busy."

"So am I," Kate had responded. Angelo's face had reflected his displeasure at being stared down by this strong-minded young woman. "A doctor's career is at stake. And I'll do whatever I have to to protect him. Even if it means destroying the reputation of this hospital!"

"Young woman, is this blackmail?" Angelo had demanded angrily.

Kate Lindstrom detected that Angelo had responded with the defensive indignation of a man protecting secrets about which he might well be blackmailed.

"Put any label on it you choose, Dr. Angelo, but I won't leave without the information I came for."

"And that is?"

"About eleven years ago a Dr. Harvey Prince resigned from this hospital. He left a thriving practice to set up again in a place where he was not known. Why would a doctor do that? Surely there must be a reason.

365

So I investigated his file. It contains many glowing letters of recommendation from this hospital. Some days ago I was assured the signatures on those letters are genuine."

"And they are," Angelo confirmed.

"Which only makes the mystery more baffling," Kate said. "A man so highly regarded, so successful, why leave and relocate? Unless . . ."

She paused.

Angelo had smiled. "Come, Doctor, you're not naive. There are always reasons. A doctor becomes personally 'involved.' Say with a nurse. Or perhaps an irate husband threatens to create a nasty scandal. Ob-Gyn men are often put in that dangerous situation, justified or not. Rather than face that, the doctor resigns, moves, sets up elsewhere. I'm not saying that happened to Dr. Prince, but it could have."

"Were you here at the time?" Kate asked suddenly.

"I was," Angelo responded, consulting his wrist-watch to indicate that the pressure of time was on him.

Determined not to permit a swift termination of the meeting, Kate had pursued, "Were you close to Dr. Prince? Did you scrub with him?"

"A number of times. Excellent technician."

"No question," Kate said. "Did you ever have any personal disagreements with him?"

"What are you getting at, Doctor?"

"Perhaps there were personality reasons why he decided to leave," Kate suggested.

"Dr. Prince is a most gracious and cooperative man. A bit of a prima donna at times, but then, which top surgeon isn't? But he was far nicer than most."

"Which makes me ask again, *why*? Why did he leave here?" Kate focused on Angelo's eyes until the older doctor swung his swivel chair to such an angle that he avoided her and stared out the window.

"I guess being a psychiatrist, you have to keep probing for devious motivations, even where none exist. I can assure you that you won't find anything in Dr. Prince's record to substantiate your suspicions."

"Exactly. Which only makes me more suspicious. I never met a man or a woman who didn't incur some criticism. But Prince's record is perfect."

"As far as this hospital was aware, his record *was* perfect."

"Good recovery rate among his patients?"

"Very good," Angelo was quick to confirm.

"Long-term survival rate among his carcinoma patients?"

"Best in the hospital."

"Even among patients who actually *did* have cancer?" Kate asked pointedly.

Angelo swung slowly back to face Kate once more. "If you're hinting that his number of hysterectomies was a bit higher than the average, I guess that's true."

" '*A bit*'?" Kate challenged.

Angelo did not reply.

"Is that why he was asked to leave?"

"I never said he was asked to leave," Angelo responded sharply.

"Of course not," Kate replied, an edge of sarcasm in her tone. "After all, the perfect doctor. The excellent technician. The lovable Dr. Prince. If we had a doctor that perfect in our hospital, we'd bar the doors to keep him. We wouldn't send him out with glowing letters of recommendation that read like nominating speeches at a presidential convention."

"You're making wild and unsubstantiated accusations!" Angelo warned.

"Wild? Perhaps. Unsubstantiated? I don't think so." Out of her purse Kate drew the well-creased slip of white paper.

Angelo scanned it swiftly as if to dismiss its importance. But his eyes betrayed him. For they flicked from the page to Kate, trying to perceive if she knew even more than she had revealed.

He attempted to deprecate the note. "An unsigned note. A bit of hospital gossip from someone who won't even reveal her identity . . ." He stopped when he realized that he had made a partial identification.

"Then you too admit it was written by a woman," Kate said.

"You're a woman; you might have written it." Angelo smiled.

"If I had to make my guess," Kate resumed, "I'd say this was written by a woman out of some personal resentment against Dr. Prince. And while it is general and broad in its accusation, it is specific in one regard: *Especially young doctors on service prior to his resignation.* I want to know *which* young doctors," Kate demanded.

Angelo responded quickly, too quickly. "It was only one man, and he . . ." He interrupted his outburst.

"That's all I want—the name of that one young doctor," Kate said, "And if you would, the reason. What happened?"

"How far do you mean to go with this?" Angelo finally asked.

"As far as I have to," Kate said. "A man's career is at stake."

"A man in whom you obviously have a strong personal interest," Angelo concluded.

"Much stronger than a strong personal interest," Kate replied.

Angelo scribbled a brief note. Before handing it to her, he warned, "Remember, I didn't give you this. Now do what you have to, but keep this hospital out of it. Agreed?"

368

"I'll try" was all Kate would promise while reaching for the note. It read simply: *Leonard Stiehl. Middlebury.*

Now she was waiting in the modest Middlebury office of Dr. Leonard Stiehl, fingering the anonymous note she had received and the slip with Stiehl's name. The phone on the nurse's desk lit up. She answered. "Yes, Doctor. Right away." She left her desk, taking with her the newly typed file on Katherine Lindstrom. Soon, the door opened: Kate was admitted.

Dr. Stiehl appeared to be a man in his early forties, blond but turning to gray, with a lean, ruddy face and almost handsome. He was studying Kate's file.

"I don't see any history of symptoms here, Miss Lindstrom. When was the last time you had a complete gynecological checkup?"

"Three weeks ago."

He glanced up over the file at her. "You don't trust your own doctor. You want a second opinion. Who's your man?"

"Angelo. Charles Angelo."

Slowly, Stiehl lowered the file and stared at her.

"He recommended I come and see you."

"Angelo?" Stiehl asked, openly skeptical.

"He indicated that you could enlighten me about events, eleven years ago, surrounding the resignation of a Dr. Harvey Prince."

Stiehl was thoughtful for a long moment. "What would you want to know? Provided, it is understood, that it didn't come from me."

"That's the first thing I want to know. Why Angelo, and now you, both say, 'I'll help you, but don't reveal it was me.'"

"Not the same reason," Stiehl said. "He's fighting to preserve the excellent reputation of his department.

I'm fighting to overcome six tough years when I couldn't get an appointment to any good hospital."

Stiehl rose from his chair and began to pace nervously. "How do you suppose I wound up in a place like Middlebury? A small town. With a hospital far smaller than the ones I trained in, served my residency in."

He turned suddenly to make sure that Kate would fully appreciate what he said now. "Mind you, I'm not faulting this town. It's been good to me. I have a wife. Two kids who are growing up well—far better, most likely, than they would be in a large city. But I wanted to be on staff at a large teaching hospital. With the best facilities. With a chance to do research. I have some ideas, good ideas, that I'd like to see tested in the laboratory. We don't have such facilities here. So I often get lonely. Lonely for other doctors to compare ideas with. To work with.

"Yes, I go to an occasional seminar when I can steal the time. To meet with other Ob-Gyn men. I keep in touch. Follow all the latest literature. I do my best."

"But it isn't the same," Kate sympathized.

"It's too late now to change that. There is a certain time in the life of a doctor when decisions he makes, or which are made for him, determine what he will do for the rest of his career."

"What kind of decisions are 'made for him'?" Kate asked.

Stiehl turned away, but glanced over his shoulder at Kate. "There's no avoiding it, I suppose."

"No chance," Kate said. Then she smiled. "But you can speak freely, say anything that comes into your mind. I'm a psychiatrist."

He returned her smile, relaxing for the first time during the entire interview. "The female psychiatrists

I met during my training were all dark, very thin, had stringy hair, and appeared very neurotic to me. You're a refreshing change."

"Thank you," Kate said. "Now?" she persisted.

"About Prince. Finest technician I ever scrubbed with. Skillful. Economical. Never a wasted motion," Stiehl began, then proceeded to relate in detail his long-ago conflict with Harvey Prince.

Finally he concluded, "He had the power and the prestige, so I ended up with a reputation for being a troublemaker. Other doctors didn't want me around. I had to go elsewhere to finish my residency. With a wife six months pregnant. And no money. But we managed. I couldn't get an affiliation with a large first-rate hospital, so eventually I set up here. It wasn't easy. But maybe it was for the best. We've got a good life here. Nice people."

But Kate could tell there was a hunger in the man that would never be satisfied. She was looking at Craig Pierson ten years from now. Except she knew that Craig would not become resigned as Stiehl had.

"There's another doctor in the same kind of trouble," Kate said. She proceeded to tell him about the Horton case.

Stiehl said, "Damn fool. He should have kept his mouth shut!"

In a moment, he added, "Look who's giving advice." He smiled ironically. "I suppose you want me to do something about it?"

"I suspect it will be painful for you, but yes. Please!"

Stiehl stared off, pondering, interrupting his thoughts only once to mutter, "Oh, Christ! Not again!"

"They can't do anything to you this time," Kate consoled.

371

"Just living through it again will be bad enough," Stiehl warned softly, with more meaning than words alone could convey.

Dr. Simmons was slipping into his topcoat. Myron Fein was at the door of the boardroom talking to Administrator Deering. Kearney was on one phone with his office to see whether any emergencies had accumulated during the two days he had been forced to remain away. Ordway had ordered Craig Pierson to come back to his office, and they were leaving when the second phone rang.

Simmons was wanted. Expecting it was an emergency call from his office, he answered with a brisk "Yes?"

"Dr. Simmons? This is Dr. Lindstrom. I must ask you to hold the hearing open for another four hours. I'm bringing another witness."

"The hearing is already concluded. And we have rendered our decision," Simmons informed her curtly.

"You upheld Dr. Pierson's dismissal?" Kate asked.

"On the basis of the testimony we had no choice," Simmons replied. "Sorry." But it was a crisp, formal, empty word bespeaking no regret.

"Not nearly so sorry as you're going to be if you don't suspend your decision until you hear my witness," Kate said pointedly.

"Young woman, are you threatening me?" Simmons accused angrily.

"Yes, Doctor. And you might as well know what I'm threatening you with. Unless you hear my witness, I am going to cause the damnedest uproar you've ever faced in your long, distinguished professional career.

372

I'll make it public that you are shielding and protecting a doctor who should have been censured and barred from practice long ago."

"You wouldn't dare!" Simmons exploded.

By now all other voices in the large room were stilled. Ordway and Craig Pierson came back into the room. Fein and Kearney gathered at Simmons' side trying to overhear the other end of the conversation. Deering and Prince waited silently, puzzled by Simmons' outburst.

Kate Lindstrom continued coolly and quite pointedly, "Dr. Simmons, make up your mind. Do you want to handle this fairly? Or do you want all the nasty publicity that will follow?"

"Doctor, I think your conduct is highly unethical. I shall report it to your superiors."

"Don't bother. I'll do that when I tell them the whole story," Kate replied firmly. "The *whole* story. This cover-up can't go on forever."

Simmons hesitated. Kate did not.

"Doctor, think of the effect not only on you. But on your hospital."

"This is outrageous," Simmons retorted, his face flushed in anger.

Undeterred, Kate persisted, "Will you give me four hours?"

"It won't change anything," Simmons warned.

"It might keep this out of the courts," Kate pointed out.

She sounded angry enough, contentious enough, so that Simmons was forced to take her last warning very seriously.

"One moment," he said. He drew Fein and Kearney aside, and after a whispered conversation, he returned to the phone. "Four hours. No more!"

"Four hours," Kate agreed. "Meantime, you might send for Dr. Prince's Personnel file."

She hung up before Simmons could inquire why.

In three hours and forty-nine minutes, Kate Lindstrom and Dr. Leonard Stiehl raced up the steps of the main building of State University Hospital. In the boardroom, the panel and all participants were waiting. On the table, before Simmons, lay the Prince file. Each of the panel members had inspected its contents, and all were now more puzzled than before. Kearney took the opportunity to compliment Prince on his excellent references.

Prince termed the entire exercise an amusing but desperate ploy by a young woman determined to protect the man she loved, who was now beyond protecting. But his smile turned to an angry glare when he saw Leonard Stiehl follow Kate Lindstrom into the room. Prince rose swiftly and shouted, "This is the damnedest piece of trumped-up libel I've ever witnessed! That man hates me. He'd say anything to avenge himself on me! He thinks I ruined his career. This is his way of trying to get back at me!"

He turned his attack on Kate. "If you brought this man to testify against me, I'll sue you. I'll have you kicked out of this hospital. And barred from practicing in this state! How dare you?"

Kate said nothing, permitting Prince's venomous reaction to settle in the room like a poisonous cloud.

Taken aback by Prince's outburst, Simmons gestured Kate and Stiehl to chairs along the table. Kate slipped into the empty seat at Craig's side.

"Now, then," Simmons said, "this hearing is reopened." He turned to the stenotypist. "I must note in the record that the only reason this hearing was

374

reconvened is due to threats made by Dr. Lindstrom. Should it turn out that her threats were without foundation and her so-called new evidence merely a ruse to benefit Dr. Pierson, this panel shall recommend the proper disciplinary action be taken against her by this hospital and the American College of Psychiatrists. Is that understood?" He directed his question to Kate.

"It is understood," Kate agreed, no hint of timidity or fear in her voice.

"Is this the witness?" Simmons asked.

"Yes, sir," Stiehl responded. "My name is—"

Prince interrupted, "Leonard Stiehl! Ask him why he's here. Ask him *where* he practices. Ask *why* he practices there. Ask him how his affiliation with General Hospital terminated!"

Concerned that Prince's highly agitated state might have physical consequences, Simmons warned, "Harvey, please don't excite yourself. We'll ask all those questions. And a good many more. Just . . . just relax."

Prince made a pretense at becoming calm, but kept muttering, "A man spends his whole life to build up a reputation and some jealous young bastards try to destroy it. Damn it, because a man is successful, must he be hounded, lied about, accused?"

"Dr. Prince," Fein quietly pointed out, "I haven't heard him accuse you."

That softly spoken fact caused Prince to realize that at that moment he had done more to impeach himself than had anyone else in the room. He grew silent, his lips twitching nervously.

"Now, Dr. Stiehl," Simmons asked, "in the interest of saving time, may we assume that you are aware of the facts in this matter?"

375

"Dr. Pierson has been discharged for insubordination and other breaches of professional ethics."

"Are you also familiar with the events out of which those charges arose?"

"Dr. Lindstrom explained the case in detail."

"We do not intend to ask your opinion on the procedure Dr. Prince followed. We feel we're qualified to have sound opinions on that. So the question becomes, exactly what *are* you here for?"

"Dr. Prince made that quite clear."

"You're here to make accusations against him?" Simmons asked.

"I'm here to state certain facts about him. It will be your duty to determine if they are accusations," Stiehl replied.

"That's the most benign description of slander I've ever heard," Prince accused. "I warn you, Stiehl, what happened last time will be nothing compared with what I'll do to you now."

"Dr. Prince, they've never heard of you in Middlebury. And they think I'm a pretty fair country doctor. So you can't threaten me; don't even try." He turned to Simmons. "Dr. Simmons, this situation may be new to you. But it is quite familiar to me. I have been here before. Except that that time I was in Pierson's place. And the same thing happened to me that has just happened to him. So I would like to relate the events."

"Proceed, Doctor," Simmons said. He, Fein, and Kearney settled back, prepared to listen.

Even before Stiehl began, Prince interposed, "Mind you, what he says is all lies. And I can prove it."

Stiehl began uneasily. It was obviously painful to reopen a part of his life that had been the traumatic turning point in his career.

376

"About Dr. Prince," Stiehl began, "I must say he's the finest technician I ever scrubbed with. Skillful. Such economy of time. His incisions were cosmetic gems. His sutures were works of art."

During his tribute he did not glance at Prince. Until he pronounced the word *"Except . . ."* and paused.

"Except . . ." Simmons prodded.

"Except that he had a tendency to get carried away with his own skill. He worshiped technique to the exclusion of his patients' total welfare. The surgery became more important than the patient. He seemed to court difficult surgery, dangerous surgery, to prove that he could accomplish it. He reveled in the praise, admiration, and envy of his colleagues."

"Envy is the answer!" Prince blurted out fiercely.

Stiehl continued, "I've had plenty of time to think about him in the past eleven years. Days when my practice was lean. Sleepless nights when I relived unfulfilled ambitions. What was it with Prince? Greed? Is that why all the unnecessary procedures? He charged the highest fees, had the most extensive practice, made far more money than any other attending at General.

"But in the end I came to the conclusion that it was more personal than that. He was in love with his own ability. He was like an actor. A star. He needed praise, applause. And yes, even envy, much as he claims to resent it. He went into the O.R. each time feeling, I am going to give them a great show! And he did. Most times. And *over*did. More than a few times. Perfectly healthy uteruses were removed. Ovaries that other surgeons would have hesitated to remove, he removed without a second thought.

"And when his judgment was questioned, he always had a ready response: 'My patients rarely come

377

back with uterine cancer, do they?' If you're content with those statistics, that argument is valid. But if you care about the patient, all those statistics fade away before the personal disaster visited on even a single patient as a result of the ruthless, if elegant, butchery practiced on her."

Stiehl had begun to perspire slightly, a glisten of sweat on his brow. Absentmindedly, he tried to brush it away in a nervous, futile gesture.

"I wasn't the only resident who noticed this tendency. I was simply the only one foolish enough to speak up. After one particularly brutal bit of surgery, I went to my Chief. I told him that a patient had been needlessly damaged. A bold accusation for a young resident to make.

"My Chief was an honest man. He confessed he'd been troubled for a long time about Prince. By the Tissue Committee reports that steadily produced findings in Prince's cases, 'no valid indication for surgery' or 'lack of pathology demonstrated.' But after all, how could he accuse Prince without at the same time accusing the hospital? And creating a scandal? The system tied his hands, shut his mouth.

"Well, I determined it wouldn't shut mine. So I collected all those Tissue Committee reports. I discussed them in meetings. Finally, I insisted a Medical Staff conference be called or I would make them public. A conference was called. The pathologists spoke up. Other residents who had scrubbed on Prince's cases. Staff men eventually felt obligated to come forward and add their opinions and criticisms."

"Staff men!" Prince interjected. "I buy and sell staff men. They're a dime a dozen. Hired hands!"

"Dr. Prince, please," Simmons remonstrated. He looked to Stiehl. "Continue, Doctor."

"Talk of that meeting got around. Eventually the

378

Trustees could not ignore it. They sent for me. I came prepared with all the Tissue Committee reports and other evidence. They listened. Respectful. But silent. Then, in their collective wisdom, they decided that Dr. Prince should be permitted to resign. That he be given a sheaf of the finest recommendations so that he could affiliate with some other hospital, preferably out of the state."

"Didn't anyone question that?" Simmons asked.

"My old Chief. Because they forced him to sign one of those letters, he resigned in protest," Stiehl said.

"And you, Doctor?" Fein pursued.

"What usually happens to the bearer of bad tidings? I suppose you could say I was 'executed.' Professionally executed. I wasn't reappointed to my last year of residency. I had to go elsewhere. It wasn't easy. Even worse . . ." But Stiehl seemed forced to avoid that subject and settled for "Finally, I ended up in Middlebury. Away from the institutional and professional politics and the hypocrisy."

There was total silence in the room after Stiehl concluded. Simmons reached for the folder before him. "Do you mean to tell us that the laudatory letters in Dr. Prince's file are, shall we say, not completely truthful?"

"*Far* from completely truthful. They were written not to laud Prince, but to protect the hospital against any possible libel suit by him and also from any adverse publicity. After all, no hospital wants to admit that a man who has been on its staff for years is inept or an uncontrolled genius once he gets a scalpel in his hands. So let him resign. Send him on his way with cheers. Let him practice his slaughter of innocents somewhere else. Let some other hospital worry about him. Unfortunately, this happens quite often.

"Gentlemen, we've been polluting our own profession and one day it will choke us," Stiehl concluded softly.

Harvey Prince brought his fist down on the table, shouting, "Damn it, I'm not going to sit here and listen to these lies! Those letters are from reputable men. Are you going to take the word of this . . . this country doctor . . . against men like those?"

Simmons handed the file to Stiehl. "Doctor, are you acquainted with the men who signed these letters?"

Stiehl examined the letters, commenting after each one: "Dr. Briscoe is dead now. And Silversmith. And so is Harrison . . ."

Harvey Prince interposed, chuckling, "Very convenient. Doctor, I can understand that because of your years of frustration you would come here and try to blame me. But I can't understand that you would be so gross and obvious about it. What happened? Did Dr. Lindstrom beguile you with the opportunity to avenge yourself? What made you come here and make such a sorry spectacle of yourself?"

Stiehl's face flushed; his lips began to tremble. He seemed desperately compelled to answer, unable to.

Sensing that, Prince decided to take a calculated risk and destroy his testimony altogether. "Tell me, Doctor, after you were forced to resign from the hospital, didn't you have a nervous breakdown? Weren't you institutionalized?"

"I was not institutionalized!" Stiehl declared.

"But you *were* under the care of a psychiatrist," Prince accused.

Stiehl did not make any denial.

"So that's why you were so amenable now to coming here and testifying under the urging of another psychiatrist," Prince asked, making obvious reference to Kate Lindstrom.

380

"I came here," Stiehl began, "to put an end, once and for all, to the kind of surgery you practice."

"And you do that by accusing honorable men of writing dishonest letters about me. Letters that conceal certain facts about me. Then, when you are challenged to prove your accusation, you say blandly, But they're all dead now!" Prince scoffed. He turned to the panel. "Gentlemen, I leave it to you to . . ." As if to reinforce his contempt for Stiehl's testimony, he did not even deign to finish the sentence.

Simmons began to nod grimly. Fein stared at Stiehl, with a combined look of pity and contempt. Kearney only gripped his jaw and glared at the nervous doctor. Stiehl could no longer control the tremor of his hand.

Kate Lindstrom leaned forward in the direction of the panel. Firmly, but in a deceptively gentle voice, she said, "I believe Dr. Prince made one error in his last statement."

Prince turned on her with a benign and disparaging smile.

"He said the men who wrote those letters were all dead now. *Not quite true,*" she said, laying out each word with great precision.

The smile froze on Prince's face. Kate had seen such smiles before, on patients who had attempted to deceive her but had been discovered. Assured, she went on.

"Two men are still alive. And can be called on to explain how these letters were written. Dr. Angelo, the present Chief of the Department. And the old Chief who felt forced to resign."

She looked across the table at Prince. "If Dr. Prince would care to call on them." Thereupon she pushed a slip of paper across the table, face down, and in Prince's direction. "Their phone numbers, Doctor."

Prince did not respond at once.

Simmons leaned forward intently. "Harvey?"

"I wouldn't take Angelo's word on anything," Prince blurted out. "He never liked me. He was jealous of my practice! He'd say anything Stiehl asked him to!"

"And what about your old Chief?" Kate Lindstrom pursued. "Why not call him and find out why he resigned right after being forced to sign this letter?"

Simmons drummed his fingers on the shiny mahogany table. He glanced at Fein, then at Kearney, soliciting their opinions. Finally he stared at Prince. "I leave it up to you, Harvey. Do you wish to make those calls, or shall we?"

No longer smiling, or confident, his face drained of its usual ruddy color, Harvey Prince was finally forced to speak the most painful words he had ever had to utter: "There's . . . there's no need. . . . I know what they'll both say."

He rose, and without a glance to anyone, he slipped silently out of the room.

Once the door closed, Simmons beckoned to Kate to hand him that slip of paper. He turned it over, stared at it, then asked, "Only Angelo's name? Only Angelo's phone number? What about the old Chief?"

Kate smiled a small innocent smile as she said, "I took a chance that he was still alive. I guess Dr. Prince believed me."

Simmons had to stifle his own smile, but his eyes confirmed his admiration for her successful gamble.

"Now," he said, "if the rest of you will excuse us, I think this panel had better reconvene in private session and reconsider our decision."

Chapter Thirty-Two

Kate and Craig drove Dr. Leonard Stiehl to the airport. Before he boarded his plane, Kate said, "I hope it wasn't too difficult for you."

"Actually, it was good therapy. I've fought that battle with Prince almost every night for eleven years now. I've hated him, blamed him, cursed him. Especially when Nancy had to go without some of the things other doctors' wives have. Always Prince was to blame. I looked forward to the day when I could even the score.

"Now I must admit when I saw him slink out of that room defeated, I felt sorry for him. He's going to relive that bitter moment every day for the rest of his life. Only he won't have the consolation I had. I was right. That made it bearable. But he knows damn well what he's guilty of. He has no consolations. So I . . . I felt sorry for him."

Touched by the man's humanity, Craig suggested, "You know, Stiehl, you don't have to practice in Middlebury the rest of your life. There are large hospitals in this city, and other cities, who'd be happy to have a good experienced man on staff. I bet Ordway would jump at the chance. Shall I talk to him?"

Stiehl smiled. "Not on your life. When I sat in that imposing boardroom, facing that panel, with all the power they represented, I said, Thank God for Middlebury, and my small hospital. Where I'm a physician and surgeon, not a politician in a white coat. I wouldn't go back to that for all the money in the world."

He laughed, a free and happy man again. They were announcing his plane when he was suddenly reminded and asked Kate, "One thing you never told me: what put you on to Angelo?"

"This." Kate handed him the unsigned note.

He glanced at it, but was still puzzled. "If you ever find out who sent you this, let me know. I'd be curious. They're calling my flight!"

Kate threw her arms around him and kissed him. "Thanks. Thanks for everything."

"Believe me, it was a pleasure!" Stiehl declared, starting for the boarding gate.

On the way back to the city, Craig drove; Kate leaned against him.

"What do *you* think?" she asked.

"I think we ought to get married right away."

"I meant, who do you think wrote that note?"

"A woman who knows more about Prince than other people do. And who, for some reason, is seeking revenge."

"Who?"

"His wife. She finally got wind of his affair with Rita Hallen," Craig said. "They tell me betrayed wives'll do that sort of thing."

"She couldn't just have got wind of it. Deep down, where a woman is a woman, she's known all along."

"Would *you* know?" Craig asked, half joking.

"Don't ever test me," Kate warned.

"If she didn't just discover his affair, why would she write that note now?" Craig asked. "To help me out? She doesn't even know me."

"You're still assuming she wrote it," Kate pointed out.

"If not her, who?" Craig asked. Then, at once, his own deduction told him, "Rita Hallen?"

"Likely," Kate said.

"But why?"

"Frustration. Menopausal depression. She's about at the age. Perhaps it was the realization that she's wasted her life in her affair with Prince. Who would know so much about his past except his wife and Rita Hallen?"

Craig said thoughtfully, "If Rita did this for me . . ." He felt a deep sense of obligation.

Kate was silent for a moment. "What do you think they'll do with him?"

"That's up to the Trustees. Prince has a lot of muscle there. And he'll use it."

Craig drove on, thoughtful, until he observed grimly, "Old Goldfingers. Still, I understand Stiehl's reaction. You have to feel a little sorry for him. To possess so much skill and betray it."

In the same room in which the professional panel had earlier voted to reinstate Dr. Craig Pierson, the Board of Trustees, the Hospital Administrator, and the Chief of the Department of Obstetrics and Gynecology were joined in an unusual, hastily convened meeting to discuss the matter of Dr. Harvey Prince.

Bruce Miller, Chairman of the Trustees and senior partner of Arthur Horton's law firm, presided.

"Madam and gentlemen, I apologize for bringing you together on such short notice. Especially since I almost feel I should disqualify myself. Because I have both an emotional and a professional involvement in this matter. The patient in the case is the daughter of one of my partners. Needless to say, I am outraged at what happened to her. *However* . . ."

Clinton Ordway flinched at the word. He knew it

usually signaled an excuse for a departure from principle.

"*However*," Miller continued, "I am also a trustee and counsel to this hospital. When I contemplate the legal effects, I must caution against any hasty or ill-advised action. There can be repercussions. A lawsuit by Prince for slander and libel. So discretion is strongly indicated."

Deering, as Administrator, as well as a friend of Harvey Prince's, took the opportunity to observe, "We have to consider the other practical effects too. If we terminate Prince, we're actually assisting the Hortons if they decide to sue Prince for malpractice. They would undoubtedly include this hospital in such a suit. Which means we're working against our own interests. Because if the Hortons win, our malpractice insurance will skyrocket. We simply cannot afford it!"

The one woman on the Board, usually timid about expressing herself, spoke up from the far end of the table: "But, Mr. Deering, if we retain Dr. Prince, aren't we exposing ourselves to even more malpractice actions in the future?"

Always affable when challenged by a Trustee, Deering replied, "Mrs. Young, I was only suggesting that we do this in an expeditious manner. We permit Dr. Prince to resign. We avoid making any statement about him that would jeopardize him professionally. After all, he's been good for this hospital. We should remember that. When you've had to wrestle with the budget as I have, and you see the amount of money Dr. Prince has brought into the Ob-Gyn Department, you can appreciate his value. Am I right, Ordway?"

Resentful of being enlisted in a conspiracy for which he had no heart, Ordway replied, "Dr. Prince has been responsible for substantial cash flow in the department. His patients are always admitted before it is necessary, and linger on after it is indicated. For the health and welfare of the patient? No. Because, by being so cooperative, Dr. Prince has assured himself of more beds in Ob-Gyn than any other surgeon. More beds mean more surgical procedures. Which mean more fees. I regret to say that, in a way, I have been part of that process. But this whole Pierson affair has caused me to do some deep and painful thinking.

"I am particularly plagued by something young Pierson said to me one day when I was trying to persuade him to drop the Horton case. He asked, 'To whom do I owe my ethical duty? To the doctor? Or to the patient?' He was right. Because other trustees in another hospital had this same discussion and decided to turn Prince loose on an unsuspecting public, we are faced with the problem now. If we let him make a graceful exit, with another fistful of 'recommendations,' we'll be doing the same thing to some other hospital. I cannot countenance that other young girls, like Cynthia Horton, may one day be stripped of their womanhood, unnecessarily, ruthlessly. To protect them, to protect our profession, I say we must finally treat with Dr. Prince in the way he deserves."

By the end of the meeting, it was unanimously voted by the Trustees that Dr. Harvey Prince have his hospital privileges revoked and his association terminated. That he be notified to that effect in a letter which would set forth in precise detail the reason for that action, including the dishonest letters of recommendation in his file.

The last was a cautionary legal step advised by Chairman Miller, who said, "Dr. Prince wouldn't dare sue this hospital and make our letter part of his complaint."

387

Dr. Kate Lindstrom was on her way from Emergency, where she had just admitted a man who had gone berserk, threatening to knife his wife and infant daughter. She was headed back to the Psychiatric Wing when her beeper summoned her to the floor phone.

"Lindstrom!" she announced hastily.

"Doctor," the operator informed her, "there's a gentleman waiting in your office who insists on seeing you."

Though she resented such unexpected intrusions, Kate was well aware of the compulsions of her patients that sometimes drove them to such extremes. She opened the door of her office expecting to find such a tormented patient. Instead she found Peter Tompkins waiting for her. Her look of surprise made him explain.

"You said to call after I had thought it over very carefully. Instead of calling, I decided to come see you."

"I also said, Call me only if you think you can do it," Kate reminded him.

"I think I can make it work, but I need assurance," he confessed. "Do *you* think it's possible?"

"If there's understanding and compassion, it's more than possible," she said firmly.

"I'll need help," the young man said.

"You'll have help. Mine. Dr. Pierson's. There are things that can be done to make your love most enjoyable and satisfying. But the most important is tenderness."

"Then will you ask her if you can treat me at the same time you're treating her?"

"No," Kate said.

"But you promised . . .," the young man started to protest.

"I think that now it would be better if *you* asked her," Kate suggested.

"Me?" He seemed a bit hesitant again.

"I'm due to drop in on her this morning. Let's go up there right now," Kate said.

She knocked gently at Cynthia's door.

"Yes?" the girl called back listlessly.

Kate opened the door slightly and peered in. "You have a visitor, Cynthia."

"Mother?"

Instead of answering, Kate opened the door wide enough for Cynthia to see.

"Pete?" she asked, tears welling up in her eyes. "Oh, Pete!"

But neither of them moved, until Kate said, "He has something important to ask you. So I'll leave you two alone."

She waited until Pete crossed the room, lifted Cynthia to her feet, and embraced her. Then Kate silently closed the door and started down the hall, confident of Cynthia's answer, confident as well of their future life together.

Of all the therapeutic agents in her specialty, Kate knew that the most potent and effective healer was being wanted, being loved.

Craig Pierson was examining a young woman of twenty-six who presented all the signs and symptoms of an ectopic pregnancy about to rupture. His beeper had been tormenting him incessantly for the past ten minutes, until he shut it off angrily and turned his full attention to the patient.

He decided on immediate surgery, and was giving

the attending nurse instructions when Burt Carlyle appeared in the doorway. Once the patient was being prepped, Craig was free to greet Carlyle.

"I've been busy every minute; I never did have a chance to thank you, Burt...."

"I didn't do that for you. I did it for me. No, I guess the truth is I did it for LuAnne. She wouldn't have it any other way. But you should answer your beeper."

"Was that you trying to raise me?" Craig asked.

"Ordway. The Board's decided. Prince has got to go. Without any nice speeches, complimentary letters, or Bon Voyage baskets. Out! Terminated!"

"Good," Craig said, deeply relieved.

"He wants to see you," Burt said.

"Prince?"

"Ordway," Burt informed him, smiling.

"I've got this emergency," Craig explained.

"Ordway will only take a few minutes. And pretend you don't know about the decision."

"Okay," Craig agreed.

"LuAnne was delighted too. She asked, could you and Kate come for dinner tonight?"

"Why don't we all go out and celebrate?"

"God, man, LuAnne's been taking a course in gourmet cuisine ever since she became too pregnant to model. Give her a chance to show off," Burt said, laughing.

"Okay. Tonight. But we'll bring the wine," Craig said as he headed down the corridor toward Ordway's office.

Clinton Ordway was scanning a research paper that one of the staff men had written and which now awaited his approval. At the knock, he called out without interrupting his reading, "Yes?"

The door opened; Craig Pierson shoved his head in. "You wanted me?"

Ordway looked up. "Oh, yes, come in, come in." He indicated a chair. Craig remained standing.

"I've got an emergency being prepped right now, sir."

"This won't take long. I guess Carlyle told you about the Board's decision."

Craig was about to deny it when Ordway preempted him. "If Burt didn't tell you, how did you know I wanted to see you? You didn't answer your page."

Craig smiled and pleaded guilty with a slight gesture.

"One thing Burt didn't tell you, because I didn't tell him. I am going to appoint you Chief Resident for your third year."

"Thank you; thank you very much."

"No thanks necessary. You're a good surgeon, on the way to becoming a better one. But that wasn't the only reason. You took a risk. A grave risk for a young surgeon. And you did it in behalf of patients, and for the good of the entire profession. I like that. I like it because, frankly, it was something I would not have had the courage to do."

Before the moment could become more personal, Ordway said brusquely, "Now get along to your emergency."

In surgery, Craig Pierson scrubbed in preparation for his procedure. At the sink on his right, Burt Carlyle was scrubbing. On his left was Willis Blinn, who seemed to scrub harder than either of them. When Craig was done, he slipped into his surgical gown, offered his hands for the surgical gloves. Safely sterile, he went into the operating room. His first glance told him that his scrub nurse was Rita Hallen. She was ready and waiting. Each sterile, glistening instrument was laid out in the order required for the successful execution of the procedure. Her mask was in place; only her deep, discerning dark eyes were visible.

"Rita, I want to thank you," Craig whispered.

"What for?" she countered, turning away to busy herself with the final preparations. Craig studied her. As if she felt his eyes, she turned back to look at him. She said nothing, but now somehow he was sure.

They were wheeling in the patient, so Craig had no opportunity to ask Rita why. He draped the patient's body, leaving only her pale abdomen exposed and presented for surgery. He held out his hand. Across the patient's body, Rita passed him a forceps at the end of which was a large cotton swab soaked in the brown betadine solution. He began to paint the field of the operation from the patient's upper thighs to her nipples.